NAPOLEON'S EXILE

Also by Patrick Rambaud

THE BATTLE

THE RETREAT

Patrick Rambaud

NAPOLEON'S
EXILE

Translated from the French by

Shaun Whiteside

Grove Press
New York

First published in English in 2005 by Picador,
an imprint of Pan Macmillan Ltd., London, England

Originally published in 2003 as *L'Absent*
by Editions Grasset & Fasquelle, Paris

Published simultaneously in Canada
Printed in the United States of America

FIRST GROVE PRESS EDITION

Library of Congress Cataloging-in-Publication Data

Rambaud, Patrick.
    [Absent. English]
    Napoleon's exile : a novel / Patrick Rambaud ; translated by
Shaun Whiteside.
        p. cm.
    ISBN-10: 0-8021-1826-7
    ISBN-13: 978-0-8021-1826-4
    I. Whiteside, Shaun.   II. Title.
PQ2678.A455A6413 2006
843'.914—dc22   2005055017

Grove Press
an imprint of Grove/Atlantic, Inc.
841 Broadway
New York, NY 10003

Distributed by Publishers Group West

www.groveatlantic.com

06 07 08 09 10   10 9 8 7 6 5 4 3 2 1

To Tieu Hong

*To Messieurs Paul Morans, Jean Renoir
and Dino Risi, les patrons*

*To Madame Arundhati Roy,
my statue of Liberty*

ON 29 MARCH 1814, the Emperor spent a sleepless night on a farm near Troyes that had been sacked by Prussian cavalry. While there, he received some alarming news: the enemy was massing on the shores of the Marne, and the reduced forces of Mortier and Marmont were turning back towards the tollgates of Paris, which they would not be fit to defend. The Marshals were yielding ground. Augereau, routed from Lyons, was retreating to Valence. Davout had shut himself away in Hamburg, and Prince Eugene's army was trudging across Italy. And Murat? He was involved in negotiations with Austria to save his Neapolitan throne.

Europe was invading France. In the south, some of Wellington's divisions, swollen by elite Spanish and Portuguese troops, had occupied Bordeaux and the surrounding region. In the north, Holland was in revolt, and Bernadotte's Sweden remained a threat. To the east, the Russians, the Austrians and the Prussians had passed through the Vosges and crossed the Rhine; converging on the capital from three directions. For two months they had been fighting a war-weary campaign; from dazzling victories to costly defeats, in frozen fog, in the rain, in the mud, they took and retook villages, bridges and hills; they were short of provisions, and the men were exhausted.

Marshal Ney, known as 'the redhead', Prince of the Moskva, knelt on the ground and fed the fire with pieces of a chair. His features tired, in a face that had grown puffy, with his paunch thrust forward and his hands held under his coat-tails, the Emperor asked him: 'How long will it take us to get back to Paris?'

'According to Macdonald's last message, the allies are at Meaux, they're holding the Marne . . .'

'We'll skirt the obstacle via Sens and Melun and make it to Fontainebleau. How long's that?'

'The army won't be there for at least four days, sire, and in such a state!'

'I'll put our battalions under your command, and I'll go on ahead. At a gallop, with an escort, I'll be in Paris tomorrow morning to organize the resistance.'

'That's madness, sire!'

'You sound like Berthier, Marshal, but I'm still capable of unnerving people.'

With cocked beaver hat pulled low over his eyes, coat buttoned to the chin and collar turned up, and with his whip fastened to his right wrist, the Emperor was ready to leave the farm at sunrise. Marshal Berthier, Prince of Neuchâtel and Wagram, had predicted his master's caprice, and was waiting in the cold grey light, wrapped in a muddy coat. Caulaincourt, Duke of Vicenza, and Lefebvre, Duke of Danzig, stood ready, along with 'virtuous' Drouot – a general and a baker's son – and Count Bertrand, the Grand Marshal of the palace. Similarly swaddled in grey or brown, the four men stamped their heels against the frozen earth. The dragoons and chasseurs were already mounted, their helmets drab and battered, their bearskin hats moth-eaten, their coats torn, threadbare and dirty, and their teeth chattering in faces blue with cold.

Berthier and Caulaincourt hoisted the Emperor on to his horse and they set off, passing through the still slumbering town of Troyes, and galloping along the road to Sens. Soon the group was stretched out and scattered: the horses were exhausted, some fell, while others couldn't muster a trot, or else they lagged and bridled; even the Emperor's horse kept to a walking pace despite the harsh digs of the spurs that drew blood from its flanks. At noon, the ten survivors of this pitiful race stopped at the inn in Villeneuve-l'Archevêque. Napoleon dismounted, and some villagers approached; passive yet suspicious, they looked at him. Meanwhile the officers embarked on a quest for coaches and fresh horses, questioning the Mayor, who had come running upon learning that the Emperor was passing through. The Russians had requisitioned the vehicles, and those that were left weren't exactly . . .

'They'll do,' pronounced the Emperor.

There were three such vehicles: a wicker cabriolet the butcher agreed to lend them, and two carts. The post-horses, which had fortunately been fed, were immediately harnessed. Napoleon climbed into the wicker cabriolet with Caulaincourt, and the Marshals shared the carts between them. The rest could fend for themselves. The postilion cracked his whip and the pathetic cortège set off back along the Sens road.

'Faster!' cried the Emperor. 'Faster!'

One

THE CONSPIRATORS

OCTAVE ADJUSTED his white English-style wig, which was combed back with fake nonchalance. He studied himself in the mirror. Pale grey eyes, pinched nostrils, a lipless mouth. His neutral face lent itself to change, and it made him smile. 'I can play any part I like,' he thought with satisfaction.

Just then there was a knock at his door and someone called his name. Octave drew back the bolt and opened the door to reveal Marquis de la Grange, the former commander of the Vendée, who had been involved in several failed conspiracies and who was now plotting in Paris, beneath the very noses of the imperial police. Tall, lean, rather severe, wearing a blue woollen frock-coat with an astrakhan collar, the Marquis had not visited Octave's apartment before.

Octave occupied a long and sparsely furnished room on the first floor of the Hôtel de Salerne, in the rue Saint-Sauveur: a candlestick on the pine table, a bed, an enormous wardrobe. The velvet of the armchairs was as faded as that of the canopy of the bed, and Octave had to make do without a valet or chambermaid, with logs piled up beside the fireplace.

'My good man,' said the Marquis, 'these lodgings of yours are a little rough . . .'

'But they are both temporary and discreet.'

'I grant you that, and in any case I'm not here to inspect you but to give you a warning.'

'Has someone spotted me?'

'No, no, don't worry about that. The bluebottles down at the Préfecture are far too stupid to do anything of the sort. I wanted to tell you that we appear to have managed a complete revolution.'

'A revolution . . .'

'In the astronomical sense: the return of a planet to the initial point of its orbit.'

'Meaning?'

'Meaning that we are about to return to our starting-point: the monarchy.'

'I still don't get what you're on about.'

'I'll take you there, and then you'll understand.'

The Marquis lifted Octave's three-cornered hat from a peg, threw him his coat, thrust his own wide-brimmed black felt hat back on and dragged Octave to the staircase.

Outside the front door, in the rue des Deux-Portes, a rented cabriolet awaited, a large number painted on its door. The coachman asked no questions, since the journey had already been decided: the coach – amid a great din of wheels, tinkling bells, hoofs and curses, all of which discouraged conversation – was taking them to the Louvre.

On that Monday, 29 March, the weather was finally clear after weeks of fine and freezing rain. Once they had reached their destination, the Marquis took Octave's arm and the two men passed beneath the wicket-gate. On the other side, behind the railings on either side of a triumphal arch, a crowd of a hundred or so onlookers stood and watched.

Squat, melancholy and austere, the Tuilerie Palace completed the two wings of the Louvre Palace and separated it from the Jardin des Tuileries. That morning, the Place du Carrousel was filled not with its usual parades, but with a great hustle and bustle. As always, there were large numbers of grey-caped cavalrymen in attendance, but they stood motionless, impatient, alert for an order.

As Octave and La Grange mingled among the spectators, a fellow with greying sideburns, dressed as a bourgeois, came over to them and murmured by way of explanation, 'Marquis, the ground-floor French windows, towards the Pavillon de Flore, were lit before dawn . . .'

'And where does that leave us, my dear Michaud?'

'The move is happening, and happening quickly, as you can see.'

In Empress Marie-Louise's apartments, valets in green livery were wrapping chandeliers, while others carried numbered cases, clocks, tables, passing gilded chairs to men clad in overalls, who were loading them on to vans and wagons. Further behind, lancers and grenadiers of the Guard stood around the twelve berlins, harnessed since morning, and the coronation carriage, covered with tarpaulins. The Marquis was delighted.

'They're sneaking off with all the silver and the crockery, like thieves.'

'But they *are* thieves, Marquis.'

La Grange turned towards Octave.

'Michaud's a printer, an active member of our Committee.'

'Very well,' replied Octave, 'but if the Empress is leaving Paris, does that mean the end of the Empire?'

'Of course it does, my dear sir, of course it does, because the government will come apart at the seams.' Then, to Michaud: 'The Chevalier de Blacé is arriving from London, he's been following our dealings from a distance.'

'Ah!' said the printer deferentially.

Standing next to them, a red-haired man in a patched waistcoat muttered, 'Off they go.'

As he spoke, a yellow-faced, bent-backed beanpole dressed in an embroidered outfit from another era descended the palace steps, accompanied by his two confidants. The three climbed into the first berlin, followed by a young woman with hollow cheeks and fat lips, and a fair-haired child who struggled in the arms of an equerry before clutching the wrought-iron railings and howling at the top of his voice. For the benefit of the London envoy, the Marquis leaned forward and commented: 'The one with the wig is Arch-Chancellor Cambacérès, the second most important person in the regime. The lost-looking young woman with the hood is Empress Marie-Louise . . .'

'And the child is the King of Rome,' said Octave.

With the armoured berlins at its head, the procession now passed slowly through the gate of the Pont-Royal, followed by the luggage carts and the vans and their cavalry escort. The onlookers dispersed, their faces uneasy; some – Octave and the Marquis among them – strolled towards the Quai to see what was left of the Imperial court leaving for Rambouillet.

'That's the end of the usurper,' said the Marquis. 'But you don't seem all that convinced.'

'Where is he?'

'Bonaparte is finished, my dear sir. So let's get going! He'll pick up a reduced and exhausted army between the Marne and the Seine; after three short-lived attempts at grand gestures he'll hesitate, he'll make a wrong move, then he'll push into the devastated Champagne region with a few children who couldn't load a musket if you paid them to, with the dubious support of a few goat-whiskered veterans. They're finished, I tell you!'

'But we haven't won yet.'

'We'll see about that. We'll run and tell our friends about the flight of the Empress, and then we can discuss what to do next.'

'You'll have to guide me, I've forgotten my way around Paris.'

'You'll see, it's filthier than London.'

'I already have: take a look at my boots.'

*

Although La Grange was delighted with a situation which he believed served the interests of the royalists, most of the rest of the population lived in fear of invasion. Carried on the north wind, the sound of cannon seemed to be getting closer from one hour to the next; gangs of beggars and wounded men wandered the streets of Paris, and contradictory rumours circulated. One newspaper supplied the name of Russian generals killed in combat, another called the people to resist, to protect the capital: 'Arm yourselves with arsenic, poison the fountains and wells, slit the throats of the Prussians in their beds with your cutlasses!'

On the Pont-Neuf, at the Palais-Royal, conmen in the

pay of the police tried to mobilize people by fear, like
this hoarse old man, standing on a stepladder: 'I was in
Rheims, I saw the Cossacks, they're raping the women
over their husbands' bodies, they're getting the girls and
children drunk before grilling them over their bivouac
fires and then throwing in exploding cartridges!' The
theatres and shops were closing; bricklayers and joiners
hurried through the streets to install hiding-places for
jewels and gold in the homes of the bourgeoisie. Crowds
gathered around the proclamation that Joseph Bonaparte
– who was now in charge of Paris – had ordered to be
posted on the walls: 'The Emperor,' it read, 'is marching
to our aid!' One sceptic improvised a song:

> Good King Joseph, pale and wan,
> Stay a while and save us!
> And if you don't, then leg it
> While the foreigners enslave us!

One had to go to the boulevards to grasp the seriousness
of the situation. Thousands of peasants were flooding
towards the capital, driven out of their homes by the
advancing allies who were ravaging the countryside, and
Octave and the Marquis found their progress hindered by
a crush of carts piled high with pots and pans, furniture
and blankets. Strapping young men in straw-covered clogs
led herds of cattle and sheep through the chaos. Weeping women and children bunched up in a horse-drawn
wagon. The most fortunate rode on donkeys but most
were on foot, all of them lamenting the loss of their homes
and fields. The sound of mooing, baaing and sobbing
swelled the hubbub of wheels and clogs. A man carrying
a mattress over his back rebuked La Grange, calling him

a toff; laments turned into insults directed against the luckier ones.

Clinging to the door-handle, a peasant woman set her little boy on the footplate of the cabriolet: 'The Cossacks are at Bondy! And you've no idea what them Cossacks are like!'

'We went and hid in the woods!'

'We've nothing but the shirts on our backs!'

'They're going to come to Paris and torch the place!'

'It's going to be like Moscow!'

'They're going to take their revenge!'

Just before they reached the unfinished Temple of the Madeleine, a shady-looking fellow in blue overalls climbed on to one of the horses pulling the cabriolet. About to whip him for his insolence, the coachman suddenly found himself threatened by a great giant of a man brandishing a pitchfork. Turning to ask his passengers for some advice, if not an order, the coachman found that they had disappeared, and his vehicle was filling up with bundles and exhausted children.

Octave and the Marquis had dodged into the rue Basse-du-Rempart, down on the north side of the boulevard. 'I caught a strong smell of the cowshed there,' said the Marquis, taking a deep breath from a little vial of eau de Cologne and pointing towards a three-storey townhouse on the corner of the rue de la Concorde. Its shutters were closed and it appeared to be deserted, but the Marquis opened the door a crack and they slipped through. Inside, a big cartload of victuals sat beneath a vaulted ceiling; porters carried bags of flour and rice up stone staircases. Provisions were piled on the landing and in the corridors – enough to get them through several weeks of siege. The

first-floor drawing-room was in semi-darkness. Silhou-
etted in the tremulous light of the chandeliers, beneath
hams suspended on ropes from the ceiling, grave-looking
men and terrified ladies prattled, agitated as sparrows.

'Europe is bringing us the disasters that we have
imposed upon it,' announced a pointy-nosed viscount.

'Nonetheless, we do have some friends.'

'That's true, Rochechouart was on the Tsar's administrative staff.'

'And Langeron, too!'

'That didn't stop their Cossacks disembowelling decent
folk who refused to serve them raw herring.'

'Raw herring? How perfectly frightful!'

'The Empress will protect us from those savages!'

Everyone thought the presence of Marie-Louise –
Napoleon's wife by an arranged marriage but daughter
of the Emperor of Austria – would be enough to restrain
the allied armies if by any misfortune they should take the
capital. The Marquis de la Grange firmly shattered these
illusions.

'Alas, your ladyship, the Empress has just left Paris.'

'Go and tell my husband!'

'So the Count of Sémallé is back?'

*

In point of fact, the Count of Sémallé had just returned
from a perilous mission with an Austrian passport that
had led him along various byways to a hostelry in Vesoul
where he had met up with Louis XVIII's turbulent
brother, 'Monsieur', the Count of Artois, who had
entrusted him with the royalist proclamations printed in
Basle and a recommendation written in his own hand:

Those who see this paper can and may place full trust in everything that Monsieur de Sémallé will tell them on my behalf.

Sémallé had drooping shoulders, a large head, and fair hair parted in the middle; he was wearing a dressing-gown, but with a tie twisted around his neck as though preparing at any moment to throw on a frock-coat to escape the merest hint of danger. For prudence's sake, he was not living in his town house near the boulevards where his wife still dwelt, but in his old, more modest house at 55 rue de Lille. He was writing and drinking hot chocolate when a valet ushered La Grange and Octave into his office.

'Empress Marie-Louise has left with her son, Cambacérès, and some members of the government.'

'That changes nothing, La Grange. The foreign forces will be making their way towards Paris as we speak. Bonaparte is away in the East, the meagre troops of Mortier and Marmont are about to reach the tollgates, but they're starving, and have no straw or wood. They won't withstand this terrible advance.'

'And what if the Parisians rise up?' asked Octave.

'Who are you?' asked Sémallé, who had until that point paid no attention to the Marquis's companion.

'The Chevalier de Blacé,' replied La Grange. 'On Wednesday he was still living in his house in Baker Street. He comes with Lady Salisbury's recommendation.'

'Fine.' And then, to Octave: 'How did you get here?'

'Via Brussels, your grace.'

'He has a Belgian passport,' added the Marquis, 'and he's registered as a lace trader.'

'What's the word in London?'

'The English are inclined towards the Bourbons, my lord.'

'I know that, Chevalier, but the Tsar has his eye on the King of Sweden, and the Austrians are looking to the King of Rome. In Rome, we failed to provoke an uprising in our favour. Last week the Prince of Hessen-Homburg, who is in charge of the city, had our partisans arrested for wearing white cockades: he saw it as sedition. In Bordeaux, Wellington is keeping the Duke of Angoulême at arm's length; he has just joined him in Saint-Jean-de-Luz ... At any rate, the King mustn't be imposed by the allies, but chosen by the French.'

'Easier said than done,' grumbled La Grange, disappointed by the Count's revelations.

'Everyone has forgotten the Bourbons,' Sémallé went on. 'What do they look like? Where are they? After their twenty years in exile, the people know nothing about them. But I do know one thing and one thing alone: *We have two days to create a popular movement.*'

'With whom? With what?'

'We have to simulate a vast royalist movement.'

'Simulate?' said Octave in astonishment.

'We must persuade the allies to support the legitimate monarchy, and the people as a whole to accept it. La Grange, have our Committee assemble tomorrow. We should be able to see things more clearly by then.'

In December, at the request of Louis XVIII, who had sought refuge in Hartwell, Sémallé had begun to put together a royalist Committee of about forty people. Having been rejected by the aristocrats, who were suspicious of police informers, he had recruited his partisans from officers, civil servants, the hardline bourgeoisie and businessmen craving peace. The committee met in the rue de l'Échiquier, in the town house of a certain Lemercier — a former banker who liked to think of himself as a man of letters — where they talked a lot, did little, and contented themselves with hoarding quantities of white cockades in all kinds of hidey-holes.

As he led Octave back, Sémallé questioned him. 'I knew a Blacé in the Tuileries, when I was one of Louis XVI's pages.'

'My father.'

'You don't look like him.'

'I've been told that before, my lord.'

'What became of your father?'

'The last image I have of him is his head on the end of a pike.'

*

Claiming to be worn out after his journey from England to Paris, Octave declined the invitation of dinner at the Palais-Royal, where some establishments were keeping their back rooms open for regulars. La Grange did not press the point, but walked him to his room and immediately took his leave.

Octave hurried to bolt the door as soon as he heard the Marquis heading down the stairs. Then he stood at the window and watched him disappear from view. There was no one else in the street, but he had some lingering doubts. The Marquis was too amiable, too confiding: a letter of recommendation had sufficed, along with some twaddle about emigrant life in London. Was he being left to his own devices so that he might more easily be kept under surveillance? If he went out again, would one or other of the members of this great Committee take advantage of the fact to tail him?

Octave threw his wig on to the table and changed his clothes; from his case he took a black tie and a long blue frock-coat which he buttoned across his chest; he put on a high, broad hat. Then, carrying a cane as thick as a cudgel under his arm, he unlocked the big wardrobe: he opened a hidden door in its base and dashed down a spiral staircase that led to the antique shop at 14 rue Saint-Sauveur. (Before the Revolution, the building had been a house of assignation run by a tobacconist's wife, and this secret exit, through the chamber that was in those days called 'the changing-room', enabled frolicking noblewomen and worthies to avoid the front door and leave the house disguised as grisettes or respectable clergymen.)

Octave walked with the quick, resolute pace of a man familiar with the district's network of alleyways. Half an hour later, at the rue de la Culture-Sainte-Cathérine, he passed through the porch of the Renaissance town-house of M. de Pommereul, the director of the library, and thus of the Imperial censors. In the sentry-box, a corporal with a wooden leg was smoking his pipe; he didn't ask any questions, as though the new arrival had an entrée into the building. Octave climbed to the first floor and found himself in a room in which files stacked on shelves rose to the ceiling, perched in chairs and tilted in unstable piles on the tile floor. Three men were busy throwing bundles of these documents into a fireplace wide and deep enough to roast an ox. One of the three men, Sebastian Roque – until recently the Baron d'Herbigny – glaced up. He was drenched in sweat, his sleeves were rolled up, and black

curls stuck to his forehead. He looked very surprised to
see Octave.

'What are you doing here?'

'I've come to deliver my report.'

'It's over, it's *over*!'

'You're my official contact with the Duke of Bassano.'

'I don't know where he's hiding, and I'm getting out
of the city like everyone else! I've bought an estate in
Normandy, and I'm retreating to it.'

'Listen, my lord, I've infiltrated a group of royalists . . .'

'Nothing to do with me any more.'

'I have their names, their addresses, they're going to
meet tomorrow evening. The most active of them, a
marquis, is staying with a man called Morin, former
secretary to Masséna, and as to the Count of Sémallé . . .'

'I want nothing to do with him!'

The Baron put a pile of files down on a sofa and stood
in front of Octave. 'Go and tell all that to the Duke of
Rovigo.'

'I'm not involved with the police,' said Octave.

'Tell that to Prefect Pasquier.'

'The loyalty of civil servants sways with the wind.'

'You must admit it's an ill wind for us!'

Octave took his heavy cane in both hands and
addressed the servants who were still feeding the flames
while pretending not to hear anything:

'You two, out!'

'Hang on a moment!' said the Baron, 'since when have
you been issuing orders?'

'Since a minute ago.'

'By what right?'

'I'm the last person here to represent His Majesty.'

Baron d'Herbigny gave a hollow laugh.

'The last person, you're right!'

'I'm going to finish what I've started.'

'Bravo! Bravissimo!' said the Baron, bellowing with laughter until a stout blow in the stomach from Octave's cane bent him double over a sofa. He regained his breath with difficulty. The office boys had fled, knocking against the shelves as they passed and causing an avalanche of stacks of files. Wheezing, d'Herbigny rose to his feet, but Octave pushed him back into the papers and cushions with the tip of his cane.

'Imagine the Emperor coming back on a forced march . . .'

'You have too much imagination.'

'That's what I'm paid for, my little baron.'

'Don't adopt that tone with me!'

'You're nothing but a draper's son!' said Octave, prodding him with his cane.

'And you of a valet and a washerwoman.'

'I make no secret of it, my little baron.'

*

It was a clear night. Columns of bare-handed workmen drifted by in silence. Octave learned that they were heading towards the Place Vendôme to ask for weapons from General Hulin, the Governor of Paris; they would get nothing and would fly into a fury, Octave knew it: the reserve muskets had been distributed to the line infantry, because the Empire was suspicious of the suburbs, where unrest is traditionally born. As to the peasants, not all of them had taken the westward road, which was still open.

They were camped along the streets in their thousands, in their carts, in stable doorways, and had lit fires on the pavement to keep themselves warm and cook poultry. Octave bought a charred pigeon at twice the going rate, and set off nibbling to the end of the rue Saint-Antoine. Just before the Charonne barrier, he turned into the rue de la Planchette, an avenue lined with low-roofed houses, gardens, railings and little walls on the edge of the fields.

With the pommel of his cane, Octave knocked at a wooden door. The sound of dragging feet came from inside, and a shrewish-looking woman appeared in the doorway, holding her lantern level with her flabby face.

'How is he?' asked Octave.

'He's asleep, sir, but he's breathing well.'

Octave took the lantern from the old woman. At the rear of the little house, in a hidden room, a fair-haired man, his shirt open, snored on a mattress. The old woman put some kindling in the stove.

'Wake him, Jeanne, I'll take him off your hands.'

'Will he be able to stand up, Monsieur Octave?'

'I'll help him. Find him a coat or a cape.'

Octave shook the sleeping man's shoulder. With a start, he opened his eyes and murmured thickly, 'Oh . . . It's you . . .' He propped himself up on his elbows and, after a moment he said, 'The other evening . . .'

'Yes?'

'You didn't say . . .'

'What?'

'If you'd seen the man who attacked me . . .'

'No, sadly, just his back. I turned up just as he was attacking you from behind. He ran off while I was picking up your bags.'

'Did I look so rich that someone would want to rob me?'

'You must have been too loose-tongued with the other people at the table. In France, Monsieur de Blacé, there are policemen or rogues everywhere you look. The minute you left that wretched inn, you became their prey.'

'I never thought . . .'

'Did you mention London?'

'I can't remember.'

'No doubt you did. And you drew attention to yourself by paying the landlord with your gold coins. That would have done it.'

Old Jeanne fetched a grey guardsman's coat, with three red woollen stripes on the sleeve.

'Put it on, Monsieur de Blacé,' said Octave.

'Where are we going?'

'To see some royalists you mentioned to me the day before yesterday.'

'I was given their address in London . . .'

'So you really don't know anyone in Paris?'

'No one. You asked me that before.'

'No relatives, not even distant ones?'

'None.'

'What about your family?'

'I saw my father's head on the end of a pike . . .'

'I know, you told me that before.'

'My mother died of tuberculosis in Soho.'

'So I'm all you've got?'

'For the time being.'

Blacé pulled on his coat, rubbed the back of his neck and suddenly came to his senses: 'Where are my clothes and my wig?'

'With your royalist friends, who are waiting for you.'

'My letter of recommendation?'

'They've got it.'

'What about my money? The money I was going to send to their Committee?'

'In safe hands.'

'Wasn't it in safe hands in this house?'

'Are you suspicious of me?'

'Not at all, but I don't even know who you are.'

'Your saviour.'

They headed outside. Blacé was still weak, his attacker had hit him hard. Octave supported him as they walked, chatting, along the moonlit avenue.

'Will we pass by the Tuileries?'

'It's on our way,' replied Octave.

'That's where I have my last memories of Paris . . .'

'How so?'

'I was eight years old. It was August, and the people were attacking the Tuileries. The King and his family slipped off through the gardens. My mother and the ladies of the court had locked themselves away with the children in a candle-lit room. I remember a lot of noise, shouting, window-panes broken by cannon-fire. Why were we spared? I can't remember. Even now I can see buildings on fire, slaughtered Swiss Guards, down by the flowerbeds, in a cloud of flies. The rioters slit eiderdowns open and shook them from the windows like snow . . . What's that noise?'

'The drums of the National Guard. Our Russian friends can't be far off. Come over this way, let's stay out of the centre of the city.'

They walked along the grassy Quai du Mail as it

sloped to the Seine. In the darkness, Octave guided the chevalier, holding him firmly by the arm.

'Where are we going now?' asked Blacé anxiously.

'You've told me what I wanted to know. I'm going to show you something in return. What do you see, at the bottom of the hill?'

'Without a lantern?'

'Without a lantern.'

'Nothing at all.'

'No, take a closer look. Lean over.'

Intrigued, the chevalier obeyed. Octave took his cane in both hands, lifted it quickly, and then brought it crashing down on the back of his companion's neck. Blacé crumpled against the embankment, his nose in the soil. Octave rolled the body down to the water with the heel of his boot, and tipped it in with his cane. The corpse floated on the surface and was carried away by the current, swifter in this part of the river, between the Île Saint-Louis and the Île Louvier. When the body had disappeared into the night, Octave went back home to bed.

*

The drums had beaten the call to arms all night and in all parts of the city. From dawn, the sound of cannon and heavy gunfire could be heard from behind the hills of Belleville, Montmartre and the Butte Chaumont, which could be seen from the upper floors of the Sémallé townhouse. The sky was dark and leaden. Nervous and corseted, the young Countess de Sémallé left the window and let her maid buckle a curious belt around her waist. At that moment the Count slipped into the room. The

Countess glimpsed him in the mirror above the fireplace and uttered a little cry.

'Jean-René, you'll give us away if you come here!'

'It's my house.'

'The police are keeping watch on the house, you know that, they'll have recognized you, they'll put you under arrest!'

'Have no fear, my dear Zoé, events are keeping them far too busy, and their masters are already confused about who they're supposed to be serving. The cannon has its charms, you see — but tell me, what's the purpose of that padded belt, which puts pounds on you?'

'I'd rather keep my diamonds with me if we have to flee.' The Countess pointed at her maid. 'Louise is wearing a belt of the same model, with my jewels and my pearls.'

'The allies are our allies.'

'And what about the hairy Cossacks who are just dying to pillage us?'

'The moment I leave, our valets will take the forage cart that I ordered yesterday and push it against the gate.'

'Will that stop the barbarians?'

'Pillagers, my dear Zoé, I know from experience, give up at the first obstacle they encounter, and go off to pillage somewhere else. In Paris, they have plenty of choice.'

'Where will you be?'

The Count kissed the hand that the Countess held out to him.

'We're going to keep a close eye on the situation before we do anything.'

'You will be careful!'

'Don't fret so, we're finally going to defeat the lackeys of the Empire.'

'May God help you!' said the Countess, crossing herself.

'God and the mandate of the Count of Artois.'

Sémallé turned on his heels, put on his big black hat and went out to meet his friend La Grange in the courtyard. They took two horses from the stable and, once mounted, set off slowly down the boulevard de la Madeleine, picking their way through an anxious and various crowd gathered beneath the lime trees. At the barrier of the Faubourg Montmartre the Parisians were preparing their defences, such as they were: *chevaux-de-frise* that had been rolled out during the night on the roads and alleyways. There were no fortifications, just a dismantled tollgate, a cannon with no gunners, and palisades manned by university students in new clothes and workers in overalls armed with sticks and carving knives. National Guardsmen were turning up as reinforcements, loaves and fat brioches impaled on their bayonets. Many of them carried picks with tricolour banners for want of muskets. They wore a few scraps of uniform, chalk-whitened shoulder straps over their frock-coats. A notary wore yellow leggings, and a grocer had his trousers tied with string at his ankles. These were the workmen, the property-owners, the shopkeepers ruined by the ceaseless war who had been enlisted to defend the city. They had little idea of the danger that faced them, and came out with a jumble of truth and wild rumour when Sémallé questioned them.

'They've attacked the Bois de Romainville.'

'There's only one column there.'

'What're you on about? There are whole armies, really there are!'

'The King of Prussia's been taken prisoner, I was told

by a sergeant on his way back from Belleville, they're going to parade him through the boulevards.'

The cannon didn't fall silent. Men on horseback circulated among the groups, distributing proclamations which they carried in packs on their saddles. La Grange took one and handed it to the Count. Sémallé put on his glasses and read in a loud voice:

> We will be pillaged!
> We will be burned!
> While the Emperor arrives
> on the arses of the enemy . . .

The appeal called the massive assault by the allies a 'helping hand', but asked for the barricades to be raised, for trenches to be dug, for loopholes to be cut in the walls, for cobblestones to be carried into the houses to serve as projectiles and for the streets to be blocked by overturned vehicles.

'A little later,' smiled the Count.

'Childish nonsense.'

'Who's going to tell us what's really happening, La Grange?'

'I only know one place in Paris, Your Lordship, where they know exactly what's going on.'

'You're right, let's go to the rue Saint-Florentin.'

This was Talleyrand's address.

*

The first floor of the unfinished Hôtel Saint-Florentin overlooked the rue de Rivoli. There, Monsieur de Talleyrand was at his toilet, following a ritual that no tragedy could alter. As ever, he had spent a large part of the night playing whist, before going to sleep in an almost seated position, wearing fourteen cotton hats for fear of falling on his head. When the clock chimed half-past eleven, he drank his camomile tea by the marble fireplace in his room, surrounded by a *corps de ballet* of valets in grey aprons, who hummed as they pomaded him, curled, combed and powdered his wig, and presented him with the silver bowl in which he dipped his fingers to wash himself. When this was done, he sucked several glasses of luke-warm water through his nostrils. He was sixty years old, with a turned-up nose, soft cheeks, clay-coloured skin and dead eyes; only his mouth was expressive, sometimes indicating irony, sometimes contempt.

One valet slipped a shirt over the rags and flannels that swaddled him, while another, kneeling, slipped silk stockings over the woollen stockings that already concealed his atrophied legs.

His entourage witnessed the spectacle.

A member of the Regency Council, the former Bishop of Autun, Prince of Benevento, and prince of intrigue, Talleyrand surrounded himself with a coterie of unfrocked abbots who hated the Emperor and admitted as much. They included Monsieur de Pradt, a disgraced ambassador who distributed the *Times* and the *Morning Chronicle* which were sent to him by a lady in Brussels; the nonchalant Montesquiou; Jaucourt, Joseph Bonaparte's chamberlain, who was very well informed about the movement of the troops; Baron Louis, now a banker, who had served mass at the Feast of the Federation during the Revolution – and others of similar stamp.

Sémallé, emboldened by the sudden impunity conferred upon him by the proximity of the enemy cannon, had entrusted his horses to La Grange and fearlessly entered this den of conspirators. He approached Jaucourt, an acquaintance of his, and whispered in his ear so as not to disturb the ceremony, 'What are Monseigneur's plans for today?'

Monseigneur Talleyrand had risen to his feet, and two valets were hoisting his black silk breeches up to his belly. Without looking at the Count, Jaucourt murmured like a ventriloquist, 'That will depend on the battle currently being fought outside Paris.'

'What news?'

'The Russian grenadiers are in Pantin, the Prussians have occupied the plain of Romainville, the Austrians are attacking Bagnolet, having already taken Montreuil. Saint-Maur and Bondy have fallen . . .'

'What has Monseigneur decided?'

'He has great respect for facts, so let us wait for the facts to speak to him.'

'Does he predict a return of the Bourbons?'

'His uncle, the former Archbishop of Reims, has become senior chaplain to King Louis XVIII, as you know, and they are in correspondence with one another . . .'

Sémallé was suspicious on principle, and his whispered exchange with Jaucourt continued. 'All the same,' he said, 'he has publicly asked the Empress to remain in Paris.'

'No doubt, but the Empress hates him. If he asks her to do anything, she does the opposite.'

'A deliberate strategy?'

'Are you surprised?'

The Count saw Talleyrand as a regicide, and was as angry with him as the emigrants were when, like them, he fled the Terror to Kensington Square: the man deserved to be broken on the wheel. Sémallé believed that Talleyrand had played a crucial part in the abduction of the Duke of Enghien in Ettenheim, and blamed him for the Duke's execution in the ditches of Vincennes, because in order to consolidate the Consulate he'd had to give a pledge to the Jacobins by killing a Bourbon. Certainly – and this was heard abroad among the royalists – it was Talleyrand who had, in a coded message, incited the hesitant allies to charge on Paris. In short, the important thing was not to trust, but to use this character, since he had such influence in the Senate.

Talleyrand stepped towards his minions on his bandy legs, his feet skating on the waxed parquet, his shirt floating over his breeches.

'My carriage? My bags?'

'They await you, Monseigneur.'

Some of those present smiled complicitly, while the others, dumbfounded, looked mutely at one another. Was Talleyrand going to visit the Imperial court and the government, now installed in Blois? If he left Paris as battle commenced, that could mean that he had been weighing up the likelihood of the Emperor's return; perhaps he had personal information on the matter. Had he ceased to believe that the monarchy would be restored? What was he playing at? Sémallé took advantage of some movement among the courtiers – fussing around their master – to leave the room. He briefly summed up the situation to La Grange, who was holding their horses by the bridle.

'So the sly dog really has decided to leave?' asked the Marquis.

'And,' said Sémallé, 'is that not a sign?'

A carriage stood by the steps, harnessed to four white horses; the lackeys were piling trunks into the van that would follow it.

'Those valets are hardly strong men,' La Grange continued.

'What do you mean?'

'Take a look for yourself.'

A valet, thin as a rake, was carrying a large trunk by the handles all by himself. He hoisted it effortlessly, at arm's length, on to the van.

'So that means . . .' muttered Sémallé with a frown.

'I sense a ruse.'

La Grange caught sight of a liveried child carrying a large suitcase on his shoulder. He casually approached the boy and, pretending to be distracted, bumped into him. The lad dropped his case.

'Clumsy!' said the Marquis.

'Hang on, monsieur, you were the one who . . .'

'Who dropped the case? Enough!' La Grange furiously bent down and picked up the case in question, which was so light that he was able to lift it with one hand.

'But sir . . .'

'Silence, rascal, or I'll tell them to throw you into the street for damaging the Prince of Benevento's luggage . . .'

'Not that . . .'

'Then keep your trap shut!'

The Marquis pressed the catch, half-opened the suitcase and glanced inside, then returned to Sémallé and the horses.

'The cases are empty.'

*

During wars, as during revolutions, when everything else is closed in the city, the cafés stay open; rakes and braggarts strut about the terraces exchanging their views on the way of the world. On this particular afternoon, a clutch of writers and out-of-work actors were getting drunk on words and punch in the Café des Variétés on the boulevard Montmartre. The establishment was next door to the new Passage des Panoramas, and the rotunda of the same name, a stone's throw from their theatre with its Greek temple façade. Preparing to interpret a tragedy of Racine bowdlerized by the censors, they ignored the sound of the cannon and the throng of concerned or curious people milling around them, in small groups that quickly formed and then dissolved again, heading off suddenly in different directions. Commandeered fiacres pushed their way through these crowds; marked with black flags that could be seen from a long distance away, they were lugging piles of blood-drenched soldiers to the hospitals.

The thespians, meanwhile, whose number included both gentlemen and several young ladies in furbelows, saw the situation as an opportunity. Their work had been badly treated by a government mistrustful of the theatre, which it considered too popular and thus too dangerous. If the Empire were to fall today, they could finally put on an unexpurgated *Britannicus*.

'What can you see?' one of them asked his neighbour, a thin tow-headed man who was directing his telescope towards the hills.

'I see troops mounting an assault on the windmills of Montmartre, coming up through the vines.'

'Bad luck on the vines, but it's all undrinkable anyway!' thundered a fat man whose face was a mass of broken veins.

'Russians?' ventured an ingénue in a feathered hat.

'Blue jackets, fur hats . . .'

'Mounted grenadiers à cheval of the Guard, probably General Belliard's men,' said Octave, who was listening at the next table.

'Come and join us, Mr Know-it-all,' suggested the red-faced man, pointing to a free chair.

'You don't look awfully military,' said the ingénue.

'I'm not, but I've learned to identify the different armies,' replied Octave, sitting down among the actors, glass in hand.

He had donned Blacé's wig and tapered frock-coat, but kept his own cane. He turned to the thin man. 'May I borrow your opera-glasses?'

'Of course, and then you can give us a commentary on the battle.'

Putting his eye to the opera-glasses, Octave could make out the seven cannons of Belleville being used by the artillery of the Guard. Some troopers were in fact climbing the hill, stumbling over the vine shoots, to liberate the gunners from a flood of Russians who were coming up from the opposite direction amid white smoke and exploding shells.

'Well?'

'You'd have to be there,' said Octave, folding up the opera-glasses, which he stuffed in his pocket.

He got up, gave a slight bow and was about to disappear into the agitated crowd when the thin actor tried to hold him back by the sleeve.

'My opera-glasses!'

'I'm confiscating them; they're of no use to you.'

'Thief!'

'Spy!' added the red-faced man.

'Fink!' cried the ingénue.

Octave swept the table with his cane, knocking scalding punch over their knees. They yelled, but amid all the commotion no one paid the slightest attention. Once outside – although jostled, harried and dragged along by the opposing currents of the crowd – Octave managed to force his way back along the boulevards until he found himself behind the derisory barricade of the Porte Saint-Denis, far from the barriers.

The local people were at their windows or on their roofs. For want of coaches, those who had fled had left their many possessions behind, piled up on the pavement, and the National Guard were carting furniture away to reinforce their defences. Planks from a building site supported wardrobes, bed-frames and chairs, all weighted down with cobble-stones. The monumental arch, whose pillars were, ironically, sculpted with royal victories, the crossing of the Rhine and the taking of Maastricht, was obstructed by carts. Skirmishers lay in wait, their eyes fixed on the long road leading from the buildings of the suburb to the gardens of the enclosure of Saint Lazare and the square buildings of the royal mail-coach service, before passing through the fallow fields scattered with farms, hamlets and hedges. The noise of the cannon was constant, louder now, and closer.

Octave perched on a tree-trunk that had been thrown across the road, and rested his elbows on the sandbags crowning the barricade. At his side, a toff was firing harmless duelling-pistols; his neighbour, a top-hatted apothecary, shouldered his hunting rifle, grunting, 'They'll taste my potion, the bastards!' In the distance, pillars of black smoke rose from bombed-out villages at the foot of the hills. A troop of men came up the road, wearing scorched uniforms filthy with mud, ash and gunpowder, their foreheads wrapped with bloody cloths. They were carrying dying men on stretchers, a blanket, a coat tied to some branches.

Octave and some volunteers leapt down from their barricade and helped the soldiers climb over it, holding the moaning casualties in their arms. The most seriously injured were immediately laid on an ammunition wagon pulled by some strong men, to be taken to a hospital if one able to admit them could be found; the remainder lay in improvised ambulances below the gates. Octave carried down a corporal with a big moustache, a gold ring in his ear and a vacant expression on his face, and entrusted him to some women who tore their aprons and headscarves into strips to serve as compresses or bandages.

'There are too many,' said the corporal, over and over again.

'The Prussians? The Russians?'

'There are too many. The more you kill, the more there are . . .'

At that moment a cavalryman emerged from the boulevard Poissonnière. He had lost his helmet, but Octave recognized him as a cheveau-léger by his green jacket and the red-and-white pennon on his lance. The man rode his mount into the crowd, knocking men and women over as he passed. He was drunk and shouting, 'Run for your lives!' This unleashed a movement of panic, a retreat into the streets running down to the Seine. Shortly afterwards, a shell crashed into the middle of the road and all the women and unarmed onlookers charged off in search of shelter. They ran hither and thither, bellowing at the tops of their voices; fresh casualties, civilians this time, crowded the paths of the houses. Octave unfolded the opera-glasses. On the Butte Montmartre, among the windmills, he saw cavalrymen with stovepipe hats and impossibly long lances: the Cossacks were turning their cannon on the capital. He saw others, a cloud of them, charging down the hills towards the blazing houses of Belleville.

*

At about four o'clock in the afternoon, a terrible silence followed the roar of battle. The injured men revealed that the Army of Silesia had occupied the banks of the Ourcq, that Marmont had forced his way through with cold steel, to retreat to the Belleville tollgate with decimated battalions. In considerable numbers, the enemy had taken Ménilmontant, La Villette, Clichy. In Paris, the shutters were going up. The crowd, once so noisy, was now scattering in silence, hoping for a truce, fearful of the even more dreadful Prussian and Russian troops. Impoverished gangs emerging from the slummiest parts of the city would lead them to the homes of the wealthy, to make off with a share of the booty.

Octave was in a hurry. He had a meeting at 36 rue de l'Echiquier, with this man Lemercier who was receiving the royalist Committee. He knocked at the door of the house, and La Grange in person opened it.

'You had no difficulty finding us, I see.'

'Thanks to the map you drew me,' replied lying Octave.

'Gracious! You have blood on your sleeve!'

'I helped carry the wounded.'

'Such self-denial, my dear man!'

'Had I refused, I would have drawn attention to myself.'

'That's true . . .'

Most of the Committee members had arrived, and sat astride tapestried chairs or lolled in gothic armchairs. The sun filtered through the little yellow window-panes. La Grange introduced Octave as Blacé, and identified his associates, Morin, Davaray, Poisson, Brigard, Laporte, Gourbillon, Imperial functionaries prepared to commit acts of treason, merchants, a couple of noblemen. They began asking Octave some questions about the mood in London, but he did not need to recite the lesson he had learned from the real Blacé, because at that moment Sémallé came into the room, rubbing his hands. One of the conspirators took his coat and hat, another offered the newcomer the comfortable armchair in which he had been sitting – but Sémallé preferred to dominate the assembly from a standing position:

'My friends,' he said, 'we have cause to be cheerful, but we are the only ones who can turn a stroke of luck into a triumph. Let me explain . . .'

Intrigued by the vanload of empty suitcases, Sémallé had, from a distance, followed the carriage that was supposedly to take Talleyrand to Blois, where he would be close to the still lawful government and the Empress. The carriage had driven very slowly to the tollgate at Faubourg de la Conférence, just short of Chaillot.

'Monseigneur clearly wanted as many people as possible to see him leave.'

'Why on earth?'

'To demonstrate, by Jove, that he had obeyed the orders of the Regency Council, because in reality, I can assure you, he did not leave. At this very moment, I would guess that he is plotting in his house in the rue Saint-Florentin.'

'A fake farewell . . .'

'All a pretence, yes. At the La Conférence tollgate, the sentry stopped him and asked for his passport, and he shouted, outraged, "Good heavens, don't you know who I am?" The performance was well orchestrated. The chief sentry, Monsieur de Rémusat, was in on it. He gave strict orders to prevent Talleyrand from getting through. Furthermore, when some guards intervened on his behalf to let him get away, Monseigneur was furious, he shrieked in his reedy voice, "That's enough! One insult is quite enough! I am prevented from fulfilling my duty, well, too bad, I shall stay!" I was on horseback, a little further along the quay, I witnessed the scene. Later on I learned the details from our indispensable Jaucourt . . .'

'What was the point of this little game?'

'Monseigneur wants to give guarantees to all parties, even Bonaparte's. You know how prudent he is.'

'Exactly,' Octave butted in. 'That might mean that he envisages the Emperor's possible return, and is covering his back.'

'Do not say *the Emperor*, my dear Blacé, say *Bonaparte* as we do. Whatever else may be the case, we have Talleyrand nearby, surrounded by the partisans of our cause . . .'

Sémallé, horrified by Octave's sadly accurate remark, chose to move straight to the agenda. Jaucourt had assured him that the allies were currently talking to Mortier and Marmont with a view to negotiating a cessation of hostilities and the retreat of their troops, who were now threatened with extermination. Joseph Bonaparte in person had ordered his marshals to sign an armistice, before galloping away. That was why the cannon had fallen silent. The remnants of the French armies would pass through Paris that night, and they would take the Rennes road to avoid running into Napoleon's troops, who were known to be to the east. Then the Count of Sémallé outlined everyone's role for the crucial hours of the following day.

'The capitulation needs to be signed,' he said, looking at the clock. Tomorrow the allies will enter Paris. It is up to us to prepare our best welcome for their sovereigns. Our demonstration must impress them. La Grange, you will take command of the Hôtel de Ville and the *mairies* of the *arrondissements*, and take with you some men who will distribute proclamations and white cockades . . .'

'Some Jacobins still dream of a republic,' said La Grange. 'The local councils could mobilize the National Guard to foil our movement.'

'That's exactly what we'll have to do: we must be able to anticipate the kind of order that any over-zealous functionary might launch.'

'There are so few of us,' Morin began.

'Remember the Malet conspiracy,' Sémallé cut in. 'Two years ago, how many of them were involved in the seizure of power? Five? Six? You were one of them, La Grange.'

'And we failed.'

'But only just! This time circumstances are on our side. Confusion works to the advantage of resolute men.'

'The Parisians have already read so many proclamations, will they believe ours?'

'It isn't a matter of telling the truth, my friend, but of creating a situation. Here is the text. Morin, see that it is printed. You will accompany him, La Grange, with whoever else you think you might need.'

Morin took the piece of paper and rolled it up. The Count continued:

'The others must keep themselves ready in the places assigned to them. They will have cockades, and the proclamations that they will collect from the printers. I will give the signal to hand them out; early in the morning, I will drape two white flags on each side of my house, one on the rue Saint-Honoré, the other on the boulevard de la Madeleine . . .'

La Grange and Morin rose to their feet and put on their coats. Octave was about to go with them when the Count stopped them.

'Langeron is in command of the Russian infantry. He is camped on the top of Montmartre. I need someone dedicated to warn him of the great royalist demonstration that is about to explode.'

'Me!' cried the Count of Douhet, a young man in a waistcoat, puffing out his chest.

'It's a dangerous mission,' Sémallé warned him.

'That's fine!'

'Here's a note I've written for Langeron. I want you to give it to him. Try to find out what the sovereigns have in mind, and what their plans are for entering Paris.'

Someone drummed on the door of the house. The

conspirators froze. Clutching a pistol, and with the Count following close behind him, Lemercier stealthily approached the door. The Count opened it abruptly, crashing it into a stout little man, liveried and breathless.

'Who are you?' asked Lemercier.

'I know him,' said the Count, 'he's one of Monsieur Jaucourt's valets. What's wrong, Ernest?'

'Monsieur Jaucourt sent me . . .'

'Catch your breath.'

'To warn you . . .'

'Get on with it!'

'The Emperor . . .'

'Yes?'

'He is . . .'

'Where, in God's name?'

'In Fontainebleau . . .'

The others had drawn closer. Because they had not heard what Ernest the valet had been mumbling, the Count of Sémallé repeated very calmly: 'Bonaparte is in Fontainebleau.'

Octave turned pale, and the Count noticed.

'Don't worry, Monsieur de Blacé, that does not conflict with our plans.'

※

La Grange and Morin set off to the printers, and Octave accompanied them. They filed along the narrow streets, twisting their ankles between the cobbles, and getting their shoes dirty because not even the bright sun could dry the black and sticky mud after weeks of rain. Instinctively they hugged the walls to avoid getting the contents of a chamber-pot on their heads, but they need not have worried: the people had locked themselves away in their houses. No one was brave enough to open the shutters; closeted indoors every sound became suspicious. The inhabitants of the houses trembled at the sound of echoing footsteps, they waited for the battle to resume – this time inside the city – because no one had told them about the surrender negotiated at the Petit Jardinet, a tavern in La Villette.

With a great wave of his arm, La Grange indicated the closed façades.

'They're about to have their last night of fear.'

'The war is over!' cried Morin.

'Perhaps,' said Octave.

'*Perhaps?*' said the Marquis, astonished.

'I'm thinking about what might happen, something that we haven't allowed for . . .'

'This is a time for deeds, my dear fellow, not doubts!'

'That's true,' said Morin.

The previous day, Octave had consulted the dossier on Claude Marie Morin that he had taken from a police file at Pommereul's house, and learned that he straddled the worlds of the bourgeoisie and the artistic milieu: Masséna's secretary during the siege of Genoa, he had written epic poems to the glory of the Emperor, sung the crossing of the St Bernard Pass, composed an elegy on the burning of Copenhagen and penned an ode to Empress Marie-Louise – all published by the printer Michaud, to whose establishment they were now setting off on a quite different mission. Despite Morin's literary achievements, the sly dog was now gloating over the fall of his god, joyfully repeating over and over again, 'Twenty years of war and it's over!'

Octave wasn't sure about that. What was the Emperor doing in Fontainebleau? He was going to assemble a motley but ferocious army, and everything was still to play for.

Taking a right turn in front of the Théâtre Feydeau, the three men heard wheels creaking over by the rue Montmartre, and could even see thin horses pulling crates. Grenadiers, heads bowed, slipped by like ghosts. To avoid these retreating regiments, the three took to the alleyways, which gave them a head start to the Place des Victoires.

There were soldiers everywhere, lying on the ground, sitting against the pyramid, some of them reminiscing about the Egyptian Campaign. Others strolled among the lounging groups, their uniforms torn, blackened with dust and soil, sad and silent, their bones frozen by the cool of evening, their stomachs empty. Some tirailleurs, perched on ladders and wielding bayonets or axes, attacked the structure concealing the statue of General Desaix, who had fallen at Marengo. It was a colossal monument, standing nearly twenty feet tall in the middle of the square, and the local prudes had asked for it to be veiled because it showed the hero entirely naked, like an ancient Greek. As the soldiers chopped away the horizontal planks to use them as firewood, the statue reappeared, first the face and the flowing hair, then the torso, and now they were down to the hips. La Grange and the others walked around the square, which was now illuminated by the fires of twenty bivouacs. They arrived near the Palais-Royal, at the corner of the rue des Bons-Enfants; it was there that Michaud kept his printing-works.

Michaud ushered them in wearing a leather apron, his shirt-sleeves rolled up to the elbows. He led them into his studio in the half-cellar, a vaulted room that smelled of ink and was lit by oil lamps, which he hurried to turn up.

'The text?' he asked Michaud.

'Here it is,' said Morin, unrolling Sémallé's sheet, which he took from his pocket.

'There's no time to lose.'

'How many could you print off in an hour?'

'About four hundred.'

'Is that all?' asked Octave.

'What? I haven't got a steam-driven machine like they have in London, Monsieur! I'm a simple craftsman, and I can't afford to go any faster.'

'I know,' replied Morin.

'Have you had any cause to complain of my services?'

'Come now! Let's have no bickering,' La Grange interrupted impatiently.

While Octave kept watch on the street through a grilled basement window, the printer began to set the text, taking the characters one by one from their wooden boxes.

'Is there anything we can do to help?'

'Absolutely not,' grunted Michaud. 'It's a craft.'

He inked the letters with a brush, and sheet by sheet he worked his machine, its noise amplified beneath the vaulted ceiling in the calm of dusk. La Grange picked up the first poster and read it in a murmur by the light of a lamp:

People of Paris, the hour of your deliverance has come.
May a feeling stifled for many years find voice in the cry,
repeated a thousand times over: *Long live the King!*
Long live Louis XVIII! Long live our glorious liberators!

'Shut up!' Octave said suddenly, nose still pressed to the basement window.

'What?'

'Be quiet, I tell you, I can see a pair of gaiters approaching.'

'It's nothing,' said Michaud, pushing down on his manual press. 'We're behind the Banque de France, and the National Guard are just patrolling as normal.'

'This isn't a normal evening,' insisted Octave, and they've stopped by the door, they're talking to each other . . .'

The sound of a musket-butt striking the door finally made them fall silent and Michaud sighed:

'Don't move, I'll go. I know the local Guards.'

He climbed the three steps, leaving the communicating door half open so that the conspirators below could follow his conversation with the officer of the National Guard, formerly a fashionable tailor.

'There's a lot of noise going on for the time of night!'

'I'm late with a piece of work.'

'In spite of events?'

'Because of them. I haven't got an assistant, so I'm doing it myself, and I'm up against it.'

'All on your own?'

'Yes.'

'Surely not,' said another voice, 'I'm convinced there was an unusual amount of activity in here, I saw it with my own eyes.'

'I was having some paper delivered.'

'Can I take a look at your studio?'

'Of course, but why would you want to? Come on, I'll give you a bottle to help you get through the night!'

There was laughter, the sound of backs being slapped and then footsteps, followed by the front door closing. Michaud returned to his press: 'They'll be back, I'm sure of it, you should leave discreetly . . .'

'But what about our posters?' asked Morin.

'There are about thirty already printed,' Michaud told him. 'Take those, I'll go on working and everything will be ready for our bill-stickers tomorrow morning.'

'But if the guards come back,' said Octave, 'they'll read our prose.'

'Don't worry, I'll tell them I'm doing some printing for a theatre that's about to reopen. I'll put older posters on top of what we've printed . . .'

He showed them a pile of posters announcing a vaude-ville by Désaugiers and Gentil, *The Ogress*, in which the comic actor Tiercelin had triumphed the previous year.

*

Octave rested his elbows against the guard-rail of an open window beneath the roofs. By leaning forward he could make out the pinnacles of the Hôtel de Ville that they were about to commandeer. Behind him, La Grange and Morin had finished a quick meal, drinking a mixture of water and vinegar in order to stay sober. The Marquis rose to his feet, stretching himself.

'Let's go and get some sleep,' he said, 'even if it's only for a couple of hours. We'll need our strength at dawn.' La Grange withdrew into the adjacent room, and Morin into his bedroom, at the end of a corridor; Octave would make do with a sofa.

Left alone in the drawing-room, he fetched his binocu-lars from the pocket of his frock-coat, unfolded them and trained his gaze on the army encampments. Very early in the morning those men would be re-forming into columns and leaving Paris for the west, but it was also possible that their officers would lead them to Fontainebleau to place them under the Emperor's orders. Octave wondered what his own fate would be. If the royalists, with their man-oeuvring and collusion, succeeded in installing Louis XVIII on the throne, then emigrants would be returning from London, people who had known the real Blacé, and when that happened Octave would have to flee the capital. Why didn't he leave that very night? He had just enough time to run along the rue Saint-Sauveur, change his clothes and his hairstyle, and pocket the gold packed away in the luggage of the cavalryman whose name and wig he had borrowed.

Octave was determined to get to Fontainebleau and meet the Duke of Bassano, his employer, but first he could scupper part of the royalist plan by eliminating two of the most active conspirators: La Grange and Morin were sleeping sweetly a few metres away from him; if he killed them, they wouldn't be able to stir up any more trouble among the functionaries of the Hôtel de Ville and the town halls. Octave took his cane in one hand, a candlestick in the other, and crept carefully into the office where the Marquis lay like a recumbent figure on a tomb, his mouth open and his hands on his belly. Setting the candlestick on a chest of drawers, and gripping his cane in both hands, he was about to bring the latter crashing down when the Marquis opened an eye and said in a cool and sonorous voice, 'Were you looking for a blanket?'

'Yes . . .'

'Can't you get to sleep?'

'Neither can you.'

'I'm resting, and I suggest you do the same: we have a hard day ahead of us.'

'I know . . .'

'And I know what your problem is, Blacé, you think too much.'

'You think so?'

'Don't worry, my friend, everything will come to pass as we have decided it should. God will protect us.'

Discountenanced by La Grange's natural manner and naïve trust, Octave abandoned his murderous project. Why had he failed? With one well-aimed blow he could have split the Marquis's head open, without giving him a chance to utter a cry and alert his accomplice; after that Octave could have executed Morin. But he felt tired, and perhaps he really was thinking too much; he no longer had the killer instinct his profession required.

Yawning, Octave decided to delay his departure – anticipating the muddle of the next few days, he would wait for, and seize, the next opportunity – and looked back down at the Seine. Firelight, far away on the left bank, past the Faubourg Saint-Denis: had some irregular Cossacks taken advantage of the truce to enter the city unimpeded?

Octave was mistaken about the nature of the flames that licked the court of the Imperial residence in the Invalides. In actual fact, Marshal Sérurier, the commander of the Parisian National Guard, had ordered the trophies stored in the chapel to be burned on a gigantic pyre; the 1,800 colours captured during the wars of the Revolution and the Empire were on no account to fall into the hands of the enemy – not the flags themselves, nor the metal of the staffs, nor even the ashes, which would be consigned to the river in the morning.

*

Octave woke before dawn. Curled up on the sofa, he had slept little and badly. Now he sat up with a stupid expression, his wig perched at an angle. Morin had filled two baskets with the white cockades that he had kept in his wood-chest, and he was pinning them to their hats. La Grange was busy loading his pistols. 'Hurry up,' he said to Octave, 'we're off.'

'Already?'

'It's six o'clock.'

'A quick wash and I'll be with you . . .'

'No time. We must surprise the rabble at the crack of dawn.'

Outside, the army had disappeared. Octave crossed the Place de Grève, flanked by the two royalists. Bah, he said to himself, I'll jot down a few names, and make a note of any about-turns and hesitations. That'll be useful to the Emperor, who likes weak people. They're more manageable than hotheads.

The three men walked through the main porch of the Hôtel de Ville (the National Guards on sentry duty didn't even think of stopping them – you don't check people who walk with such a determined stride) and climbed the large stone staircase on the right, which led to the single upper storey. A bald clerk, dressed in black, raised his hands to block their way: 'Gentlemen, gentlemen! Where are you going?'

They did not reply; Octave pushed the clerk aside with his cane, like a walker bending back a branch in his way.

'Messieurs!' cried the man, gawping and staggering in their wake.

A second clerk tried to obstruct their path by pressing himself against both wings of a large door:

'No one comes in here, this is the Prefect's office!'

'But he's the man we've come to see,' said La Grange.

'Our of the question!'

'I beg to differ,' said Octave, catching the man by the lapels.

'The Prefect is not in his office!'

'Where is he?'

'He's at the Ministry of the Interior, where the mayors of the *arrondissements* are meeting at this very moment.'

'Who is taking his place?'

'The Secretary-General . . .'

'Go and get him.'

'I'm sorry?'

'We urgently need to speak to him.'

'Who's that making such a racket?' said a stocky, short-legged individual emerging from a corridor?

'Monsieur Walknaer,' mumbled the clerk, 'these gentlemen wanted to meet the Prefect . . .'

'Are you the Secretary-General?' asked La Grange.

'Precisely so,' said Monsieur Walknaer, alarmed by the intrusion and the appearance of these unshaven visitors.

La Grange moved to stand in front of the Secretary-General, parting his frock-coat so that the latter could see the handles of the pistols sticking out of his belt: 'How can the Prefect absent himself under such circumstances? It's insane!'

'Monsieur de Chabrol is in a meeting . . .'

'In any case, he is no longer the Prefect of the Seine, he has been replaced.'

'By whom?'

'By Monsieur Morin here, who has come to take his post and occupy his office. Ha! Let us in! No? If you are not willing to serve your new Prefect, I can have you replaced as well.'

'I didn't say I was refusing . . .'

'A fine idea, if I may say so, and much the better for you: the allied sovereigns have just recognized Louis XVIII as King of France.'

'I didn't know . . .'

'Of course, you were here, either shut away or asleep! Here are the proclamations, and some white cockades which you will immediately distribute to your staff.'

Morin held one of his baskets out to the Secretary-General, who ventured a question: 'What if they don't want to wear them?'

'Then throw them out! Right now, we have work to do.'

The three conspirators entered the Prefect's office, shutting the door in the clerks' faces.

'Here is your office, Morin. Lovely location. First of all, reprint our appeal using the Prefecture's services, and order them to be posted up in every district.'

'If they obey me . . .'

'This pack of cowards is under your orders.'

'But what if Monsieur de Chabrol comes back?' asked Morin anxiously.

'What? Are you going to give up on us now?'

'No, no . . .'

'You've got plenty of time, those windbags from the councils and the ministries will go on endlessly nattering, they haven't a clue where their interests lie, and anyway, as of this evening, Paris will have a Russian or Austrian governor.'

Octave pricked up his ears:

'Did you hear that? Sounds like horses, a whole troop of them.'

'Here we go!' said Morin gloomily. 'The Prefect's back.'

Octave and La Grange opened one of the windows.

A detachment of cavalrymen, in blue uniforms and black shakos, was coming from the quays, led by a general in a plumed cocked hat. 'The Prussians!' said the Marquis. These good people will help us.' La Grange seized the second basket of cockades and dragged Octave over to the big staircase, where some terrified officials were holding hasty confabulations.

Down below, Monsieur Walknaer was negotiating with anyone who still refused to wear a royalist cockade. When he saw La Grange and Octave slipping off towards the front steps, he joined them. They reached the court-yard together just as the dragoons of Brandenburg were marching in. At the sight of them, the General dismounted and introduced himself. He was a middle-aged man, covered with medals and gold badges, with a thin goatee and a smartly curled moustache.

'I am General Baron Plotho, Chief of Staff to the King of Prussia . . .'

'Where are you going, General?' asked the Marquis.

'To see the Prefect.'

'I am the Prefect.'

'*Sehr gut*, Meuzieur! I have come to reach the agreement with you for the living places of the Emperors of Russia and Austria, my sovereign and some princes who are with them.'

'Secretary General!' cried La Grange.

'I'm here, sir, there's no need to shout,' said poor Walknaer.

'Who is in charge of the accommodation of the foreign sovereigns?'

'Monsieur Monnet, the head of department.'

'Drop your basket and call him this minute!'

Walknaer ran off and came back almost immediately with a fat, maggot-like character who, adjusting his white tie, began to speak without waiting.

'Everything has been sorted out. His Majesty the Emperor of Russia wants to live on the Champs-Elysées, the Emperor of Austria in the boulevards, the King of Prussia has demanded the Faubourg Saint-Germain . . .'

'Have the *mairies* of those *arrondissements* been warned of this?'

'Not yet, but . . .'

'But I am dealing with it myself,' said La Grange, 'along with the General.' And the Marquis gestured to the coach-driver who was waiting on his box in the courtyard. The coach pulled in at the bottom of the stairs.

'You can't take that carriage!' Monsieur Walknaer protested, embarrassed.

'And why not?'

'It's Monsieur de Chabrol's . . .'

'He is nothing now!' And then, to the Prussian: 'Get in, General, together we must go and recognize the residences of our liberators.'

'This is a very good idea, I think,' said Baron Plotho, climbing into the berlin.

Octave joined him with the cockades, and La Grange issued an order to the coachman: 'Rue de l'Echiquier, number 36!'

*

'My friends, I have been successful! Morin is in the Hôtel de Ville, in the Prefect's chair!'

'Bravo!'

'I have with me a Prussian general who believes I am a higher authority: he is going to serve as guarantor!'

'Bravo! Bravo! Bravo!'

The Committee members still present at Lemercier's had risen to their feet, and they applauded as one might applaud a resolute deed in a play. La Grange, in a state of boundless jubilation, continued.

'I am going to the *mairies* of the *arrondissements* with our Prussian friend, to prepare the accommodation of the sovereigns and their retinues. Come with me, let us announce that the allies have recognized Louis XVIII!'

There were more volunteers than would fit in the carriage (from which the conspirators were to throw handfuls of royalist cockades at passers-by), and Octave seized upon this as an excuse: he would go to the Count of Sémallé and tell him about their dawn raid. La Grange approved; he climbed into the real Prefect's berlin, pressing against Baron Plotho, and the two set off, escorted by sky-blue dragoons, who were surprised by being thus welcomed into a conquered capital. Octave set off in the other direction, towards the boulevard.

It was almost ten o'clock, and the smarter districts had

very quickly reassumed their normal appearance once the Parisians had learned of the capitulation. They had dreaded the possibility that the city might be put to the torch: over the past few days, *La Gazette de France* and *Les Débats* had recounted so many horrors that, since the worst had failed to materialize, there was a great sense of relief. Yesterday, the walls of the houses had been bare and black with soot; today they were covered with gaudy posters, advertisements for music-halls, for concerts, lotteries, hotels and magic potions, but also with insults against Napoleon, jubilantly scribbled caricatures (one showed the Emperor on all fours, with his buttocks in a broken drum, and a Russian general beating the march with a birch whip). All of a sudden life was reborn, light and muddled. The boulevard once again filled with people. Fear had fled.

Octave approached a crowd who were laughing delightedly at two bourgeois in threadbare suits being manhandled by members of the National Guard armed with picks. 'Let me go!' screeched one of the bourgeois; held firmly by the collar, he was wiggling and waving his arms around, but they were too short to reach the stout, uniformed fellow who was holding him. Octave recognized a conspirator from the royalist Committee, and he remained apart, hidden by the growing crowd. As he watched, one of the guards tore the white cockade from the hat of the other bourgeois, threw it on the ground and stamped on it; as his victim protested, another guard picked up the posters the royalist had been carrying, plunged them into his bucket of glue and smeared the man's face with them. Octave quietly removed the cockade that Morin had pinned on his hat, and sloped off.

Over by the Madeleine he noticed a white flag flapping,

as predicted, from one of the balconies of Sémallé's house.
If the passers-by did happen to look up, no one complained, no one saluted – and it looked as though they
were getting away with it. The flags no longer made the
Parisians tremble, either with shame or joy; they were
waking from an improbable dream, the air was sweet, and
they wanted to dance. The shopkeepers imagined that
business would pick up, that the invaders would make
their fortunes for them by buying huge quantities of
fabrics, necklaces and wine; others were convinced they
would fill their theatres or their taverns: the foreign
officers would distribute gold pieces without counting
them, they were so pleased with their victory after such
rough treatment throughout the winter.

Not far from the Count's house, a group of about twenty
young people in white scarves were waving handkerchiefs
on the ends of their canes, shouting, 'Down with the tyrant!
Long live the Bourbons!' In the suburbs they would have
been soundly thrashed, but here, in the elegant part of the
boulevards, the indifferent crowd simply opened up so they
could pass. These excited folk, Octave thought, had never
known kings. They didn't even understand their own
slogans, which they were barking out as though issuing
commands, inspired by hatred of the Imperial order.

Behind the youngsters he saw Marquis de Maubreuil –
recognizing him by his plum-coloured silk clothes: he had
tied his Cross of the Légion d'honneur to the tail of his
horse, and was singing in a tenor voice, *'Vive le roi!'*

*

The allied armies had entered Paris by the Pantin tollgate
at eleven o'clock. They had passed beneath the Porte

Saint-Denis, now cleared of its pitiful barricade. In the suburbs, the people had watched the impeccable squadrons passing by without much of a murmur, but in the capital the National Guard was acting as a police force, its officers holding back those who wanted to spit and curse at the young soldiers in their bright uniforms. There were even some cries of *'Vive l'Empereur!'* which were barely drowned out by the military fanfares. Then, though, as the armies passed through different districts, the nature of the crowd had changed: from the boulevard des Italiens onwards, the windows were covered with bed-sheets or white towels, elegant ladies waved handkerchiefs, and cheers rose by several tones as the marching men approached the Place de la Concorde.

'They're coming!' said the young Countess of Sémallé at her balcony. Deeply moved, she brushed a tear from her made-up cheek with a fingertip. Heralded by an impressive brass band playing an unfamiliar anthem, the red Cossacks of the Guard came first, followed by cuirassiers with gleaming boots, then the hussars, and the pearl-grey regiments of the King of Prussia.

'Eleven, twelve . . .' murmured Octave.

'How comforting they are!' remarked the dazzled Countess, beside him.

'Fourteen, fifteen . . .' said Octave.

'Fifteen what?' asked the Countess, clapping her hands.

'The cavalrymen, madam, fifteen deep.'

'How handsome they are!'

'Control yourself, my dear,' the Count rebuked her.

'We've been waiting so long for this liberation!'

'Of course we have, Zoé, but a countess doesn't hop up and down.'

'The Count is right,' hazarded Octave. 'All the same, it's the first time since the Hundred Years War that foreign armies have defiled our capital . . .'

'But they aren't foreigners, Monsieur, they are our European cousins! Isn't that so, Jean-René?'

'Yes,' replied the Count. Then, to Octave: 'They won't stay, Blacé, they will restore power to us and then they will go home again. The people of Paris understand that, look at them.'

Down below, in the boulevard de la Madeleine, the crowd was surging in the direction of the procession, shouting: 'Long live our liberators!' Among the keenest of them, Octave thought he recognized the apothecary who had been so patriotic on the Saint-Denis barricade. His neighbour in that potential battle was now raising his hat, mouth open wide, to acclaim the very men whom he would cheerfully have massacred with his hunting rifle the day before. Meanwhile some hysterical women dashed towards the orderly ranks of the marching Russian cavalrymen, grabbing their boots, kissing their gloves and calling them 'saviours' and similar extravagant names.

Octave was not at all surprised to see a population turning in the blink of an eye to kneel before its conqueror. He was accustomed to the fickle feelings of his contemporaries, but one thing still intrigued him: the enemy soldiers were all wearing white armbands on their sleeves, as though parading for Louis XVIII. Octave leaned towards the Count and yelled loudly in his ear, for it was not easy to be heard among all the commotion:

'How did you persuade them to wear the symbol of our royal family?'

'Pure chance, my dear friend,' replied Sémallé in the same tone, 'a happy coincidence, a sign of Heaven, a misunderstanding that's bloody useful to us!'

Count de Langeron, who served the Tsar, had just told him the reason for the armbands. The other morning an English officer had been wounded by a Cossack who mistook him for one of Napoleon's grenadiers – because the allied soldiers had trouble telling French uniforms from Austrian, Russian, Prussian, English and German – so the staff had decided that they would wear armbands to avoid killing each other. However, the Parisians actually believed that the occupying forces were supporting the King of France and, lest they be importuned at a later date by this invading army, more and more were themselves wearing armbands, scarves, and the white cockades that Sémallé's men were now distributing without fear of harm. The Count had won his wager – the allied sovereigns would be convinced that the French were, in chorus, reclaiming their legitimate king. And he threw great handfuls of cockades like grain to pigeons.

A valet appeared on the balcony and whispered a few words to the Count, whose face lit up: 'My dear Blacé, the miracle continues! The blind can see, the deaf can hear!'

The heads of the aristocratic party had disdained or rejected Sémallé's overtures, but as events had progressed they were now jostling in his antechamber, aware of his connections with the Count d'Artois, the King's brother. Octave couldn't get over it: harebrained the day before yesterday, the Count's calculations had proved correct, and his far-fetched ideas were fast becoming reality.

*

Count Ferrand, the Duke of La Rochefoucauld, Doudeau-
ville and Chateaubriand were all in the drawing-room.
They wanted to take Sémallé to Mme de Mortefontaine's
house, where they had just set up a second Committee of
members of the senior aristocracy. Standing apart from the
rest, Octave watched and listened to them chirruping,
especially Chateaubriand, feverish, pale as a winding-
sheet, his head a mass of crazed little curls. Everyone knew
that he was writing a pamphlet against Bonaparte, that he
hid the manuscript under his pillow and went to sleep
every night with a pistol close at hand: he could breathe at
last, and had joined the others to request an audience with
Tsar Alexander and the King of Prussia, to persuade the
two sovereigns to recall Louis XVIII from exile.

The Count listened to the group with sardonic detachment, tempering their recent ardour, and hoping all the
while that La Grange, who had been out and about since
dawn, would soon return to tell him how the situation
was changing, what attitude to adopt, and when. In the
meantime he dragged the interview out as long as possible,
asking endless questions, and giving evasive answers to
those questions asked of him. Exhausted by the endless
waffle, one of the emissaries of the aristocratic party left
the group to chat to Octave, under the impression that the
latter knew the Count's secrets. The man had the face of
a little bird, lost amid the lace of his jabot, and a solemn
voice that was at odds with his appearance. He introduced
himself.

'Champcenetz. You must have heard of me, Monsieur
de Blacé.'

'Champcenetz, you say?'

'But of course, in London!'

'In London? Ah, yes, how silly of me!'

'Lady Salisbury, I was told, recommended you to our precious Sémallé, and indeed, she is a great friend: it is to her that I owe my life and my good fortune.'

Champcenetz did not look especially sly, but Octave's interest was kindled when he mentioned his career as an emigrant in England. This irritating character was all thumbs, but by observing his cooks he had learned how to toss a salad in the correct manner – by hand – and that was enough to establish his reputation. Brought into society by the Countess of Salisbury, he'd been in demand at the big houses, where he was asked to mix lettuce or cress in public, and he was invited to the upper-crust circles and restaurants that were then so fashionable. He'd trained up a number of pupils and returned to France, in around 1802, with an income of 150,000 francs.

'You're too young,' he said to Octave, 'to have known those times, when we arrived with nothing, driven out by the Jacobins who wanted to cut our throats.'

'To be fair, I was eight years old!'

'We were ruined, we became door-to-door salesmen, acrobats, water-carriers like Madame de Montmorency. You remember? Countesses sang in cafés, they sold fish from the Thames . . .'

'My mother made straw hats.'

'Terrible times, weren't they? But over there they have no guillotines – only sash windows!'

Champcenetz hiccuped at this quip, which he had repeated a thousand times, and then, with a sniff, asked Octave, 'And incidentally, how is that dear woman?'

'The Countess of Salisbury? Well, goodness me, she's quite well.'

'I assume she received you in her lovely house in Kensington . . .'

Octave didn't need to reply, as the Count of Sémallé, who had abandoned the gentlemen he had been speaking to, took him by the arm and dragged him into a little office nearby, where La Grange was waiting for them.

'We are at the helm,' said the Marquis, in an excellent mood. 'Baron Plotho, our Prussian friend from this morning, has introduced me to the new Governor of Paris, Sacken, a general who expresses himself in impeccable French, and now I'm his deputy. What do you think of that?'

'Perfect,' said Sémallé. 'We'll have to take care of the press without wasting a moment. Bonaparte has helped us: he banned most of the newspapers, we only have five to work on, those in Paris, which are responsible for public opinion. Appoint Morin Censor General, and let him appoint editors for each of those papers . . .'

'Michaud for *La Gazette de France*?'

'As you wish.'

'One other thing,' said La Grange. 'The Tsar is staying at the Hôtel Saint-Florentin.'

'Wasn't he supposed to be staying at the Elysée?' said Octave.

'Yes, but word reached him that the palace was mined, so he accepted the offer made him by Talleyrand . . .'

'. . . who sent that letter to bring Alexander to his residence, oh, the sly fox!'

'The worst thing is,' La Grange continued, 'that Caulaincourt is in the rue Saint-Florentin as we speak.'

'Damn! The Duke of Vincennes!' This was the name the royalists gave to the Duke of Vicenza, Caulaincourt;

they accused him of being involved in the abduction of the Duke of Enghien, who had been murdered at the Château de Vincennes.

The Count remained thoughtful, his eyes fixed on the patterns in the carpet. Caulaincourt, Grand Equerry to the Emperor, had known the Tsar in St Petersburg when he had been ambassador there, and they had liked one another. Bonaparte had sent him to negotiate, but to negotiate what? His throne? A regency? The Tsar admired Napoleon, he might consent to be swayed, and influence the other sovereigns. That was hardly something the royalists were about to organize.

'How could we find out what Bonaparte has in mind?' asked Sémallé. We have a spy in Fontainebleau, don't we?'

'A servant, Chauvin.'

'Has he been struck dumb?'

'He's worried, he will have to be replaced. In his last message, he said he was ready to take in one of our men. He would pretend the man in question was his cousin, and make sure he was given a job.'

'Who were you thinking of?'

'What about me?' suggested Octave, jumping at the chance to return to Fontainebleau.

'You?' the Marquis and Sémallé spoke simultaneously.

'Why not? I have one advantage: no one in the imperial entourage knows me.'

'That much I admit, my dear fellow, but could you really play the part of a servant?'

'As an émigré in London, you know, we survived by practising a thousand and one trades that had little to do with our rank. We became door-to-door salesmen, I even knew one viscount who was an acrobat, and Madame de Montmorency was a water-carrier . . .'

'Maybe. It's not such a bad idea.'

The Count opened one of his desk drawers and took out a cameo – a Negro's head on an agate – which he held out to Octave.

'When Chauvin sees this ring, he will understand. Then we need only arrange your departure from Paris and your journey to Fontainebleau. The city has been closed off since this afternoon.'

'I shall see to it,' said La Grange.

*

Monsieur de Sémallé hated wasting time. He was good at waiting, certainly, but when he had made a decision, he could not bear to delay its implementation; Octave did not have time to collect any personal effects from his rooms in the rue Saint-Sauveur, nor the booty of gold coins that he had taken from the luggage of the dead cavalryman whose outfit he had adopted.

The Count called in his valet and handed Octave over to him, with instructions to transform him into a thoroughly credible servant. To that end, Octave was given a grey morning-coat, a pair of stout travelling boots, and a flat, narrow-brimmed hat to lend him a provincial air, and a barber shaved his chin (but spared his nascent sideburns).

La Grange witnessed the transformation: 'I can already imagine you in livery,' he said. 'Basically, a livery and a duke's outfit are worn in similar fashion, wishbone protruding, like a turkey. Did you not notice that La Rochefoucauld has the bearing of a *sommelier*?'

Octave repeated the question he had asked the Marquis a few moments before: could they not, even just for a moment, call in at the rue Saint-Sauveur?

'You must leave as quickly as possible,' said La Grange, 'to pass through the enemy lines surrounding Paris. But give me your key, I will put your belongings out of harm's way myself.'

Octave resigned himself to handing over his key — his gold. This would be a loss to him; since the ill-fated Russian expedition, Napoleon had ceased to pay wages and salaries, or else had paid only very small amounts.

In the rue Saint-Honoré, La Grange himself opened the door of a dusty coach hitched up with ropes; the Russian coachman, who had a thick beard and was wearing a dark coat, did not bother to turn his head. 'Forgive the awful state of the vehicle,' the Marquis said to Octave, 'it's the only one the governor will make available to his new deputy . . .'

Inside, one of the Tsar's officers was waiting for them, his hair emerging in waves from beneath his flat cap and falling to his shoulders. He leaned forward to issue an instruction, and the coach set off.

'Where are we going?' asked Octave.

'To see General Sacken. While you were being disguised as a valet, Sémallé wrote a pass in your name, or rather, in the name of the servant whose cousin you are to become. Sacken has only to sign it, and then we will consider the manner of your departure.'

Along the length of the rue Saint-Honoré they saw Germans and Asians, Cossacks with sheepskins and red beards, brick-coloured Tartars with small whips around their necks, blue-uniformed uhlans from Silesia, stiff in their high collars, reining in their horses and leaving trails of dung behind them. They reached the Palais-Royal at nightfall just as lamps and windows were being lit around the gardens. There was a party at the Savoy Café, the royalist hideout where the Imperial police had never officially shown their faces. Beneath the wooden arcades the prostitutes strolled once more, luring the soldiers with a swing of the shoulder and a flash of the eye. Under striped awnings, wine was being served up from the barrel. Smoke from the roast-meat stalls stinging their eyes, Octave and the Marquis progressed through greasy fog that stuck to their clothes, past shops where pretty girls, dressed as sellers of knick-knacks, tried to persuade the passers-by to come inside, behind the screens, and entered a restaurant filled with braying officers in green frock-coats. The porter greeted La Grange, pointing towards the stairs.

Reaching the first floor, they found General Sacken, with his powdered wig and a strip of leather over one eye, his collar open, sitting at table with his entourage. The drawing-room was decorated in the oriental style; multiplied in the mirrors along all four walls, and engulfed by incense smoke that rose from braziers, the soldiers stabbed forks into the dishes before them, greedily tearing at their partridge casserole, stuffing their gullets with cucumbers and bone-marrow or sautéed white beet with ham – all of which, amid laughter and bellowed exchanges, was amply washed down with thick wines that burned the stomach. Some of the men, drunk already, staggered to the wide-open windows, guffawing between belches, and threw gold coins to the citizens assembled beneath the trees. Coloured lanterns, hanging from the branches, lit the beggars in a red light, making them look like a swarm of devils, as they elbowed each other out of the way, fought one another and held out their hats to collect the money raining down on them.

Sacken's chin glistened with sauce, and his eye was cloudy. Waving a drumstick he had been chewing on, he gestured to the colonels on either side of him to give up their seats to the new arrivals: 'Sit down, Monsieur, and you too, Deputy,' he said to Octave and the Marquis. 'Are you hungry?'

'We just need your support,' La Grange replied as he took his seat.

'A drink for my guests!'

A servant turbaned like a pantomime Bedouin immediately charged the glasses.

'What can I do for you?'

'Place your signature at the bottom of this pass. We're sending your comrade to join our provincial partisans.'

'Semanow!'

The General's orderly, who had been sitting behind him, stood up with a click of his heels, his chest thrown out to emphasize the garland of the yellow aiguilette on his blue double-breasted spencer. The General requested some writing materials, and as the man disappeared, his master read what Sémallé had written. When Semanow returned with a pen, an inkpot and some dusting powder, Sacken signed.

'There you are, Monsieur Chauvin,' he said, holding out the document to Octave.

'General?'

'Your name is Chauvin, isn't it?'

'Yes, yes, of course,' said La Grange. 'And now, about leaving Paris . . .'

'Semanow!'

After a brief exchange in Russian, the General told his guests, 'Semanow will come and lead you out of the tollgates.'

The Marquis got to his feet with a word of thanks, and rested one hand on Octave's shoulder as he put down his glass. 'Good luck. I'd got used to you.'

'Me too,' said Octave.

'Aren't you staying, Marquis?'

'No, General, I am going off to earn my post as Deputy Governor. I have a thousand things to do tonight.'

Then Octave found himself in the midst of the partygoers. To beguile the time he accepted a plate of fried goujons. Suddenly the ceiling slid open, and a gilded chariot descended majestically between the chandeliers. Inside it, about fifteen nymphs struck poses; they let the transparent veils covering the curves of their shoulders slip, each revealing a pink or brown nipple. At this spectacle, the drunks hammered their heels and clapped, and it seemed as though the shaking floor was about to collapse. The girls, with practised smiles, emerged from the chariot, which had come to rest among the tables; they swayed their hips, darted the tips of their tongues between their painted lips, and sat down simpering on the knees of the most decorated men. One of them put her arms around Octave's neck and, through the general hubbub, whispered some unexpected words in her suburban accent.

'What're you doing with these rats?'

'I'm working, Rosine,' said Octave.

'Like me?'

'Regimes change, but you and I stay the same.'

'Sure!'

The time for conversation had passed, and Rosine wrapped her arms around Octave so as not to attract the attention of the General, who was himself encumbered by a plump little naiad. Octave asked:

'Can you help me?'

'If you protect me, as you once did from the cops, then sure. Do you want more information about my regulars?'

'I'd like you to take my spare key.'

'And put it where exactly? As you can see, I'm wearing nothing but bracelets.'

'I'll hide it under this cushion, and you can pick it up once this heap of savages have rolled under the table-cloths. You go to my place before dawn, through the antique shop, through the wardrobe door that you're familiar with, then open the trunk and take out a brown bag. It's for you.'

'What's in it?'

'Gold.'

'For me, you say?'

'I don't want anyone to steal it from me, I'd rather give it to you. I've got to leave tonight, and I won't be able to go back to the rue Saint-Sauveur, do you under-stand?'

'I don't, but why me?'

'Because I've met you, Rosine, and I owe you that at least.'

'Is there a lot of it, this gold of yours?'

'Enough for you to set yourself up.'

'Open a dress shop?'

They were interrupted by Semanow's return.

*

Framed on either side by lancers, like a prisoner, Octave trotted quickly along the quays on a Prussian mare. Semanow led the troop and set its speed. To reach the Versailles road, on the left bank, the horsemen turned at the Pont de la Concorde. The public baths – which offered tubs at 230 sous – were illuminated. The imposing wooden construction floated on the water, with orange-trees in pots arranged around the terrace. Silhouettes were outlined against torches, amidst a cacophony of laughter and songs.

On the other side of the Seine, Semanow's troop continued on its way, guided by the lights of the allied camps. Too large to be lodged in the central districts, the armies were bivouacked on the edge of the city, spilling out into the countryside. Enterprising soldiers had converted arbours into cosy tents. Some Cossacks had built huts by supporting bales of straw between their crossed lances; elsewhere, men from a Berlin infantry regiment lounged about in the grass around their cauldrons of soup.

The war had not touched the west of the city, no splintered shutters hung from the windows, no shrubs had been mown down by case shot as they had in Belleville. On the contrary, in every village, farmers and bourgeois mingled with soldiers to celebrate the peace. They had rigged up tables on barrels, sheep-fat crackled on the spits, and young peasant girls danced with hussars. Semanow stopped his men on the edge of a large village and said to

Octave, 'I shall leave you now, but don't dismount, you'll be setting off again straight away.'

He entrusted his companion and his pass to an Austrian officer. Octave changed escorts at every village, from staging-post to staging-post, until he reached the hills of Juvisy and the headquarters of the Count of Pahlen. The 6th Corps of the Army of Bohemia occupied the summit; the enclosures for the horses and the rows of tents were lit by torches tied to flagpoles. Octave was blindfolded before being led across the fields. When an officer untied the blindfold, it was nine o'clock in the morning and Octave recognized the clock-tower of the town of Essonnes.

As he walked, alone now, on a beaten path, Octave reflected that he was in a curious situation: the royalists were sending him to Fontainebleau to spy on the Emperor, while in Paris he had been spying on the royalists on behalf of the Emperor. An opportunist would take advantage of the chance to spy on both camps, but Octave didn't feel as though he had a traitor's soul, and anyway, if the Bourbons did successfully establish themselves, they would still be haunted by the ghost of the Chevalier de Blacé, whose name, showy outfits and life Octave had appropriated. When he met his first French patrol, grenadiers whose greatcoats had faded in the rain, he said in a commanding voice: 'Take me to Fontainebleau, to the Duke of Bassano.'

'And why would the Duke wish to see you?'

'Tell him that Octave Sénécal has come to deliver his report.'

Two

CAGED

IN THE LONG marble gallery of the Palace of Fontaine-bleau, a man dressed in black was walking at a measured pace, holding a letter. He had thick eyebrows and a permanent smile on his lips like a rictus, and wore a curly white wig and a high collar to underline his ponderous air. Adjutants, chamberlains in scarlet silk highlighted with silver, quartermasters and various degrees of valet all stopped as he passed and greeted him with a bow. He didn't reply, he didn't see them. He was Hugues Bernard Maret, the Duke of Bassano, Secretary of State in charge of civilian affairs, the Emperor's closest confidant. He alone had permission to enter Napoleon's ordinary apart-ment unannounced, and the guard officer, a captain in the voltigeurs, merely held the door open for him. From the antechamber, Maret passed into the study; his master had been bent over his maps since five o'clock in the morning, along with Major General Berthier.

'His Majesty has left, your grace,' said the first valet, very tall, very respectful, and still wearing his travelling clothes.

'I know, Monsieur Constant. How is he this morning?'

'In fine fettle,' said the valet before withdrawing.

Napoleon refused to accept defeat, and Fontainebleau

was merely a garrison; he had scorned the big apartments, still closed, for more military accommodation in a mezzanine on the corner of the palace, at the end of the François I gallery. The study overlooked a gloomy clump of fir trees. The maps were scattered higgledy-piggledy on a bare wooden table set on trestles, and some aloe twigs smoked in the incense-burner like an Egyptian statue. Maret took the unsealed letter he held in his hand and threw it in the fire, then consulted the maps, with all their pencilled scribbles, to try to guess his Emperor's plans.

After a frenzied outburst of rage two days previously, because he had arrived at night, four hours too late, on the hills beside the capital, he had questioned General Belliard's retreating cavalrymen and noticed the thousand fires of the enemy camps. Then the Emperor had regained control of himself, and decided to mass the remaining regiments along a river that ran from the left bank of the Seine to the Orléans road. He had gone to inspect that natural defence and order the fortification of the towns of Essonnes and Corbeil, with their powder mill and flour warehouses. Maret knew that the Emperor was hoping to attack Paris in four days' time, when Ney and Macdonald had brought their armies back from Champagne; they were exhausted, barefoot and demoralised, and Napoleon hoped to inspire them with his mere presence.

Maret's smile concealed his faith. He endured his master's dangerous whims and furies without flinching; if he had a doubt or a criticism he voiced it when the two of them were alone, never in a meeting (unlike the more brutal Caulaincourt), and because he appeared never to disown the Emperor he was seen by everyone else as a servile cretin. He didn't care. He had been skilful enough to manufacture the absolute trust of the Emperor and maintain it both by his attitude and his manoeuvres. He sometimes dictated letters to the pretty Duchess of Bassano, for example, in which she confided in him her jealousy of the Emperor: he was too fond of the Duke, and the Duke was too fond of him. Napoleon, who always read his entourage's correspondence, was delighted by such devotion – and upon returning from his morning inspection, at which he had received great acclaim, he was therefore neither surprised nor angry to find the Secretary of State sitting in his chair of gilded wood. The Emperor threw his hat on the ground, shook his frock-coat into Constant's waiting hands, and appeared in the green uniform of the chasseurs of the Guard, the modest garb that his soldiers revered. He opened a snuff-box, stuffed a pinch into his nose and sneezed. Maret held out the letter he had brought.

'Sire, we have just received a dispatch from the Duke of Vicenza.'

'What does he say?'

'He has had difficulties meeting the Tsar.'

'But he got there?'

'Yes.'

'Go on.'

'The allies refuse to negotiate with Your Majesty.'

'Go on.'

'The Senate has confirmed a provisional government around Talleyrand . . .'

'The Senate! A government! Has Caulaincourt given us the names of these pygmies?'

'Beurnonville, Jaucourt, Dalberg, the Abbé de Montesquiou ...'

'*Coglioni!*'

'The Prefect of Police is said to have joined them ...'

'Him too? Already?'

'But Pasquier owes his job to me; you will recall that
he allowed me to win at billiards to support his nomina-
tion from your Majesty.'

'Pass on a message to him, ask him for some details,
and his reply may enlighten us.'

'The Duke of Vicenza adds: "I am rejected, I have not
seen a friendly face."'

Appalled and concerned, the Emperor took out his
lorgnette, picked up the piece of paper that Maret was
holding and skimmed it quickly, before crumpling it into
a ball and dropping it on the floor. He paced back and
forth with his hands behind his back, deliberately tipped
over his snuffbox and went and stood by a window to
gaze out at the motionless fir trees.

'A blow struck at Paris could have a terrific effect.'

'Sire?'

'Can you imagine those traitors, oozing hatred, if I
were to return to the Tuileries?'

For a moment the Emperor enjoyed the exaggerated
sense of panic, and then pursued a train of thought that
he had begun with Berthier at dawn.

'The Tsar and the King of Prussia are wondering what
I've got up my sleeve. They suspect me, and they are right
to do so. They have just lost more than ten thousand men
in the ditches of Paris. They're tired now, and basking in
a false sense of security. Their generals are pampering

themselves, they've taken over our town-houses, and their marauders are getting lost in our streets, which they know no better than they know our language. How many of them are there, inside and outside, and where are they? How are the Parisians reacting? Who's taking charge of this chaos?'

'We can find out something about that, sire. One of my men, how can I put it? Trustworthy, that's it, trustworthy and attached to the Empire . . .'

'Your spy, go on, don't shy away from it.'

'Well, sire, my spy, then, my spy is on his way from the capital. Last night he crossed enemy lines and he knows all about them. I have just received him at the Chancellery.'

'Why isn't he here? What were you waiting for?'

'Your permission.'

'What a buffoon you are!'

And the Emperor gave Maret's cheek a resounding but affectionate slap.

*

Musket at slope arms, a grenadier whose bearskin made him appear even taller than he was in reality accompanied a green-suited valet. They passed along the buildings that lined the cobbled courtyard until they reached the guard room at the corner of the railings that surrounded the Palace of Fontainebleau.

'So what's this cousin like?' asked the valet, slightly concerned.

'You don't know your own cousin, Monsieur Chauvin?'

'I have several of them. Cousins, that is.'

'This one here has come from Paris, that's all I know, and you're to go and see him. He gave your name.'

Octave was waiting on the bench in the guard room. After reporting to the Duke of Bassano on what he had seen over the past few days, he had presented himself at the main entrance to the palace, on foot, without luggage, as though he had just come from Paris on a series of backroads; he had asked to see the valet Chauvin, passing himself off as his cousin as the royalists had suggested. During that exhausting night, he had had time to prepare his story, and looked so innocent that the soldiers were happy to believe him. The search had revealed nothing, but Octave realized he had left behind his cane, his favourite weapon, while being transformed into a provincial at the home of the Count of Sémallé. It made him downcast, and his morose expression gave his character a touch of authenticity, since he was in fact about to inform Chauvin of the severe illness of his wife, who had stayed behind in the suburbs: it was sufficient reason to risk arrest or capture by foreign soldiers.

The soldiers formed a circle around Octave, sitting backwards on chairs and with their elbows resting on the arms; a sergeant puffed clouds of tobacco smoke from his clay pipe as he talked about Cossacks, whom he called 'the ruthless ones'.

'So are you trying to tell me they didn't do any looting, those demons of hell?'

'If they had broken down the doors in the fine districts, word would have got around in the city.'

'I passed by in their wake, not far from the Marne. It

wasn't a pretty sight, not pretty at all, the charred bodies of the farmers, lying twisted in the ashes.'

Monsieur Chauvin and his grenadier appeared in the open doorway. Octave rose to his feet and held out his hand to the valet, palm down to give him a good view of the Negro's-head stone given to him by Sémallé, which he wore on his ring finger. At the sight of it, the valet immediately began to play his part.

'Your visit catches me off guard!'

'Alas!' said Octave, putting his arms around Chauvin, 'I bring you grievous news . . .'

'What is it?'

'Your wife . . .'

'My wife?' said the valet, apparently alarmed.

'Marie is very unwell.'

'Is it serious?'

'Serious enough to justify a journey to Paris, in spite of the danger.'

'It is not the danger that holds me back, heavens above! But I cannot abandon His Majesty!' cried Chauvin, pretending to be virtuous.

The soldiers, moved to pity, let the two alleged cousins move to the courtyard unchaperoned. Once the two were on their own, walking side by side towards the palace, their conversation changed register.

'We knew you wanted to go back to Paris,' said Octave, 'so I've come to take your place, if that's possible.'

'I can arrange it with Monsieur Constant, the first valet. It will be his decision.'

'Can you persuade him?'

'Perhaps by tugging at his heartstrings,' said Chauvin with a chuckle.

'Tell me, weren't you at all concerned when I told you of your wife's imaginary illness?'

'I'm not married.'

'Neither am I,' said Octave. 'I am entirely devoted to our cause.'

'Is it true that the King is returning to Paris?'

'I'm afraid so.'

'You're afraid so?'

'I'm sorry?'

'You just said you were afraid so.'

'You misheard me, Chauvin, I was using a form of shorthand: yes, *I think* that Louis XVIII will finally take the throne, thanks to the support of the allies, who have given me a pass that I will in turn give to you, it's in your name.'

'Didn't the soldiers search you?'

'Yes, but they were looking for a weapon, a pistol, a knife, a dagger, not a folded sheet of paper. I slipped it into the top of my hat at the last Austrian checkpoint.'

As they climbed the the horseshoe steps in the middle of the Renaissance façade of Fontainebleau, an aide-de-camp in a pair of maroon trousers drew alongside them and asked Octave: 'Are you the gentleman who has just come from the capital?'

'Yes.'

'Please follow me.'

*

Octave had already seen the Emperor, but only from a distance and as part of a crowd. That had been on the Place du Carrousel, when Napoleon had been swaggering on his horse in front of the lined-up battalions of his Guard. Now here he was, standing right in front of Octave, still talking to the Duke of Bassano and Major General Berthier, as though the summoned visitor did not exist. Octave felt silly in his ill-cut clothes, hat awkwardly clutched in his hands.

Napoleon's head was lowered, and his chin spilled in rolls over his cravat. He was a rotund little man, with his hands held under the turnbacks of his colonel's uniform. The gold fringes of his epaulettes trembled every time he twitched; his white waistcoat, one button of which was undone, tended to creak under the pressure of a belly that spilled from the top of his breeches. His face was round, his complexion bilious; his thinning hair flopped across his forehead; his nose and mouth, set in his fat face, were surprisingly fine. When he looked up, Octave felt as if the Emperor was casting a spell over him: his eyes were as blue as the Mediterranean, they had a magnetic, sorcerous quality. He spoke quickly, swallowing his words.

'Were you in Paris yesterday evening? How are the occupying forces behaving?'

Octave was paralysed, stupid as a greenhorn.

'This chap of yours is a useless great lump!' the Emperor said to Maret.

'He hasn't slept, sire.'

'Neither have I.'

'It's the first time he has the honour of finding himself in Your Majesty's presence . . .'

'Do I frighten you, my boy?'

Getting over his unease, Octave managed to stammer in a monotone, 'Not as much as you frighten our enemies, sire.'

'Tell me about them.'

The Emperor was issuing an order. If Octave had never known a more disconcerting situation, he had faced more dangerous ones, had dodged dagger thrusts and whistling bullets. He took a deep breath and choked down his saliva.

'I saw them in our streets, sire. They have not been sowing disorder. For the time being, they are taking advantage of their conquest, singing, going to see things, distracting themselves and drinking in the salons of the Palais-Royal.'

'Let them dull their senses! We'll wake them up. How many foreigners do you think there are within the walls of Paris?'

'About forty thousand, sire, according to the royalists who are collaborating with the Russian governor. They are also holding the hills of Montmartre and Belleville with cannon.'

'And between the Seine and the shores of the Essonne?'

'I took that route at night, part of it blindfolded, past Juvisy, but I saw the lights of their camps, I heard their columns marching. On this side, there are at least twice as many enemy troops as there are in Paris.'

'That makes sense, doesn't it, Berthier?'

'Yes, sire. They're concentrated to the south, directly opposite our own front.'

The Emperor mumbled as he thought to himself, and cast an eye over the maps with his lorgnette.

'How many are there right now, Berthier?'

'A hundred and eighty thousand, three times as many as we would be if we regrouped our scattered regiments . . .'

'Forty thousand in Paris, twice as many ahead of us,

that would leave about sixty thousand on the right bank of the Seine and in the east.'

'Probably.'

'Definitely! If we attack in the south, as they expect us to, will the Parisians rise up behind them?'

He looked at Octave, who replied, 'The workers in the suburbs are grumbling, and the occupying forces won't dare go to their districts, but they have no weapons.'

'Why not? And what about the artillery park in the Champs-de-Mars? Haven't the muskets and the ammunition been distributed?'

'I don't know, sire. The young people from the university got shells instead of roundshot, roundshot instead of shells, and then, when they opened them up, they found that the cartridges were full of clay or coal . . .'

'So we may expect nothing from them?'

'No, but possibly from elsewhere. Some Russian officers, very surprised at having been able to invade the city so quickly, assured me that the allies had only enough ammunition left for sixteen hours . . .'

'I knew it! The partisans in the Vosges and Lorraine are still sabotaging their communications, and the armies on the right bank are cut off from the ones on the left. Let's head east, along their line of retreat.'

Berthier anxiously studied the maps over the Emperor's shoulder. As far as Octave was concerned, the interview was at an end, and Maret pushed him into the antechamber.

'You haven't met His Majesty. You were simply questioned: that is perfectly normal, because you have come here from Paris. And you have said nothing out of the ordinary. Reassure Chauvin, cajole him, I want to know how that sly dog communicates with the outside world. And untangle the plans of the conspirators you have left behind, in short, stick with the routine that you know by heart.'

*

The staff had their sleeping quarters in the dark and stuffy outbuildings in the east wing of the palace. A quartermaster had added a bed, or rather a bed base, to one of the partitioned cells, which became Octave's bed-room. Exhausted, he had slumped upon it without taking his shirt off, and had dozed there until evening. He was just slipping on his ugly boots when Chauvin came in, quivering with excitement.

'That was easy,' the delighted valet announced, 'I'd have to say that we're living through unusual times here in Fontainebleau.'

He had been granted permission to return to Paris and the bedside of his invented wife. He had asked to pass through enemy lines in the garb of a rustic, the get-up that the messengers had been using for two days. Chauvin was in a hurry, but first he had to clothe and train his replacement, having very convincingly vouched for him.

'Tonight,' he told Octave, 'I've been given permission to take you to a tailor in town. He will adjust one of my suits to your measurements, a few little touches so that you will be able to wear the regulation livery by tomorrow.'

'Isn't there a tailor at the palace?'

'Hell's bells, we're at war, not on holiday! The sooner you're ready, the sooner I'll be able to leave.'

'You won't really be safe in Paris.'

'Ah, but I'm not actually going to go there, I plan to head down to Orléans, where I have relatives.'

'Our friends will be worried, they'll have to be told that I've managed to meet up with you, that I'm going to take your job . . .'

Chauvin didn't reply, he was too busy wrapping one of his embroidered frock-coats in paper, and consulting his watch.

Without any unnecessary chatter, they left the palace in plain clothes, via a side door that led out to the forest. They followed the park wall towards the town that stretched along the road. As they walked, Chauvin delivered his instructions in a few brief sentences.

'In the morning, a cup of orange-flower tea that you will bring on a silver-gilt tray . . . The main thing is that you should keep your ears open at all times. We servants listen to everything, we see everything, and no one notices us, we are pieces of furniture, the masters feel they can go on talking in confidence.'

Octave had already recited stories of his emigrant past to Chauvin, and pretended this was the first time he had ever heard of flunkeys picking up on echoes, whims and secrets. (In fact, he had known it from birth: his father had been valet to a duke under Louis XVI, a publican after the Revolution, and an informer to the Committee of General Security. Before Thermidor, because he had good instincts or good sources, he had turned himself in to the very same Jacobin that he had served as an agent, saving his own head just as Robespierre was losing his. After that he had served the police of the Directory, then the police of the Consulate, before dying in his bed, his liver ravaged by endless carafes of wine. Octave had learned everything he knew in his father's tavern. The former domestic servants of the nobility frequented it, and exchanged useful information. It was there, in his youth, that Octave had met Monsieur Nicolas, known as the Owl because he roamed Paris at night with his blue cloak and his picklock's stick. He too had survived all this political upheaval, and was allowed to publish forthright essays in return for precise reports on the nightlife of the city, high and low, which he delivered under false names. When Octave first befriended him, Monsieur Nicolas was working in the office that kept watch on the correspondence of emigrants and foreigners. He had initiated Octave into his trade, its mischiefs, its hidden pleasures, its risks; he had also taught him grammar and a love of language, which was how the young man had found himself working for the *Journal de l'Empire*, where he wrote literary articles, copied out Plutarch, shamelessly distorting him for the edification of the public: Brutus no longer stabbed Caesar, Nero showered his mother with gifts and titles rather than having her throat slit for conspiring against him; under the Empire, even Antiquity had to serve as a model. Octave's zeal, his ironic talent, had attracted the attention of the Duke of Bassano, who took an interest in the press. He had set up the *Bulletin de l'Assemblée Nationale*, which published the ultra-official *Moniteur*. They talked together and the Duke recruited Octave when he worked out that he must, by virtue of his job, have considerable knowledge of royalist circles . . .)

Octave and Chauvin reached the town of Fontaine-bleau. Before crossing the main street, they let the cavalry squadrons pass. They were coming from the east, thousands of armed men in uniforms so dirty it was hard to see quite what they were – although they were definitely the Guard, because Chauvin recognized General Sebastiani among the officers. The soldiers were flooding into Fontainebleau, filling the squares, which had been turned into improvised camps. The citizens locked themselves up in their houses and only crept out furtively if they absolutely had to; even if they were on your side, hungry soldiers could rob you, empty your attic and your cellar, and chop your linen chest to smithereens to feed the fires in the street.

'Here we are,' said Chauvin, gesturing with his chin to a shuttered shop. A wooden silhouette of a boot swung over the window. Octave was rather surprised, since the sign seemed rather unusual for a tailor, but he allowed himself to be guided by Chauvin. Passing through a door next to the shop, Chauvin led him upstairs. He knocked, with a warning: 'Remember: three knocks, a pause, two more knocks.' They heard footsteps and the clatter of several bolts. A smell of cabbage steamed from a pot hanging from the trammel. Sitting on stools, with their backs towards them, two women were cutting up vegetables and throwing them into the soup; a rabbit that would shortly be eaten nibbled at the peelings. The host, a sly-looking little man in a waistcoat, with hunting gaiters laced up to his knees, listened to Chauvin as he outlined the situation to him. Then he grunted, the younger of the women stood up, and Chauvin held out his livery which he had just unwrapped, and which Octave was to try on. It was an almost perfect fit – just the sleeves were slightly too long. The nimble-fingered girl pulled back the fabric and stuck pins in the armholes.

'Boiron is a shoemaker,' Chauvin explained to Octave.

'Shoemaker,' repeated Boiron.

'When Bonaparte is in Fontainebleau and I have secrets to divulge to the Committee, he's the one who takes the messages.'

'I'm the one.'

The girl was now restitching the livery that Octave was wearing, but he suddenly started back and she pricked him in the arm.

'Ouch!'

A chasseur of the Guard, bearskin cap in his hand, came out of the neighbouring bedroom. This apparition had startled Octave, and as the soldier approached the lamp, his face reminded him of someone. He had seen that hollow face, that veiled expression before, but what clothes had the man been wearing then? The soldier addressed Octave in a slow and haughty voice.

'Are you the Chevalier de Blacé?'

'And you?'

'Marie Armand de Guéry de Maubreuil, Marquis d'Orvault.'

Maubreuil, the same Marquis who had tied his Légion d'honneur to the tail of his horse the other morning, when the allies were processing through the boulevards, Maubreuil disguised in a uniform taken from the shops of the military school, an adventurer, a *Chouan*, a relative of the Caulaincourts through his brother-in-law, former equerry to Jérôme Bonaparte, a speculator on army supplies . . .

From the pocket of his dolman Maubreuil drew letters stamped and signed by the new Parisian authorities, an order from Sacken to have foreign troops placed at his disposal, a passport, a permit authorizing the holder to commandeer post-horses as a matter of priority.

'Fine,' said Octave, taking off his altered clothing, 'but why are you showing us these documents?'

'So that you too will help to make my task easier. I have come to carry out a confidential order from Monsieur Talleyrand, head of the provisional government. He has reached an agreement with the entourage of Monseigneur the Count of Artois. That is to say, with the members of your Committee.'

'So what is your mission?'

'To kill Bonaparte.'

*

On the morning of the following day, Saturday 2 April, Chauvin had received his wages and was buckling up a saddlebag beneath Octave's amused eyes. Taking the lackey's place, Octave had adopted his unruffled manners along with his suit – that most excellent green suit with its gold embroidered collar, black breeches and white stockings. As agreed, Chauvin would go into town; shoe-maker Boiron would find him a greengrocer's cart to take him away from Fontainebleau. If he happened to bump into foreign solders on the Orléans road, as was entirely possible, the pass Octave had given him would prove very useful. Before disappearing, happy to escape the worrying noises of war, Chauvin left a number of recommendations.

'You will start your service at midday, in place of Monsieur Hubert, who will have been keeping watch in the antechamber throughout the night. You have only to carry out the orders of Monsieur Constant. The Emperor's timetables are not currently as regular as they have been in the past, you will have to be prepared for anything, at all times. You'll get used to it, and you will no longer need to know to the last minute how the tyrant's normal days are organized. Things are breaking down, my friend, everything's breaking down . . .'

The two men's footsteps echoed down the corridor as they passed beneath ceilings with coffers of gilded wood that framed bucolic and irrelevant mythological scenes. The entrances leading into the ceremonial rooms were closed with dark velvet doors and, among the unlit candelabras, in the pale daylight, groups of officers and servants spoke in muffled voices. Caulaincourt had returned from Paris, they were saying, he had spent a long time last night talking to His Majesty, that was all they knew, but they were absolutely sure that the offensive would be launched within three days – as Chauvin would hurry to confirm with shoemaker Boiron.

'Monsieur de Maubreuil is going to need to have his ambush prepared as soon as possible,' he said to Octave.

'It's no longer anything to do with you, Chauvin.'

'Are you up to the task?'

'I'm dealing with this man Maubreuil.'

As they passed a high window opened by some curious members of staff, they heard delirious cries: 'Long live the Emperor! To Paris! Down with the traitors!' Over the heads and shoulders of the soldiers and valets, in the courtyard of the White Horse, they saw grenadiers and chasseurs in bearskins standing at attention: they were presenting arms and shouting enthusiastically, grey with dust and soil from their shoes to their wool epaulettes, but clean-shaven, chins pressed into their horsecloth ties.

Napoleon was passing them in review, his hat in his hand to salute them, and they wept with joy as they called, 'To Paris! To Paris!' before setting off in perfect columns, their feet striking the cobbles to the sound of the drums. The Old Guard was in the town, and had detached two battalions to serve the Palace.

'That's not going to make your work any easier,' Chauvin murmured into Octave's ear. 'Will the Marquis de Maubreuil be able to kill the usurper if he's surrounded by all these people?'

'He's got his uniform.'

'That's true,' Chauvin agreed, failing to reflect that Maubreuil would be the only person wearing a clean, new uniform, and that this would render him conspicuous and suspect, but Chauvin's thoughts were focused entirely on his escape. When he left by one of the staff entrances, he whispered faintly, '*Vive le roi . . .*' and winked. Octave crossed his arms and sighed as he saw him trotting down the road; he would happily have strangled that pest, had his disappearance not risked alerting shoemaker Boiron, Maubreuil and the members of the Committee.

*

The Emperor was dining in the heavily gilded salon of his aides-de-camp. His appetite tended to reflect his mood, and on this particular evening he was hungry. The loyal Dunan, son of a cook to the Prince de Condé, who had served aristocrats in the past, was setting down covered silver platters on a pedestal table with a napkin thrown over it as a tablecloth. Napoleon lifted the lids, poked his fingers into the various dishes, and swallowed down partridge crépinettes and macaroni under a layer of parmesan. Between mouthfuls he wiped his hands on his white breeches, and chatted and joked as though he was sure of sending the foreigners packing to the border. The members of his entourage were more serious, and stood around him as ceremony had so far decreed. A prefect dressed all in pale green, hat under his arm, checked the sealed bottle of Chambertin and the food that was arriving from another room, where the butler kept it warm over bains-marie. The Emperor gulped down big mouthfuls. Reinvigorated by his Guard's applause, he took pleasure in hearing the latest news that reached him from the invaded capital, and in hearing it over and over again.

'Read me again the proclamation by that damned fool Talleyrand,' he said, stuffing down two chicken dumplings at the same time.

Count Bertrand, Grand Marshal of the palace, with his hang-dog expression, nodded his bald pate, wiggling the corkscrew hair that fluffed from his temples:

'I shall read it, sire: *You are no longer the soldiers of Napoleon; the Senate and the whole of France free you from your oaths . . .*'

'The whole of France! The Senate, that ragbag of revolutionaries that I trounced! By what right? You knew Lodi, Bertrand, and the Pyramids, you took command at Austerlitz, can you imagine Talleyrand's bunglers faced with my troops? He can barely make it from his bed to his chair! Can you see my soldiers taking commands from the King of Prussia?'

Since Caulaincourt's report the previous day, Napoleon was aware of the climate in Paris, but he did not let it trouble him. The newspapers were insulting him, calling him an ogre and a tyrant, but that was in the order of things: the new government had installed editors who would do what they wanted. He also knew that the Tsar had been acclaimed at the Opera. Did the people go to the Opera? The belles in the balconies had thrown white ribbons into the auditorium; the morning-coated spectators had yelled, 'Down with the bird! Down with the eagle!' so loudly that a machinist had had to cover over the emblem adorning the pediment of the Imperial box. A former convict called Vidocq, who was in charge of a police brigade, had climbed up the Vendôme column to topple the statue of the Emperor wearing a toga. (It had not fallen, however, but merely leaned over to taunt the hooligans and threaten the passers-by, and all of a sudden the Russians had stopped people getting anywhere near it . . .) Napoleon disdained even the suggestions of Caulaincourt, who was trying to save him: What? Was he proposing that he abdicate in favour of the King of Rome? The Emperor was discussing the matter when his butler served him his daily cup of coffee.

'The Regency is a decoy, Bertrand, do you hear me?'

'Yes, sire, I hear you: a decoy.'

'The Duke of Vicenza is devoted, but he still doesn't understand! My son is a child, the Empress knows nothing about the running of things. The truth is that our enemies want me to disappear, Bertrand, because they know they're sunk, without ammunition, trapped in Paris! Who can they trust, eh? There may well be lots of them, but they're divided. I've got the Guard, Bertrand, the Guard, the mere sight of whom scares the living daylights out of them. My Old Guard stretches all the way to Étampes.

The regiments of Oudinot and Gérard have arrived, Macdonald's cavalry is at Melun. Marmont is holding Essonnes and Corbeil, with Mortier further to the west.'

The Duke of Bassano came in just as the Emperor was finishing his coffee. He had received a reply from Prefect Pasquier, to whom he had sent a note: a man from the countryside had pierced the Austrian lines by travelling along forest paths. He told the Emperor that the Senate had announced his defeat, and that some generals were preparing to rally the new government. As Napoleon did not blink, the Duke broke off and looked at him, but at a gesture he continued reading.

'"*We are assured that there are a number of plans to approach the Emperor and that the individuals thinking that way include Jacobins. The bankers are offering twelve million . . .*"'

The Emperor held out his hand, took the letter, recognized Pasquier's handwriting and shrugged his shoulders.

'It's not the first time people have wanted to "approach" me, as this chap Pasquier writes so cautiously. Do you remember that old clown in the Tuileries who was hauled out from behind the curtains of my study?'

'Ah yes, sire, he had got past the patrols and the sentries . . .'

'He claimed he had found his father's soul in the lights of the palace!'

'A lunatic, we sent him to Charenton, sire. But we are dealing with lunatics no longer.'

'The bankers' money is dreadful in a different way, isn't it?'

'Many people are betraying us. Even Pasquier adds at the end of his letter that we shouldn't even turn to him.'

'Let's see. He who warns does not betray.'

*

Octave would never forget 4 April. It was a Monday. He had spent the night doing Chauvin's job. His work consisted of placing a plate with two glasses covered by a napkin, a silver sugar bowl with a shell-shaped lid, a small spoon and a jug full of water on the chest of drawers in the Emperor's bedroom. Apart from that, Octave had to be available at all times. He had seen officers going gloomily in and out of the study; he had heard the sound of voices, but had been unable to make out what they were discussing, or what orders were being given. He had already warned Bassano of Maubreuil's murderous plans, but the Duke was convinced that the Emperor was in no immediate danger. Octave would talk to him again in the morning so that they could put their heads together and weigh up the threat, which was confirmed by Pasquier's letter.

As soon as Napoleon was safely shut up in his bedroom, Octave had taken off his livery to avoid creasing it, and lain down on a sofa, still wearing his waistcoat. The Mameluke Roustan also laid his velvet turban and his curved sabre on a chair, and pushed his trestle bed against the door. Fat, flirtatious, foolish, usually this child of Tiflis – a sultan's slave before becoming General Bonaparte's lapdog in Egypt – talked tirelessly about the lottery office that the Emperor had just bestowed upon him, but on this occasion he spared Octave this tale by quickly going to sleep. Alas, the chap started snoring; he snored in changing rhythms, and the night was an ordeal, the kind that stirred discordant thoughts in a maddening half-sleep that tugged reality out of shape. Was Maubreuil telling the truth? He was famous in Paris for his boasting, after all. If his word was to be trusted, though, why was Sémallé's royalist Committee now supporting the idea of a murder it had not dreamed of two days ago? Talleyrand must have something to do with it. And what about the Count of Artois? There were connections there, because Maubreuil had used the royalist network in Fontainebleau. Why had Octave not had a note to warn him? Who was he to believe? By his night light, everything blurred and then came into perspective.

Hubert, the polite and cultured valet, relieved Octave at dawn. Finally able to leave that uncomfortable antechamber, Octave passed through the line of grenadiers who ensured the safety of the Imperial apartments, and set off down the corridors, rubbing the small of his back. He encountered more soldiers and over-excited servants; patrols of soldiers were circulating in the courtyard intoning battle-hymns to the sound of fifes, or shouting, 'To Paris! To Paris!' to maintain the spirit of excitement that precedes a battle. When Octave reached the door, a young wardrobe attendant was waiting for him with a cloth bag that he held out.

'It's for you, sir.'

'For me?' asked Octave, surprised.

'Yes, yes.'

'Are you sure?'

'Damn right!'

'So you know me?'

'Course I do, you're Chauvin's cousin.'

'Chauvin's cousin, fine, but how do you know that?'

'In the castle, word gets round.'

'And have you been waiting for me for a long time?'

'Oh no, I found out.'

'About what?'

'About your hours.'

'From whom?'

'The Palace Prefect, of all people.'

Octave had taken the bag and opened it to see what was inside.

'Boots?'

'Wouldn't be surprised.'

'Why so, brat?'

'Old Boiron left 'em here for you at the sentry post, yesterday evening.'

'So you know old Boiron as well?'

'Everyone knows him, everyone in the staff here in the castle.'

'Does he come often?'

'He does services, that's all.'

'Of what kind?'

'Well, he's a shoemaker, so he repairs things.'

'Has he ever been inside the palace?'

'Only when His Majesty ain't there, otherwise . . .'

'Otherwise?'

'Some of the soldiers ain't from these parts, and they don't let him through.'

'They wouldn't let him through?'

'Like I said, but I was there and I took your parcel.'

'Did the soldiers look inside?'

'Yeah.'

'Well?'

'They saw some boots, I said they were for you and I said who you were. Did I do the right thing, sir?'

'Yes.'

'Can I go?'

'Be off with you!'

Octave threw the bag on his bed and took out a pair of new boots. Inside the turned-down top of one of them he found a sheet of paper, which he unfolded:

Monsieur le Chevalier, it's about this evening. Our allies are in a hurry. They know that Bonaparte is going to attack them on Tuesday, and they are keen to avoid a new and uncertain war. They are even talking about abandoning Paris and retreating to Meaux. It is therefore a matter of urgency. If my uniform allows me to enter the castle, yours must surely allow me to enter the tyrant's apartment at night. I have a sword.

Maubreuil

*

The Duke of Bassano put Maubreuil's note down on his desk. He smiled faintly, as he always did, but at the same time he wrinkled the fat black eyebrows that caterpillared across his forehead. Octave stood behind him, in civilian clothes. With a slow and composed movement of his head, for he was copying the disdainful manners that he thought typical of the true aristocracy, the Duke said in his unctuous voice: 'Your Marquis is a dilettante. What a ludicrous idea, a message in a pair of boots; even a farce-writer like Désaugiers wouldn't have risked that. And his plan is the plan of a fantasist.'

'Fantasist or not, your grace, his intention is clear.'

'Certainly . . .'

'His family is dedicated to the royal cause; he is related to the La Rochejaqueleins.'

'The fact that he's from the Vendée proves neither his courage nor his skill. How can he imagine that a valet might open the doors to the Imperial apartment in the middle of the night? There are the aides-de-camp, there's Monsieur Constant, whose bedroom communicates with the Emperor's via a spiral staircase, that fool Roustan down below, the corridors full of soldiers . . .'

Ever since that infernal machine had exploded in the rue Saint-Niçaise fourteen years previously, all attempts on Napoleon's life had been foiled. The aristocratic hired killers dispatched from England by the Count of Artois had been swept away, all of them: the Cadoudals, the Rivières, the Bouvets, Burbans and Polignacs. Those attempted assassinations had in fact benefited the Empire; as a result, public opinion had been happier to accept the strengthening of measures taken by the police and the censors, the assertion of authority, the plethora of banishments or executions   but could this one, which was bound to fail, be exploited? Octave dragged Bassano from his reflections.

'I have come to ask your orders, your grace.'

'Let your Marquis approach, if he will.'

'And then?'

'The Emperor wishes to attack tomorrow, our enemies know that and they are quaking with fear at the thought of it. According to your man Maubreuil, the allies intend to pull back to Meaux: that is the only interesting piece of information in his note, and I shall pass it on to His Majesty.'

'But what about him?'

'He can fail when he is near to his goal, can't he?'

'Without a doubt.'

'If he is killed, would that not harm your reputation with the royalists?'

'I don't think so.'

'Neither do I.'

'So, if he turns up . . .'

'If he turns up you kill him. Word will circulate outside the palace that an over-excited marquis has failed, and you will remain uninvolved in the eyes of his partners, whom you will still be able to keep under surveillance. Are you armed?'

'No.'

'I will give you a few men, you will just have to point out our prey to them.'

'I'd prefer to deal with it on my own, your grace.'

'As you wish.'

'But . . .'

'But?'

'I'd need a hunting knife.'

'That's easily done.'

Bassano called for a servant, and asked for a knife to be brought immediately. As they waited for the weapon, the Duke asked: 'This man Maubreuil, do you think he's a hard-liner?'

'Better than that: he's being paid.'

'With promises or gold coins?'

'Promises. From what he told me the first time, at Boiron the shoemaker's, Talleyrand himself has offered him the title of duke, the governorship of a province, an income of two hundred thousand livres . . .'

'Pffft! He'll faint at the first obstacle.'

'How can we know that?'

'If he's hoping for a title, a province and an income, it means he's fond of life.'

'And if he's fond of life?'

'He's not going to risk death.'

A chamberlain came in, bringing a knife in a leather case. Octave slipped it under his belt, beneath his frock-coat, saluted and left the room. Maubreuil, this supposed murderer, this elegant hired killer, barely worried the Duke of Bassano. In any case, Octave would do what needed to be done. On the other hand, Prefect Pasquier's remarks about the Jacobins were spinning around in Bassano's head. He thought about Fouché. The former Minister of Police, who had been dismissed, could play the Jacobins' game, and he was fierce. He had retained the names of his informers in the Faubourg Saint-Germain as though they were in the army or at court; but events happened to be keeping him in Lyons. And the rest? Small fry. It was the marshals that worried Bassano. If they couldn't rely on the marshals, the Empire was lost.

Napoleon wasn't suspicious enough of them, he thought they were obedient, he told them time and again that without him they would fall. However, two weeks previously, by the flames of Arcis-sur-Aube, some of them had begun to conspire in the face of the enemy, those 40,000 Bavarians and Austrians that they could no longer contain; Ney had even called the Emperor a scourge. The marshals were grumbling. Their wives, their town-houses and belongings were in Paris: would they march on the capital to destroy their own possessions, and risk the deaths of their own families? An intrepid rogue, jealous and choleric, self-seeking, Ney was becoming dangerous. His brother-in-law lived in the Faubourg Saint-Germain, that den of aristos, and while his wife Eglé had been at school with Hortense de Beauharnais, she was also the daughter of one of Marie-Antoinette's chambermaids, Madame Auguié, who had thrown herself from a window to escape Robespierre's detectives, a few days before 9 Thermidor that would have saved her life.

*

Michel Ney, Prince of the Moskva, had a face as red as his unruly hair. He was furious, and strode around the gallery, spurs clanking. 'I'll tell him, oh yes, I'll tell him!' He repeated those words as a litany to fire himself up. The other marshals lengthened their steps to keep up with him, feathers quivering on their hats. They had donned their gold-embroidered costumes, their brightly coloured silk sashes, rows of medals awarded in the past; their riding-boots gleamed with wax. Old Lefebvre grumbled, wheezed, clutched his side. Oudinot looked lost, round-eyed, his eyebrow raised in a circumflex. Honest Moncey, who used to love weapons so much, was not so fond of them now. Marshal Macdonald, Duke of Tarentum, joined this group on the threshold of the Imperial apartments. He had been running, and his anxiety was apparent on his normally placid face.

Caulaincourt had walked ahead of them into the drawing-room adjoining the Emperor's study; he stopped talking to Bertrand and Bassano when the marshals entered the room in a single determined block. They looked at one another and said nothing, tense and quaking. Finally, Major General Berthier, more taciturn than usual, his back bent, sighed and half-opened the communicating door.

'Gentlemen, His Majesty awaits you . . .'

Jostling one another, they silently entered the study together, cocked hats under their arms, huddled like schoolboys fearing punishment, not so strong all of a sudden. The only sound was their panting breath and the rustle of the maps that Napoleon, at his desk, was moving about and marking with a pencil. The Emperor cast a distracted eye over the group, noticed the latest arrival to Fontainebleau, Macdonald, who had just come from Melun, and stared him in the eye.

'Greetings, Lord Tarentum, how are your men bearing up?'

'Very badly, sire.'

'And?'

'Having failed to save Paris . . . We're all devastated.'

'What do your men say?'

'That you're calling on us to march on the capital.'

'They're right.'

'Sire, they don't want to expose Paris to the same fate as Moscow . . .'

'Moscow was deserted, Paris isn't.'

'Exactly, sire, no civil war!'

'The Senate has just pronounced your deposition,' ventured Marshal Ney, gritting his teeth and hissing like a rattlesnake.

'The new government is calling the Bourbons back,' added Moncey, who had fought fiercely on the Paris barricades.

'The provisional government, gentlemen, is provisional: it admits as much itself! Those scoundrels will soon be bowing down to the Bourbons, certainly, but they'll be doing it in England!'

'Sire,' Macdonald went on, 'my soldiers are dying of hunger, they are discouraged. Many of them have gone home, and what are the others going to live on in Fontainebleau, in the middle of a forest?'

'Are you refusing to fight? I have sergeants enough to replace you.'

'The army will not march on Paris!' stated Marshal Ney furiously.

'The army will obey me!'

'No, sire, the army obeys its generals.'

The Emperor fell silent and studied them one by one. They lowered their eyes, even Ney, and then, in a dry voice, Napoleon asked, 'What do you suggest?'

'Your abdication,' replied Ney, studying the slats of the parquet.

'You may go.'

They backed out of the room. Marshal Ney's eyes revealed that he was at once frightened and proud of his refusal. The Emperor kept Bassano and Caulaincourt behind.

'Has the Guard been paid?' he asked in a calmer voice.

'Yes, sire, but from your personal funds. We haven't a penny left for the other regiments.'

'And what about the Treasury?'

The great treasurer, Peyrusse, who made grammatical errors but never miscalculated, had been sent to Orléans to recover the booty removed from the Tuileries by the Empress and Cambacérès, about twenty million in all. Peyrusse had not yet returned, and there was no news of his mission. The Emperor leapt to his feet.

'The regency! Have you heard! It's all they can talk about! The regency! No one believes in it! The allies aren't as naïve as that!'

He paced around the room, hurling to the ground all the objects his hand happened to rest on — the oval snuff-box, a monogrammed pencil-box, some maps — then he abruptly asked for writing material. An aide-de-camp brought paper, Caulaincourt uncorked the inkpot, and Bassano held out a finely trimmed crow's feather. The Emperor took up position at his desk and wrote, for once without making too many mistakes.

'Abdication! We'll give them abdication all right! Everyone will be reassured, cajoled, rocked to sleep! The allies will believe that we're not going to attack, *bene*! Let's gain some time.'

He spoke and wrote at the same time. His pen scratched nervously.

'Caulaincourt, go to Paris, negotiate their damned regency as best you can, play the part, take that great idiot Ney with you, and Macdonald, that'll calm them down ...'

'Recall the marshals!' called the Duke of Bassano, half-opening the door of the antechamber. Shortly afterwards, the marshals came back; some valets had caught up with them by running down the gallery to the steps of the external staircase. Taken by surprise, the group were unsure about what attitude they should adopt. The Emperor could have had them shot for disobedience, but no, Napoleon stood there, letter in hand, waving it around to dry the ink, and his voice was soft.

'Am I an obstacle? So be it. The Duke of Bassano will read you the note that I have just written.'

Bassano took the letter held out to him by his Emperor, and deciphered his small, jerky, sloped hand, all in lower case with words joined to one another. He read in a loud voice, amid a heavy silence.

The allied powers having proclaimed the Emperor Napoleon to be the sole obstacle to the re-establishment of peace in Europe, Emperor Napoleon, true to his oath, declares that he is prepared to descend from the throne, to leave France and to leave even his life for the good of the fatherland, which is inseparable from the rights of his son, those of the Empress's regency and the maintenance of the laws of the Empire.

The marshals were dumbfounded. They surrounded Napoleon, clutched his arms, kissed his hands. The Emperor looked at them with a certain disdain, but they didn't notice.

*

That accursed day was not over. Octave was sitting on a green taffeta love-seat, head on his folded arms, fighting fatigue, forcing himself to be vigilant. On the other side of the partition he heard the Emperor pacing around his study, ceaselessly, like an animal in its cage. Octave thought of the following day's reply. It seemed inevitable, even with battalions reduced by death and desertion, and soldiers many of whom seemed very young, but who had seen active service in the plains of Champagne; their rage stood in for experience. Waiting for Napoleon to head for bed, to brood over the imminent battle, Octave would then go into the study and put everything away, and sweep up the coarse-cut snuff that His Majesty scattered around the place.

A vague sense of unrest somewhere in the palace shook Octave from his dreamy torpor. Sounds were getting closer, faint voices. Roustan had risen to his feet and gripped his sabre. Octave patted the hip where he had attached his knife; he parted his livery to draw it at the first sign of danger. Doors slammed. Calls rang out in the corridors. A stamping of feet, now, in the François I gallery. The aide-de-camp suddenly pushed wide the door to the antechamber. General Belliard and a helmeted cuirassier, serious and annoyed, urgently asked to see the Emperor. Octave tapped at the door to his study.

'Who is it?'

'Belliard, sire!'

'In the middle of the night?'

'It's eleven o'clock, sire.'

'What's so important, Belliard?' said the Emperor, opening the door himself.

'Bad news.'

'Bad news is your lot.' (This was the same Belliard who had announced the capitulation of Paris to Napoleon when the Emperor arrived too late to enter the city.)

The General entered the study, and the door closed once more. Octave saw some officers hanging around in the gallery: what was going on? The officers themselves were very keen to know, but the General was clearly keeping his information to himself. Further off, some colonels had turned a drawing-room into a gambling den, and decided to keep watch while frittering away their last gold coins, perhaps before dying in a few hours' time. Octave thought he could make out the silhouette of Maubreuil, in the uniform of a chasseur of the Guard. Did Maubreuil see him?

Rather than coming over to him, the figure made off and disappeared around a corner in the corridor. Octave set off in pursuit. Soldiers and servants carrying lanterns were arriving, perhaps in response to Bassano's news. Octave pushed against the current: he didn't want to lose Maubreuil, and spotted him at the bottom of the staircase. He raced down the steps, dashed through the doors and down the grand staircase, forcing his way past cheveau-légers and hussars with great queues hanging down their necks coming pell-mell in the opposite direction. Could the enemy have launched a night offensive on the Essonne front? Octave found himself wondering what all this agitation was about: he hoped it would help him eliminate Maubreuil discreetly, and thus solve the problem. Clearly the royalist was fleeing because there were too many people around the Emperor; he didn't much fancy being torn to pieces, but even if he had abandoned or postponed his enterprise, he still had to be liquidated.

Octave concentrated his attention on this pitiful would-be assassin, who was now crossing the main courtyard, his back illuminated by the chandeliers that were currently being lit behind the palace windows.

Octave quickened his pace. It was a moonless, starless night, and there was similar confusion in the streets of the town of Fontainebleau: soldiers forming processions, brandishing smoking torches, burning branches covered with dry leaves to cook their grub. Octave kept his eye trained on Maubreuil's shoulders as he pushed his way through the yelling and indignant columns. Threatening-looking grenadiers with walrus moustaches, muskets sloped, were heading towards the castle yelling, 'To Paris! To Paris!'

The young conscripts, admonished by their elders, broke away from their officers and joined the free-for-all. For a moment Octave lost sight of his quarry, but no, there he was, over there, turning into a side-alley. Octave speeded up once more, and the two men emerged almost together into a little square lit by campfires, where the chasseurs of the Guard were saddling their horses. Octave reached Maubreuil and was about to raise his knife when his foot slipped in the stream of dung flowing through the middle of the cobbles; he tumbled to the ground and dropped his knife. The chasseur turned around at the sound of his pratfall.

'You look a sight, Monsieur, with your four paws in the air!'

It wasn't Maubreuil. And besides, from close up and in the light of the flames, his uniform was less shiny than the assassin's. Cavalrymen gathered around them to look at the valet sitting with a sore bottom in the gutter. Octave started explaining himself.

'Forgive me, Lieutenant, I mistook you for someone else . . .'

'And what grudge did you bear against that someone else?'

'The individual I was chasing wears the same uniform as you do, he's stolen it, and his plan was to approach His Majesty . . .'

'Well, blow me! Since when have servants been acting as detectives?'

'I'm a detective acting as a servant.'

'Have you come from the palace?' asked someone else.

'Indeed I have.'

'Has the betrayal been confirmed?'

'What betrayal?'

'You're coming from the palace and you don't know what people are saying?'

'I thought only of the man I was attending to.'

'False valet,' said the false Maubreuil, 'the 6th Corps have just defected.'

Octave struggled to his feet, white stockings and boots stained with Fontainebleau mud. The chasseur explained.

'Eleven thousand of our men have gone over to the enemy, monsieur.'

*

The 6th Corps, which Marmont had regrouped along the river Essonne, after passing through the Russian and Bavarian camps in the middle of the night, were marching on Versailles to give themselves up to the provisional government. The soldiers were loyal but their leaders were not; Marmont had negotiated his renunciation with the allied staff, who had skilfully flattered him; the men had obeyed because their generals had lied: 'The army is going to attack at dawn, we must cover them.' Thus duped, the regiments had set off, but in the wrong direction. Some soldiers had noticed, like the cuirassier captain that Belliard had brought to the Emperor: he had escaped across the fields and travelled the eight leagues to Fontainebleau.

When the defection became known, Napoleon did not react. Outside, his Guard were storming furiously through the town; some emissaries had told them they still had the weak division of the incorruptible General Lucotte on their side, that the rearguard squadron of Polish cavalry-

men had refused to go along with the suspicious deploy-
ment; that Mortier was requesting instructions, that he
was stretching out his corps as far as Corbeil to protect
Fontainebleau.

The Emperor had gone to bed.

He had not risen by late morning, when Caulaincourt,
looking distraught, climbed out of a barouche from Paris.
The Duke hurried towards the mezzanine apartments,
and bumped into Napoleon's chief valet.

'I've got to see the Emperor straight away!'

'But he's asleep . . .'

'I don't care! Wake him, Monsieur Constant, wake
him!'

As the valet didn't dare do anything so familiar,
Caulaincourt burst into the room and roughly shook the
sleeping man until he opened his hooded eyes and sighed,
'Ah! Caulaincourt . . .'

Very unkempt, his complexion yellow and puffy, the
Emperor struggled to sit up on his pillows, then sat down
on the edge of the mattress, his feet on the little stepladder
that he used to climb into bed. Constant ran over to
him, put his ugly red slippers on his feet and helped him
into a dressing-gown. Caulaincourt explained his unhappy
mission; he described how Tsar Alexander had changed
his mind on learning of the defection of the 6th Corps,
how he had rejected the regency that he, unlike the other
sovereigns, had until then supported, and now joined
the rest in demanding an abdication pure and simple,
and exile — but the Emperor was barely listening, for he
could think only of Marmont, the Duke of Ragusa, whose
loyalty he had never doubted.

'Marmont!' he said. 'Deserting in the face of the

enemy! And when did he do it? Just as our victory was certain! He is trampling the national cockade underfoot to wear the mark of the traitors he has been against for twenty-five years! Who could have believed that of him? I loved him, Caulaincourt, he was a man with whom I have broken bread, a man I dragged from poverty, a man whose fortune and reputation I made! The ingratitude of it! He will be unhappier than I, you'll see.'

'Talleyrand did everything in his power to make him abandon us.'

'Talleyrand? For him, betrayal was a means of escape. His role was written for him. He knew I wanted to stop him, but what interest could the others have in betraying me? And it's those I have raised highest who are leaving me first: within the year, Caulaincourt, they will be ashamed of having yielded rather than fighting, of having been handed over to the Bourbons and the Russians!'

Caulaincourt told the Emperor that Talleyrand had sent Marmont his old aide-de-camp from Egypt, Montessuy, dressed as a Cossack, to persuade him. Montessuy had flattered the vanity of the Duke of Ragusa, showing him that by deserting with his army he alone could spare the pillaging of Paris and consolidate peace in Europe. The Marshal had signed an agreement with the allied staff, but upon learning that the Emperor was abdicating in favour of his son, and that the regency was possible, he changed his mind and returned to Paris in Ney's coach to plead his own case to the foreign sovereigns. Alas, he had entrusted the army to his generals; in his absence they had carried out the original plan and delivered their regiments to the enemy.

'When he learned of the defection, at the same time as we did, the Duke of Ragusa felt dishonoured.'

'And he is!'

'General Souham, who replaced him, has convinced his peers . . .'

'Souham?' said the Emperor. 'Yesterday he asked me for six thousand francs, and I gave it to him. Money, ambition, their positions, that's what guides them, the birdbrains! What about the soldiers?'

'When they reached Versailles they worked out that they'd been trapped, and mutinied. They wanted to join you, sire.'

'It was too late . . .'

'Yes.'

Caulaincourt returned to his mission, explaining that while the allies hoped to send Napoleon to the ends of the earth, he and the Tsar had sought to negotiate an exile for the Emperor that might not be quite so harsh, on an island off the coast of Tuscany, because the coasts were fortified, and that . . .

'Thank you, Caulaincourt.'

With a gesture of his chin, the Emperor dismissed the Duke of Vicenza.

*

Ney arrived a few hours later with Macdonald, having called in at his Paris town house on the bank of the Seine and sworn to his wife that he would make sure that war didn't break out, and sworn to Talleyrand that he would very soon bring him the unconditional abdication of the man he called 'the tyrant'. The Marshal was like that, always treading a path between two extremes, fundamentally irresolute, more courageous with a sabre than with words. His mind teemed with ideas, certainly, but standing before the Emperor he mumbled, standing with the others and delivering his report. Napoleon had regained his composure, but kept his hands firmly behind his back, beneath the turnbacks of his colonel's uniform; he had forgotten that the occupying forces wanted to send a quarter of his army to Normandy. To reopen that wound and watch him crack, Ney handed him the latest issue of the *Journal des débats*, hot off the press, the front page of which began:

> Marshal Marmont, Duke of Ragusa, has abandoned the colours of Bonaparte to embrace the cause of France and of humanity . . .

The Emperor folded up his lorgnette and very calmly put the paper down.

'Gentlemen, I have been thinking.'

Silence.

'All is not lost. Soissons is putting up resistance, and so is Compiègne. Some places are holding out against the invader: Strasbourg, Antwerp, Mantua, Barcelona, the garrisons in Germany. Partisans are harrying the rear of the enemy—'

'But in Paris,' Marshal Ney broke in, 'peace has become a magic word . . .'

'Peace! With the Bourbons? Louis XVI's brother is old and crippled, and he needs a machine with pulleys to lift him into his barouche! The Bourbons! The people around him are nothing but passions and hatreds dressed in human clothing!'

'Do we have any other choice?' Macdonald ventured.

'Yes, Marshal, we do have a choice other than a king brought back from England by foreign regiments. Let's head for the Loire.'

'Sire,' intervened Major General Berthier, 'I have shown you the latest reports from our light cavalry . . .'

'I know. The enemy is advancing along the Orléans road, they have taken Pithiviers and they are trying to surround Fontainebleau. The Russians have crossed the Loing. So?'

'Can we break through that encirclement and reach the Loire?' asked Macdonald.

'Soult has fifty thousand men beneath the walls of Toulouse, Suchet is bringing fifteen thousand back from Catalonia; in Italy Prince Eugène has about thirty thousand soldiers, Augereau commands fifteen thousand in the Cévennes. Let's not forget the border garrisons, and General Maisons' army, and my Guard, the twenty-five thousand of my Guard!'

The marshals were dismayed and made no secret of the fact. Their faces darkened and they averted their eyes.

'Do you want a rest?'

'The army is finished, sire,' said Macdonald. 'More and more people are deserting, the men are demoralized by the defection of the 6th Corps . . .'

'Poor Marshals! Poor heroes! Poor dishonoured people thinking only of my death!'

'Sire!'

'Do you know how many kinds of grief and danger await you on your feather beds?'

The Emperor moved to sit down behind a little mahogany pedestal table on which the Duke of Bassano had arranged pens, ink and paper. Pale, and with a nervous hand, Napoleon began to write a text that he had already pondered; the ink blotted on the paper, which was wrinkled by his passing pen. He crossed out the word 'nation' and replaced it with 'France'.

'Read!'

He held the paper out to Ney, but his scrawls were barely legible, and Bassano read for him:

> The allied powers having proclaimed that the Emperor Napoleon was the sole obstacle to the re-establishment of peace in Europe, the Emperor, true to his oath, declares that he renounces the thrones of France and Italy, both for himself and for his heirs, and that there is no personal sacrifice, even that of his own life, that he is not prepared to make in the interests of France.

Ney and Macdonald, who had ceased to believe that this would happen, eagerly approached the Emperor with great relief, and gripped his hands: 'Sire! Never have you shown more greatness!'

Ney took advantage of Napoleon that same day, requesting a large sum of money from the monarch he had helped to sell. The Emperor let him have it.

*

The marshals left again that evening to arrange an honourable treaty with the conquerors in exchange for the Emperor's abdication, and to defend as best they could the interests of Napoleon, his wife, their son, the army and the servants of Empire. Octave saw them setting off as he returned to the palace (after asking shoe-maker Boiron about the intentions of the royalist party;

Maubreuil seemed to have abandoned his planned assassination, and had disappeared).

In Fontainebleau, the feverish atmosphere of the past
few days had subsided once more. The palace had emptied, and all of a sudden it seemed vast. Octave sometimes
came across shadows in the deserted galleries; no one
ventured a comment or a greeting, they were all thinking
of their imminent departure, constructing noble and credible excuses, a sick relation, funds they had to find, an
invitation. Even before the treaty had been drawn up and
ratified by the allies, generals and dukes were declaring
their allegiance to Louis XVIII — meaning Talleyrand —
in order to gain privileges. First Oudinot, then Mortier,
the oh-so-republican Jourdan, Kellermann, Ségur, Hulin,
Latour Maubourg: almost everyone.

Even in the midst of so swift a collapse, the Emperor still
put up a good show, and altered none of his domestic habits.
When he got up, Constant presented him with a basin filled
with soapy orange-scented water and he plunged his hands
up to his forearms and moistened his chin, splashing his
flannel waistcoat, everyone present, and the floor. Then, by
the mirror that Roustan was holding in the light from a
window, he began to shave, sliding his mother-of-pearl-
handled cut-throat razor down his face, contrary to the
practice of barbers. He had always shaved himself, perhaps
as a precaution, refusing to allow anyone else to wield a
blade anywhere near his throat. He'd often joked about it,
referring to Hieron of Syracuse, the tyrant in Xenophon,
who never turned his back on a window for fear of a dagger
or an arrow — but his thoughts were becoming ghoulish
with the passing days, while his fate was being decided in
Paris among strangers, hard-line royalists and traitors.

'I can think of lots of people who would like to use this razor to open my throat. Of course, they're annoyed that I'm still alive! And besides, so am I. If those runts had any idea! I don't give a damn about power! A throne is nothing but a bit of gilded wood to park your arse on!'

As Octave arrived with the steaming infusion, the sound of wheels was heard in the courtyard. The Emperor froze mid-gesture.

'What's that?'

'A coach by the steps,' said Octave, glancing out of the window.

'Is it Berthier? Is he coming back?'

'No, sire, it's General Friant leaving.'

'Friant . . .'

Napoleon washed his hands with almond paste and said not another word; he felt under-occupied, which he hated. Meanwhile Bassano brought him the latest news from Paris, always in the same fashion: pamphlets, gazettes, a booklet by Chateaubriand attributing to the Emperor every vice in hell and earth, while painting an angelic portrait of Louis XVIII; printed songs, a swarm of caricatures (one of which showed him as a spinning-top whipped by the sovereigns of Europe; on another, the north wind blew to scatter his victory bulletins and decrees). Some jokers had discovered that Napoleon was the name of a devil in the *Acts of the Saints*, others mockingly claimed that his first name was really Nicolas. He was only moved by one drawing showing the King of Rome: the child passed a rope around the neck of a bust of the Emperor beneath the legend *Papa's tie*.

'Everything's shrinking,' he said with a moue of disgust.

Then he voiced his astonishment to Bassano at the fact that he had stopped receiving notes from the Empress; he had written to her every day while he had been in Fontainebleau, and hand-selected officers regularly carried letters between the two, but what had happened? The road to Blois was blocked, the messengers intercepted, Napoleon lamented, he knew that Marie-Louise was weak and ill, prey to insomnia and to fits of weeping. She was sorry to have left Paris, she was sorry no longer to be near him. The Emperor was alone. His family had fled. His mother was probably in Rome, and Louis was in Switzerland, where Joseph and Jérôme were preparing to join him.

While his enemies were agreeing his destiny, the Emperor ventured out of his bedroom and went for a walk in the little garden near the chapel, solidly enclosed by thick stone walls.

From the old deer gallery overlooking the garden, the Duke of Bassano and Octave observed the Emperor: he paced along the avenues, taking great strides, a stick in his hand, breaking the branches of the shrubs, mammocking the flower-beds, decapitating the flowers with lashing blows, leaving petals flying in his wake.

'You will keep an eye on His Majesty at all times,' said Bassano, placing a familiar hand on Octave's shoulder. 'I'm sure there were many occasions during the last campaign when he wanted to die and I heard he sought out dangerous situations, as though to make an end to it. In Troyes, I know that he drew his parade sword against some uhlans who had surrounded him, and that he looked utterly devastated when he was saved in the very nick of time. At Arcis-sur-Aube, when the situation was becoming disastrous, he spurred his horse towards a shell that had fallen a moment before. The shell exploded and disembowelled his horse, and it was only by some miracle that he managed to get away. It all worries me, Monsieur Sénécal, unlike your pompous fool Maubreuil, who vanished into thin air as I predicted he would.'

'I have just learned that he is recruiting killers . . .'

'Let him recruit as he will, the worst of the Emperor's murderers is the Emperor himself.'

Down below, Napoleon had interrupted his walk and was prodding his stick into a pile of sand, like a sword into a belly.

*

In Fontainebleau the days passed, empty and tense; everyone was spying on the Emperor, puzzling over his slightest words in search of a double meaning, and interpreting his every gesture as a cause for concern. Roustan had noticed him dreamily turning a powder horn around in his hand, and took advantage of a moment when His Majesty had left his room to filch the bullets lined up in his pouch. Then Constant was about to hide the powder horn, but the Emperor caught him at it.

'Monsieur Constant! My son! Do you think I'm planning on killing myself? Suicide is for gamblers! And anyway, death wants none of me, as you know . . .'

His tone sounded false. Napoleon had no reassuring words for those around him. When he was splashing in his bath and called for a brazier of coal, his valets found reasons not to bring it to him. Did he want to asphyxiate himself? He regained a degree of self-control when a liaison officer who had managed to penetrate enemy lines gave him a letter from Marie-Louise which he read and reread. The Empress suggested joining him in his exile: 'All I desire,' she wrote, 'is to be able to share your ill fortune.' She also told him that she would soon be leaving Blois to see the Emperor of Austria, her father, in the Palace of Rambouillet, which did not please Napoleon at all. He asked the Duke of Bassano if the chasseurs of his Guard still had a general; yes, they did. Napoleon immediately summoned him to one of his drawing-rooms. Pierre Cambronne came straight away, one leg stiff and his left arm in a sling; he had been wounded at Craonne and at Bar-sur-Aube. His face was wrinkled from top to bottom, with a wide thin mouth that resembled a straight line drawn with a pencil, and the round, mobile eyes of a bird.

'General,' said the Emperor when he saw him, 'can you still ride a horse?'

'I live on horseback, sire!'

'In spite of your recent wounds?'

'Forgive me, but you are getting muddled. I took a bullet in the buttock at Austerlitz. My leg and my left arm don't stop me getting into the saddle or wielding a sword!'

'Thank you,' said Napoleon, smiling for the first time in weeks. 'General, I am pleased that you have not left Fontainebleau.'

'Where would I have gone?'

'To Paris, like everyone else.'

'I'm not like everyone else!'

'I know, Cambronne, but you will have to leave anyway.'

'To prostrate myself before the Bourbons! In that, sire, if you will forgive me, you are asking too much of me after twenty years of war! If anyone else suggested abandoning you, I would take it as a mortal insult!'

'Assemble two battalions of the Guard, take four cannon with you and bring my son and the Empress back from Blois.'

'Will she agree?'

'If she hesitates, kidnap her.'

It was an order. Soon, the Emperor would be issuing no more.

*

The palace became a prison. Napoleon waited dejectedly, unable to make a decision. He who had governed all the people, all the subjects of his vast Empire, now made only trifling decisions. He reserved his commands for commis chefs and underlings, and only lost his temper over too hot an infusion, a crumpled blanket, cold lentils. He couldn't even complain about the noise: the few occupants of the castle walked silently around like monks. When he heard a coach, he knew it meant that another of his men was leaving. He didn't try to restrain those who had served him; on the contrary, he encouraged them to join the new government and make themselves known to the Bourbons – they were not to miss the opportunity of a job or an income because of some pointless sense of devotion. Even his Mameluke went off to see his wife in Paris, swearing to come back – but what did it matter? Each hour the Emperor passed merely reinforced his humiliation and his helplessness. Indolent, absent-minded and broken, he barely reacted to anything. Octave never took his eyes off him, in accordance with Bassano's instructions, and one morning, coming into the bedroom, he saw

Napoleon slumped in his armchair with blood on his white breeches. He had lacerated his thigh with his fingernails.

On the morning of 12 April, the bad news started coming in thick and fast. First of all Peyrusse, the official paymaster, returned without having recovered any of the diamonds or the millions from the civil list that had been confiscated by the court: in the name of the King, a certain Marquis de la Grange had boarded and inspected the convoy near Orléans and taken the money to the Tuileries; under the eye of the National Guard, the vans had still not been unloaded because Treasury servants were arguing with the royalists who wanted to hang on to the loot. Later that day, General Cambronne also returned empty-handed. By the time he had reached Blois Castle, the Empress had already left for the Palace of Rambouillet, where her father was waiting for her.

Finally, in the evening, Caulaincourt and Macdonald brought in the treaty drawn up by the allies. As long as the ex-Emperor fled immediately, most of his wishes had been respected, except for one which concerned Marie-Louise; she would not be given Tuscany as a place of retirement, since her own father's delegation opposed the idea. 'Those Austrians have no guts!' said Napoleon. All that was missing now was his signature, and his kingdom would be reduced to a rock in the Mediterranean, the island of Elba that he had been granted after dreaming of Corfu or Corsica. He balked at the idea. 'To force me to sign this treaty,' he maintained, 'is to prolong my agony . . .'

*

Octave replaced Roustan the Mameluke outside the Emperor's door. He was lying on the trestle bed when he heard a voice calling. He gave a start, leapt up, grabbed a torch and walked unceremoniously into the room. Napoleon was sunk amid his pillows. By the faint night-light his bed, raised on its velvet platform and overshadowed by a tester, looked like a catafalque, but the prostrate figure was murmuring: 'Monsieur Sénécal, I am going to get up.'

As he set his torch down on a table, Octave noticed that the clock read four in the morning. He brought slippers, helped the Emperor into his damask dressing-gown, stirred the dying fire, put the broken logs back on the firedog, then, crouching on all fours, blew on the embers.

'Fetch me some paper.'

Octave headed to the antechamber. Paper? Where on earth from? He bumped into one of the aides-de-camp, who directed him, voice thick with sleep, towards the desk in the adjacent study, where the writing-case was kept. Octave took out a bundle of papers and returned to the bedroom: Napoleon was sitting on a loveseat, near the chimney where sparks licked at the wood. Octave laid down the sheets and writing materials, but the Emperor was staring into the distance. Octave dawdled, hoping for an instruction that never came, then glanced around to check that everything was in order, but no, Monsieur Hubert, who had been on duty before him, had forgotten to put the sugar-bowl on the chest of drawers beside the jug of water. Octave said nothing, but just backed slowly out of the room and returned to his antechamber, but he did not close the door completely, so that he could watch the Emperor through the chink.

Lit by the fire, which cast a giant, trembling shadow on the wall behind him, Napoleon dipped a pen into his crystal inkpot; he frantically scratched the paper, then tore up the page, crumpled the pieces and threw them into the fire; he started over again, and again he burned the results – and did so a third time before rising to his feet with a wheeze. Octave could no longer see him, but he could hear him, because the floor creaked and the footsteps came heavy and slow. Then came the sound of running water; he must have been filling a glass. There was also a more metallic sound, the little spoon stirring sugar. What sugar?

Octave was beginning to worry when the bedroom door opened abruptly and the Emperor appeared in the gloomy doorway. The untied belt of his dressing-gown hung like a rope, his body was gripped with spasms, and he clutched his stomach with one hand and the door frame with the other. His face was distorted into a grimace. He managed to issue an order between the violent hiccups that shook his body.

'Call the Duke of Vicenza and the Duke of Bassano . . .'

'Sire! First I will help you to sit down,' stammered Octave.

'Call them! Call the Duke of Vicenza . . .' Napoleon insisted, leaning against the door as though he were about to slide and fall into a heap.

'Gentlemen!' cried Octave, panic-stricken, shaking awake the other valets and waking the guard officers slumped on the uncomfortable sofas in the drawing rooms. They jumped to their feet, grew agitated, and

finally worked out what was going on. Soon the interminable corridors were filled with people, and candles were
being lit all over the palace. Some of the servants dashed
to the chancellery where Bassano was staying, while others
went in search of Caulaincourt and Dr Yvan. Marshal
Bertrand had been roused from sleep, and was hastily
getting dressed. Everyone was unkempt, some had managed to put on waistcoats, most barely had time to slip on
their shoes or plonk their wigs on their heads. Octave
stayed by the Emperor. Constant came running at the
sound of all the activity. He made some tea to calm his
master, who had dropped into his armchair, downcast for
a moment, then nervous again, tense and panting.

When Caulaincourt arrived, he turned away the
younger palace attendants, who were groaning or sobbing
more or less sincerely. News spread and distorted; they
were already burying the Emperor.

'Quickly,' said Octave. 'He's calling for you.'

'What's wrong with him?'

'Nausea, shivering, when I helped him to the armchair
(God, but he was heavy!) I felt his freezing hands, his dry
skin, he's unsteady, he's green in the face . . .'

Caulaincourt looked at Napoleon. The Emperor was
tormented by hiccups, his lips were flecked with foam.
Constant tried to make him swallow a few mouthfuls of
tea, but he spat it all over himself.

'A vase!'

Octave caught sight of a piece of Dresden china and
handed it to Caulaincourt, who placed it beneath His
Majesty's mouth. Napoleon began to vomit a disgusting
grey liquid; calming down, he looked up at the Duke and
said with a sigh, 'Your grace . . .'

'Sire, I'm here.'

'I've poisoned myself.'

'Have you called Dr Yvan?' Caulaincourt asked Octave, who was holding the revolting vase and didn't know where to empty it.

'Right away, your grace.'

In came the doctor, along with Bassano, who had just finished knotting his tie.

'He tried to poison himself,' Caulaincourt explained.

'I see!' exclaimed the doctor wearily, with a hint of anger.

Yvan immediately checked the glass that the Emperor had used; there on the silver-gilt tray he discovered the empty capsule in which the pharmacist had prepared, on his orders, the same poison that the Emperor had, in Russia, worn around his neck in a black satin heart. Napoleon grumbled: 'You miscalculated the dose, Yvan...'

The horrified doctor felt the Emperor's pulse.

'Sire, when you want to kill yourself you're better off picking up a pistol, and then you're sure to get the dose right.'

'Give me something stronger.'.

Yvan did not reply, but congratulated Constant on his initiative: 'Now that he's back from the dead, give the patient some hot tea to wash out his stomach, and let him rest.' With that, Yvan turned on his heels, forgetting his hat, and parted the groups of servants clustered in the corridors and antechambers. He answered questions with only a single sentence: 'It's all an act, that's all it is, an act!'

Meanwhile Octave had passed the vase to a clerk,

and opened wide a window. Caulaincourt and Bassano dragged the Emperor over so that he could breathe in the cool night air, which revived him a little. In the courtyard, Dr Yvan untethered a horse, jumped into the saddle and set off at a great gallop.

'How difficult it is to die in one's bed,' said the Emperor, his face pallid. 'When so little separates life from war . . .'

'Sire,' asked Bassano, 'why did you take the poison?'

'I'm going to throw up again.'

Another vase was spoiled before the Emperor explained that he found any other kind of death repugant, it left traces of blood, it left marks on the face. He was sure that his body would be displayed after his death, and he wanted the soldiers to recognize his face smooth and calm, as they had seen it a thousand times in battle.

It was dawn. Wrapped in his dressing-gown, the Emperor sat in an armchair by the now extinguished fire, his head in his hands, his legs bare, his feet in his worn slippers. He didn't move. Caulaincourt ventured to remind him that he still had to sign the ratifications of the treaty demanded by the allies, which Macdonald would take to Paris. And so it was that Napoleon signed, without rereading it, the long text that would keep him far from France on an island, a tiny island, which smelled of rosemary – but which was really a cage.

Three

ON THE ROAD

'A man has no calling; he has no more duty or vocation than a plant or an animal.'

Stirner, *The Ego and His Own*

THE EMPEROR WAS resigned. After a day on a light diet, entrusting Bassano and Caulaincourt with the task of arranging the stages of his journey, he took refuge in books. Shutting himself away in his study, which he now hardly ever left, he organized the pillage of the palace library, drawing up a list of the authors to be taken into exile: Cervantes, Fénélon, La Fontaine, Voltaire, his dear Plutarch in the translation by Jacques Amyot, a collection of the *Moniteur universel*. The Emperor browsed, consulted, marked pages, sorted through the volumes that were to be put in the cases – and, because the regular librarians of Fontainebleau had fled and because he was well-read, Octave was appointed to assist Count Bertrand in this diverting task. If Napoleon went on unfolding maps, he no longer did so to plan his army's retreat, but to study geographical landmarks. He looked up and asked, 'Do you know this island, gentlemen? Does it have a palace? A castle? A suitable dwelling-place? A reasonable one?'

'We just know where it is, sire.'

'Show me, Bertrand, I can't find it . . .'

'Here . . .'

Count Bertrand pointed with his fingernail to a forlorn little dot in the sea next to Corsica.

'It looks like a greenfly.'

'It's the island of Elba.'

'That's supposed to be an island? That's a rock.'

Napoleon pouted, peering through his lorgnette at the map of the Mediterranean.

'The coast doesn't seem far away,' he said.

'Piombino is about three or four leagues from Elba. Look, sire . . .'

'I can see the shores of Tuscany. The Tuscans can't stand me, they're still in mourning for their Grand Duke Leopold. They live in a garden, but I know they are hostile to me.'

'They are as cowardly as they are rebellious, Your Majesty has nothing to fear.'

'Ha! My kingdom isn't all that far from Rome . . .'

'Forty-five leagues away, in fact, and Naples eighty-five.'

'That opens up some prospects . . .'

The Emperor was smiling, and nibbling dreamily at the handle of his pince-nez. He clapped his hands when Octave handed him a booklet he had just dug out from the bottom of a drawer, *Notice on the Island of Elba*, by an anonymous author, and, more importantly, Arsène Thébaut's larger and more recent *Journey to the Island of Elba*. 'Right, then!' he said. 'Let's learn about our kingdom!'

He read until evening, sometimes meditating out loud: 'These stout fellows, sailors and fishermen, have rather coarse manners . . .' or: 'If the hares eat all those aromatic herbs in the scrub, they must taste extraordinary in a fricassée, don't you think, gentlemen? Let's get going! This little island doesn't sound all that bad . . . It even has unexploited goldmines.' Nothing that he learned from Paris held his imagination now: it mattered little to him that royalists had put the statue of Henri IV back on the Pont-Neuf; in his mind's eye he was wandering among the juniper bushes and fig-trees that grew twisted among the rocks of Elba. He had already left.

His regrets now became more historical and distant in tone, he spoke of the Etruscans who had exploited the island of Elba, flushed from the *Aeneid* 300 warriors who had come from the island to disembark with Aeneas on Ausonia's shores: 'Both iron and soldiers Elba did supply,' Virgil sang. 'Nonetheless,' Napoleon added quietly, with a frown, 'when Diocletian abdicates to retire to his villa in Savona, he is returning to the Dalmatia of his birth, and by then he is sixty years old, and power has exhausted him. All the same!' he continued. 'I'm fifteen years younger than that, and it isn't power that exhausts me. What I lack is men.'

Once again Octave changed clothes without changing his role. As he was unattached, Bassano had easily persuaded him to pursue his surveillance work close to the Emperor. Octave would follow him to the island of Elba. In the phoney court that would be set up there, he would protect Napoleon against his enemies, whether paid or fanatical. Besides, by visiting shoemaker Boiron, as he had done several times in search of information, Octave had learned that Maubreuil was assembling a team of paid thugs, and was planning to launch an ambush in the forest when the procession left the castle and took the road into exile; chasseurs of the Guard would therefore escort His Majesty at least as far as Briare, the first expected stopping-point. Boiron had also given Octave a parcel of the belongings he had left at the rue Saint-Sauveur, which the royalists had managed to pass on to him. As well as his favourite cane, which he had left behind at Sémallé's, Octave recognized his blue suit and his wide-brimmed hat. Octave wanted to pay the shoemaker for his new boots, which could have been made to measure for him. So it was in civilian dress that, on the night of 19 April, he checked the loading of the 100 vans which would travel ahead of the Imperial carriage – because this wasn't a hasty escape, but a noble departure planned out in the minutest detail; His Majesty would want for nothing.

Preparations went on for hours. The open coaches were lined up in the palace courtyard, by the bright light of the torchères and the coachmen's lanterns. The servants, and some grenadiers who had been called in as reinforcements, loaded the numbered boxes according to their content. The Emperor's personal silver took up little room compared to the military munitions, wrapped statues, furniture, bronzes, paintings large and small, and the books designed to render the unknown dwelling on the island of Elba inhabitable.

'Take care with that, damn you!' cried Octave, raising his cane like a sergeant major.

'Me?' asked a dazed groom, who was tangled up with a peculiarly shaped package swaddled in coarse cloth. He was having trouble holding it in his arms.

'It's a Cupidon!'

'I swear I've done nothing . . .'

'That statue, there – you nearly broke the bow it's holding! It's fragile!'

'What's going on?'

Count Bertrand had turned his head at the sound of the altercation, interrupting the advice he was giving the Polish officers who would be acting as guides and protection for the convoy. The groom put his burden down on the cobbles, nearly knocked over the Cupidon again, and explained to Bertrand: 'It's the Pubidon, Chief Marshal.'

'The what?'

'The Cupidon from the green salon,' said Octave, 'whose bow could have been broken by such rough treatment!'

The groom didn't understand a word, but picked up the trussed object again and carried it like a sacrament to the designated van. There, valets crammed the statue in between a bust of Socrates (whose beard poked from a sack) and a marble-eyed Venus. There was no real accident of any kind, however, and even the silver-gilt plates were intact as they faced the jolts of the journey. Soon the coaches were covered with tarpaulins; they passed through the castle gates just before midnight. Octave and Bertrand nostalgically considered the interminable procession as the vehicles disappeared into the Fontainebleau night.

'Don't you think there's something funereal about the echoes of the wheels and hoofs?'

'I was about to say just that, your grace, but look over there . . .'

Two figures were outlined against the metal base of a

torchère. The first was furtively throwing his luggage into a cabriolet; smaller and rounder, the second followed him with a coat-rack.

'By the size and shoulders of the first one,' said Bertrand, 'I recognize Monsieur Constant.'

'So he's creeping off as well . . .'

'And the other?'

'I think it's Roustan, but how can we be sure, when he isn't wearing his Mameluke's outfit?'

'I thought he'd come back from Paris?'

'Then he's setting off again, your lordship, this time for good.'

'The rats! There won't be many of us serving His Majesty in the new place.'

*

There were not many of them the following morning, in fact, in the Courtyard of the White Horse. By nine o'clock, only thirteen coaches were lined up for an imminent departure. Most of the privileged or devoted people who were to accompany the Emperor had already taken their places in the queue of berlins: the pharmacist, the two cooks, the farrier – about twenty people at the most who had been selected to recreate the household of the exiled sovereign. On General Petit's orders, the First Regiment of the Grenadiers à pied lined up; the trumpeters awaited the order to play 'Pour l'empereur', the drummers held their sticks poised above the instruments they wore on sholder-straps, standards hung like fringed and gilded rags at the end of poles whose eagles held their beaks lowered. No sound, no wind. Serious faces, smoke-dried by the bivouacs and the gunfire, expressed nothing but a void; it was the end of an adventure.

Octave was daydreaming, boots in his stirrups on a post-horse. He thought of his past as a penpusher and a paid informer (complementary activities since in each case the task was to give an account of what one knew or wished to understand). He was just reflecting that the fall of a great man was a blessing to its immediate witnesses, and that he had, thanks to his gifts as a writer, a subject that would surely bring him to prominence, when a voice dragged him from his ambiguous thoughts.

'Monsieur Sénécal, can you tell His Majesty that everything is ready?' Count Bertrand was sharing the six-horse sleeping-carriage that was to take the Emperor away. He had opened the door and called to Octave, who quickly dismounted.

'Straight away . . .' Clutching his cane and hat like a master of ceremonies, Octave walked along the line of grenadiers at ease, climbed the horseshoe steps and walked mechanically along the route that brought him to the mezzanine apartments, through the long vestibule where aides-de-camp and starchy servants were waiting impatiently, although they didn't show it, stirred by the idea of joining their families, getting back to Paris and working for new masters.

The Emperor stood in the middle of an antechamber gesticulating, stamping his heels and, for the umpteenth time, throwing his cocked beaver hat (duly picked up by Bassano) on the floor.

'I'm not going!'

'Sire . . .'

'Sire! Sire! Sire! Oh, fine, you treat me with such concern, as though I were already in my grave, Master Campbell!'

In front of the other foreign commissioners Sir Neil Campbell, a colonel of Scottish origin sent by London, stood impassively in his blood-red uniform. He had the milky complexion of the British and a pattern of broken veins on his nose and cheeks; the lobes of his large ears protruded from beneath his rolled wig, which was fixed at his collar by a velvet band. The Emperor knew nothing of the Russian, hated the Prussian and despised the Austrian, speaking only to Campbell.

'Your King George is mad, he climbs the curtains, he babbles baby-talk, he crawls on his belly along the carpets of Buckingham Palace like a grass-snake; his son, who is going to replace him on a vacant throne, is no better, he's a hedonist, a whoremonger, a softy at the mercy of his entourage of shopkeepers! And as for me, Campbell, who do you take me for?'

'You have signed the treaty . . .'

'A dischcloth that I can denounce if the terms are not respected!'

'How are the allies failing to respect the treaty?'

'They are stopping the Empress from joining me!'

'It was her decision . . .'

'No!'

'The provisional government . . .'

'I don't give a damn about the provisional government! It breaks its promises!'

Campbell had come to the palace four days earlier, to present the document that required his current commander to hand the island of Elba over to Napoleon.

Those orders stipulated that the forts were to be disarmed and gunpowder supplies were to be repatriated. The Emperor irritably returned to that clause.

'And those cannon that they want to take from me! Without artillery, how could I defend myself against Algerine corsairs? Do they want me to be captured? Who would pay the ransom? Do they want me to be disembowelled? Why don't I just go along nicely and retire to England, Campbell? All I need is a bed and a corporal's wages!'

Mingling with the impatient onlookers, Octave listened to His Majesty's recriminations as he passed lightly from one theme to another, listing his grievances, until his fury subsided and he lowered his voice to augment its effect.

'The people are unhappy, I'm told. I can hear it from here and I know it. I have thirty thousand men, I can get a hundred thousand more. Without foreign troops, what are your Bourbons? How long will they hold out?'

'The provisional government is French, sire.'

'Come now! Talleyrand sold me the Directory, now he's selling me to the Bourbons, but are you sure that tomorrow he won't sell me Louis XVIII and his whole family? What's next?'

Napoleon had just noticed Octave, and repeated, staring him evilly in the eyes: 'What's next, Monsieur Sénécal?'

'Count Bertrand . . .'

'. . . wants to tell me everything is ready?'

'Yes, sire.'

'I will leave when I want, and if I want.'

*

Octave mounted his horse again near the gates leading out of the grand courtyard – beside some young couriers whose task it was to run ahead before each staging-post to ensure the Emperor would be given the best possible welcome. He saw the officers of the Guard pacing up and down in front of a silent regiment. He saw General Drouot, the commander-in-chief of the artillery, climb aboard the berlin at the head of the procession and draw the curtains to block everything out. The foreign commissioners did the same, skirting the troops at the foot of the buildings to avoid, by their conspicuous presence, turning sad faces into furious ones. The morning was interminable.

At last!

At noon the Emperor came out on to the steps. Bassano and Belliard surrounded him amid a cluster of aides-de-camp and barons. A clamour rose up like sea-swell. Napoleon took off his hat to salute the soldiers, who raised their heads towards him, then he quickly descended the horseshoe steps and advanced towards the troops who stood to attention even though no order had been given. Some grognards had tears in their eyes, others sniffed. The Emperor raised his arm, but the usual delirious acclamation in response was not forthcoming; a terrible silence fell. He began to speak; only the officers massed in front of him could really hear his words. They repeated them, as they came, to the ranks behind, and the phrases ran in scraps from mouth to mouth, strengthened by their simplicity: '*I . . . am leaving . . . You, my friends, continue to serve France . . . I will write about the great things we have done together . . . Goodbye, my children!*'

The drums began to beat a ruffle, a steady, raging roll

that drowned the sound of sobbing. Fists pressed to the pommel of his saddle, Octave raised himself up for a better glimpse of the Emperor among the rows of caps and shakos and plumed cocked hats: Napoleon was delivering an accolade to a white-haired general. Hiding his face behind a hand, a grenadier lowered his flag towards him; the Emperor kissed the fabric – on which tremendous victories were inscribed in letters of gold – before swiftly turning on his heels to be swallowed up by the carriage where Bertrand had been waiting for him for several hours. At that signal the procession immediately set off, trumpets playing a military march.

Octave trotted at the front, among the chasseurs who were led by the lieutenant he had mistaken for Maubreuil the other night. Octave had told him of his concern about Maubreuil and, now riding at a full trot, they both kept a close eye on the verges of the road. When they advanced into the forest, having sent some scouts ahead, they knew that beyond the chaotic rocks, the sandy ravines, the dense curtains of oaks and pines, lay the Seine; the Cossacks occupied the right bank, and it would be easy for Maubreuil to recruit from among their number; but no murderous mob burst suddenly from the undergrowth.

The procession sped up as it passed through Nemours and Montargis, stopping only at the obligatory relays; they spent a long time at each, because they had to change sixty horses every time. In the main square of Briare, General Cambronne and his battalion of grognards presented arms. They had left the palace two days previously, and were preparing to travel through the whole of France before setting sail for Elba. This was the whole of the Emperor's army: the allies had allowed 300, but there were twice as many as that. The Emperor reviewed them with visible emotion, wishing them a pleasant journey. Cambronne had drawn his sabre from its scabbard to salute him, and his master thanked him for his extreme loyalty before going to dine at the Hôtel de la Poste. It was eight o'clock in the evening.

*

In the sovereign's service, Octave learned how to waste time. It all hung on a word, a whim. He was not as used to this as other members of the reduced staff that was following the Emperor into his exile, for whom lazing around had become a full-time occupation. So Octave sat in a chair all morning, bored, distracted only for a moment by a plump serving-girl whom he wouldn't be inviting up to his garret, wink as she might. Octave felt as though he was bound hand and foot. Previously, he had been in charge of his own timetable and his own movements, he had led a life both secret and active in his pursuit of information, a life that took him to slums and housing offices, always tailing someone, his eyes as multi-faceted as a fly's. He had acquired the instinct of danger, a special flair that he could scarcely exercise on a morning such as this. When he got up, the Emperor appeared as though he were still in the Tuileries, resolute and authoritarian. He refused to wolf down his lunch, inspected his convoy, and talked to the coachmen and cavalrymen who were escorting him. At midday he gave the order to leave. Even the foreign commissioners complied with his wishes: for one last time they let him have the illusion that he was governing men.

But in Cosne, in La Charité-sur-Loire, the villagers

lining the main road hailed Napoleon, identifying him by his famous hat as he passed, while he held his hand open through the carriage window. It was as though he were visiting his provinces, accepting the normal submission of his subjects and giving them his blessing.

In the evening, Octave was riding with the lieutenant of the chasseurs when he spotted the spire of the Cathedral of Saint-Cyr on the horizon, with the old town of Nevers rising up the hill to meet it. The day had been tiring and monotonous, but this staging-post promised to be a little more active: the closer he came to it the more clearly he saw the people crowding into the middle of the road, barring the gates of the town.

'What do you think, Lieutenant?'

'I think we might finally have some work to do . . .'

'What are they shouting?'

'I haven't a clue, but they're certainly shouting!'

'I'd like to go on ahead . . .'

'As you wish. Hugonnet! Fournier! Ride on with Monsieur Sénécal!'

Octave and the two chasseurs of the Guard galloped off towards the town. Half-way, they stopped abruptly. A horseman was coming out of Nevers, one of the convoy's messengers who had been dispatched as a scout two hours before. He was breathless, red-faced and sweating. With a smile on his lips he told them: 'They're like devils.'

'What are these excitable characters yelling?'

'Vive l'Empereur!'

'Go and tell the Lieutenant, we'll go to Nevers.'

The people of the town had come down into the streets, and processions were coming to the gates to welcome the convoy. When the two chasseurs arrived in front of that tightly packed crowd, the sight of their uniforms prompted a further eruption of cheers. Their horses waded through the dense tide of men and women, children sitting on their parents' shoulders, who raised their hats, their umbrellas and their canes. Trooper Hugonnet noticed a bourgeois who had come out of curiosity and was now looking rather alarmed; he reached down and tore the white cockade from the man's top hat to cheering and applause.

'Clear the way! Clear the way!' yelled Octave, although no one paid any attention. It took the arrival of the whole of the escort to contain the enthusiasts and force the thirteen carriages through the crowd. They slowly climbed the sloping streets, rattling their way up the hill to the old palace of the Dukes of Cleves. At the risk of being trampled, some excited townspeople slipped under the horses' bellies, and managed to touch the emblazoned door of the Imperial carriage, the palms of their hands flattened against the glass. They had to be pushed away, not too harshly, but firmly nonetheless, and shoes were crushed beneath hoofs, dresses were crumpled, people were jostled and shoved at random. Fortunately, a battalion of the line had emerged from their barracks, and forced their way through to the cavalrymen by swinging the butts of their guns.

The Emperor, protected from these people who missed him so, left his carriage behind a stout cordon of soldiers. He climbed the steps that led beneath a Renaissance tower and into the palace, ordering the officer of the local detachment to 'Call the Chief of Police and the Mayor, bring me the newspapers, and let's get a fire going!'

'Sire, you were to be lodged in a hostelry very close by . . .'

'I want some fire in this damned fireplace!'

Octave and the lieutenant joined the Emperor and his retinue in a vast, unfurnished – and cold – room. As the evening light passed faintly through grilled, ogival windows, the garrison soldiers quickly set to work with the Emperor's valets, lighting torches, organizing lamps, getting a flame going and bringing in various bits of furniture from elsewhere in the building to form a sort of drawing-room. They were going to camp that night, and Napoleon was growing impatient: where on earth was the Mayor? And the Police Chief? They'd had to part the crowd, and arrived now looking very dishevelled, their ties crooked, their faces deferential, as they withstood the Emperor's rapid flow of questions.

'Public opinion?'

'You must be aware of it, sire, listen to the street . . .'

'To calm them down,' added the Police Chief, 'if you would appear at a window . . .'

'And what about the former aristocracy?'

'They aren't much in evidence, sire, but they have insisted that the fleur-de-lys flag be flown from the balcony of the Hôtel de Ville . . .'

'Do the people here obey them?'

'As one might obey a directive from Paris, sire.'

'The garrison?'

'They refused to give the oath to the King . . .'

There was more about this in the newspaper, which made Colonel Campbell and his commissioner colleagues turn pale. In Clermont-Ferrand, the soldiers had burned the white flag which was being carried in procession by the council. The royal insignia had been destroyed in Rouen, Orléans, Poitiers and Moulins. In Lyons the troops were on the brink of mutiny, and were beating up allied patrols. In Paris, workers were helping the soldiers to run Cossacks through with their swords in broad daylight. There were attempted uprisings in Antwerp, in Mayence, in all the Eastern garrisons. The Emperor stood by the fireplace rubbing his hands, growing more animated as the foreign commissioners grew more alarmed. Once the worthies had departed, Napoleon sat in an armchair and called for his pharmacist. The man came running with a case marked with an eagle, took out a syringe which he gave to the Emperor, uncorking a flask so that Napoleon could fill his syringe himself with a mixture of zinc and copper sulphate, lead acetate and mercury, weighed out and dissolved in distilled water and laudanum. The Emperor had to undergo this daily injection because he suffered from a venereal disease, a gift from an actress during his first stay in Paris. Unconcerned about the foreign commissioners, who were unaccustomed to such intimacy, he pulled his breeches below his knees and, punctuating his phrases with the full syringe held between his fingers, he launched into a lesson in strategy *a posteriori*.

'Luck abandoned me on the twenty-first of March, gentlemen, and it was my fault! Around Saint-Dizier I thought I held all your armies before me, but all I was hunting down was a Russian corps . . . If I had withdrawn to Paris, you wouldn't be with me this evening . . . Oof!' (He had just given himself an injection in the penis.) 'On the way I would have rejoined Oudinot's and Macdonald's corps, Compans' infantry in Sézanne, Ledru-Dessarts' men in Meaux!' (He waved his empty syringe around like a sword.) Marmont's and Mortier's regiments would not have been slaughtered in Fère-Champenoise.' (He held out the syringe to the pharmacist.) 'What a disaster! That infernal storm that blinded the men and drenched the powder!' (He reflectively pulled up his breeches.) 'In Paris, I would have found the garrison and the National Guard, I would have had almost a hundred thousand men under my command, pressing down on the capital — and you would have been crushed, gentlemen!'

Napoleon rose to his feet to dismiss the commissioners. 'Go and sleep wherever you can, tomorrow morning we will leave at six o'clock.'

They disappeared in search of somewhere to stay in the chilly palace. The Emperor put on his hat and his green jacket, cocking his ear to the continuing hubbub outside.

'Is there a balcony from which the citizens might see me?'

'Just above this room, sire,' said Octave, who had reconnoitred the building.

'Take a torch. You too, Bertrand.'

On the first floor, the Emperor himself opened a double window and commanded: 'Each of you take up position on one side of this guard-rail, and light me.'

He emerged from the window between the two lanterns, held out his arm in an Imperial salute and intoxicated himself on the endless ovation unleashed by his appearance.

*

Octave had resolved to take notes. At each stop he pencilled down a few lines in his notebook so he would not forget the details that he would later assemble into a story: '*Saint-Pierre-le-Moûtier, Villeneuve-sur-Allier, Moulins, Roanne, Tarare, Salvaguny, wherever we went the population gave His Majesty a warm reception, wherever we went he stopped and chatted with the priest, the doctor, the Mayor, a shopkeeper. In Lyons, honour was paid to him as though he was still on the throne. On Sunday we reached Vienne at dawn, and we breakfasted in Péage-de-Roussillon. Slates made way for Roman tiles.*'

In Valence everything changed. The town was silent, no one came to meet the convoy, no one tried to hamper their progress. The Emperor would have liked to visit the furnished room where he had lived with his young brother Louis when he was a lieutenant in the 4th Artillery Regiment; he had been pleased to see the rue Perollerie again, and the Three Pigeons inn where he had taken his meals in those days – but the Bourbon flag flapped from every monument, on every statue, and he chose not to stop.

They passed beyond the town. Napoleon was stretching his legs by walking up a hill when a carriage overtook him; it parked on the verge not far away. A man wearing a travelling cap got out and stood in the middle of the road, with his hands behind his back. The Emperor walked straight towards him. It was Augereau, the Duke of Castiglione, in civilian clothes. A marshal and adventurer, this fruiterer's son from the rue Mouffetard had been a fencing master in Naples, had sold watches in Constantinople, given dancing lessons, served in the Russian army and abducted a young Greek girl to live with him in Lisbon. The Directory had crowned him with laurels and Napoleon had showered him with gold. He was the champion of Arcola, having taken the place of Bonaparte (who had fallen into a ditch before he reached the bridge) and the undisputed hero of Millesimo, Ceva, Lodi, the head of the Army of the Rhine and then the Army of Catalonia; before the Austrian advance he had abandoned Lyons without a fight, exhausted by the war.

Count Bertrand told Octave the identity of this famous marshal, whom he knew by his name alone. Octave dreamed of having the power of Gyges, the King of Lydia, whose ring granted him invisibility. So many significant scenes went unwitnessed, like this random encounter which he was unable to observe at close quarters; he could merely guess its progress at a distance, from the attitudes of the two old comrades at arms. The Emperor had taken off his hat, and the other man insolently kept his on. Had he been invisible, Octave would have slipped between them and heard a brief and brutal conversation.

'Good day to you, Lord Castiglione,' said Napoleon.

'Lord of what? A lousy village that I held against the Austrians in spite of your orders? Castiglione, oh, yes, it has a ring to it, but it rings hollow, like all that you give and all that you have done.'

'I have been deceived about people.'

'No, it is you who have deceived them.'

'You owe your fortune to me, your grace.'

'You always bring everything down to yourself.'

'Go and spit on me in Paris, your grace, the Bourbons will pay you handsomely for it.'

'You're as rapacious as your eagle! Look what you have brought us to.'

'Be off with your grudges!'

'I'm not your puppet!'

Augereau put two fingers to the visor of his cap. Napoleon pulled his cocked hat low over his forehead and, turning his back on the marshal, strode to his carriage. Later, when all the passengers had disembarked from the berlins that were about to cross the Isère, Sir Neil Campbell showed the Emperor an order signed by Augereau, which some soldiers wearing white cockades had handed to him in Valence. Napoleon asked Bertrand for his glasses and read it emotionlessly:

> You have been freed from your oaths ... You are freed by the abdication of a man who, having immolated thousands of victims in the service of his own cruel ambition, could not die a soldier's death. Let us swear loyalty to Louis XVIII and wear truly French colours ...

The Emperor ripped this proclamation into shreds and, saying to the Englishman, 'The Duke of Castiglione has confirmed all that to me,' he threw the pieces of paper into the wind, which carried them to the swift waves of the Isère.

*

In Montélimar at sunset, the Emperor had a long discussion with the Sub-Prefect, M. Gaud de Rousillac: he was entering hostile territory, and was sorry to have dismissed his escort of chasseurs in Nevers. The Midi had always been royalist in its soul. Napoleon had forgotten that, but deep down he did not need to be reminded of it. The day after the Thermidor coup, the inhabitants of Tarascon had hurled sixty republicans over the castle walls. In Aix and Nîmes, the people of Provence had indiscriminately slit the throats of the occupants of the prisons. Wolves had returned to attack the hamlets; armed bands of deserters marched by night and laid waste the region from the Alpilles to Les Landes. The people of Marseille were learning Russian so they could talk to their liberators, because Suvorov was coming back up from Milan towards the Alps. Napoleon remembered those times. He thought he was back there when he reached Donzère, which was celebrating the Restoration. 'Down with the tyrant! Long live the King!' they shouted at the carriages with their eagle insignia as they quickly passed by. Wishing to be spared mockery, and to avoid musket fire, the Emperor transferred to the barouche of the Austrian commissioner, General Koller; he asked him, 'Does your postilion smoke?'

'Probably, but not if he's carrying Your Majesty.'

'Quite the contrary! Such familiarity will prove that I am not aboard your carriage. And why don't you sing a little? Vienna is the opera capital of the world, is it not?'

'Sire, my singing is appallingly out of tune . . .'

'Then whistle! Anyone can whistle! Show a lack of respect, for God's sake, to conceal my presence!'

General Koller tried to whistle a bit of Mozart that was so distorted as to be entirely unrecognizable. Napoleon sat sullenly in a corner of the seat and pretended to sleep as they passed through the streets of Orange – but they had to stop at the post-house on the way out of town to change horses. A fleur-de-lys flag hung from the roof of the stables. While the Emperor hid himself away, Count Bertrand took advantage of this forced stop to reach an agreement with Campbell.

'Colonel,' he said, 'our convoy is attracting too much

attention. For the sake of prudence we should divide it in two.'

'You're right.'

'You go on ahead and open up the road for us. Your English uniform will protect you – the southerners seem to like your compatriots.'

'I believe that is so, your grace.'

'You take the two carriages of cooks and valets, with their provisions, if necessary; they may have to set up a canteen in open country if the towns are too turbulent. Monsieur Sénécal will go with you on horseback, ensuring contact between you and His Majesty. In two days' time we will all meet up, if possible, at the port of Saint Tropez.'

'That seems like a sensible plan.'

So Octave set off with Campbell and the two administrative barouches. They entered Avignon at four o'clock in the morning. The city was not asleep; on the contrary, it was celebrating. People were dancing to the sound of discordant bands, beneath garlands of multicoloured Chinese lanterns. They were dancing the farandole, singing at the top of their voices and drinking a heavy wine that made their heads spin. Some recently liberated Spanish prisoners played the mandolin and rattled their castanets. Draft dodgers who had been hunted by the Imperial gendarmerie had emerged from the mountains where they had been hiding, and passed through the streets to cheers, with pine cones in their hats. Outside the door of the *mairie*, a large portrait of Napoleon was ablaze. Some worthies threw his bust out of a window. It shattered on the cobbles to cries of joy. Bells rang out, white flags hung from the windows of all the buildings, and the whole population was wearing the Bourbon cockade – on their hats, on the lapels of their jackets and pinned to the dancers' hair.

Not far from the Place de la Comédie, where armed men were keeping guard, the berlins lined up beside a coach decorated with a string of little white flags that was leaving for Lyons at daybreak. The town guard checked the travellers.

'Hey, look!' said a boy. 'The bird of ill omen!'

He pointed at the Imperial coat of arms painted on the sides of the administrative coaches. A crowd gathered immediately. A shaggy shepherd wearing a rough woollen jacket opened one of the doors, and dragged out a terrified cook by the throat. His faint protests met with a shower of curses. From his pocket, Octave took the white cockade that he had worn with Sémallé in Paris. He fixed it to the ribbon of his hat and was able to intervene.

'My friends! My friends! What are you looking for?'

'The tyrant isn't hidden under one of your cushions, is he?'

'If you're talking about the former Emperor, he's not with us.'

'And who might you be?'

'A representative of the provisional government of his Majesty Louis XVIII.'

'That's fine!' said the shepherd.

'Then cry *Long live the King!*' said a joker.

'Long live the King!' cried Octave, who was used to doing just that.

'Long live the King!' cried the little crowd.

'And the rest of them!' the shepherd continued.

Valets and cooks complied as cockades were fixed to

their hats, and the residents of Avignon, armed with buckets of tar, daubed the hated eagles that gleamed too brightly on the carriages. Colonel Campbell, who had also alighted from his berlin, negotiated with a captain of the city guard. Free to do as he pleased thanks to his usurped title and the royalist colours that he wore voluntarily, Octave rode over to Campbell.

'Captain Montagnac is in command here,' the Englishman explained. 'He's telling me about the risks that the Emperor runs.'

'I'm sure that's so, but he can't avoid Avignon; a detour would be too long and no less dangerous.'

'Does he have sufficient escort?' asked the Captain.

'It's non-existent.'

'Give us reinforcements,' Campbell suggested.

Octave went on, 'Can you assure us that His Majesty will be protected while the horses are being changed?'

'I'll try . . .'

Loyal Captain Montagnac rounded up his feeble detachment of guards. They were wearing clogs, held rusty old guns and had dented swords wedged in their belts. Most of them were yawning or rubbing their eyes – they had taken part in the celebrations that had been turning Avignon upside down ever since the newspapers from Paris had confirmed the Restoration.

The Emperor's sleeping car and two accompanying carriages arrived at six o'clock in the morning, and waited behind those of Campbell and the administrators. By that time fresh horses had already been prepared. Farriers quickly harnessed them beneath the concerned but vigilant eye of Captain Montagnac. How would he contain the drunk and excited people who were now crowding around the travellers, very interested and much too close? They became furious at the sight of the imperial coat of arms, pushing back the guards who showed barely any resistance, looking for the tyrant to tear him limb from limb — and thought they had glimpsed him in the depths of the Austrian general's barouche. One bystander put his hand on the door-handle, but Octave held him back by the shoulder, and was just raising his cane to knock him out, when Montagnac moved him aside.

'You rascal! Stop that this minute!'

'Calm yourself, Monsieur Sénécal,' advised the Emperor through the open window.

'Let the carriage set off!' the Captain ordered his guards. 'And you,' he said to the coachman, 'go at a gallop!'

'Thank you, Captain,' the Emperor said. 'I will remember you.'

'For God's sake, go!'

As soon as the horses were harnessed, the procession of six carriages hurried forward, dust rising, volleys of stones flying in their wake. Mounting his horse, Octave noticed Count Bertrand, impassive and alone in Napoleon's carriage. The window was broken. With his glove he was brushing splinters of glass from his sleeve.

*

Napoleon had examined the administrators' map of the region, crossing out those towns that were too large, and from which only violence could be expected. But he had circled the name of Orgon: he planned to lunch in that village, which reminded him of an episode from his youth as a soldier. It wasn't a girl, not that, but a punitive expedition against recalcitrant aristocrats. With the help of their peasants they were ruthlessly murdering the soldiers who came and went from the Italian army stationed on the outskirts of Nice. The situation had barely changed despite the passing years, as Napoleon learned when one of the messengers who had gone on ahead halted the convoy before they reached the town.

'The villagers are waiting for us in the square, I didn't dare get too close, but it looks as though some hotheads are stirring things up.'

'Is there any other way to get to Aix?' asked Bertrand, with his nose to the door.

'Sadly no, your grace, you'd have to head back towards Avignon.'

'Oh, no!'

The Emperor had climbed out of General Koller's barouche, and was walking along the road to the first carriage.

'In that case,' said the messenger, 'you'll just have to head into the crowd as quickly as you can and hope for the best . . .'

'What's your name?' asked the Emperor.

'Antoine Loisellier, sire.'

'Undress, Monsieur Loisellier.'

'Sire?'

'Do as I say, you wretched ass! I will take your place and you will take mine.'

'Me?'

'Well, yes, you idiot! Is your life worth more than mine?'

'I didn't say that, but . . .'

'No buts!'

Loisellier, poor Loisellier, dismounted and obeyed. Napoleon dismounted too, and held his cocked hat out to Bertrand, followed by his grey frock-coat and his colonel's uniform; he took off his riding boots and even removed his waistcoat and his white breeches. Then he dressed in the clothes he had asked for, ordering the messenger to get into the sleeping-carriage next to Count Bertrand.

First, however, Napoleon wanted to inspect his stand-in. 'Let's take a look at you,' the Emperor said. 'Yes ... That should do it, I hope, but my clothes are huge on you, and I can barely breathe in yours ...' With one final flourish, the Emperor donned the blue greatcoat and the round hat with the white cockade. He climbed on to the nag with the help of Bertrand and a coachman.

'Sire,' said the Count, 'are you sure this is wise?'

The disguised Emperor spurred the beast on without replying, and launched into a gallop.

'Monsieur Sénécal!' cried Bertrand. 'Go with His Majesty and don't let him out of your sight!' Octave immediately followed the Emperor, amid whip-cracks and the sound of the postilions' bugles.

Two kilometres further on, the horsemen slowed to a trot. They saw the first buildings of Orgon, low and long, whitewashed and with pink roofs, surrounded by little dry stone walls beneath the parasols of a grove of pines. Some noisy activity in front of the post-house disturbed this peaceful vision: as soon as they spotted the procession, the villagers had congregated, brandishing their pitchforks and old rapiers, bludgeons and butchers' knives. A mannequin made of cloth and straw and drenched in ox-blood dangled from a tree. It bore a piece of cardboard with the word *Bonaparte* scrawled upon it. Napoleon and Octave waited until most of the cortège had forced its way through, then filed in behind, the Emperor instinctively tugging on the reins to let Octave catch up with him: to crash into this crowd at a gallop would be to risk getting a pitchfork full in the chest.

'What scum!' Napoleon said to Octave in a trembling voice. 'I can't bear the mob, Monsieur Sénécal, I have never been able to bear the mob; the mob is idiotic and monstrous, it frightens me. You should never see it from too close up, unless you have cannon . . .'

They were now advancing at the same pace as the berlins, which acted as a shield; the people of Orgon seemed to be devoting their entire attention to the carriages they thought contained Napoleon, whom they wanted to get their hands on. There he is! The raging crowd rushed towards the sleeping-carriage at the front of the procession. Some tall fellows grabbed the horses by the bit to immobilize them; the animals foamed and whinnied, shied, striking the dusty ground with their hoofs and shaking their harnesses, making the couplings jolt. The postilions lashed out with their whips to beat back the peasants who were assaulting them from all sides. Hurling curses and death-threats in a patois that needed no translation, so distorted were their sun-bronzed faces, they pounced on Bertrand's sleeping-carriage, sticks raised. They threw large, sharp stones that dented the bodywork and broke the last remaining windows, while the Emperor and Octave trotted on ahead, because the savages of Orgon let the two supposed scouts – with their white cockades – continue on their way unmolested. Octave turned on his saddle: a group of shrieking harpies had dragged out the hapless Loisellier in his enormous uniform, mistaking him for the Emperor. They clutched him by the collar, screamed in his face, tore the medals from his clothes and threw his cocked hat in the air like a ball. Octave could see Colonel Campbell, waving and shouting sharply at the shrewish women, then he dug his spurs into the side of his mount to join the Emperor; the two rode along the road to Aix in the blazing sunshine.

*

The mistral rose. It blew sideways at the horsemen as they plunged into swirls of dust. Their noses deep in the wind-stirred manes of their horses, Octave and the Emperor passed pine forests, rock-piles, isolated farms in a stony desert without seeing any of them. They picked their way up and down steep mountain tracks, and a hundred times risked breaking their necks. The road narrowed. In single file, they trekked through the gorge that opens up in the Roc de Valbonette, they rode through Lambesc, and skirted meadows and groves of grey olive trees. They had to change horses in Saint-Canat, but they didn't linger there, leaving on empty stomachs, riding hell for leather. No hills now, the road was flat and straight, hamlets came and went, then vines, clusters of almond-trees and chalk quarries. They were hungry and thirsty, and they were exhausted, finally allowing themselves a halt at about one o'clock in the afternoon, in an inn identified by a sign nailed to a post as La Calade.

With some difficulty, the Emperor managed to get his leg over the saddle. Octave jumped down from his horse and helped him dismount because he didn't have his usual ladder.

'Sire,' said Octave, holding both bridles, 'I'll lead our horses to the stable, you go in and find a seat.'

'You're going to let me go into that den of cut-throats alone and unarmed?'

'Sire . . .'

'Stop calling me that! Enough of this madness, Monsieur Sénécal! Call me Loiseau, like the real messenger!'

'Loisellier.'

'As you wish, but forget my rank! So you don't want to lose me?'

'No, monsieur.'

'Not even *monsieur*, you idiot three times over! I'm wearing fancy dress, fine, but what if someone were to recognize me?

'No chance, rigged out like that.'

'You can be polite, all the same!'

The Emperor shook the dust from his greatcoat. His tight trousers refused to button up beneath his imposing belly, and he'd had to tie them with a piece of string – but such a ludicrous arrangement, so unworthy of a sovereign, deflected suspicion. Nonetheless, Napoleon continued to look distrustfully around him, and followed Octave to the stable, sticking to him like a leech.

They returned together to the courtyard, which was dominated by a gigantic poplar, and entered the inn. On a spit, some fat capons were turning, being basted with stock by a fat woman.

There were no other customers, and the landlady pointed to a table with her ladle.

'Wait a bit over a carafe, you two. My birds ain't cooked yet. You all right?'

'Oh yes, madam,' said Octave, offering a chair to the

Emperor, who muttered between clenched teeth: 'No stupid deference, Sénécal, you'll get us noticed.'

Napoleon sat himself down, angry but anxious, with his elbows on the table and without taking off his round hat. The old woman drew a jug of wine from the barrel, and set it down abruptly on the table with two glasses.

'Have you come from Aix?' she asked.

'No, madam,' said Octave, pouring himself some red wine. We've been galloping through the wind from Avignon.'

'If you're coming from the north, did you see Bonaparte? He's supposed to be passing this way.'

'Haven't seen him.'

The Emperor lowered his head over his glass, which he didn't fill. The woman, returning to her task of basting the capons, picked up a long carving knife and sharpened it on a stone beside the stove on which some beans were boiling. She worked herself into a fury.

'I tell you, that ogre isn't going to make it to that bloody island of his! He'll be thrown in the sea on the way! If he doesn't get killed first, he'll be back before three months are up, you'll see, and he'll start bleeding us dry all over again!'

She turned towards the table and pointed her knife towards Napoleon.

'Touch the tip of that, mate.'

The Emperor was obliged to run his finger along the blade.

'If someone wants to slit the pig's throat, there's the tool to do it with!'

'What has Bonaparte done to you?' asked Octave, who could see the Emperor changing colour.

'He killed my son, the monster! And my nephew, and so many young people! There's no one left in these parts but old people and widows.'

Frozen, the Emperor hid his face in his hands.

'Your friend looks exhausted,' the hostess remarked to Octave.

'Small wonder! We've been riding since dawn.'

'S'pose,' she agreed, waddling towards the fireplace to see how the cooking was getting on, 'and fat blokes tire quicker . . .'

*

The mistral had started gusting again, tilting the poplar in the courtyard, rattling the windows, and blowing gravel, sand and leaves into the inn. Just then the door opened with a clatter to a group of warmly wrapped-up men, their hair and wigs sticking out in all directions. The tallest of them removed his grey cape – it was Campbell – then asked for a rag to wipe his polished boots because he couldn't bear to look untidy. The landlady, a little alarmed at first by this sudden entrance, was impressed by Campbell's red uniform, and her initial fear subsided when the Englishman spoke to her in a very respectful, almost flirtatious tone, with that hint of an accent that had, in its day, seduced French baronesses and prostitutes alike; she duly brought him a rag. He thanked her and asked, 'Do you have anything for us to eat?'

'I'll set on enough chickens for you all, Milord,' said the woman, wiping her hands on her apron.

The other commissioners and Count Bertrand took off their coats and laid them across a table while the valets, the pharmacist and the coachmen who arrived in their

turn seated themselves at different tables. Octave had
risen to his feet. His eyes met those of Count Bertrand,
who had been the first to notice the prostrate Emperor
and who now came to sit opposite him. Napoleon took his
hands away from his face. It was drenched with tears. He
sniffed and closed his eyes. The landlady reappeared from
the farmyard and her husband followed her, bent, perhaps
even hunchbacked, and wearing wooden clogs. He held
some chickens by their feet, cackling and complaining.

In the inn, no one spoke; they had all seen the
Emperor, and they joined in his silence to the surprise of
the landlord and landlady, who were accustomed to
more unruly gatherings. The husband threw the chickens
into a cage where they fought and pecked one another,
while he dragged them out one by one, wrung their necks
and handed them to his wife. Sitting on a stool, she
plucked the birds over a large sack. The two cooks from
the Imperial retinue went to work, setting full carafes
and slices of ham down on the tables. Bertrand had just
served the Emperor when the latter knocked his glass
over with the back of his hand.

'Bertrand . . .'

'Sire?'

'Fetch me my Chambertin from your carriage. They're
going to poison me here, I'm sure of it.'

'Monsieur Hubert,' cried Bertrand in ringing tones,
'bring His Majesty's Chambertin!'

The innkeepers stood and gaped, having just worked
out that the fat fellow with the white cockade was the
monster whose death they so devoutly wished for. The
woman had said too much a moment before, and now she
hesitated between fear and disgust. She looked Napoleon

up and down as she gutted the chickens, pulling out heart, liver and gizzard with a single crisp gesture, her fingers red with blood – and she saw the hated figure, gnawing on an end of bread, give a start when her husband dropped a dead chicken on to the block and chopped its head off with a dull thud. The rest of the room drank in silence, waited patiently and ate ham and bread; the old woman turned the spits and stared at the fallen sovereign; the chickens cooked and time passed.

'Do you hear that?'

'The mistral, sire.'

'No! Voices, creaking, wheels. It's an ambush. They're going to kill me, I tell you!'

'I'll go and look.'

Standing by one of the windows overlooking the courtyard, Octave realized the peasants of the region were assembling in large numbers outside, with entire families sitting in carts. The Emperor gave a start at the slightest sound, but it was quite possible that he was not mistaken; after all, the convoy had been stoned at Lambesc; by Saint-Canat, not one berlin had a single window left intact, and two postilions had been wounded. Octave returned to the table.

'The road is blocked by people from the hamlets and the neighbouring farms . . .'

'Let's wait for nightfall,' said Bertrand, 'until they've gone.'

'And what if they attack?' asked the Emperor. 'Could I get out through that window at the back?'

Octave examined the window in question, which turned out to have a grille over it. Meanwhile Campbell tried to reassure the trembling exile.

'They're just curious.'

'They're furious, is what they are, not curious!'

The Emperor was prevailed upon to drink a glass of Chambertin, half of which he spilled over his waistcoat. He refused to taste the capons and the chickens when they were finally cooked, and shivered intermittently as though electricity were passing through his body.

'I want to leave before they hang me!'

'Let's wait for nightfall,' repeated Campbell.

'But didn't you see that scarecrow effigy of me this morning, hanging from a tree?'

'We'll surround you, sire,' said Bertrand to calm him.

'You haven't even got any guns!'

'These people will go, Sire, they aren't going to put you under siege . . .'

'How do you know that? When they've had enough of standing waiting in the wind, they'll come back *en masse* to the inn, and they'll run one of those spits through my belly!'

Napoleon pointed towards the spits in the fireplace, which gleamed with stock and chicken juice.

*

As soon as he had the opportunity, Octave took out his notebook and pencilled some notes about what he had just experienced. Later he would flesh out the rather dry information, which he saw as an aide-mémoire. From being a subaltern, who would never play the most important role in the team, he would become a witness. Thus, under the date of Tuesday 26 April, he wrote the following: *Because of the peasants who had us trapped in the inn of La Calade, we had to wait for nightfall before we could set off again. The postilions, some of them armed with loaded pistols, slept in the stable to watch over the horses, encircling the berlins, which were subjected to no further damage. The people just wanted to see His Majesty, out of curiosity, according to Campbell, or to insult him, because I clearly made out some cries of "Down with Corsica!" After the meal, which he did not touch, suspecting that he was being poisoned with arsenic, the Emperor called for a room. There was one, low-ceilinged and not very clean, which was enough for him. Once his injection had been administered, he went to sleep sitting on the straw mattress, which was crawling with insects, his head leaning against my shoulder. I know he had nightmares, and his sudden starts and the inaudible phrases he muttered woke me several times. The foreign commissioners shook us awake at about three o'clock in the morning to tell us that the road was free and the carriages were ready. We would be passing through Aix before dawn. The authorities had taken the precaution of locking the gates to keep the armed mob from running into the road and attacking us. The Sub-prefect, a messenger told us, was walking to join our cortège and offer us a squadron of police. His Majesty gave the unfortunate Loisellier back his uniform, thanking him for his help and the risks he had taken, and, in response to an idea of Campbell's, the messenger was kitted out more nobly, although rather strangely, with a white Austrian tunic, a Prussian cap and the pale grey coat of the Russian officers. A foreign major took his place next to Bertrand in the sleeper. We avoided Aix, which was in turmoil, but heard a great hubbub behind the ramparts. At La Grande Pagère we lunched with the Sub-prefect, whose policemen helped us to pass through Saint-Maximin, Brignoles and Tourves by first light . . .'*

Once they had passed through those towns, they felt they had reached safety. Imposing Austrian garrisons had been set up throughout the region, and troops were spread over tens of kilometres all the way to the coast. At Le Luc de Provence, where the carriages appeared in the middle of the afternoon, some hussars from Lichten-stein had erected their tents in a park. The park faced the château of Bouillidou — the home of the former Deputy Charles — where Napoleon found Pauline, his favourite sister. She was supposed to have gone to a spa in the Basses-Alpes but, having been alerted to the Emperor's impending arrival, she had chosen to wait in this country mansion.

A severe figure in a cassimere coat with a v-neck (in line with the latest Parisian fashion) opened the door as Napoleon approached: Montbreton, a highly professional equerry and chamberlain, dealt with everything, sorted out all kinds of problems, issued advice and generally made Pauline's life easier.

'The Princess?' Napoleon asked.

'I will take you to her room, Sire.'

'Is she still unwell? Be frank, Montbreton.'

'She's hot, she's cold, she has vapours, she sweats, either she eats nothing at all or else she eats too much . . .'

'Oh, Paoletta! She just needs to be taken dancing or introduced to a nicely turned aide-de-camp! Tell me, Montbreton, how do you find me?'

'In perfect health, sire.'

'I mean: what do you think of my new style?'

The Emperor opened his coat as he walked, revealing his composite uniform, over which the chamberlain cast an expert eye.

'The chasseur's uniform suited Your Majesty ... in a different way.'

'Do you think so?'

'I certainly do.'

'It would have been too conspicuous, and I have just travelled through a land of murderers!'

In the corridor Napoleon removed his Prussian cap and held it out to Bertrand, before handing his Russian coat to Octave. Together the three men entered a darkened room, the walls striped with sunlight that passed through the slats of the closed shutters. Two servants ran lit candles back and forth along the door and window frames to find the draughts that Pauline could not bear, while she lay on a swan-shaped sofa, rolled up in a priceless cashmir from Leroy in the rue Mandar, her feet wrapped in a blouse that belonged to an ample-bosomed lady's maid. She turned her head. She had the straight nose of the Bonapartes, long eyelashes and luscious lips. Bertrand thought she looked unusually thin, but Octave felt a sudden flood of warmth pass through him; red as a crayfish, he studied the Borghese princess, all of a sudden scornful of his rustic amours.

'Nabulione!' exclaimed the goddess, rising to her feet.

She spread her arms, her cashmir fell, and she was cold no more. Octave saw her round shoulders and her legs showing below her fashionable Venus tunic. She had long, firm muscles, tender, warm, the colour of ivory. Her movements were languid, but her nerves were clearly on edge, and she was more savage than princess. The candle-light played on the coils of her dark hair as brother and sister hugged one another to the point of suffocation, he laughing, she weeping.

'Nabulione, why, tell me why you abdicated!'

'The legitimacy of the Bourbons, Paoletta, is formidably powerful . . .'

'But!'

Pauline had pressed her cheek to the Emperor's Austrian jacket, and now she pushed him away with both hands, rolling her black eyes.

'What is this uniform?'

'I'd be dead without it.'

'Take it off! Take it off or I'll never speak to you again! Take it off immediately!'

'Monsieur Sénécal, rather than standing there gawping at us like an idiot, get me a uniform of the chasseurs of the Guard.'

In his ordinary uniform once again, the Emperor closed himself away with Pauline until evening. In the meantime, his retinue and his commissioners prepared for the night ahead, a proper, peaceful night in real sheets — and about time too — but late that same day an anxious chamberlain appeared, informing Bertrand in a quavering voice: 'Your master is exposing himself to danger, your grace.'

'I'll deal with it, Montbreton.'

Napoleon was standing on a terrace surrounded by honeysuckle, facing a crowd. The locals were grumbling, and one excitable voice demanded, 'Where is the wretch?'

'Here I am!' replied the Emperor, towering over the scene.

'So you're the monster?' a market gardener asked.

'Do you doubt it?'

Napoleon threw down a coin bearing his effigy, which was picked up by an urchin. Everyone wanted to compare the profile engraved upon it with the fat man above them.

A good few people had their doubts – the real one wasn't so puffy, he had a thicker curl on his forehead, a more noble air – until an old man with grey whiskers raised his cocked hat and called in a stentorian voice: 'I saw you at Marengo, my Emperor! I was a dragoon under Kellermann! And under Bessières at Wagram. We shot hares in the burning corn! A bullet in my left calf, a bayonet in my right thigh! Cuts everywhere! Lost an eye at the Moskva, but I can see you with the other!'

The Emperor chose to address only this heaven-sent old soldier, although as he talked to him of glory, his words spoke also to the crowd. He was busy winning his audience over when Bertrand tugged him by the sleeve. He groaned.

'You exasperate me, Bertrand! They were about to shout *"Vive l'Empereur!"* '

*

'Wednesday 27. Since Princess Pauline (who is even more beautiful than the very beautiful Duchess of Bassano), since Princess Pauline, as I was saying, has promised the Emperor she'll come to the island of Elba, he has been acting up. We parted ways before St Tropez, where we waited for the other berlins in the convoy, along with little General Drouot and the vans that had arrived safely from Fontainebleau. And we didn't stop at Saint Raphaël, that fishing port where His Majesty had once landed on his way back from Egypt, and where some ships awaited him for a crossing of a different kind, but at Fréjus, "the home of Tacitus", he said. At the inn of the Red Hat, Bertrand announced the visit of an Englishman whom Campbell wished to introduce to him. This Captain Thomas Ussher commanded a frigate, the

Undaunted. *The Emperor stood there with a book in his hand as they talked about the island of Elba, and how the Spanish had once fortified it against the Ottoman corsairs. His Majesty was to board the brig* Inconstant, *but, inspired by Campbell, he preferred to go to sea in the* Undaunted. *Captain Ussher's frigate was better equipped and faster, it had special comforts and, more particularly, the Emperor felt safer under an English flag than on a boat that had formerly been controlled by the King of France.'*

In almost overloaded boats, the sailors of the *Undaunted* ferried the various bits of luggage, statues and crates from the vans and the berlins to the ship, and hoisted them on board the frigate with thick ropes. The departure was scheduled for the following day, Thursday, with no time yet specified — but in the middle of the night Captain Ussher ran down to the apartment in the Red Hat where Napoleon was staying. Octave, who was sleeping outside the bedroom door on Roustan's old trestle bed, woke violently and was astonished at what he heard.

'What time is it?'

'Nearly five in the morning, monsieur, the Emperor will have to get ready, we have to weigh anchor.'

'So early?'

'The wind is falling and that worries me. The commissioners of the allied powers don't want us to spend whole days lying at anchor.'

'Count Bertrand has ordered carriages for seven o'clock . . .'

'Wake up your butler now, sir, if you will!'

'What's all this racket?' croaked a voice behind the bedroom door, which opened to reveal the Emperor in a nightshirt, with tired eyes and a grumpy expression.

Ussher was not giving the real reason for his zeal. Campbell, in fact, had received some information: soldiers dismissed from the Italian army were returning to France, shouting, *'Vive l'Empereur!'* There was no time to lose. Those troublemakers could turn away from the coast and prevent or hinder the departure of the *Undaunted*; Ussher was nervous and Napoleon was apathetic.

'It's because of the wind, sire,' explained Octave.

'The wind?'

'It could change,' said the captain.

'Let it change. That's the wind's job.'

'My frigate asks only to get under way, Sire.'

'And I, captain, ask only to rest, I feel queasy, I have a bad stomach and a sore leg, I'm about to go down with something, it must be that lobster I ate . . .'

Napoleon took his time; Octave helped Hubert the valet to perform the ritual of the Emperor's toilet, and once he was shaved and dressed he began walking meditatively around the room. Angry sounds rose from the street, and he raised an eyebrow.

'The French populace is the worst in the world,' observed the Englishman.

'They're fickle.'

'They don't look particularly aggressive to me,' remarked Octave, who was watching them from the open window.

'That's exactly what I mean, they're fickle! In the evening they want to hang me, in the morning they adore me.'

Bertrand came to announce that the carriages had arrived. Napoleon picked up his sword, which was lying on a table, and slipped it into his belt.

'Let's go,' he said.

The captain checked that his own sword was moving properly in its scabbard, so he could draw it in case of trouble, but the moment the Emperor appeared in the doorway of the inn, the crowd that had gathered fell silent. Respectable bourgeois, ladies in all their finery. These provincials felt they were taking part in a historical event that they would tell their friends and children about for years to come. They parted before the Emperor, who, noticing a pretty girl, asked, 'Are you married? Do you have children?'

As always, he continued on his way at a measured pace, without waiting for her reply. Waving and smiling, he climbed into a carriage that set off at a gallop for Saint Raphaël. It was a brilliant moonlit night. A soft breeze blew. Along the bay, among the pines and palm trees, a regiment of Austrian cavalry was presenting arms. The Emperor took Ussher's arm and walked towards the launch. The sailors raised their oars like halberds.

*

With a boiled-leather sailor's hat pulled low over his forehead, and his frock-coat floating in the wind, Napoleon leaned on the hammock-netting and looked at the waves of foam thrown up by the prow.

'Where's Bertrand?'

'I haven't seen him all morning,' replied Octave, who was discovering life at sea. He had never been aboard a ship, having only ever taken the occasional little boat out on the Seine to go from one shore to the other, between the wine market and the market gardens near the Bastille – but here the roll was working its way through his intestines, and he held a handkerchief to his mouth for fear that his hiccups might get worse, and he might vomit up the little food he'd had the strength to swallow. Bertrand was presumably in a similar state. As to the Emperor, he was clearly in a good mood and taking deep breaths.

'Bring him to me, Monsieur Sénécal, the fresh air before dinner will do him good.'

'Dinner? Are you mad?'

Octave did not press the point. He took advantage of the break to read an article from the *Courrier*, cut out and glued into one of Ussher's books, which gave a detailed description of the Emperor: a few months previously, some reports from London had warned the commanders of the English vessels that Napoleon might try to escape to America. Octave shrugged his shoulders at this out-dated cutting, and Bertrand's seasickness; mutely he returned to the Emperor, who was talking to Captain Ussher.

'We're barely moving,' Napoleon was saying. 'If you were chasing an enemy frigate, would you have set more sails?'

Looking up towards the masts, Ussher agreed, 'Probably . . .'

'There's a sail missing from the quarter-deck.'

'Ah, yes . . .'

'So unfurl it, it'll be useful to us. Ah! Sénécal, I expect our great marshal is on his last legs? Too bad! The Captain has invited us to his table, you can take his place.'

On the deck, the sailors stopped mending sails or cleaning their muskets, and lined up instead to receive their rations, after which they squatted down, each with a bowl of cocoa.

'Since when have your men had cocoa and sugar, Mr Ussher?'

'They owe that to you, sire.' (He pronounced it 'sir'.) 'Your blockade stopped us from selling on the Continent, so they're taking advantage of the fact.'

'They must think I was right to close our ports, then?'

Napoleon joked as far as the officers' mess, where he alone ate with the Captain, chatting about English trade, the navy, the constant lack of discipline among the men in his fleet. Over dessert he added some pointed remarks about the Bourbons, in a mocking tone.

'Poor devils! They're happy to be back in their castles, but they can't bear those factories I've set up; they'll be driven out within six months! In Lyons, in those parts of central France where I've encouraged the construction of factories, the people have celebrated me. You remember that, Campbell?'

'Oh, yes . . .'

Then they talked about Spain which, the Emperor said, would do well to bomb Gibraltar day and night to dislodge the English.

'But you invaded that peninsula,' Campbell replied, rather shocked.

'Yes, to abolish the Inquisition, feudal rights and the privileges of certain classes.'

'They didn't see it that way in Madrid and Saragossa.'

'I am not always understood, Campbell.'

Life on board proceeded in this way, amid cordial discussions in which no topic was out of bounds, dull walks on the deck and interminable hours spent inspecting the sea or birds that indicated the proximity of the coast. On Monday 2 May, Octave couldn't get to sleep in steerage and he visited Napoleon before daybreak, since the Emperor rose at four every morning. The ship was being tossed about by a storm and Octave had difficulty walking without falling, or rolling from port to starboard and crashing into the cannon.

'If the storm gets any worse, sir,' said Ussher, 'we'll have to drop anchor.'

'Why not off the coast of Ajaccio?'

'It's not on our route.'

'What about Calvi? The water's deep around there, and the port is sheltered from gales.'

At the sight of Calvi, the Emperor grew feverish. Despite the big waves, he stayed with his bodyguards. As the coast drew nearer, he remembered one accursed day in June 1793.

'The nationalists accused my family of having been bought by the French, but at the same time they wanted to sell Corsica to you lot, the English. My mother had to flee with the children at dead of night, through the tracks and potholes of the Campo dell'Oro, through streams swollen by the showers, to the Genoese tower of Capitello stuck up there on the rocks ... I was a captain; I had bombed the citadel of Ajaccio, and I was in retreat ... I put out a launch and gathered up the fugitives, and together we climbed up towards Calvi where the partisans of the republic were gathering ... Pauline was thirteen ...'

The *Undaunted* rounded a rocky cape three cables' length away from the coast. 'Why don't we explore the cliff, Captain?' the Emperor suggested. 'A good walk would stretch our legs and clear our heads, don't you think?'

He received no reply. But the ship lay to off Calvi for seven hours before setting sail again. On the fifth day of sailing, a dot was seen on the horizon. The ship made straight for it. A block of jagged black rocks loomed out of the sea. It was the island of Elba.

Four

IN EXILE

PORTOFERRAIO FACED away from the sea. Its Levantine houses, grey or ochre, with pointed windows, were tiered along the slopes of a rocky amphitheatre. On the other side, a series of belvederes and Florentine walls fell to the sleepy waters of the port. Most of the streets climbed the hill; they finished in crude steps, without railings. As Monsieur Pons de l'Hérault had lived on the island for five years, his calves had grown very big from all the climbing he'd done — and he was climbing that morning, towards the Forte Stella, which gave a view of the Mediterranean; the lookout had signalled an English ship, and Monsieur Pons wanted to find out more. He stopped in the middle of a steep alleyway, which formed a kind of landing before the next flight of steps. The sun beat down. Monsieur Pons was sweating. His thin, lank hair stuck to his forehead. His glasses had slipped down his not inconsiderable nose, and he slid them back into place with one finger, wiped his face with his handkerchief and looked across at the flat, pink roofs and the harbour below. Then he recommenced his climb with the regular pace of a mountain-dweller, joining General Dalesme, the Governor of this poor Sub-prefecture, on the tower of the crenellated fort. It was then that he saw a motionless three-master next to the keep that defended the narrows leading into the port.

'Did you try to blow it up with your cannon?' Monsieur Pons asked the General.

'Warning shots.'

'And?'

'And nothing, see for yourself.'

Dalesme lent him his spyglass to study the unflagged ship. Before administering the iron mines on the island of Elba, which he had restored, Pons de l'Hérault had served as a navy captain. The General said in his broad Limousin accent, 'It's an English frigate, do you agree?'

'By the shape of the sails, there can be no doubt.'

'Damned *rosbifs*! What do they want from us this time?'

An English squadron had blockaded the island for a long time, since London coveted Elba for the island's strategic position as much as it did Corsica. For five months, they'd had no news from the Continent. British agents had driven the islanders to rebellion, encouraged mutinies, delivered weapons on the sly; a press-ganged regiment of Corsicans, Tuscans, deserters and draft-dodgers had revolted in April. These crooks had murdered their commander, and Dalesme had ordered them shot by his 35th Light Infantrymen. Some survivors had seized a merchant ship to make their getaway, while others had been forced aboard and dumped ashore in Italy. Meanwhile the French garrison, 400 strong, had barricaded itself up in Portoferraio and lived on biscuits and salted meat from the store.

The British had laid claim to the island, the Bourbons returned to power in Paris, and an emissary announced that Elba now belonged to the vanquished Emperor, who was about to take possession of it. Dalesme was suspicious. What did they want, the occupants of that frigate anchored in the roads, refusing to answer and threatening to stay there if the wind did not rise? The garrison had taken up arms, the loaded cannon on the ramparts were trained on the intruder; the Sea Gate was closed to bar the dock, and so too was the Land Gate, at the outlet to the tunnel beneath the fort of Sant'Ilario. On that side, they had only to pull up the drawbridge over a sea-water canal to cut off the island completely.

'Fire!' ordered General Dalesme.

Waves splashed the hull of the frigate, as the cannon-balls fell short of their target.

'If they don't react next time, I'm going to break the masts!'

'Oh!' exclaimed Monsieur Pons, who had taken off his glasses to put an eye to the telescope. 'He's furling the sails, he's going to cast anchor . . .'

'Let me see, administrator.'

'Wait! They're hoisting a flag at the main-mast . . . a white flag . . .'

'With a fleur-de-lys?'

'No . . . A launch is being lowered from the davit, at the stern . . . Some uniforms . . . A blue uniform . . .'

'A Frenchman?'

'It looks that way, but all I can see from here are patches of colour . . .'

'Perhaps they're bringing us our new king.'

'You must be joking, Dalesme! I can hardly imagine the English handing us Bonaparte like a common prisoner.'

'I'm going down!'

The General ran the length of the rampart walk and jumped on the horse that was waiting for him in the courtyard. By galloping along the sloping street he could get to the harbour more quickly.

*

Monsieur Pons de l'Hérault, meanwhile, took the alternative route – the steps of the alleyways – to reach the harbour, grumbling as he hurried on his way lest he miss the docking of the foreign launch. He was nettled by the idea that Napoleon might come and settle on the very island where he had taken refuge specifically to get away from him.

What did Napoleon know of the people of Elba? Nothing. Monsieur Pons, on the other hand, was respected because, having been placed in charge of the local mines, he had put his republican ideas into practice by treating his workers as citizens. He had allowed them to build suitable housing, there was a full granary, warehouses, boats to deliver the mineral to Piombino, and he paid them in grain. Bonaparte, by contrast, had substituted the power of soldiers for the power of citizens, a coup d'état for which Pons had never forgiven him, writing ferocious pamphlets against the Emperor's omnipotence. And now a decision in Paris was bringing the man to Elba, turning the island into an absurd kingdom. The other man – his contemptuous name for the defeated Emperor – was going to spoil everything. (Pons had known Captain Bonaparte very well at the siege of Toulon. At that time – when he had insisted on being called Marat Lepeletier Pons, in honour of two eminent patriots – he'd been a member of the local Jacobin club, and had commanded the artillery of Bandol. Robespierre's brother, Augustin (known as Bonbon), had protected both of them, since they tried to outdo each other in republican ardour. But Pons had been intransigent on the basis of principles that events had done nothing to change. He had found Robespierre's hauteur almost impossible to bear when they had met briefly in Paris, and he had been horrified by the corruption of the members of the Directory who'd tried to bribe him. He even considered that the Thermidorean Reaction, the revolt against Robespierre, had been worse than the Terror. Should Pons leave? And where would he go? To live on what? At the age of forty-two he found it hard to imagine drifting hither and thither with his wife and his two little girls. But if they stayed, would he be forced to apologize for not having betrayed (as Napoleon had, in his view) his republican ideals? Either option was unthinkable.

Brooding over his misfortune, he joined General Dalesme at the end of the wooden dock. 'Take a look at what's in the launch,' said Dalesme, handing him the telescope again.

Monsieur Pons gave a cry of astonishment: 'Drouot!'

'If that man Drouot sets foot on dry land, Administrator, it means that the Emperor is on board . . .'

'I fear so.'

'Paris has made our decision for us. Go on! It must be our great man.'

'It's easier to be a great man in a vast empire than in a small state.'

'You hate him that much?'

'I certainly do!' replied Monsieur Pons.

*

From a distance, with its Italianate appearance, the pastel tones of the houses against a rocky amphitheatre, Portoferraio looked rather charming. Octave liked it already; the sky was solid blue, the water translucent, and shadows stirred on the mole. Octave had a premonition of discovery and joy.

The previous day, at sea, a fisherman had told the *Undaunted*'s passengers about the brutality of the people of Elba: as in Provence, they had burned an effigy of Napoleon, and their hostility remained intense, despite English attempts to calm the troublemakers. Informed of this unfortunate situation, the Emperor agreed to come ashore only once his security problems had been resolved. With this in mind, a delegation fronted by Drouot was dispatched to the island. Octave, although not part of this official deputation, accompanied them nonetheless, keen to see the town and its inhabitants for himself.

The oars rippled regularly as the launch approached the quay, and Octave contemplated the landscape with delight. The muted colours and the mildness of the air rendered him naïve: how, he thought, could violence erupt in such a paradise? Stepping on to the dock, though – while Dalesme and Drouot hailed each other as old accomplices from a hundred battles – Octave found himself reconsidering his initial impression: dilapidated buildings, generally topsy-turvy, climbed towards the ramparts, and in places even loomed above them. Past the Sea Gate, the façades of Via San Giovanni sweated, paint

that had once been pink was flaking away, and pistachio-
coloured shutters dangled from their hinges. Channels of
dirty water emerged from adjacent alleyways, streaming
together in the middle of the road, forming bubbling
puddles where insects buzzed. A strong smell of excre-
ment, urine and soap hung in the air, but this did not
appear to upset the onlookers who had assembled to watch
the delegation pass by. Bourgeois in shirt-sleeves and
women fanning themselves with palm fronds appeared at
balconies filled with flowers and reddened foliage. Tanned
fishermen with mistrustful eyes gathered by the gates and
along the walls. Octave noticed a bevy of girls, who hid
their faces and shook with silent laughter beneath their
black straw hats. Dressed in very short red or blue skirts,
they had solid, brown legs, their feet bare in the mud.

The delegates climbed towards the parade ground.
Following in the wake of Generals Drouot and Dalesme,
both in full dress, came a colonel of the Polish lancers in
heavy scarlet cloth, collapsing with the heat, and a stoical
Austrian major dressed entirely in white. Octave brought
up the rear with Campbell, who was discreetly holding
his nose. Monsieur Pons followed them, head lowered,
dawdling like a carthorse resigned to being led to the
knacker's yard. Beneath the plane trees in the square, the
group turned towards the town hall, where those worthies
who had already been alerted were waiting by a small
flight of steps. These gentlemen introduced themselves at
the invitation of the Mayor, Monsieur Traditi, and the
delegates were led inside, up a very cramped staircase
and onto the first floor, where they passed into a drawing-
room, its shutters lowered to keep out at least the worst
of the heat. The local authorities stood because there were

not enough chairs for them all, while Drouot showed them the official documents that placed the island under the Emperor's rule. Then General Dalesme read aloud the letter sent by the Emperor himself:

Dear General,

 I have sacrificed my rights to the interests of the fatherland, and I have reserved to myself the sovereignty and the ownership of the island of Elba, as agreed by all the Powers. Please inform the inhabitants of this new state of affairs, and of the fact that I have chosen their island for my sojourn, in consideration of the mildness of their customs and their climate. Tell them they will be the constant object of my keenest interests . . .

The Sub-prefect, the Mayor, his deputy and Monsieur Pons de l'Hérault had listened with pursed lips, but no obvious sign of effusion, reluctance or objection. Stunned by the news, they knew that their lives, which until then had been idle and free of any real turmoil, were about to be turned on their heads. Drouot mopped his brow and the back of his neck with a lace handkerchief that he drew from the embroidered sleeve of his Imperial general's uniform. He spoke to break a painful silence.

 'Gentlemen, what is the current state of mind of your inhabitants?'

 'Not very favourable to His Majesty,' ventured Monsieur Pons in a hoarse, deep voice.

 'They will have to submit to the French provisional government,' the Austrian major replied crisply.

 'I hope we won't need to fight,' said the Polish colonel, reaching for the pommel of his sword.

'Fight? No, no!' gasped Monsieur Traditi, rolling eyes that were wide with alarm.

'The Emperor must come ashore tomorrow,' explained Campbell.

'Make sure there is applause for him,' continued Drouot.

'We'll try.' The Mayor was trembling.

'Generate some enthusiasm!' Drouot ordered.

'What?' said the Sub-prefect, who thought he had misunderstood, and didn't see how one could generate enthusiasm in a rebellious population.

'General Drouot,' Octave broke in, 'expects you to supply a reception worthy of His Majesty. You have until tomorrow afternoon to prepare it.'

'Twenty-four hours?'

'It can be done.'

He was thinking of the Count of Sémallé. There was a man knew how to play the game – within only a few hours he had managed to launch a movement to give the impression that the people of Paris were demanding the return of Louis XVIII, when most of them were in fact unaware of his existence – Octave had learned much from him.

In the confusion and the embarrassing silence that followed his trenchant statement, Octave suggested he speak to the worthies of the island, because he was, he claimed, quite skilled at swaying opinions; he also knew that southerners were quick to move from one extreme to the other. In the meantime, the authorities of the island would go on board the *Undaunted* to greet their new prince.

As everyone else dispersed, Monsieur Pons de l'Hérault and Octave were left alone in the drawing-room. Monsieur Pons waved away some irritating flies, dropped his heavy jacket and slumped on to a chair, unfolding a fan.

'Do as I do,' he suggested. 'You must be boiling in that get-up.' At ten o'clock in the morning it was already as hot as a baker's oven.

*

'It has a strange taste,' said Octave with a grimace.

'They call it vermouth. It's the national drink, herbs macerated in the white wine of the island.'

Monsieur Pons had taken Octave to the Buono Gusto café. Dug like a cave into the ramparts, it provided shelter from the violent sun. By an arrangement of open doors, the landlord had cleverly engineered a through-draught – although the fetid smells of the street drifted in along with any supposed freshness. Octave set his terracotta cup on the table; sweat trickled down his forehead and into his eyes, his skin was damp and his drenched shirt clung to his back.

'You know' – Monsieur Pons was describing the Elban mentality – 'there aren't as many Elbans in the world as there are Italians. The people of Milan bear no resemblance to the people of Naples, who are utterly unlike the people of Rome. It's the same thing here. The people of Portoferraio are witty but envious, while the inhabitants of Porto Longone, in the south, are both ignorant and superstitious. In Rio, in Marciana, they're conceited but very energetic.'

'I suppose the mayors and priests have the same characteristics as the people they administer.'

'I would say so.'

'But are they malleable? How can we win them over in a single day?'

'By playing on their weaknesses. For months, the agents of London have presented a warlike and bloody Napoleon. Now we must reverse that image, show them a man who is going to improve their wretched condition, we must use the terms that your Emperor used in his letter to General Dalesme. Tell them he prefers Elba to Corsica, the place of his birth, or to Parma.'

'Is there a printing-works in Portoferraio?'

'We're not savages!'

'Could we get some posters printed overnight?'

'The printer is a cousin of Traditi, the Mayor.'

'Fine, but that's not enough . . .'

'Another drop of vermouth?'

'No, thanks, I'm worried I might fall asleep.'

The young waitress diverted him, however, by bringing some grey bread and a sheep's cheese that smelled off. 'Thanks, Gianna,' said Monsieur Pons. She had swarthy, copper-coloured skin, and raven curls that fell over her eyes; a white corset hugged her waist and emphasized her breasts, and as she departed her skirt swayed with her hips. Monsieur Pons was amused to see Octave watching her retreating figure: 'If you are so interested in the customs of the people of Elba, I'll ask Gianna to put you up in her family's house tonight.'

Octave was oblivious to the other man's mockery. 'An excellent idea.'

Monsieur Pons returned to the matter in hand. 'We will establish the text of the posters in a moment with Dalesme. He'll have to sign it. He's the Governor.'

'Yes, and we should stress the fact that the Emperor has *chosen* the island of Elba, but we'll also have to put word about.'

'That's easy, my dear man. In a small town like this, news spreads like wildfire. Look, those two men over by the barrels, forcing down some chestnut cake (our speciality) for politeness' sake. They've just arrived from Piombino.'

'Italians?'

'From Turin. They have taken a room in Mademoiselle Sauvage's inn.'

'You know everything!'

'There's only one inn in Portoferraio.'

*

Anxious not to displease his host, who kept wickedly refilling his cup, Octave ended up drinking two jugs of aromatic wine, so that the back of his neck prickled, and his legs felt like lead when he rose from the table. Returning to the town hall, dazzled by the sun and alcohol, failing even to notice the stench of the streets, he walked unsteadily, stumbling slightly, but refused to take his companion's arm. However, Octave's somnolent state didn't stop him writing the first version of a proclamation that Monsieur Pons considered lively and precise – although for form's sake it had to be approved by the worthies. The dignitaries in question had earlier departed, concerned and hesitant, to visit the Emperor aboard the English frigate. They reappeared in a state of excitement. Napoleon had wooed them by speaking unctuously of the misfortunes of France and the good fortune of their island – so beautiful, so calm, so industrious – which he promised would increase under his benevolent protection. Thus aroused, they read what Octave had written, adding a few inflated words here and there, and amending some turns of phrase to give a clearer sense of the submission of the island authorities.

General Dalesme did not wish to sign. He was still the Governor, certainly, but henceforth he was dependent on the goodwill of Paris, a city to which he would shortly have to return; the Sub-prefect, Balbiani, was happy to sign in his superior's stead, and the Mayor hurried to his cousin's printing-works with the proclamation that would be posted up on every wall during the night:

To the inhabitants of Portoferraio

The happiest event that could ever bring fame to the history of the island of Elba has taken place this day! Our august sovereign, the Emperor Napoleon, has arrived among us. Our wishes are accomplished: the happiness of the island of Elba is assured.

Listen to the first words that he deigned to address to us, speaking of the functionaries who represent you: 'I will be a good father to you, be good sons to me.' They will be engraved for ever in our grateful hearts.

Let us unite around his holy person, let us vie with one another in zeal and loyalty to serve him. It will be the sweetest satisfaction for his paternal heart. And in this way we will make ourselves worthy of the favour that Providence has pleased to bestow upon us.

The Sub-prefect:
Louis Balbiani

The Sub-prefect was delighted by what he thought of as his prose (those who put their names to a document often imagine that they have written it themselves), but Octave still had his doubts about the usefulness of the posters, and the dignitaries set about reassuring him. Certainly, the people of Elba had wanted to kill Napoleon only the previous day – because they dreaded his reputation as a warrior – but he had come unarmed, so his image had changed, and the local people were saying as much to one another at this very moment, prattling on their front doorsteps or in the café. They now hoped that Napoleon's fame would enrich them, there was no doubt about that, and seductive rumours of this kind would spread very quickly around the island.

'But will the population of Portoferraio alone, even in a state of jubilation, be able to give an impression of a large crowd?' Octave asked. 'We need shouting and cheering along His Majesty's route, between the mole and the church where the Vicar-General will chant a Te Deum.'

The Sub-prefect immediately dispatched letters to the villages, instructing the Mayors to come to the capital with as many local people – wine-growers, sailors – as they could muster. Meanwhile General Dalesme departed to inspect the uniforms of his troops and mobilize the National Guard. The deputy followed the instructions of Octave (whom he treated with deference because he represented the new authority of the Emperor), and gave a simple, cheerful text to the town crier, who set off to declaim the news that was already spreading from the harbour to the hills.

Leaving preparations for ceremonies in the municipality to the others, Monsieur Pons de l'Hérault pushed Octave outside: he would see with his own eyes the good humour of the island's inhabitants, he would see how the rumour had softened them, how easy they were to persuade, how swift to enthusiasm. In a courtyard they encountered some stout fellows who were busy lugging up various items of furniture to adorn the town hall, where the Emperor would be spending the first part of his stay.

'You see,' said Monsieur Pons, 'the bourgeoisie are providing their most comfortable armchairs for the imperial buttocks.'

Octave didn't spot the irony, or the fact that the phrase did not include the speaker among the Emperor's loyal subjects.

Evening fell. The town, which had a moment before been slumped beneath the sun, was suddenly filled with movement. Crowding on street corners and beneath trees, noisy groups commented on the day's events. Carpenters hammered together platforms and pavilions. Half-closed shutters opened to let in the warmth of the night, revealing the members of the bourgeoisie in their homes, brushing down their evening wear. Women were making garlands together, men hurrying about the place, carrying parcels of candles under their arms; Monsieur Pons's own wife was busy working with some seamstresses to make the new flag, the design for which Drouot had given them that morning.

Monsieur Pons brought Octave back to the Buono Gusto — now full of chattering people — with a view to handing him over to Gianna's family for the night. The two men crammed themselves behind a table, at the back near the barrels, elbow to elbow with drunken sailors who were jawing away in their Tuscan dialect. Never mind the noise — Octave was starving, and wolfed down a plateful of marinated tuna, a dish that dries the throat, and drank cup after cup of a local wine, clearer than the one he had had that morning, with no herbs floating in it. After the sixth cup he grew homesick, Monsieur Pons could tell from his distant gaze. After the seventh he started talking about himself. His mentor took advantage of the fact to reverse their roles and begin questioning him.

'I saw you drafting the first version of the poster, at the town hall, all in one go, and one thing surprised me . . .'

'Tell me?' said Octave, filling the empty jug from the barrel.

'It was a phrase. A phrase you put in Napoleon's mouth, yet one which he did subsequently utter to the Sub-prefect, aboard the English frigate, when neither of us was present.'

'Which one would that be?'

'"I will be a good father to you, be good sons to me . . ."'

'Yes?'

'Had he said that before, to anyone else?'

'I don't know, it just came to me quite naturally.'

'What?'

'Quite naturally, I tell you! What do you expect me to have him say? *To your cannon! Fire!*'

Octave laughed, started choking and downed another glass.

'Where do you get this talent from, Monsieur Sénécal?'

'It isn't a talent, it's a habit. I have learned to second-guess him. You know, you have to keep second-guessing him all the time – all the time, I tell you – you get used to it, it's exhausting but you get used to it, you become familiar with his turns of phrase, his manner, it's not that hard when you're with him all the time.'

'Yes, you have that good fortune . . .'

'Good fortune? I don't know about that. Good fortune if you like, but I would say – well, I would say that the closer you are to him the less existence you have yourself.'

'Really!'

'Don't you think so?'

'I'm prepared to believe you. Explain it to me.'

'I wasn't so important before, perhaps, but I was freer, I had my own life. I strolled around Paris, I opened my eyes and ears, and jotted down anything abnormal. I drew up reports, I knew some nice girls and they helped me out, or rather we helped each other out – and well, now that I'm near him I no longer have a personality. That's what he wants. He likes to surround himself with puppets. And within only a few weeks I've become a perfect puppet myself. Oh, he's good at that all right, he orders you about without a word, and you're trapped, however cunning you may think you are. Your Sub-prefect is a puppet already, and the Mayor, after a single conversation, do you understand? And everyone else here, all puppets!'

Octave's speech was beginning to slur, and he knocked his cup over twice, but he carried on drinking. Monsieur Pons waved to Gianna, who was walking by with plates of dried meat.

After negotiating with the waitress and the landlord of the Buono Gusto to find a bed for Octave, he returned to his pied-à-terre in Portoferraio, where he'd lived full-time since the English blockade had stopped his barges from carrying ore to Piombino. He could see no reason, he reflected, why Napoleon shouldn't let him resume his activities, and start extracting iron again, but that meant submitting to the Emperor. Contradictory thoughts waged war within him at that prospect: he had let Octave babble away to himself about his misfortunes, while he dwelt on his own.

Later that night, when the last sailors were leaving, braying and merry, Gianna, who had the strength of a peasant girl, helped Octave to his feet. He was swaying and mumbling to himself, and took out a gold coin and threw it on the wine-stained table. The landlord whisked it away in a flash: '*Piace molto, il denaro del nostro sovranno, è tutto d'oro...*' Octave, eyes glazed, struggled to keep his balance. He could see two Giannas, now, and attributed this to an excess of drink. But no, the waitress had called her sister to help her, and they were incredibly alike, except that Luisa had coloured ribbons tied in her hair. The two girls dragged the drunk by the wrists, guiding him through the door.

As he breathed in the contaminated air of the Piazza Gran Bastione, Octave imagined that he was in Paris, emerging from a certain little restaurant by the tollgate, where the dustmen carted the city's refuse into the countryside and left it to rot beneath the open sky. It was there that Octave used to meet some of the ladies of the night who acted as spies for him – and he was so befogged he genuinely believed that the two Elban girls plied the same trade. When he freed a hand to rest it on Luisa's brown shoulder, however, he got a resounding slap and heard the two sisters chuckling. Letting them guide him, Octave stumbled on the steps, missed one, found himself first on his knees and then on all fours, clutched at a girl's

ankle and received a kick from a heel to his cheek — not a
hard kick, more of a playful one. He rolled aside, bumped
his elbow, and felt himself being lifted and carried like a
soft-legged puppet.

The two girls carried Octave into a dark lair where he
could see nothing, but was aware of the sound of clearing
throats, a dry cough, breathing. It smelled like a den of
wild animals. Gianna stripped him of his frock-coat, his
waistcoat and his shirt. Luisa deposited him on a kind of
straw-stuffed sofa, before pulling off his boots and everything else. Next, he heard the sisters removing their corsets
in the dark, heard the slide of their short skirts, their
quiet laughter. And he went to sleep with his mouth open.

*

At noon the next day, 4 May, the flag of the new kingdom
was raised over the Forte Stella: it showed three bees,
stitched on to a white background cut from a sail. (The
Imperial bees had actually been part of the old coat of
arms of Cosimo de' Medici, Elba's first benefactor, who
had fortified the island against the Barbary pirates.) A
single cannon-shot saluted the flag, followed by 200 more
along the length of the ramparts, with salvoes fired from
the *Undaunted* in reply.

This was the signal.

Napoleon climbed down the ladder into the barge,
which was bedecked with carpets. To his colonel's uniform he had pinned the orange ribbon of the Iron
Crown, and the silver embroidered plaque of the large
eagle of the Légion d'honneur, which caught the sun like
a mirror. Manning the yards, red-jacketed English sailors
hailed the approaching Emperor, their cheers adding to

the general din: blanks fired by the cannon, the peals of bells, shouts and cries from the town, music from everywhere. A multitude of barks and tartans, their bowsprits garlanded with banners and pennants, hid the water of the harbour almost completely. The sailors waved their hats on the ends of their oars and yelled, women in brightly coloured dresses hurled handfuls of flowers that floated in the water, a choir sang *Apollo exiled from heaven comes to dwell in Thessaly* ... Some girls, wasp-waisted in their traditional corsets, struck little drums with their bracelets, and flautists did their best with various musical scores. By now, the Emperor was standing so he could clearly be seen, deafened but heroic amid the heat and the noise; he had fixed his Elban cockade to his cocked hat, which he held under his arm.

The barge drew alongside the jetty of Ponte del Gallo where the Mayor, the Vicar-General and a line of dignitaries stood in silk breeches and pale frock-coats. The moment he stepped upon the landing stage, the Emperor's heart leapt briefly at the sight of this enthusiastic crowd. His new subjects were bellowing at the tops of their voices, like a tribe of Iroquois, or a band of hysterics who had escaped *en masse* from their asylum.

Mayor Traditi held the keys of Portoferraio on a silver platter. The Emperor looked at them. A fly was dancing about on them, and the mayor leaned slightly over his platter to shoo it away. It flew on to the Emperor's sleeve, and walked about on his epaulette throughout the ceremony.

'Your worship,' said the Emperor, making no move to take them, 'these keys could not be in better hands than yours.'

Traditi was very annoyed about this, because he didn't have a free hand to slip into his pocket and pull out the speech he had spent much of the night composing. To his aid came the Vicar-General, Arrighi, a sanguine, gossipy character, a great trencherman who enjoyed a drink, and who had now been taking advantage of his kinship with Napoleon, established the previous day, on the grounds of their shared Corsican background. Arrighi borrowed some words of the Church to glorify the Emperor, who bowed to custom and touched his lips to his pectoral cross. Two children from the choir, urchins in surplices and worn-out shoes, stood on either side of him; one of them swung his censer on the end of its chain as though it were a sling-shot, the other had a finger half-way up his nose.

Meanwhile other boats from the *Undaunted* had docked. Bertrand climbed out – his face long, sad and sulky – then came plumed little Drouot, Campbell, stiff in his ceremonial apparel, and the treasurer Peyrusse (jovial, curly-haired, a native of Carcassonne who preserved the cheerful tone for which that town is celebrated, even in the most terrible circumstances – it was said that when Moscow was burned, he was surprised not to be able to find anyone to iron his linen); General Dalesme mingled with the quartermasters, the pharmacist and the secretary.

The cortège could now form, and begin its march to the cathedral. With this in mind, the dais was brought forward. The dais! Held by four ragged villagers, trembling and overwhelmed by the honour, it consisted of wooden handles supporting a piece of decorated fabric, stuck with bits of scarlet cloth and paper cut into motifs and fringes.

'What a farce!' thought the Emperor. 'What a lamentable farce!'

Images of his coronation stirred in his memory in contrast ... It had been both snowy and foggy, the princesses had been wearing very low-cut dresses despite the cold of Notre-Dame, there had been dozens of bishops in attendance, and the Pope had worn his gold cloth cope, the dignitaries had bowed their heads in costumes devised by David and Isabey: puffy, slashed breeches, velvet berets, ostrich feathers, wide-brimmed Renaissance hats; antique drapes, gold, a lot of gold – and Josephine had been so moved. A real dais carried along by canons, the silver-gilt sceptre ... And here he was today, fat-bellied under a rickety parasol ... The gunfire, the music, the bells and the shouting had not subsided; those flies of ill-omen buzzed everywhere as though around carrion.

The Emperor settled under the dais to escape the scorching sun, and the procession rattled off, both moving and grotesque, drums at the front, three dull blows then three rolls, more funereal than solemn.

Past the Sea Gate, in the town itself, Dalesme's infantry supplied reinforcements for the National Guard, who were unable to cope with the event by themselves; with some difficulty they managed to create a path through the middle of the crowd. There were people at the windows, on the balconies draped with silk shawls, crowds filled the stands and there were even people on the roofs. There were ladies in turbans and short jackets, wild-looking girls wearing nothing but flowers, rags and jangling jewellery. *Evviva l'Imperatore!* Handkerchiefs flew threw the air, rosepetals rained down, men raised their top hats or tricornes. Terrified by the cannon, swallows swirled around in a flock above the crowd, sometimes getting caught in the festoons of paper stretched between the houses, the branches of palm trees, or the rough flags sewn in the night. To add to the cacophony, little tearaways threw fire-crackers, some of which exploded between the Emperor's legs; Monsignor Arrighi, his face bright red with fury, shook his fist and kicked the boys in the pants. The procession advanced with some difficulty over scattered armfuls of box and bayleaves, and despite the short distance it was almost an hour before it reached the Piazza del Duomo.

The promised cathedral was nothing but a small, sober church, with white walls and a mosaic façade. The Emperor finally entered, framed on either side by two petrified chamberlains. Disguised in theatrical costumes, they tried to strike a pose.

*

'Thank you! Well done! Ah, you've made a proper fool out of me!' croaked Octave, shaving his chin over a basin.

'You wanted to see some indigenous people close up,' Monsieur Pons defended himself with a flash of irony.

'Well, I've certainly done that! Savages, they are! Monkeys!'

'You aren't being very nice about your new compatriots . . .'

'I've been to slums in Paris, I swear to you, but really, that takes the biscuit!'

'Don't exaggerate, now, Monsieur Sénécal, and anyway, you're going to help the Emperor to civilize them.'

Octave had woken at first light, because Gianna's family home had no shutters. Looking around him, he'd thought he was still asleep and having a nightmare. In a large rough bed with neither sheets nor blankets, seven or eight people, infant to grandmother, lay sleeping, all completely naked – as indeed Octave was himself. He had leapt up, pushing aside Gianna's arm and her right leg, which had pinned him to the palliasse (she was buxom, certainly, but so what?), rummaging around for his clothes, which he found among others, on the beaten earth floor. Shaking the dust from them, he had dressed in silence and escaped into the steep deserted streets. He'd had to wait for ages on the steps of the town hall, because it was so early that the door was locked. Finally, however, shutters opened, blinds were raised, activity resumed. Workmen were checking the solidity of the platforms by jumping up and down on them, and men on ladders were hooking up garlands. A cart covered with mauve flowers passed by.

It was Joseph Hutré, the Deputy Mayor, who opened the town hall to Octave. Hutré, a musician from Toulon, had fled the Republic in an English sloop, chased by Captain Bonaparte's cannon, but he had compensated for that regrettable episode by marrying a woman from Elba, and he now kept the prestigious salt-works store on the Piazza Gran Bastione. He showed Octave the apartment the council had reserved for the sovereign: four austere rooms where, in the days of the Consulate, a disgraced colonel, Hugo, had lived with his three little boys, their nurse and a fat mistress. Together, Octave and the deputy helped some English soldiers, and Hubert the valet, to unload the first pieces of furniture from the *Undaunted*. As they worked they saw the mountain people trekking down into the town behind their priests, and massing near the port.

Early in the afternoon, just as the Emperor was being subjected to an interminable Te Deum in the neighbouring 'cathedral', Monsieur Pons had surprised Octave in the tiny room where he was doing his best to shave, because if there was one thing His Majesty could not bear it was an untidy chin. They had barely exchanged three rather sour phrases when the Sub-prefect announced: 'He's coming!'

The Emperor was walking beneath the plane trees of the parade ground, through the middle of a crowd, amid ceaseless hubbub, and he had only a few more yards to cover before entering the town hall, where he expected to hold an audience. The official drawing-room had been modified for the purpose. The Mayor's throne, decorated with gold paper, was perched on the school platform. Some letter 'N's cut from cardboard were stuck to the wall, a number of crystal candelabras had been arranged around the place, and a large painting, showing tuna fishermen in the Gulf of Procchio, had been hung in pride of place. Some musicians who had taken refuge in a corner of the room were tuning their instruments – three violins and two harps.

Octave and Monsieur Pons stayed in the background as Napoleon, by now seated on this fantastic throne, gave an audience to the people of Elba. Handpicked by the Sub-prefect, and channelled along cramped corridors, these privileged folk stepped forward to hear the Emperor. They were curious and deferential, and Napoleon, as much at ease as he would have been in the Tuileries before a panel of princes, spoke to them. So familiar was he with the problems and geography of the island that his listeners were won over. Monsieur Pons, however, knew that the dignitaries had, only that very morning, talked the Emperor through their record books, and he had simply assimilated everything they told him.

In French or Italian, depending on who he was responding to, Napoleon gave confident and pertinent replies to everyone; he found solutions for the development of the sardine trade in Porto Longone, the exploitation of salt or the growing of wheat, which was sadly restricted to the single canton of Campo; he spoke of the excellent chestnut purée that was a staple on the island, the black lodestone used for magnetizing compasses, the medicinal plants that could be collected nowhere else. He spoke of the Etruscans, and the Romans who had cut the columns of their porticoes from the island's greenish-grey marble. He told the story of the Lombards, the Vandals, the Genoese, the King of Naples who had given up this rich but arid land to France.

The whole affair lasted till nightfall.

Outside, people who had not been invited to the audience set off fireworks and danced at the crossroads. The town was illuminated, but the mountain people were already lighting torches to return in long processions to their provinces.

Monsieur Pons identified the bigwigs for Octave: the chief justice, surrounded by magistrates like a hen and her chicks, the archpriest, some smiling curés, the garrison officers, the handful of French residents (some of whom had, only a day before, been wearing white cockades and who would be leaving by the first boat), the town councillors, a few shopkeepers. Octave nudged his mentor, having spotted the two Italians Pons had pointed out to him at the Buono Gusto café: they were talking in an undertone to Count Bertrand, unfolding documents and showing them to him. As they were still there when everyone else had gone, Bertrand immediately led them into the drawing-room to speak with the Emperor. Before the door closed on their discussion, Octave caught a phrase: '*Dite si faccia l'Italia, e l'Italia si farà!*' which Monsieur Pons translated for him: 'Say that Italy should form, and Italy will form.'

'Meaning?'

'That they are patriots, and would like our Emperor to be theirs. After all Napoleon is Italian . . .'

The two Turinese conspirators left the drawing-room a quarter of an hour later, pulled their hats down over their eyes and slipped out without a word. The Emperor followed them thoughtfully, stopping in the corridor and noticing Octave. At once his mood changed.

'Shut that window, Monsieur Sénécal! I have already put up with those dreadful violinists and their wretched ritornellos, but enough's enough! Can't we ever have any peace and quiet around here?'

A girls' choir was giving a serenade outside the town hall, and Napoleon, aghast, retired with Bertrand and Dalesme to a more soundproofed room. Meanwhile Octave was waiting to show the Emperor his excessively modest apartment. Hubert, the valet, had brought up the camp-bed used on expeditions, and set out some familiar trinkets on the chairs and rustic chests of drawers that had been donated by local families.

Monsieur Pons saw no point in keeping watch, since it

was midnight, and was just preparing to take his leave when the door opened.

'Mr Mining Administrator, will you allow me to lunch with you, at Rio Marina?'

'Yes, sire.'

'At nine o'clock in the morning?'

'Yes, sire.'

'Grand Marshal Bertrand tells me that the mines have not worked for weeks, that you have abandoned your lovely house for a dwelling in Portoferraio, and that my desire cannot be satisfied in such a short time . . .'

'On the contrary, it's very easy.'

'You see, Bertrand, killjoy that you are!' said the Emperor, then, addressing Pons once more: 'Tell me frankly if it isn't too much of a disturbance for you . . .'

'It doesn't disturb me at all, it's just . . .'

'Just what?'

'I crave Your Majesty's indulgence.'

'And I grant it you, but what about Madame Pons? Wouldn't it be an abuse of her kindness?'

'It will make her very happy.'

'You see, Bertrand!'

'At nine o'clock, Your Majesty will find his table laid.'

Even more sullen than before, Bertrand left with Monsieur Pons and told him to mobilize a beaming populace to acclaim the Emperor.

*

At five o'clock in the morning, when the sky was still black, a group of horsemen entered the tunnel of the Land Gate, at the bottom of the curtain walls of the Forte

Sant'Ilario, the portcullis of which was reached by a steep path. The vault of the tunnel was wide enough for large berlins to get through, but it was gloomy and cold, lit only very faintly by the glow from a grilled niche containing a statue of the Madonna. Suddenly, though, a flickering light illuminated the walls at the first bend in the tunnel, and the horsemen had to press themselves against the wall to make room for a religious procession. Penitents in pointed hoods carried smoking torches, walking ahead of a bald priest and a coffin carried on a litter decorated with biblical scenes, bringing a Brother of Mercy to the cemetery. Other penitents followed behind them, then women dressed in black, hidden behind floral wreaths. The Emperor removed his hat and whispered to General Dalesme, who was escorting him and his entourage to the Rio mines, where Monsieur Pons awaited them, 'A funeral? At this time of day?'

'Because of the heat, sire, burials take place before dawn or at nightfall . . .'

Once the last of the penitents had passed, the horsemen were finally able to leave the smoky tunnel, emerging on to a stony road at the entrance to a valley tinged red by the rising sun. They didn't have far to travel, but had to stop often to receive the tributes of the peasants at every village, every hamlet. After that the roads were bad, narrow and poorly marked. At the foot of the mountains they rode along the gulf, and then beside ravines, they climbed into wild pine forests, and back down a road lined with aloes. Beyond the fortress of Porto Longone, built on granite blocks, battered by the waves, the land of iron began: no more trees, and not a tuft of grass;

instead they saw grey houses, and hillsides left ashen by
slag from the mines. The path was pitted by the carts that
brought the ore to the barges.

Evviva l'Imperatore! On the ridges, workers unfurled
their new banners, and at Rio Marina, 150 miners, picks
shouldered, hailed His Majesty. Boatmen lit the fuses of
their antique culverins and local girls, their black hair
entwined with ribbons, ran to meet him, throwing flower
petals, squealing like mad things and trying to kiss his
hands. Pons de l'Hérault, who was quite nervous, and the
representatives of the local councils – some of whom had,
the previous week, cried *Death to Napoleon!* and set fire to
effigies of him – now welcomed him with open displays
of emotion. When Bertrand and Dalesme helped the
Emperor from his horse, the ovation rose a notch, but
the endlessly repeated cheers of *Evviva l'Imperatore* were
now joined by clear cries of *Viva il nostro babbo!* –
which Napoleon understood perfectly well – directed at
Monsieur Pons.

'I get a sense that you're the King,' said the Emperor
irritably, as the two men walked beneath the inevitable
triumphal arch of chestnut and oak leaves.

'Oh no, I'm not their sovereign . . .'

'But you are their father, isn't that what they're
shouting?'

'I am their father, yes . . .'

'That's even better.'

The day had not started well.

Monsieur Pons kept the ceremonies to a minimum, cut
short the compliments that Napoleon had heard twenty
times already since his arrival and, after a brief stroll on
the rocks, took his visitors to lunch at the mine adminis-

tration mansion —where he lived under normal circumstances, a sad but spacious mansion by the sea. He had
not been idle. He'd galloped to Rio at dead of night,
woken his workers with a lantern, asked the gardener to
bedeck the front steps with flowers, ordered nets put out
at the first light of day. By some miracle his fishermen
had caught a twenty-five-pound fish, and others besides;
enough to prepare a bouillabaisse every bit as good as the
one he had given Captain Bonaparte in Bandol, the first
Napoleon had ever eaten. Would he remember?

None of Monsieur Pons's efforts were rewarded, however, and were in fact seen as pure insolence because the
gardener, who was a fine man but ignorant of symbols,
had arranged white lilies very conspicuously at the bottom
of the steps. This was not greatly to the Emperor's liking.

'This insignium bodes well!'

Inside, Napoleon asked his host, 'Isn't Madame Pons
here?'

'She stayed in Portoferraio,' Pons replied uneasily.

'Couldn't she receive me?'

'She's still making flags . . .'

'You will thank her for the care she is taking . . .'

'Certainly, monsieur,' stammered Pons, forgetting the
correct form of address.

His guests passed into the dining-room and poor
Monsieur Pons wondered what blunders he was going
to commit next, but His Majesty had stopped talking to
him, preferring to direct questions about iron extraction
at General Dalesme — or that imbecile Taillade, a naval
lieutenant without a vessel, who had settled on the
island but was so pretentious that the people of Elba
simply laughed at him. Now he acted as though he knew

everything, and tried to puff himself up by explaining things Napoleon already knew: that the name Elba came from the Etruscan *ilva*, iron; that the Medici had sent their convicts to the citadel of Porto Longone, and it was from them that the mine-workers were descended.

Bertrand himself had arranged the seating of the guests, placing Monsieur Pons far away from the Emperor, as though he were being punished. Dalesme, clearly exasperated by the situation, kept an eye on the administrator, gesturing him to be calm. The worst moment was when the Emperor expressed surprise that the ore could not be transformed on the island, for want of wood to feed the kilns. 'Then we will plant forests,' he said, adding cheerfully that he felt himself turning into a peasant. When the bouillabaisse was served, he asked what the dish was, and claimed never to have eaten it before – glancing at Monsieur Pons out of the corner of his eye as he did so. Pons could hardly contain himself, and almost left the table several times, but the Emperor then began talking about transforming the island, building real roads, sewers in the towns; he thought it wrong that Elba was unable to produce enough wheat for its own needs, and had to import its grain.

The conversation thus turned to nearby Italy, which was occupied by the Austrians: Napoleon thought that all the nations in the peninsula would one day have to merge into a great Italian fatherland. To do so they would have to forget their rivalries, and Rome, Florence and Milan would have to reach an agreement if they were to be strong together. When the war was mentioned, Napoleon replied abruptly.

'Don't talk to me about war! I've had enough of war

... You see, I've thought about it a great deal ... We have waged war all our life, the future may force us to do so again, and yet war will in the end become an anachronism. These battles? The confrontation of two societies, one which dates from 1789 and the *ancien régime*. They couldn't live together, and the younger devoured the older ... Yes, war has brought me low, *me*, the representative of the French Revolution and the instrument of its principles. None of it is of any import. It's a lost battle for civilization, but civilization, believe me, will take its revenge ...'

His bouillabaisse, which he had not yet touched, was going cold but, waving his knife in the air, the Emperor pursued his theme, his eyes half-closed.

'There are two systems, the past and the future: the present is merely a painful transition. Which, in your view, must triumph? Surely the future? Well, the future is intelligence, industry and peace! I say once again, gentlemen, don't speak to me of war, it is no longer one of our customs ...'

Monsieur Pons thought this speech was directed at him, that His Majesty, in neglecting his bouillabaisse, was needling his own republican convictions. Was this despot going to lecture him under his own roof? He fulminated, but he stayed sitting where he was.

When the Emperor rose before coffee, he deigned to ask his host for precise details about the working of the mines and how much they yielded, but Monsieur Pons merely said he would provide all the information in writing. (This reply was something he regretted, however, when, just as they were walking past the very place where the ore was piled for loading, a group of clerks and miners approached the Emperor, knelt before him and handed him a petition to keep their beloved administrator in his job. The Emperor frowned as he read it and Monsieur Pons, very embarrassed, said, 'Monsieur, I know nothing of this inappropriate gesture.')

'Are you still a Republican?'

'A patriot, yes.'

'Do you want to stay with me?'

'I ask only to be of use to you.'

'That wasn't the question, I was asking only if you want to continue with your administration. Are you staying, or are you not?'

'I will do as you wish.'

The visit had got off to a dreadful start, and finished as it had begun. Monsieur Pons made one gaffe after another, couldn't bring himself to call the Emperor 'sire', stammered as he called him 'monsieur', 'your grace', 'your worship', and the general feeling of unease was heightened because he did not travel with the sovereign on the boat back to Portoferraio, as etiquette required.

Monsieur Pons was unhappy, and that evening he thought of the jobs he might be able to do in Italy, working for one or other of the buyers of his ore, once Napoleon expelled him along with his family.

*

Octave was already on to his second notebook, dated Sunday 22 May: *'I can write only what I see, and show it to the Emperor without explanation. His character is clearly visible in everything he does. When he is not waging war, he puts the same amount of energy into travelling. It took him only a few days to turn the island into a building site. Anyone*

*who can dig, lay bricks, nail, cut, terrace, paint, sew or plant
has contributed. Foreigners are now arriving as back-up for
the Elban workers; there is talk of Italian sculptors who
will open studios and exploit the neglected marble quarries.
Everything, up to now, has been abandoned, everything is to
be built or restored, like the salt-marshes and the tuna-fish
pounds. The coral will not be reserved for the Neapolitans,
and wheat will be permitted to enter the island. The old roads
will be broadened, and new ones opened up. Already, avenues
of young mulberry trees surround Portoferraio, whose streets
are slowly being paved. The warehouses of the saltworks will
be turned into stables, the forts will be equipped, a hospital is
planned and customs will be reorganized. His Majesty finds
water tanks unsatisfactory, and wishes to bring mountain
water into the town. He has identified a spring from which
the sailors of the* Undaunted *draw their supplies, and one of
them has even given him some of it to drink, serving it to him
in a dent in his hat. He found it delicious. Through the
French window I can see His Majesty talking to the architect,
no, the engineer, Monsieur Bargigli, beneath the palm-trees
and the cypresses in the garden . . .'*

The Emperor now had a palace, right at the top of the
town, between Forte Stella and Forte Falcone; from his
terrace he could see Italy. He had not been able to bear
life in town for long, amid the people, the nauseating
smells, the constant serenades beneath his windows that
drove him out of his mind. It was his conviction that an
emperor should live apart from his subjects, and avoid any
kind of familiarity with them, that he should set up a
court as soon as possible, and enforce a strict code of
etiquette. On his nocturnal strolls (for his days began at
three o'clock in the morning) he'd kept his eyes open for

an ideal site for a palace, and had liked this place as soon
as he'd seen it; it overlooked Portoferraio on one side, and
on the other plunged down to a shingle beach largely
inaccessible from any other direction. The house itself was
an old gardener's cottage, flanked by two pavilions accom-
modating artillery officers. Its name, the Mulini Palace,
came from recently demolished windmills whose ruined
foundations could still be seen amid brambles and weeds.
Shacks and bits of useless dry-stone walls had been cleared
away very quickly, and a building constructed between
the pavilions, a storey higher than the old house. Avenues
had been paved between the palm trees and myrtle bushes
as far as the parapet of the covered rampart walk that
connected the two forts at the top of the cliffs. The
Emperor had drawn the plans himself, and they'd been
implemented by builders, joiners and upholsterers over-
seen by engineer Bargigli, with whom His Majesty was
chatting on this particular day.

'Is the road into these mountains passable?'

'Which mountains, sire?'

'Are you blind? Over there, on the right!'

'But they're on the mainland, sire.'

'Aha? My island really is very small . . .'

Impatient to live in his palace, the Emperor had moved
in before work was completed, and so lived amid dust,
paint, damp cement, hammer-blows and the song of the
nightingales. To speed up the pace, he helped the builders
with the most menial tasks. Octave had seen him using
a pick and getting his white breeches covered with soil,
he had seen him sitting on a pile of rubble eating a boiled
egg, and clinking glasses with the workers who were
painting the façade pink. For the sake of economy, Napo-

leon had launched a raid on the palace of Piombino, which could be seen through binoculars from the terrace of the Mulini Palace: Elisa, the Duchess of Tuscany, the sister who had betrayed him, had left her furniture there while fleeing the Austrians. With the amused complicity of the English sailors, a quartermaster had managed to strip the place – even dismantling the sycamore parquets and removing the shutters from the windows – transporting everything to the Mulini Palace where white and gold stools and roll-top bedside tables were now stacked chaotically next to ladders and pots of paint.

In the room that would soon serve as a library, Octave closed his notebook on the insignificant details of this life that was more bohemian than Imperial and looked through the bay window. Outside, two Elban National Guards were placing a statue of Minerva on a plinth that was barely dry. At that moment one of the English NCOs in charge of the running of the house came to announce the arrival of a visitor. Monsieur Pons appeared shortly afterwards. Octave guessed the tenor of the conversation from their gestures and facial expressions: Napoleon was looking scornfully at the mine administrator. Monsieur Pons stood as straight as a sword. He must have been giving crisp replies to the questions or orders of the Emperor, who was clearly irritated because he belched, twisted his mouth and gesticulated. But the scene was short, and Monsieur Pons turned to depart while His Majesty kicked the parapet violently, beneath the startled eyes of engineer Bargigli.

Octave went into Napoleon's bedroom, which was filled by Elisa Bonaparte's bed, its wooden uprights spiky with claws and gilded beaks. From there, through the antechamber at the bottom of the stairs, he emerged near the street and found himself face to face with Monsieur Pons – pale, furious, his jaw set – leaving the Mulini Palace at a furious pace. Octave tackled him.

'I glimpsed you in the garden . . .'

'Your Bonaparte does not know how to behave!'

'Did he dismiss you?'

'No, he summoned me, but it comes to the same thing, because I am going to hand in my resignation!'

'As serious as that!'

'Yes, my dear fellow, I refuse to spit on people who have placed their trust in me!'

Together Octave and Monsieur Pons crossed the stepped street that a squad of workmen was digging up to replace it with a ramp, so that vehicles would be able to pass along it.

'What a mess!' groused Monsieur Pons.

'What did His Majesty ask of you?'

'Money, for heaven's sake! The money from the mines to satisfy his whims!'

'The mines belong to him . . .'

'From the 11 of April, fine, but not before then! I also told him that the coffers were empty, and he said, "You have reserves, I know you do." How does he know that, if you please?'

'And is it true?'

'What?'

'That you have reserves.'

'Of course it is! Since we learned of the fall of the Empire, I hurried to pay my creditors and set aside the rest of my takings.'

'A considerable sum?'

'More than two hundred thousand francs, but it's going back to the Order of the Légion d'honneur that employed me, so from the moral point of view it's not at my disposal! Your master has claimed not to understand, or perhaps he isn't used to meeting honest people. He yelled right in my face: "Are you refusing to obey? Do you know the consequences? I can easily find another admini-strator!"'

'He's right there: you have the best-paid job on the island . . .'

'My word is my bond!'

'The Emperor will send his gendarmes to get you.'

'They'd better be strong, then, because I'll greet them with my miners! Force, that's all Bonaparte understands! And money to corrupt the weak!'

Monsieur Pons was in a rage. The presence of the Emperor was going to attract all kinds of crooks to the island; communication had already been re-established with Piombino and Italy. Every day ships brought build-ing materials, strangers were disembarking at random, trade would spread and money circulate; the Emperor already employed Elbans as chamberlains or ordnance officers on salaries they had never dreamed of.

'No one is rich here,' said Monsieur Pons, 'and this luxury will spoil men and women accustomed to a simple life.'

*

As part of his duties, Octave spent the morning wandering about the quays. He checked the arrival of boats unload-ing merchandise and passengers at Portoferraio. Genoese businessmen, an architect from Livorno, artists seeking sponsors, adventurers or entrepreneurs in search of building sites, a man who had constructed a village of wooden houses for when the neighbouring islands were colonized, ordinary visitors, most of them English or Italian, and Roman countesses hoping to obtain an audience with the great man; when they were not received, they consoled themselves by buying alabaster busts of Napoleon in the shop recently established by a Florentine craftsman. A new twenty-room inn had opened to accommodate these bountiful strangers. The fishermen and shopkeepers were beginning to become wealthy. Nothing was free now, nothing was spontaneous, and prices were rising along with temptation: the Elbans all hoped to profit from it. Each passing day confirmed to Octave that Pons de l'Hérault was right. The customs of the indigenous people were changing quickly, and they even turned into thieves when the occasion presented itself.

In his rooms at the Mulini Palace, Monsieur Peyrusse had kept a quantity of bags, each containing 1,000 gold napoleons, which he had brought from Fontainebleau. When the treasurer had finally got around to putting his hoard in safe keeping, a member of the National Guard by the name of Paolini, a shoemaker by trade, and very poor, stirred the straw with his boot to check that no coins had inadvertently rolled into it. He found a whole bag. Would he give it back? Not at all. He hid the bag and its contents in his shako. Naturally enough, his sudden and insane spending spree announced his larceny, but no one dared to punish him.

Now everyone was claiming his share. The peasants who accompanied the Emperor on his nocturnal rambles with their lanterns wanted a salary to walk the dug-up streets. The supernumeraries demanded by Count Bertrand, who were herded all over the island whenever they were needed to hail the passage of the Imperial cortège, had to be paid as well.

Napoleon himself was setting a bad example, Monsieur Pons had suggested to Octave. On the evening after a storm, a ship had sought refuge in the gulf of Porto Longone. The vessel was carrying furniture belonging to the Borghese prince; Pauline's lover was having it transported from Genoa to Rome, where he now lived. The Emperor ordered that it be requisitioned, and justified the act with a quip: 'It'll be staying in the family.' All of a sudden Bertrand had to turn Elbans out of their homes, to transform the buildings into furniture warehouses, just as he had turned the tuna-fishing warehouses into stables. And then, Monsieur Pons had elaborated, there was such insolence in that display of silver-gilt, of gold, of horses, landaus and barouches, some of which carried nothing but fruit and eau-de-vie. And the costumes, the uniforms, the postilions' green morning coats with gold braid, the Imperial eagle on the horses' harnesses, the red-jacketed grooms who watched the people from on high. Such contempt! Bourgeois and dignitaries were running up debts trying to emulate the Emperor, and the ladies were forever wanting smart dresses to show off at parties. How could one move from economy to extravagance, from frugality to so much gluttony, without doing damage to oneself?

Octave understood that a sleepy Sub-prefecture could not be turned abruptly into an operatic principality, but he had nothing to say on the matter. He never had anything to say. He carried out orders. He did his job, and was careful never to express the merest hint of a personal judgement out loud. However, the growing numbers of visitors worried him; the Emperor was in exile, but he was close to the coasts of Europe and Octave was sure the royalists' Committee, from whom he'd received no news, would try to join him, that they would send an emissary, whom Octave would have to provide with verifiable information in order to retain his credibility. Consequently, he kept his eye on strangers, suspecting them all of being enemy agents, even killers, and his permanent watchfulness exhausted him while at the same time giving him a reason to be near Napoleon.

Late in the morning, when the ships had disgorged their contingent of tourists, it was Octave's custom to go to the Buono Gusto to find out what was happening. He kept his ears pricked. He sometimes engaged in banal conversation with anyone who spoke French. The Via Gran Bastione had been recobbled, and tables had been placed outside the café, which was always full. The landlord had bought his neighbours' house so he could rent rooms at outlandish prices; he never complained about His Majesty – oh no – and neither did Gianna. She had other girls to help her now, including her sister. With their short, brightly coloured skirts they effortlessly titillated the customers.

At the Buono Gusto now Octave looked for a seat, but couldn't find one. Gianna was chatting in dialect with some Tuscans. She was wearing shoes, and a gleaming bracelet flashed on her wrist.

'Where did you get the jewellery?'

'Someone nicer than you,' she replied to Octave in his own language

'Oh? So you're having a go at speaking French, then, Gianna?'

'I learn from a officer.'

'More than one, isn't that right?'

'*Lasciami!*'

Grumbling to himself — Monsieur Pons's predictions even involved the girls of the port; the money of the sailors and the foreigners seemed easy, never again would he see Gianna without giving her presents, but her venality stripped her of some of her charm, and of the illusion that she liked him just for himself — Octave went down to the docks.

'The air of Portoferraio,' said the mine administrator, 'will become just as vicious as the air at the Palace of Versailles, you'll see!'

Octave had already seen, but he was not interested in jeremiads, turning his attention instead to a Neapolitan frigate that had arrived the previous evening. Parcels were piled in front of a platoon of suspicious grenadiers of the Guard supplementing the contingent of customs officers. That was something else that had changed: Cambronne had managed to transport his battalion across France and over the Italian coast; his 600 grognards had come to replace Dalesme's garrison, most of which had returned to the metropolis. Cambronne's fine fellows, employed on tasks that were less than warlike, sweated beneath their fur hats and intensified their zeal, roughly interrogating an Elban who had taken delivery of a mountain of barrels. Seeing Octave, the man waved wildly at him.

'Monsieur Sénécal! Come and tell them who I am!'

Octave picked his way through the barrels and sacks of grain. Like everyone else, he knew the merchant, a man just short of middle age, five feet tall, with a round face and a flat nose, and very black hair. His name was Alessandro Forli, and he made oil with olives he bought from the farmer Vantini.

'Are you having problems, Monsieur Forli?'

'Don't talk to me about problems, your lascars won't listen to anything I say!'

'Are your customs papers not in order?'

'Of course they are! They think there's something strange about me receiving empty barrels! I can't help it if we have neither wood nor coopers on the island, can I? And I'm hardly going to deliver my oil in a handkerchief on the end of a stick!'

Octave resolved the difficulty, and was joking about it with Forli when a familiar voice rang out behind him:

'I see that you have found your cane, my dear Blacé.'

Marquis de la Grange climbed out of a launch dispatched from the merchant ship, and stepped on to the gangway. His collar was open, and his face was hidden beneath a vast and very plebeian straw hat.

'Blacé?' Octave hoarsely. 'I know no one of that name . . .'

'Chevalier! Signor Forli is our friend, so what does your new name matter, whether it be Chauvin or Sénécal?'

'It's Sénécal.'

'Fine! That sounds authentic enough.'

The three men strolled along the rampart walk, which was usually blocked off – but Octave enjoyed special privileges and the sentries gave him a military salute. La Grange was quite taken aback.

'My word, Chevalier, you've come up in the world . . .'

'I have little merit, Marquis, if you knew . . .'

'Knowledge is precisely my purpose in coming here, Chevalier. Tell me all.'

'The Emperor, that is, Bonaparte, is surrounded by idiots. When he asks the time of the old gendarme who acts as his batman, do you know what that ass tells him? "Whatever time pleases Your Majesty."'

'Basically I've come here to assess the standard of his entourage,' said La Grange with an explosion of laughter, 'What's your role in all this now?'

'I'm a kind of butler; I observe, I can go anywhere I like, sometimes I recite appropriate verses . . . The other day, Bonaparte was grumbling about his court, so I gave him a riposte I had taken from a Shakespeare play in the library: 'He that can endure to follow with allegiance a fallen lord does conquer him that did his master conquer.'

'Lovely!'

'It's from Act III of *Antony and Cleopatra* . . .'

'Monsieur Sénécal is playing down his role,' broke in the oil merchant. 'He also has police powers, and everyone knows about it.'

'Is that true?' asked La Grange, astonished.

'Yes, if you like,' Octave replied immediately. 'I'm well read, and it's been useful to me.'

'Ah, yes, the old education . . .'

'I'm supposed to ensure good order among both things and people, but I have no official title.'

'Perfect! You are precious to us, Chevalier.'

Far away from eavesdroppers by now, they began to swap confidences of a more serious kind. La Grange had travelled in person to establish a connection between Paris and his agents on the island. He supplied information before he asked for it: thus Octave learned that the formidable Maubreuil was rotting in prison: rather than attacking Napoleon in the forest of Fontainebleau, as he had been commissioned to do, Maubreuil had robbed the Princess of Wurtemberg, the wife of Jérôme Bonaparte, on the road to Nemours, as she took eleven coffers of gold and diamonds to Germany. Tsar Alexander had been furious about this affront to a princess of royal blood and ordered an inquiry. The police had found one of the diamonds on Maubreuil's bed, in his lodgings in the rue Neuve-du-Luxembourg. Octave also learned that the Count of Sémallé was suspicious of Louis XVIII, who was too much inclined to listen to the perfidious advice of Talleyrand and reformed Jacobins. Sémallé believed this would lead to disaster, and devoted himself exclusively to the Count of Artois, the Lieutenant General of the kingdom and the only person – in his eyes –who could maintain a real monarchy.

Having listened to these details, it was obvious to Octave that he was, in turn, expected to inform the Marquis about life in the Mulini Palace and the behaviour of the Emperor, but he delivered only selected truths, and breathed easier for knowing La Grange was leaving again that evening on the Neapolitan ship. He now looked on the oil merchant in a different light, fortunately, and thought of ways of using the man for his own purposes, providing him with distorted information to pass on to Paris.

Wanting to deliver his report on the day's events to the Emperor, Octave discovered that Napoleon had gone in search of a country residence; he did not return to the villa until morning, after exhausting his aides-de-camp and valets by riding at a gallop.

*

The unctuous Foureau de Beauregard, physician to the imperial stables, had taken care of Napoleon's health since the defection of Dr Yvan in Fontainebleau, after the attempted poisoning. The man was unpopular because he sought to display his knowledge on every occasion. A pedant, as chatty as a blackbird, always delivering quips that were a whisker away from slander, he emerged from the kitchens carrying a steaming bowl, walked the length of the ground floor, and entered the bathroom at the end of the east wing. The Emperor was relaxing in an enamel bathtub coffered with exotic wood. Foureau held out the concoction in both hands.

'Your Majesty should drink it very hot, this brew is excellent for cleansing and firming the innards.'

Napoleon took the receptacle, brought it to his lips, took a little sip and bellowed: 'Ah! Do you want to burn my tongue and my throat with your infernal mixture?'

'Chicken, sire, clear stock . . .'

'Clear but scalding!'

'It has to be drunk that way to have any effect . . .'

'It's had its effect!'

'Only the heat can overcome and dispel the diseased element. Hippocrates is quite clear on the matter.'

Up to his chest in salt water, the Emperor inhaled the scented steam of the consommé, and the doctor immediately grew alarmed.

'No, no! Not like that!'

'What is it this time, Monsieur Purgon?'

'By inhaling the fumes, Your Majesty is swallowing columns of air!'

'Really?'

'It's very bad for you. That air will whirl around the intestines and give you colic.'

'By my age I ought to know how to drink!'

'Sire, those vapours can be harmful, the bouillon needs to be liquid to provide relief, and besides, Aristotle himself . . .'

'Would all three of you kindly bugger off, Hippocrates, Aristotle and you!'

Despite the fact that civil affairs remained a matter for Count Bertrand, Octave had officially replaced the Duke of Bassano, and this gave him the privilege of entering the Emperor's room unannounced. He arrived via the valets' room, which opened on to the garden, just as the eloquent medic had the bowl and its contents hurled at his waist-coat. Hubert the valet, silent and practised, picked up the pieces of faience before sponging down the tiles.

'Charlatan!' the Emperor yelled at the departing doctor, who was annoyed but still obsequious. Columns of air indeed!

The Emperor struck the bathwater with the palms of his hands.

'Columns of air!' he went on. 'Did you hear that, Monsieur Sénécal?'

'No, sire.'

'Just as well! And invoking Aristotle to make you swallow soup that boils your entrails!'

Octave never disturbed the Emperor without good reason. When Hubert the valet had left with his pieces of bowl and his wet rag, Napoleon said, 'Shut the French window, Monsieur Sénécal, the walls have ears in the Mulini. What news do you bring me?'

'It's precisely on the subject of eavesdroppers, sire . . .'

'I know! They're listening to me, they're watching me, they're repeating my words, distorting them, interpreting them, worrying about my projects, noticing my every mood, my every movement, what I eat, if I have backache or a stomachache, they follow me when I go for a walk – ha! I've got eyes: the moment I venture outside, Campbell is hot on my heels, I sometimes wonder if he doesn't hire English dwarfs to hide under my bed, in my drawers, in my pocket, in my snuffboxes!'

'Your Majesty insisted that Colonel Campbell stay on the island of Elba.'

'Of course! I know him. Although he isn't aware of it, that idiot is telling London precisely what I want him to.'

'It's not just the English . . .'

'Pass me a hot towel, Monsieur Sénécal, help me climb out of this bathtub and let me hear what you have to say.'

While the Emperor, wrapped in his towel, sprayed himself with eau de Cologne, Octave told him what he had learned the previous day by going to the harbour, describing his surprise at bumping into La Grange dressed as a Neapolitan businessman and detailing the arguments between the King's entourage and the partisans of Louis's brother the Count of Artois – and the double game being played by Signor Forli, the oil merchant who was sending news to Paris.

'He's a nice enough chap, about thirty, he gets on very well with his many customers. I saw him delivering olive oil to the Forte Stella the other morning, although I didn't know what he was up to at the time, and he seemed to be very good friends with General Cambronne.'

'He'll be sending reports to Italy, I expect. How? And to whom?'

'Forli writes his messages in lemon juice, between the lines of anodyne letters to his family. The reports end up in Livorno, with the French consul, Chevalier Mariotti, who reveals them with the help of a candle, writes them out again, sending one copy to Talleyrand and another to the Count of Bussigny in Rome . . .'

'Pussini?'

'Louis XVIII's ambassador.'

'Well, Sénécal, let's treat your man Forli like my Campbell. Does he trust you? He does? Does he think you're the royalists' envoy? Perfect! You'll feed him information. We'll invent stories for him as we see fit. Of course, you will report only to me.'

'Not a word to Monsieur Poggi?'

'Not a word, I tell you, not to anyone!'

'And yet you've put Monsieur Poggi in charge of the police and . . .'

'And he distracts me with his gossip, he helps me gauge the temperature of spirits on the island, no more than that. So, just to me, you stubborn mule!'

Hubert had silently returned and was dressing the Emperor, who continued talking to Octave without worrying about the presence of the loyal valet.

'When you see your chap again, Monsieur Sénécal, just to show the resigned and inoffensive side of my character, tell him that I read no newspapers from the Continent. Tell him that some do reach me, but I scorn them, and have no interest in France.'

'That will be easy, sire, because you really do refuse to read those papers.'

'I don't need to, and you know it! Our visitors keep me sufficiently well informed, especially the English, who are less than enchanted by the King of France, and who come and peer up my nose as they might the dromedary in the Jardin des Plantes!'

Napoleon was just buttoning his white piqué waistcoat before climbing to the first floor – to see how the Florentine painters were getting on as they decorated the trompe-l'oeil ceilings with laurel garlands, victories and gauze held by bundles of lances – when, looking out the window, he noticed Bertrand walking across the lawn.

'Here comes our great marshal with his doleful countenance. I bet you, Sénécal, that he is about to announce the arrival of Countess Bertrand and her children, that he likes his apartment in the town hall either a great deal or not at all; in short, some domestic matters that I couldn't give a fig about.'

The Emperor went out into the garden, jacketless, putting on a straw hat.

'Has your wife arrived, your grace?'

'Yes, sire, this morning...'

'Is she well?'

'As well as possible, sire, but she is pregnant and the journey has tired her...'

'I will pay her a visit.'

'Thank you, sire, but...'

'But come upstairs with me, I am going to see how our painters are managing, because I'm taking a great interest in the decoration of the Empress's apartments!'

'The Empress...'

'Do you bring me news? And my son?'

'No, sire, no, I meant the ex-Empress.'

'Josephine wants to join me?'

'Not any more . . .'

'Then finish your sentences, damn it!'

'Fanny, my wife, tells me she was very ill.'

'Is she better? No? Does she want a good doctor, if such a creature exists?'

'She has died in Malmaison.'

Napoleon sat without leaving his armchair till evening. He fiddled with his watch-chain, plaited with Josephine's hair, as though it were a rosary and quietly rejected the audiences he was supposed to be giving; he ate nothing and went to bed early, a thousand memories beneath his closed eyelids.

*

With much to do, the Emperor forgot his grief. The following day he wanted to climb the Monte Giove, dedicated to Jupiter, from which he would look down on both his island and the Tyrrhenian Sea. For that, however, he needed a local horse, one that knew where to set its hoofs among the stones along the edges of the ravines. Octave was at his wits' end: how could he ensure the Emperor's safety in a land of dense forests? Assassins could so easily ambush him and disappear. The Emperor didn't care; his need of pure air, of mountain-tops, was too great, and up there, if the chestnut trees were bushy, so much the better, as it meant there would be shade and wind (for summer in Portoferraio was stifling). Nonetheless, Napoleon did not refuse the escort of the Polish lancers; they would abandon their usual mounts to ride, as he did, those safe animals, accustomed to the scrubland and its many hazards.

The troop galloped for a long time along stone-battered hairpin roads, not stopping until they reached Marciana Alta. This was a village perched half-way up the slope, the kind often seen in Corsica, where severe-looking houses push their way into poorly cobbled, rocky streets. There the horses had to be abandoned to the care of the lancers, who watered them from a spring that flowed among the lichen.

'Could you make yourself useful, Campbell?' asked the Emperor.

'Certainly.' Campbell had insisted on accompanying Napoleon on this trek, and had been granted permission to do so.

'Give me your arm.'

Campbell, his back aching from hours of riding, began the climb, limping slightly as he struggled to keep up with His Majesty. Napoleon was not tired in the slightest, and was taking comfort from terrain like that of his childhood.

Clutching sticks carved from branches, the two men climbed a path lined with low walls, at intervals drinking water from their leather beakers, scooped from springs that bubbled among the rocks; treading on moss and bracken, they entered a primitive forest and, after walking for some time, they finally reached a chapel dedicated to the Madonna, daubed with naïve frescoes and framed by knotty hundred-year-old chestnut trees whose roots pierced the ground and re-emerged like snakes. Next to the chapel stood a hermitage, the home of the sanctuary's guardian. He indicated the path and pointed out the peak, a hundred yards higher, at the end of a pile of fallen earth.

Napoleon and Campbell clambered up there with one last effort, panting, their legs heavy. From the ridge they could see Corsica to the west, and the lacy peaks of the Monte d'Oro. The Emperor sat down on a rock, and Campbell threw himself on the ground.

'Do you know this perfume, Master Campbell?' asked the Emperor, taking in a big breath through his nostrils.

'Perfume, sire? What perfume?'

'Breathe in, for heaven's sake! You northerners have your noses blocked! You can't smell anything but mud from the top of the white cliffs of Dover! Even with my eyes closed, I can recognize Corsica by its perfume. Why go anywhere else, Campbell? I've come home to take root.'

'I understand . . .'

'Pfft! No, no, you can't understand. Your moors are odourless! My scrubland is filled with the smell of wild thyme and the essences of paradise.'

The Emperor got to his feet, resting an arm on the shoulder of his breathless companion, who, red as a well-cooked lobster, was sponging himself with his sodden handkerchief. Napoleon returned to the rock he had used as a seat, and gazed across at Corsica. He came from that land of mountain folk, rough and ready, families ready to murder each other at the first hint of a slight, taking refuge behind the loopholes of their farms. He remembered his nurse Illaria, telling him about the baby-eating vampire, and the *uspirdo*, the bird that announced death by descending with the fog. To protect him against bad luck, she used to place a dish of water on his head and pour three drops of olive oil into it, chanting as she did so. In her language, a mixture of Tuscan and Berber, she told him that Satan had struck the peak of Tafonato with a hammer, that the cemetery of the Île Sainte-Marie, in the pool of Diana, was cursed. The barren land beyond the valley of Lozari was the revenge of a three-headed monster. She also told him that curé Gabrielli had summoned up the devil to save the members of his clan who'd been besieged by a rival family, and that the devil had turned the rivals into grey sheep; and that some witches had taken possession of the cemetery above Cuttoli, that the twisted, flickering flames seen on some nights in the hamlet of Busso, *i fochi di u Busso*, were the souls of the damned. These fables were a mixture of Greek myths, Islam and Christian martyrology, because over the centuries Corsica, like its neighbour Elba, had passed through the hands of the Spanish, the Greek, the Etruscans, the Saracens, the Romans; Seneca, who had been exiled there, had worried about the dark forests where the elves danced. Napoleon recalled a group of shepherds, great stout fellows with pointed hats who slept on bracken and were thought to be soothsayers. He'd seen them throwing the keys of a chapel into the midst of their flock to cure sick animals, and they had told him that two months before his birth, near the point of Parata, above the Bloody Islands, a comet had been sighted.

When he returned to the hermitage, deliberately placing all his weight on Campbell's shoulder, Napoleon seemed happy. Rather than losing himself in nostalgia, he regained his strength, and chivvied the colonel into the guardian's cottage. He wanted to live there, he wanted to escape Portoferraio and the phoney palace that was being renovated in the countryside, isolated on a peak, but far from trees and exposed to the sun.

'Remember, Colonel, that we will have to install a kitchen in this shed, at the back, and build a stable under a canopy.'

'I haven't brought anything to write with,' said Campbell.

'Then engrave it on your brain! Look, there are three shutters missing. Allow for three lanterns, and a torch, outside. And some curtains, the rails are up already. And then shovels and tongs for the fires in the hearth.'

'Fires?' queried the Englishman, dazed by the heat.

'Up in the mountains it gets cold in the evenings, Monsieur, as cold as it is in your hovels in London.'

*

'Monday, 25 August. I barely have the strength to keep this diary on a regular basis. For weeks, the summer has been exhausting me. A scorching wind from the south-east is bringing us a heat-wave from the African deserts. At night, it often rains, and the drops are hot. I was even caught in one of those sudden heavy showers: water poured and streamed, becoming a raging torrent whose current dragged me several yards. I went down to Gianna's, on Via del Gran Bastione; she's playing at being a lady with dresses brought on boats from Naples. I'd bought skirts and stockings from some sailors who were selling them at auction in the port, and was looking forward to watching her try them on, but I wasn't the only one, and Gianna didn't open the door to me; she was too busy with a lieutenant-commander. I had to take shelter for part of the night, not far away, in the shed that's used for the Imperial coaches, with my soaking silk and laces, drenched to the bone.'

In his notebooks, Octave stuck strictly to the facts. No

one reading them would learn anything of his thoughts. He recorded events, never appraising them or delivering a judgement, so that his scribblings, were they to be seen by malevolent eyes, could never be used against him or against the Emperor. Octave reported, for example, that His Majesty was ordering books from Venice or Genoa, that he was having them rebound in Livorno; or that in his unfinished villa in San Martino, which was being built out of a farm and a barn, he was arranging souvenirs of Marie-Louise, knick-knacks and portraits, that he had torn the engravings from a book about Egypt to mount them on the walls too, that one of the rooms was decorated with hieroglyphics and painted palm groves. It wasn't very interesting, perhaps, but it was innocent.

Octave also recorded the movements of the staff. Hubert had gone back to France, to be by his wife's bedside, and Monsieur Marchand had come to replace him. Marchand had given Napoleon news of the Empress, facts gleaned from his mother, who was a governess to the King of Rome. Marie-Louise's doctor, he said, claimed that the air of Elba would be harmful to her, and that the Austrians had even refused to let her travel to Parma, which was too close. And what about the King of Rome? The Emperor of Austria had apparently scooped him up in his arms, at Rambouillet, but the boy had said, 'He isn't handsome, grandpapa!' — a piece of gossip that had delighted Napoleon, even while he understood his chances of seeing his son and the Empress again were rapidly fading away.

In a few lines, Octave had also recorded news of Princess Pauline, who had visited Portoferraio. She had stayed for only one night before embarking for Naples

where, it was said, she had gone to negotiate an alliance
with Murat, in an attempt to reconcile her brother and his
impetuous brother-in-law. Octave contented himself with
repeating the rumour, although without giving it the
slightest foundation. Did he know any more than that?
He had seen the Princess Pauline giving her brother a
handful of diamonds, but had no idea whether their
purpose was to finance the model farm in San Marino,
or whether Napoleon was hoping to grow wheat on the
island's stony ground. The Emperor dispersed his secrets.
What he said to Drouot he didn't repeat to Bertrand,
Cambronne was kept in the dark about his confidences to
Bertrand, and so on. Each man collected discrete confidences that he was never able to link up with anything
else. In his writings, Octave sorted, refined, held things
back. His horror or his criticisms were left to the imagination. The installation of Madame Mère on the island in
a house rented from Monsieur Vantini, a hundred yards
down from the Mulini Palace, seemed to leave him cold,
and he recorded not a word of the Emperor's outpourings
on the subject. Octave did not greatly care for the crabby
old lady in black, who expressed herself only in Italian,
ate Italian food, surrounded herself with Italian servants
and wanted to install Corsicans in the best positions in the
kingdom, even going so far as to squander on them part
of the million and a half francs that she kept in a little
box – until the Emperor became angry because he needed
the money himself. Madame Mère grew resigned, and
Octave wrote this about her: *'She rarely leaves her house,
she spends her days with music and embroidery, goes up to
the Mulini Palace on Sundays for dinner, and often in the*

evenings to play revers with her son – and lose small sums,
because he cheats.'

These insignificant details could only have excited a
historian, but Octave left out the main thing: boredom.
They were all idle, that devoted little colony from France,
who were given miniature tasks to do. They passed the
time, they withered away and yawned – apart from the
treasurer, Peyrusse, who kept his accounts with exasperat-
ing equanimity. The daily walks and the inspection of the
building-sites became as monotonous as the soirées held
by the Emperor, to which he invited the dignitaries and
their wives so that he could demonstrate to them the
importance of the breeding of silkworms, or boast of the
exploits of his guards, who were reluctantly widening the
roads and planting vegetables. When the clock struck
nine, the Emperor would dismiss his guests by approaching the piano and, with the tip of his index finger, playing
notes that were always the same: CC GG AA G, FF EE
DD C. At this signal the guests would rise and rustle out
into the night.

Napoleon appeared content with this routine, even
imposing his own timetable upon himself, a typical day
unfolding thus: rising at three o'clock in the morning,
he read in his library (works of geography and Pluto's
life of Galba, which began with a warning to princes:
undisciplined troops are dangerous – perhaps recalling
his grenadiers who had been left behind in France,
ill-treated by the new powers, certainly prepared to
mutiny if the opportunity presented itself); after that,
imagining Louis XVIII suffering the same terrible fate as
Romanus, who was slaughtered by his own legionaries,

Napoleon would go for a walk, smiling at his kitchen garden, plucking a tomato or worrying about the size of his courgettes. He would retire to bed again at about eight o'clock, and sleep until lunch – usually served in the countryside on a table-cloth thrown on the grass – before a quick siesta under an apricot tree or one of the fig trees whose branches hung down to the ground. It was during one of these trips that the Emperor and Monsieur Pons de l'Hérault were reconciled.

*

At the bottom of his blossoming garden in Rio Marina, Monsieur Pons had a small shed where he often meditated on republican or moralistic tracts. He read to his two young daughters, Hermine and Pauline: in this instance, the text in question was a passage from Fénelon's book *Télémaque*, in which the author set out the nature of the ideal king in the simplest possible terms. Accustomed to his sermons, for he took charge of their education, the children listened to their father without moving from their stools, fanning themselves in the heat.

'Telemachus and his guide, on a Syrian ship . . .'

'What's Syrian?'

'Syria is a country in the East. So, they're on their way to Crete, a happy island where King Minos, famed for the wisdom of his laws, reigned long ago. The guide, who already knows this island, tells Telemachus what happens if you have a good government. I shall read: "*There is never any call for the repression of excess and flabbiness, for they are unknown in Crete. Everyone works there, and no one thinks of enriching himself . . .*"'

'So it isn't like the island of Elba, then, Papa?'

'You are right, Hermine, it isn't at all like the island of Elba. I shall continue: "*Everyone thinks that he receives enough pay for his work in a sweet and ordered life, where peace is enjoyed, and an abundance of all that is truly necessary for life . . ."*'

He read until he reached the passage in which Fénelon expatiates upon the virtues of a king: '"*He must have nothing more than anyone else, beyond that which is necessary, or to help him to perform his painful duties, or to win the people's respect for the one who must sustain the laws*" . . .'

'What's sustain?'

'Have them respected. "*The king must be more sober, more hostile to softness, more exempt from extravagance and arrogance than anyone else . . ."*'

'Are you alluding to our Emperor?'

Pons gave a start. Octave was standing against the door of the cabin, enjoying the lesson.

'We're studying Fénelon, Monsieur Sénécal.'

'I've read him. We brought that very same book from Fontainebleau.'

'I wouldn't have believed it.'

'Why? Because he speaks of wisdom? The Emperor will confirm as much himself. He awaits you.'

'You mean I have to go to Portoferraio right now?'

'No, he's here, on your terrace.'

'Really! To extort money from me, or put me in prison?'

'Perhaps to make you hear reason.'

'Reason? Ah, that lovely word. He had only to accept my resignation.'

The Emperor knew of the friendly relations that existed between Octave and Monsieur Pons, and had on several occasions sent Octave to Rio to soften the character of the mine administrator, but fruitlessly. Today he had made the journey himself and he really was waiting on the terrace, in the blue uniform and white lapels of the Elban National Guard – to show he was the master of this island, its inhabitants and its resources. On the coast road, Monsieur Pons could see Bertrand, Campbell, the treasurer Peyrusse, some lancers, horses and the carts carrying the tents and comestibles required for a lunch; Napoleon also stared towards the Italian coast, but saw a multitude of sails dancing by the port of Piombino. Without looking at Pons, he said: 'Are you going to let me have those two hundred thousand francs?'

'No.'

'Ah! So you've still got them.'

'But of course . . .'

'I was afraid you might have sent them to Paris.'

'The chancellor of the Légion d'Honneur is aware of your demand. I wrote to ask his advice.'

'You will wait a long time, Monsieur Pons.'

'He's a friend of mine, he'll answer me.'

'He won't.'

'We'll see.'

'It's already sorted out. Your friend Lacépède is no longer chancellor.'

Pons was thrown, and Napoleon took advantage of the fact.

'The Abbé de Pradt is replacing him. Have you heard of that traitor, who is up to something with Talleyrand? He's wished me dead since I dismissed him from his embassy in Poland. An incompetent! Did you know that he boasted of having hastened the victory of the foreign armies? Do you want to give the money from our mines to the royalists you have always fought against? The *ancien régime* has returned, Monsieur Pons, as though neither of us had ever existed.'

The administrator thoughtfully wiped his glasses.

'Fetch your horse from the stable and come with me.'

Monsieur Pons obeyed mechanically, joining the outing to the countryside, trotting beside Octave. He was torn in two. Did his principles still apply? The allied sovereigns had formed a league against the Emperor, and given France to the Bourbons, ousting the man they still saw as the representative of the Revolution, the man who had terrified them so. The kings had never treated Napoleon as an equal, but rather as a parvenu, a gaudy representative of the middle classes, the accomplice of regicides. Whom should he serve? The Bourbons? Anything but that. The coaches stopped by the only real forest on the island, where the road narrowed to a path.

'Give me your cane, Monsieur Sénécal,' said the Emperor. 'I wish to climb on to that high plateau. Come with me, Pons, you can tell me about the landscape.'

Leaning on Octave's cane, which had broken many a neck and crushed a good few skulls on behalf of his cause, Napoleon was in a state of delight. He identified each variety of tree, he leaned forward to breathe in the scent of the plants whose virtues he listed. At the top, in a jaunty mood, he considered the panorama and then, looking at a pile of carved stones, he observed to Pons, 'They're the remains of a Roman temple, I was told . . .'

'Whoever told you was exaggerating, sire, it was only

a tower built in the Middle Ages by the inhabitants of Rio. It was from here that they watched the Barbary pirates.'

'Whatever the truth of it, stones wear down as men do, isn't that right? What will remain of us, monsieur? A pile of stones? A legend if we're lucky? Certainly not the reality of what we were. Was Tiberius as monstrous as Suetonius claims? Suetonius was a viper, an aristocrat jealous of power, and there you have it. The image of Tiberius has been fixed for eternity by a jealous man. Whom do we trust? No one, you see, no one is safe from the blows of fate . . . Pons?'

'Sire?'

'What do we see there, on the horizon?'

'The Gulf of Spezia, and then, following the ridges, you reach Genoa, and here are the Livorno roads, there, at the tip of my finger . . .'

'Filled with fishing boats, yes, at least a thousand of them. They look like butterflies. This place is divine, you could plant a garden here.' (Napoleon pointed to a corner of bare ground.) 'Next to it I would place a tank, in that grove, and a covered path under the trees down to the sea, with little farms down below, and cattle . . .' (He sat down on a pile of broken stones.) 'Ah, Pons! See how busy my mind is, spending money that I haven't got.'

As Pons said nothing, the two men walked towards the clearing where the valets had thrown the tablecloth for their meal. The Emperor grew bucolic and quoted Latin poets, but also spoke of more practical matters such as his farming projects, the fields of wheat on the little island of Pianosa where no one lived now but wild horses, the revival of coral-fishing . . . Everyone noticed that he was speaking only to the administrator, who was dazzled by such familiarity. Because of his many acts of disobedience Monsieur Pons had fully expected to see his iron mines confiscated; instead, the Emperor was offering him – and only him – a glass of pink champagne. The Emperor even let him share his own cup of mocha: 'Let us drink to the health of our island!' Monsieur Pons was oblivious to the fact that the Emperor knew how to woo the most recalcitrant people if his menaces failed. Smiles and acts of kindness had often been more effective than cannon and Monsieur Pons duly succumbed to this offensive. The very next day he gave Peyrusse the 200,000 francs that he had been keeping for the Légion d'honneur.

*

Octave was violently awoken by a series of explosions. Gunfire, he thought immediately, getting up and parting the curtains to see Elbans running in the street. 'Whassa goin' on?' Gianna asked him, in that groggy voice that people sometimes have when they're dragged prematurely from sleep. 'Gunfire.' Octave quickly dressed, his face anxious, and when Gianna said to him, 'You goin'?' his reply was emphatic: 'Yes, I'm going. I've got to know.' She threw the blanket over her face, bothered by the bright light, and sighed; Octave stroked her hair and left the room, depositing some gold coins on a pedestal table.

Downstairs, he passed through the Buono Gusto café, which the landlord arranged as a dormitory each night for travellers who had not found lodgings elsewhere. Octave stepped over some rolled-up mattresses and over some late sleepers and out into the Via Gran Bastione. The people gathered there were animated but not frenzied, chatting quite cheerfully about a rumour that was going around. Octave was mingling with a group of people, hoping to learn more, when he spotted the deputy mayor.

'Who were they shooting at?'

'No one, Monsieur Sénécal.'

'I'm not deaf!'

'Some tearaways lit firecrackers.'

'Why?'

'To celebrate, I think. An unflagged brig has dropped anchor in the bay.'

'So?'

'The customs men have gone aboard.'

'As usual.'

'Not exactly, Monsieur Sénécal.'

'What have the customs men found that's so unusual?'

'The Empress and the King of Rome, that's what, and our island is preparing to salute the event. As we speak!'

Octave stood gawping. He couldn't believe it. The previous week, he knew, the Emperor had dispatched one of his Guard captains to Aix-les-Bains. The husband of one of Marie-Louise's ladies-in-waiting, he was to reach the Empress through her, and persuade her to set sail for Elba – but how could he have achieved his goal so quickly, without a hitch? Nonetheless, some customs men had talked to the Neapolitan sailors on the brig: among their passengers were a fair-haired young woman and a little boy of four or five who talked about his 'Emperor Papa'.

Octave walked beneath the trees to the town hall, passing through clusters of chattering people, each repeating the news and amplifying it with a thousand invented details. Count Bertrand was in his apartment, in his uniform, very alarmed.

'A plague upon the gossips, and upon this island!'

'How would one go about stopping them, your grace?'

'I don't know, and that's what's irritating me.'

'Can't you deny it?'

'No.'

'Because it's true?'

'Not that either.'

'But the customs men didn't make it up . . .'

'No.'

'And it's not about the Empress?'

'No, no, and thrice no!'

'Then what is it, your grace?'

'Madame Walewska.'

Octave had not heard these details before, but Bertrand was obliged to tell him now so he could help him defuse the false news without revealing the truth. In Fontainebleau, while the Empire was collapsing, only Marie Walewska had come to give Napoleon her support. Shaken by events, he had not received her; she had waited a whole night, on a sofa in a corridor, but that was not the end: in early August, her brother Teodor had come incognito to Elba to prepare the way for another visit. Then, just a few days ago, the Emperor had travelled to the hermitage of the Madonna, above Marciana Alta where he'd found a home for his mother; Portoferraio was blazing hot and airless, and the mountain seemed to provide a milder climate for the old lady. Sheltering behind that excuse, Napoleon was in fact waiting for his young Polish mistress. He had even sent her a letter in his own hand, which ended 'one hundred tender things'. It had all remained secret. On no account was anyone to know anything about the journey. The Emperor kept a close eye on the morals of his subjects, fulminated against cohabitation, drove his officers to marry Elban girls and refused to receive unmarried couples at the Mulini Palace. Since that was the case, how could he officially receive his mistress?

'Do you think we'll be able to quash the rumour?' asked Bertrand.

'Once a rumour is out, you can't hush it up, your grace . . .'

'Nonetheless, Madame Walewska won't be able to play the part of the Empress!'

'I can try to put the gossips on the wrong track . . .'

'Do as you wish, Monsieur Sénécal, but sort this matter out! Come and see me in two hours in the Imperial stables.'

On the parade ground, the townspeople were already hanging Chinese lanterns from the branches of the chestnut trees. Octave walked towards the deputy, who was in charge of the operation.

'These illuminations are premature, Monsieur Hutré.'

'What? You mean the good news is bad?'

'Somewhere in between . . .'

'Is it the Empress or is it not?'

'Yes, it is she, with her son, aboard the Neapolitan ship, but they will not be staying for long.'

'What?'

'They're stopping here briefly before going to Parma, or Rome, I can't remember, but anyway, they'll be back this winter when everything is ready to welcome them properly.'

The mayor's deputy, crestfallen, indicated that he understood, but added, 'How are we going to explain this disappointment to our compatriots?'

'Simple. You need only take down your lanterns, and when the people ask you why, you will tell them what I have just said to you.'

'They'll never believe me.'

'Lower your voice. Say to anyone who asks, "Just don't repeat it." In an instant, the whole island will know.'

*

A coach and four was waiting in an olive grove, near the hamlet of San Giovanni beside the bay. The coachman and his valets, lying in a heap in the shade of the coach, were drinking warm water from a leather bottle, passing it from hand to hand. Further away, saddled horses and mules were tethered to tree-trunks. On the pebbly beach, meanwhile, Bertrand and Octave stood about kicking their heels.

As dusk fell, Bertrand used his tinderbox to light a wood fire, already prepared on the shore. At that sign, a launch was lowered from the ship that lay a hundred yards off the coast. There was not a breath of wind, and the only sound that could be heard was the oars dipping rhythmically into the calm water. The coachman had sat back on the bench, and the valets were untethering the horses and the mules; Count Bertrand walked beside the waves, holding a lantern. The sailors, meanwhile, had reached the shore, carrying the first of the passengers, lest she wet the hem of her grey faille dress. Her face was hidden by a little veil, but Bertrand recognized her frail figure, her manners and her way of holding her son by the hand – it was Marie. Next came her sister Emilie, then Teodor, her brother, soaked to the knees.

They wasted no time. Once their luggage had been tied on to the back of the mules, they drove along the shore, two grooms pointing the way with their lanterns. Cliffs, valleys and hills, for two hours; a vineyard, lined with cactuses, led down to a creek. The procession passed through the village of Biadola and stopped further along, on the road to Proccio, where a lantern was seen swinging in the darkness. The Emperor, seated on his horse and wearing his ordinary colonel's uniform, handed the light to a lancer escort, before dismounting and opening the door of his berlin. Marie lifted her veil and Napoleon kissed her hand, hugged little Alexandre, their son – who barely stirred from his sleep – and greeted Teodor and young Emilie. The caravan then continued at a trot, trusting to the moon and the pale glow of the lanterns.

Not long after midnight, in Marciana Alta, the party had to abandon the berlin to make their way down a track of flat stones with streamlets trickling through it. Napoleon took little Alexandre, who might easily have been mistaken for the King of Rome, and wedged the sleeping child between his fat belly and the saddle. On they rode in file, the Emperor and the ladies on mules, the men on foot carrying torches. Finally, at the end of a tunnel of chestnut trees they emerged outside the hermitage of the Madonna. The chapel's crenellated bell-tower, with its Moorish arrow-slits, stood out against the moon. There was no sound, except for the fountains bubbling in their sculpted basins. All the birds were sleeping. The air was mild, and smelled of mint and turpentine. The Imperial tent was set up outside. Supper awaited the travellers.

Sitting at table by torchlight, they talked of their crossing, the calm of the island, the late summer heat. Napoleon complimented young Emilie, who, despite his famous uniform, thought he looked like a large landowner. The Emperor said to Marie Walewska: 'Countess, why would your sister not marry a French officer?' They laughed, ate and drank cool drinks. Raised up on cushions, little Alexandre sat sleepily on his armchair, and his father teased him.

'Let me eat!' the child protested with his mouth full. His directness amused everyone, but Napoleon had eyes only for Marie, blonde and graceful, an ermine scarf around her shoulders. She was to take the waters at Lucca or Pisa, she had not yet made up her mind, she said — but in fact she was going to Italy for the sake of Alexandre, who had come into an endowment in the kingdom of Naples. (Marie was planning to visit Murat: he was the one who was responsible for Marie's relationship with Napoleon, for it was he who had selected her to distract the Emperor during the rainy winter of 1806 in Warsaw. Now she wanted Murat to give her the payment due to her son, and ensure that he did not sequester the income previously granted by the Emperor.)

Eventually everyone withdrew, tired after a long day; the visitors to the modest bedrooms of the hermitage — the caretaker having been relegated to the cellar — and Napoleon and Bertrand to their tent. Everyone else, the chamberlain, the valets and the guards, climbed down the path to Marciana, while Octave chose to spend the night under the open sky, more or less, to keep watch on the surrounding area from one of the wooden workmen's huts that lined the route of the village's annual procession, and which were used as storehouses for the rest of the year. When rain started falling, gently at first, but soon turning into a storm, he was happily sheltered from the lightning and the rain.

*

'Sénécal!'

Napoleon came out of his tent half dressed. Octave came running, with shaving foam on his chin.

'Where were you?'

'Sire, I was shaving in the sacristy.'

'In the sacristy? Scoundrel! Hurry up, we're going to Marciana.'

No doubt he planned to visit Madame Mère, and Octave wielded his cut-throat razor with such haste that he nicked one of his cheeks, cursing and splashing himself with spring water. Just as he reached the tent, Dr Foureau de Beauregard was arriving astride a donkey. He was glistening and red in the face; a handkerchief protruded from his hat to shield the back of his neck from the sun. He proffered his services in a distinguished voice.

'Sire, here I am.'

'Unfortunately, so I see!'

'I thought the queen and the heir to the throne might need a doctor.'

'They're absolutely fine. But how do you know they are with me?'

'I have ears, sire, and good eyes. The inhabitants of

Portoferraio are talking only of this, and are preparing their reception as we speak.'

Napoleon turned to Octave. 'The Grand Marshal swore to me that you had sorted this problem out, and yet the gossips are still at it?'

'I tried to throw them off course, sire.'

'And where is the Grand Marshal?'

'Count Bertrand has joined his wife in town, sire; she may be about to give birth . . .'

'I had forgotten. Go and get me Count Alexandre.'

Octave slipped into the hermitage and reappeared with the child, who was pouting just as his father did. The Emperor sat down on a chair he'd placed in the grass, and took his son on his knees.

'What do you think of him, you charlatan?'

'The King has grown . . .'

'Go back to town and don't talk to anyone. The boy and his mother must set off again, but they will be back.'

Drenched in sweat but happy to have discovered a secret, the tedious doctor left the company amid a flurry of little bows, and mounted his donkey. Octave was amused: the Emperor had used the same argument and almost the same words as Octave himself to throw off the rumour. People who have a secret like to repeat it to win the praise of those around them, but there was no point in doing that here because the people of Elba heard only what they wanted to hear, and denials, however well disguised, went nowhere.

Nonetheless, the doctor's visit changed the plan, and there was no longer any question of going down to Marciana. The meal, cooked in Madame Mère's residence, was already being carried up from the village in large baskets strapped to the backs of mules. Traditi, the Mayor of Portoferraio, led the food convoy; he had been promoted to chamberlain, and his breast swelled in his new embroidered costume. They lunched in the tent, His Majesty carving the meat like a bourgeois entertaining in his country retreat. The conversation remained determinedly trivial – much was said, but it was all about nothing – and the Emperor left before dessert because he needed to be alone.

Accompanied by a batman and one of the grenadiers in charge of security, Octave watched after his master, not losing sight of him until the moment he entered the chapel. It was there, at about one in the afternoon, that the chamberlain brought the Emperor his son and Countess Walewska as he had requested. Soon afterwards, Octave saw them emerging together. Marie had opened her umbrella, and the Emperor carried little Alexandre on his shoulders. They walked up a path lined with the bright green prickly pears that grew in the dry earth among the rocks; they breathed in the perfume of late mauve cyclamens, and walked like any family taking a Sunday stroll.

Alone, and spied upon only from a distance, they were neither sovereign nor countess, they spoke without protocol, which is to say that Napoleon set off on long monologues inspired by the landscape of his tiny kingdom.

'These colours, these smells, are Corsica, Marie. If you had any idea how lost I was the first time my father dispatched Joseph and me to the Continent. We were very isolated, but he was older than I and destined for the seminary. I was not then ten, and locked away in a boarding school, in Autun, to learn French, which I didn't speak at all. No orange trees flowered in the spring, there were no mountains, there was no sun, no scrubland smell. We ate heavy meat, drowned in brown gravy to hide the fact it had gone off. I was puny and wild, I wanted to run in the forest, I wanted to throw stones. The others laughed at my small size and my accent; oh, Marie, how I loathed the French!'

They had reached the promontory from which Corsica could be seen, to the left Capraja, on the right Pianosa, and far behind, Montecristo. 'From Bastia too,' Napoleon said, 'you can make out the islands.' A strong breeze gusted in from the sea, and, on the way back, the Emperor interrogated his son, who was striking the bracken with a switch.

'Do you have any friends, Alexandre?'

'He is as serious and solitary as you were,' his mother replied.

'Which do you prefer, learning to read or horse-riding?'

'I have a little horse, but I've fallen off it twice.'

'I've fallen off a horse as well.'

'But if you fall it's not the same.'

'Why's that?'

'Because I don't get hurt.'

The Emperor burst out laughing, as he did only with children. He had often surrounded himself with them, especially in Saint-Cloud, where they had played around him as he had his lunch – first his official son, who was allowed to get away with anything, and who was allowed to drink the Emperor's Chambertin mixed with water, and then his nephews, whom he enjoyed teasing. Everyone at the palace knew that if you wanted something done, the best idea was to send a child. Napoleon continued interrogating Alexandre.

'I'm told you never mention my name in your prayers?'

'Never.'

'So you never think of me?'

'Yes, I do, but I say "Emperor Papa".'

Napoleon opened the box of sweets that he always carried in his pocket, and took out a piece of liquorice.

'I want some too!' said Alexandre.

'You won't like the flavour.'

'I will!'

The child took a piece of liquorice and spat it out, but when the Emperor laughed at him he got annoyed.

'I want to try it, to find out if I like it or not!'

'He's quite right,' said Napoleon to Marie. 'Splendid fellow!'

The family continued on its walk, calmly bantering. Down below, a shepherd was guiding his flock. Napoleon called to him and the man ran away.

'Did you frighten him?' Alexandre asked in surprise.

'I frighten lots of people, you know . . .'

'I'm not afraid of you!'

'That's lucky.'

They took advantage of this rare time together by making up games. Alexandre's parents spent ages pretending to look for him as he hid behind a big round brown rock, then it was the turn of the Countess, the child finding her straight away because her dress was sticking out from behind a pine trunk. As the boy was counting to ten, wrapped in his mother's arms, the Emperor lay silently beside an enormous clump of tree-like ferns. The boy ran hither and thither calling out to his father. All of a sudden, the Emperor, still prostrate, found himself surrounded by people he had not heard approaching; registering their scarlet breeches with double blue stripes, Napoleon recognized his Polish lancers and said, in a low and very discontented voice, 'What the hell are you doing here?'

'We thought Your Majesty had taken a bad fall . . .'

'Idiots! Can't you see I'm busy?'

'We didn't know . . .'

'I'm playing hide and seek, and I don't need you!'

The lancers sheepishly withdrew, but treasurer Peyrusse, who was with them, put his account books down on the moss and helped the Emperor to his feet.

'Peyrousse! You too! Will you never leave me in peace?'

'I wanted to give Your Majesty a report on our tax revenue, and the fines that we're imposing on the prostitutes in the harbour, who are growing considerably more numerous . . .'

'Couldn't that wait for a couple of days?'

'Got you! Got you!' cried Alexandre, gambolling towards them.

*

At dawn the following morning, Octave went into the tent where the Emperor was calling for him. He had a sore head, because dinner under the chestnut trees, to which he had been invited as a replacement for Bertrand, had gone on for ever. A Polish officer of the lancers had played a nostalgic tune, and the guests had joined together to sing songs that sang the praises of Warsaw and the

Vistula. Emilie had danced like an angel, in short boots, and her skirt held up above her knees. Marie had even persuaded the Emperor to dance a mazurka, laughing at his ungainliness.

Once the mists had cleared, Octave found the Emperor in a feverish state; he was waving a letter from Drouot that a dispatch rider had just delivered.

'Monsieur Sénécal, get me a pen from my case, quickly! Portoferraio is decked with flags and they aren't allowing the woman they think is the Empress to leave! Even the Guard have signed a petition! It's infernal! Write!'

'I'm ready, sire,' said Octave, pen in the air above a pedestal table.

'The Neapolitan brig is to head for the high seas.'

'The ... high ... seas ...'

'She is to turn to the west ...'

'West ...'

'Follow the coast and heave to off Marciana Marina, three miles from our hermitage.'

'Hermitage ...'

'No! Stop at the name of the fishing port, cretin! Countess Walewska and her family will leave at nightfall from the nearest port. Copy and send to Drouot.'

Emerging from the tent, Octave stepped aside to let Marie enter.

'You didn't tell me you were short of money,' said Marie.

'I'm not short of anything,' replied the Emperor, surprised and brittle.

'Yes, I know.'

'Ah, you've been talking to that damned Peyrousse!'

The Countess set a well-wrapped package on the same

pedestal table that Octave had used to write his missive for Drouot.

'What are you doing, Marie?'

'Since you're sending me away, I won't be wearing these jewels any more.'

'I'm sending you away?'

'All right, then, give me a little house, and I'll stay with our son.'

'Elba is a village, it's impossible, you would be the subject of all kinds of awful gossip . . .'

'The Empress and the King of Rome will never join you.'

'Marie-Louise wants to, and my son is demanding it.'

'Austria is opposed to it.'

Once the Countess had left, the Emperor opened the package. The cases contained brooches, earrings, brace lets, even the necklace he had given her after the birth of Alexandre. He closed the boxes, and no one saw him again before evening. He had gone hunting, he claimed, with an officer and some guns – but he had found no game, not a single hare, not even a partridge.

The last dinner was sadder than the ones that preceded it, and more serious. The Emperor talked ceaselessly, seeking no replies, and speaking on various topics, passing from one to the other without transition. He explained the necessity of clearing undergrowth from the forests, and raising sheep. He commented on the reports that partisans were bringing from France, where royalists were arousing the people's hatred with their haughtiness and abuse. He quoted newspaper articles and spoke of Marie-Louise.

At last the time came for the Polish family to leave.

The weather was sultry, the clouds black; a mackerel sky, swollen with rain. The coach bounced along from Marciana Alta to Marciana Marina, from the mountain to the sea, and the horses were nervous. The sound of squeaking wheels and the clip-clop of the hoofs rang out, amplified by the deceptive, heavy calm that comes before a storm. After a quarter of a league, the Emperor said his goodbyes and handed out presents: to Marie, he offered the envelope containing her jewels, which he did not wish her to part with. She was not to open it until later on. Then he gave a trinket-box to Emilie, and toys and sweets to little Alexandre, who, alarmed by the distant thunder, was huddled in the depths of the berlin. Napoleon then returned to the hermitage, leaving a cavalry squadron as an escort. He was in his tent when the rain lashed the canvas, filling it with pockets of water. The storm burst, the thunder grew more intense and came ever closer, while flashes of lightning cast a blue glow on the tiles of the chapel. Napoleon grew worried: his lips trembled and he wrung his hands. Would Marie be able to embark without putting herself in danger? Would the brig be smashed to pieces on the reefs, so numerous all along the coast? The Emperor became furious as he imagined the disaster. He slipped on his frock-coat, put on his hat and called to his servants. Once again he happened upon Octave, who was playing cards in the chapel with some guards, by a faint night-light. Following orders, Octave straddled a mule – less swift than a horse, but safer – and set off in search of news, his vision blurred with rain and a lashing wind. He hurtled along in the darkness, skirting the wall and the densely packed trees, down the narrow path with which he was by now so familiar, to Marciana

Marina. He couldn't see the ship's lights. Could the ship have cast off already? Where was she? And what about her passengers? The captain of the port, dragged from his bed, informed him: 'They've gone, Monsieur.'

'But where to? On the brig? In a storm like that?'

'No, they couldn't board, Monsieur, but before the clouds broke I gave signals to warn the boat to make for Cape Vita and anchor at Porto Longone. The bay is sheltered, Monsieur, in Porto Longone.'

'And the passengers?'

'It's just that the sailing boat was turning over her anchors . . .'

'I understand! *What about the passengers?*'

'They were caught in the gale, weren't they? It even put out their torches, but they left anyway, for Porto Longone. They may even have reached the ship by now, but I can't tell you about that, Monsieur.'

His clothes drenched, his hat dripping with water, Octave retraced his steps and informed the Emperor, who was impatiently striking the chairs in the chapel with his whip. Then Octave called to a lieutenant of the lancers: 'Round up ten men, we're going!'

Thunder, lightning, a deluge, panicking horses, the road slipping beneath them in the downpour, they rode for the rest of the night and arrived at dawn, exhausted, mud-caked, by the bay of Porto Longone. The hurricane had not subsided, but Marie's ship was already bound for Naples.

Five

IN HELL

'Shepherds, shepherds, the wolf is wrong
Only when he is the weaker:
Shall he live a hermit's life?'

La Fontaine, *The Wolf and the Shepherds*,
Tenth book, fable V

IN NOVEMBER, life on the island changed. The Guard's
bugles, which rang out in the fortresses, still woke
Portoferraio, and in the evening the rubbish-collector's
trumpet, outside every door, brought the day to a close.
But everything softened once Princess Pauline had been
definitively installed on the island. The life of the people of
Elba became less military. A Paris fashion-designer opened
a trinket shop near the harbour and it prospered, because
there was a succession of parties. There was dancing at
the Mulini Palace, in the drawing-rooms and the public
squares newly lit by new street lights. *'His Majesty is
devoting himself to the decoration of the town, as well as
road-building and defence,'* Octave wrote in his notebooks.
*'Princess Pauline is setting the tone. On a little square, half-
way up the slope, the church of St Francis was used as a store
of food and clothing for the garrison, and now the Empress*

has decided to turn it into a theatre. As we are not rich, because the salt-works and the vines bring in little revenue, and more particularly because the King of France is not paying the two million promised in income by the Treaty of Fontainebleau, the Emperor has listened to good old Peyrusse, who has wonderfully imaginative ways of saving money. The treasurer has invented a company of purchasers, appropriately named the "Academy of the Fortunate", which allows the Elbans to buy a box or a seat in the theatre for life. This dodge will have to finance the works, because they are going to cost a fortune, just think: four tiers of galleries! An artist has come from Piedmont to paint the curtain, and he has already presented his designs: they will show Apollo instructing some shepherds; feature for feature the god will resemble His Majesty, who really is giving agricultural advice to the peasants he has met on his walks. The other morning the Emperor told one of them what to do to ensure that his radishes were neither tasteless nor too peppery, for he draws his gardening knowledge from assiduous reading of La Maison Rustique . . .'

There were picnics in the countryside, fruit-picking, farandoles, outings in boats full of oranges and cool water, masked balls. Pauline also persuaded the prettier Elban girls and young officers to perform light comedies with her. The Guard band gave concerts. Each day at noon, children marched on to the parade ground alongside grenadiers, grave-faced with wooden swords and paper hats, to the applause of the tourists.

Octave filled his notebooks with accounts of these anodyne festivities, but anxiety lurked behind that carefree façade: Napoleon's adversaries were relentlessly conspiring against his life. Since contact with the Continent had never been fully severed, messages reached Octave's ears, and foreign visitors became a marvellous substitute for newspapers. Lord Douglas, Lord Ebrington, Nordic princes and noble Prussians brought the Emperor confidential messages about the latest events. Others issued warnings. Some Bavarians claimed to know of a German league that was planning Napoleon's execution. Others confided that a group of fanatical monks, who had journeyed from Rome dressed as innocent bourgeois, were waiting for the right moment to stab the Emperor to death. Poggi, the Chief of Police, had learned of the presence of agents of the Great Duke of Tuscany, but spies were swarming on the island in a thousand different disguises. Octave reflected with a smile that they were gleaning only distorted and unusable scraps of gossip; amateurs spying on each other, while he alone controlled the real informer of Talleyrand and the Bourbons, Signor Forli, whom he showered with reassuring and fabricated confidences.

Nonetheless, there were still many very serious threats, so Octave had helped Poggi to reinforce security, as discreetly as possible in order to preserve that climate of deliberate nonchalance for the eyes of the outside world. Monsieur Seno, who owned fisheries, had been appointed as a batman, and now accompanied the Emperor everywhere he went, carrying two loaded pistols. When the Emperor travelled, gendarmes were posted along his route, and five cheveau-légers, armed with muskets, followed his coach. Vigilance was never relaxed now, even at the Mulini Palace. The guests at Napoleon's official dinners were the first to notice.

Such a dinner took place one Sunday evening in

November. The guests were the regular visitors to the Imperial table: officers, traders, owners of salt-works or tuna-fish pounds, town councillors who sometimes brought their daughters along in outrageously costly muslin dresses. They showed cards bearing Bertrand's signature and passed through a double row of light-cavalrymen, whose bare sabre gleamed in the torchlight, and into the drawing-room. The chamberlain arranged them around the table, where they sat slightly stiff, exchanging meaningless formulas in an undertone. On Monsieur Pons's arm was his wife, who was not fond of parties, but who attended out of politeness, not once opening her mouth because of her southern accent, which she considered too singsong and inappropriate for this kind of soirée.

'I can't see His Majesty,' Pons said to Cambronne.

'He's over there,' the General replied, pointing to an open double-door.

The Emperor was sitting at his table in the adjacent library. Next to him sat Madame Mère, her cheeks painted heavily with rouge. The room was more easily observed from the garden outside, where Pons noticed sentries pacing about; he could also make out Octave's broad-brimmed hat.

Light from the upstairs window fell on the garden, and Octave asked one of the sentries, 'Has the Princess not come down for dinner?'

'She is unwell, Monsieur Sénécal.'

'What's wrong with her this evening?'

'She has the vapours as usual.'

'Go and get me the list of guests. Your officer must have kept the cards . . .'

'If it's an order . . .'

'It is.'

The grenadier departed. Octave stood by the half-open French door, able to view the Emperor from behind, chatting as he chewed on his game fricassée.

'I've had some good news, I must tell you . . .'

Napoleon rose to his feet, napkin knotted around his neck, and — after swallowing down a nice mouthful of rabbit in sauce — moved into the drawing-room, whereupon the guests automatically rose to their feet, each in turn. The Emperor motioned to them to sit down and continued, circling behind his guests, who no longer dared to eat, and simply stared at the food cooling on their plates.

'We're about to solve the wheat problem. The island, as you know, takes in only two months' worth of stores per annum, and has to import grain, which is costing our treasury dearly. This will have to stop: we must strive for self-sufficiency. This week I met a man from Genoa, and I am going to give him the land on the island of Pianosa to colonize with at least a hundred families from the Continent. In return for that concession he will grow wheat and that, by my calculations, should provide five additional months in the granaries . . .'

No one stirred. The guests had come to listen to His Majesty, and didn't risk giving their own opinion unless the Emperor specifically requested it.

'We must also buy some olive trees to replace the fig trees. We have too many of the latter, and they are damaging the vines. Pons?'

'Sire?' The administrator rose from his chair, fork in hand.

'You will go to the mainland and address this problem, returning with nurseries of olive and mulberry trees.'

'As Your Majesty wishes...'

'Stand where you are, since you are standing already, and tell us what you heard the other night on the rampart.'

'Well,' said Monsieur Pons, clearing his throat, 'there I was walking on the rampart, just beneath the windows of my apartment in Portoferraio. Down below, as you know, there is a sentry post, and the soldiers talk to one another, and voices rise. A corporal from Marseille was talking about our return to France.'

'Listen carefully to this, Campbell,' said the Emperor with a laugh. 'You'll be able to tell them in London!'

'Oh, sire...'

'None of your airs and graces, now, Colonel. Go on, Pons.'

'The corporal was saying to the others, who were heatedly encouraging him: "We are leaving for Malta in our flotilla, we'll take galleys there, and disembark at the mouth of the Danube. Constantinople will turn a blind eye. Afterwards, the Greeks will join us, we'll enter Belgrade, the Hungarians will come and swell our ranks, then the Poles, we'll take Vienna – and after that it's easy, we know the road from Vienna to Paris by heart!"'

'My soldiers have a vivid imagination, don't they?' joked the Emperor, sitting back down beside his mother.

'Our men have a lyrical spirit,' acknowledged Cambronne, whose undertaker's face failed to evince much enthusiasm.

'They're getting bored,' added Drouot, cutting up a cold rabbit-leg.

'Ah!' the Emperor resumed. 'People rebuke me for abandoning the fatherland. Perhaps they're right...'

*

The *Inconstant* dropped anchor in the roads. She was a square-sailed two-master, painted yellow and grey, and all that the allies had allowed the exile by way of a fleet. She had eighteen guns, but was used for freight; she would sail to Genoa or Civitavecchia, where she took on livestock, trees, visitors and message-carriers. Octave was standing on the jetty, watching the first launches leaving the ship, when Signor Forli, the jovial olive-oil merchant, gripped him by the shoulders.

'Hey! Anyone would think you were a policeman – you've got the right posture for it, the way you thrust your chest out, the way you carry your cane. Haven't you got anything for me today?'

'I'm waiting for some acorns.'

'Acorns?'

'The Emperor has ordered them from the Black Forest, he wants to plant some oak trees.'

'My word! Oaks take a long time to grow!'

'He's in no hurry.'

'Who knows what the future holds? I can't imagine him staying on our island for ever.'

'When you plant oak trees, you hope to see them grow.'

'He's just pretending.'

'Are you better informed than I am, Forli?'

'My friend Cambronne invited me to dinner in the Mulini Palace, on Sunday, and I'm not hard of hearing.

The Emperor is thinking of going to France. He's been dropping hints to that effect.'

'It's just a little joke to annoy Campbell.'

'Perhaps ... But accidents will happen.'

'Of what kind?'

'The Chevalier de Bruslart has just been appointed Governor of Corsica.'

Octave was stunned, but instinctively adopted a stupid expression, which provoked Forli to ask, 'Didn't they talk about Bruslart in London?'

'I vaguely remember something ...'

'It's simple. He has an ancient grudge to work off: Bonaparte ordered the shooting of his friend Frotté, the commander of the Norman insurrection, and Chouans like Bruslart don't forgive such things.'

'I see.'

'You should also understand that Bruslart has sent an emissary to Algiers to have a word with the pirates there, I have it from a good source ...'

'Pirates? What for?'

'Bonaparte sometimes goes sailing. If he disappeared, *in one way or another*, we could always blame the Algerine corsairs.'

'The Emperor hardly ever strays far from the coast.'

'But he does go to Pianosa. Tell me when he next goes to inspect the island.'

'So that you can tell the pirates?'

'No! We know he never sleeps on land, but always aboard the *Inconstant*.'

'That's true.'

'And that's where everything becomes possible.'

At that moment some launches drew up alongside the

mole with their passengers, including Lieutenant Taillade, who was commanding the brig only because no one else could be found. (It was said that this braggart went and hid in his cabin with the most terrible sea-sickness at the first hint of a squall.) As the oil merchant moved to greet the captain, things began to fall into place for Octave: the two men had an agreement. So His Majesty was no longer safe aboard his own ship? Apparently Taillade, the little squirt, was easily bribed. The crew? Hard to tell: some sailors might be persuaded to betray the Emperor – those press-ganged in the ports along the coast, in the taverns of Genoa or the dives of Capraia, badly paid, alert to the sound of gold coins. In addition, Octave couldn't help thinking about the damaging proximity of Bruslart: the oil merchant was a spy, but the *chouan* was a man of action. Octave knew him very well. The police had been after him for years, and even at the age of sixty his reputation had not diminished in the slightest. He was small, stocky, hairy as a black bear, and the police imagined they saw him all over the place, but hadn't been able find him anywhere. He drove the Prefects to distraction. sightings of him had been reported, always too late in each case, at the Auberge de la Poste, in Caen, and then in a *traiterie* in Bayeux, in Jersey, in Scotland, at the Palais-Royal. He was known to have spent the night with the languid and red-headed Madame de Vaubadon, or with one Demoiselle Banvelle, or with Mademoiselle Berruyer, who was believed to be his wife. He played hide and seek, he teased the cops, he made *beignets* with acacia-flower water for his lovely lodgers, and moved from manor-house to château under multiple identities. One day he was Petit, a Belgian merchant, the next, who knows . . .

Some grenadiers were unloading mail for the Mulini Palace from one of the *Inconstant*'s boats, along with sacks of grain and seed, but Octave made them pile the packages on to their carts and stand near the customs office, at the entrance to the Sea Gate. There he routinely kept an eye on the day's arrivals – often a good hundred of them, standing in a line – who would be directed towards the Forte Stella, where Cambronne's department would examine their passports. Some of the visitors would head for the town hall and request an audience with the Emperor.

That morning, to Octave's eyes, everyone looked like a possible criminal in the pay of the Chouan. Did that chap in his bourgeois clothes carry a stiletto in his waxed boot? Did that woman not hide a blade in the handle of her umbrella? Octave tried to detect any detail that did not match the person; a distinguished-looking sailor immediately aroused suspicion – and why was that fat man sweating? Was he apprehensive, as he prepared to commit his crime? Octave listened to the customs official who was now interviewing the man. Were there forests near Genoa? Did he have an accent? An NCO approached Octave.

'Everything's been loaded, Monsieur Sénécal.'

'Then let's get moving.'

Almost regretfully, Octave abandoned these tourists, who seemed to him as dangerous as vipers, to their own devices. As he left the mole, however, he noticed the oil merchant and Lieutenant Taillade laughing – which reinforced his fears – as they entered the Buono Gusto. To reassure himself, he gripped his cane more tightly, like a cudgel.

*

The Emperor's face was powdered, his mouth adorned with lipstick, and he wore a gaudy circus costume cut from garish coloured paper. Blindfold, he ran breathlessly among the tamarinds and oleanders in the garden. Pauline's pretty friends, her readers and dressers disguised as sylphs or columbines, darted away from him, uttering amused little cries. He caught one by the arm and drew her towards him; while she pretended to struggle and protested, with a little giggle. The Emperor tried to kiss her, and she twisted her head in all directions as he smeared her lips with his comical big mouth, exclaiming, 'It's Charlotte! I'm sure it's Charlotte!' Finally the Emperor let go of his prey and pulled off his blindfold.

'I win!'

'Bravo, sire! Bravo!' laughed the girls of his harem, dressed in gauze and yellow cardboard wings. Campbell had been observing this scene, and now Octave appeared at the edge of the lawn, and came to join the Colonel. Campbell's face was serious, and he said with consternation, 'The man who won the Battle of Austerlitz is playing Blind Man's Buff.'

'Aren't you going to join in?'

'The very idea!'

'But why are they all got up like trollops?' asked Octave.

'It's an idea that Princess Pauline came up with for her Thursday masked ball.'

'What are you coming as, Colonel?'

'Monsieur Sénécal, please!'

'You can't be serious all the time.'

'Don't you find this spectacle appalling?'

'His Majesty must be allowed to relax.'

'There are a thousand other ways, all the same!'

'Don't you like my new uniform, Campbell?' asked the Emperor, coming to stand in front of them, while the belles fled up the hidden staircase behind the pots of myrtle and geraniums in the kitchen, to Pauline's bathroom. The Englishman sighed, stammered an incomprehensible phrase that delighted the Emperor, saluted, and withdrew.

'Doesn't he like innocent games?'

'He thinks you're reverting to childhood, sire.'

'Excellent. I'm reverting to childhood. Excellent! The people must be told, Monsieur Sénécal. Do you bring mail? News? Both? Come to my study.'

The Emperor fell into an armchair. His make-up was running because he had been exerting himself. He looked like a ham actor at the end of his career. With his harlequin sleeve, he wiped away the sweat pearling on his forehead.

'All this slap and tickle is exhausting!'

'As regards that girl Charlotte . . .'

'I guessed right, did you see that?'

'Sire, we know she has affiliations with Police Headquarters in Paris.'

'You told me that last week. That's fine! That proves we still have some loyal people in this house, and they keep us informed. The girl is very appealing, though, so why shouldn't we let her earn her livelihood with a bit of half-cocked spying. And anyway, I caught her on purpose – I had a hole in my blindfold – and now she'll write a report, she'll say I'm a great big child with the lecherous tastes of an old man. A pretty portrait that will reassure Louis XVIII.'

Octave mentioned Bruslart. At the name, the Emperor struck out at his roll-top desk and then tore up his paper tabard. He took a deep breath, closed his black-rimmed eyes tight and regained control of himself.

'Let's go through our mail.'

Two grenadiers had set the sack down nearby, on the tiles; Octave untied and opened it, pulling out armfuls of letters and brochures which he deposited on a trestle-table pushed against the wall. As in the Tuileries or at Saint-Cloud, as in the days of the *cabinet noir*, the censors' office run by Monsieur de Lavalette, his Majesty greedily read the correspondence of his entourage before they did. The difference was that in Portoferraio if he broke the seals, there was no need to stick them back together to put people off the scent: the recipients would simply blame the French or the Austrian police. Gloating as he discovered the love affairs of a general or the moods of a baron, Napoleon momentarily forgot Bruslart in Corsica, forgot the threat that he posed. Octave, meanwhile, sorted the newspapers into two packages: for and against. (While Campbell brought the English newspapers, Bertrand had subscribed under fantastic names to the main journals of France, Germany and Austria, which were sent to an address in Naples. A dispatch rider then brought them to Piombino, and from there they set off for Elba, in the packet boat or aboard the *Inconstant*.)

'Help me, Monsieur Sénécal,' said the Emperor, pushing a pile of unopened letters in front of Octave. 'Find me something spicy.'

Octave opened a letter that had come from Verdun — the mother of a garrison soldier replying to her son. After reading a few lines, Octave began to laugh gently.

'What foolishness have you discovered, Monsieur Séné-cal, that amuses you so?'

'Some news from France, sire. It's hardly academic, but you might like it . . .'

'I'm listening.'

'It's a good peasant woman, sire. She's writing to Sergeant Paradis, her son. I will decipher her words for you:

> I love you all the more for knowin as how your near our
> Loyle empror. Thats what Good people do. I can ashure
> you that their comin from the fore corners of the town to
> read your Letter, and that Evryone says your an honrable
> Man. The bourbons arent finished and we do not like
> these People. Marmont was kild in a Dual by one of ours,
> and France has divorced him. Ive nothing to tell you
> just that I Pray to God and make your Sister pray for the
> emprar and King.

The Emperor asked for the letter to be read three times, but did not laugh, he was touched. After a silence, he said to Octave: 'See to it that Cambronne gives ten gold coins to that soldier.'

'Why, sire?'

'Because of that letter, for heaven's sake!'

'You aren't supposed to have read it . . .'

'Ah, yes. Let's wait for the soldier to read it to his comrades to give them a sense of what's going on in the country. The others will talk about it, we'll pretend to catch wind of it, and then we'll be able to reward him quite naturally . . .'

*

Twice a year on Elba, tuna-fishing provided an opportunity for a party. Monsieur Seno, the orderly, was still the owner of a major fish-pound and had invited the Emperor and most of the worthies of Portoferraio to participate in his autumn fishing expedition. At daybreak, a multitude of boats crossed the roads in all directions – and in apparent confusion – but the men, hammering the water with the flat of their oars, were in fact driving the fish into a vast system of nets stretched on stakes they had secured in the sea bed. Caught in this meshy labyrinth, fish could not escape to the open sea, and so were forced towards the coast, where fishermen, up to their waists in the waves, were watching for them, harpoons at the ready. The moment the fishermen spotted the armour plating of large, steely blue scales in the clear water, they struck, grazing or wounding the fish; in a sea red with blood, the tuna thrashed with pain, twisted away and surged back, trapped; they writhed, collided with the stakes, got tangled up in the nets, squirmed and struggled until they were exhausted, and let themselves drift, half-dead, to the weapons that finally pierced them through. Then the fishermen had only to catch them by the tail or the gills to throw them on to the sand where they wriggled and opened their mouths for one final gasp. Other men then bundled the bodies on to carts that took them to the fisheries, long single-storey buildings that looked like sheds; there the fish would be scaled, cut up and marinaded in the olive oil bought from Signor Forli – who was doubtless already rubbing his hands with glee.

Standing on the shore in the shade of parasols, Monsieur Seno explained this practice to the Emperor and the guests, most of whom were unfamiliar with the manner in which tuna were caught in the Mediterranean. Words were not enough for Napoleon, however: he wanted to join in. A boy brought him a harpoon, which the Emperor brandished like a lance. He strode into the water – with his boots still on – and, clutching the weapon in both hands, as though charging an Austrian division all by himself, jabbed the waves at random as soon as he spotted a gleaming shape, guffawing each time he plunged the weapon between the fins and felt the tuna resisting or getting away. He yelled, 'I'll get you! I'll get you and I'll eat you raw!' When he did succeed in stabbing a fish, he rejoiced at his catch, blood and water drenching his National Guard uniform. He returned, soaked, bloody and breathless, to the parasols.

'Doesn't that make you feel like having a go, Bertrand?'

'Far from it, sire.'

'Nonsense! You don't get nearly enough exercise! It would do you a power of good.'

Count Bertrand only came to the Villa now if the Emperor invited him; he seldom accompanied him on his walks around the island, and hid instead in his apartments in the town hall with Fanny, his wife. The couple's youngest son had suffocated in his cradle at the age of three weeks, and since that tragedy Bertrand was a sorry sight. He had never been a cheerful person, but now his face was growing longer and longer with this recent misery. Nonetheless, the Emperor went needling, 'For his own good,' he said; but every day Napoleon visited Fanny to console her.

Monsieur Seno suggested a visit to his fishery, which was very close by. On the hills, lancers could be seen cordoning off the site with the help of gendarmes. Inside the main fishery, the Emperor went into ecstasies over the dexterity with which the Elban women filleted the tuna; he distributed gold coins, and the women knelt before him to kiss his hands, and shower him with scales. As Monsieur Seno described the various tasks, the Emperor bent down, took a handful of fresh sardines from a tub and slipped them into Count Bertrand's pocket. The Count, listening to Monsieur Seno's disquisition along with everyone else, failed to notice a thing. Shortly afterwards, as they came out into the daylight, the Emperor sneezed: 'My word, I've caught a cold in the water! Lend me your handkerchief, Bertrand.'

Bertrand put his hand in his pocket – and removed it quickly at the slimy, wriggling touch of the sardines; the Emperor fell to the ground in a fit of wild laughter that left him breathless. No one else seemed amused, and many people, particularly Campbell and Signor Forli, wondered at this childish joke. Meanwhile Bertrand had taken off his frock-coat and emptied the contents of his pocket out on the white, wet, fishy sand.

'Boats,' Monsieur Seno said at that moment.

The Emperor wiped away his tears of mirth with the back of his sleeve and looked towards the high sea. Three frigates lay at anchor off the coast.

'Bertrand! Your spy-glass.'

The Count handed Napoleon his telescope.

'French vessels. Call Cambronne, Drouot, Monsieur Poggi and Monsieur Sénécal. They are to be at the Mulini Palace in an hour.'

*

Because of the three French warships cruising round the island, the Emperor doubled the garrisons of the forts and put them on alert: lookouts worked day and night in relays to train their glasses on the intruders. In a single morning, some grenadiers set about demolishing the hovels that clung to the ramparts, where they blocked the loopholes and obstructed the cannon. The gunners were exercising all out, frantically firing red-hot shot into the sea. Dressed as a sailor on a vessel that was supposed to be carrying salt to the neighbouring islands, Octave observed the ships at close quarters. He learned little from the officer of the watch, with whom he had a brief exchange, except that the French were going to sail to Italy, and were ensuring the safety of traders in the Mediterranean; there were dark mutterings of pirates.

On the third night, Octave patrolled the ragged coast-line with a group of gendarmes. He visited abandoned shacks on the headlands, questioned shore-dwellers, and reassured himself that no one had clandestinely disembarked on the deserted beaches or the creeks. Then, as the moon, round and glowing, appeared between two black and hurried clouds, one of the gendarmes took Octave's arm, drawing his attention to a triangle of white canvas advancing across the water. It was a medium-sized fishing vessel, which appeared to be coming from Genoa and was approaching the shore. The clouds covered the moon once more, but the gendarme had the practised eye of an old poacher: he had caught plenty of rabbits in these parts, and could see in the dark like a cat. Octave and his crew said not another word, but crouched motionless behind the rosemary bushes.

A boat was dispatched from the vessel, and as it

reached the shore a tall, bare-headed man climbed out, with a bag over his shoulder. The oarsmen silently waved him goodbye, before setting off once more for their ship. The solitary figure walked through the darkness, guided by the streetlights shining in Portoferraio, cursing as he trod in a muddy puddle. Octave and his gendarmes waited for the sailors to reach their vessel and for the ship to set sail, before leaping to their feet and sprinting across the sand, guns levelled, to surround the suspect – who made no attempt to resist, and spoke in French: 'I've come from Paris to see the Emperor.'

'And you come ashore like a smuggler?' asked Octave.

'I have a special mission.'

'Search him!'

Octave took the man's bag.

'What are you carrying?'

'Dispatches from Paris and Rome for General Cam-bronne, General Drouot . . .'

One of the gendarmes lit a lantern. Octave checked his fob watch – it was three o'clock in the morning – and inspected the open bag, which appeared to contain sealed letters.

Meanwhile a fat gendarme patted down the relaxed and confident stranger himself, checking likely hiding places. 'There are no weapons, Monsieur Sénécal,' he confirmed.

'What about this?' said Octave, pulling a long object from one of his pockets.

'That's my pipe.'

It was indeed a meerschaum pipe, in a case decorated with Napoleon's profile. The stranger smiled.

'You can find objects with the Emperor's image on

them all over France, absolutely everywhere. His picture's on plates, on tobacco tins, and even flat-irons. At the Palais-Royal last month someone etched *Vive l'Empereur!* on a shop mirror with a diamond, and within a few days others had added *Yes, yes, yes . . .*'

'Follow us.'

'I am delighted to, gentlemen.'

For caution's sake, the man's hands were tied behind his back with a belt, before he was led towards the rocks where a customs boat was moored.

The group climbed aboard and headed towards the harbour. 'On foot,' Octave said to his prisoner, 'it would have taken you hours, there are ravines and collapsed paths, and you'd have fallen or got lost.'

'Perhaps.'

'Your name?'

'Marceau.'

'A soldier? You look like one.'

'I was. I was a commander at Jemmapes, and that's not exactly yesterday.'

'Republican?'

'Republican officer, monsieur. Before that, I was a pastry chef.'

'You say you've come from Paris?'

'Via Burgundy, Lyons, Avignon, Marseille, Toulon, where Marshal Masséna gave me a letter, and Nice, and Genoa, and here I am.'

'How long from Paris to Nice?'

'I will give the details of my journey to the Emperor. I have orders to.'

'From whom?'

'I will tell the Emperor. I am not armed, and that should be enough for you.'

Octave asked no more questions until they reached the Mulini Palace, where Napoleon, who was awake at that time of day, was standing on the terrace singing 'If the king had given me Paris' and contemplating the sea that crashed against the rocks and the fortifications.

*

His Majesty received the messenger alone. The man had been appointed by Italian patriots – who had once formed a rebel government in Turin and who were now scattered around the peninsula – and their French correspondents, close to the old Imperial court. The first wanted a King of Italy, the second were preparing for a return to the Tuileries.

The Emperor sat in his study and examined the grey-haired, battle-scarred officer, and he, standing almost to attention before him, had ready replies to each of Napoleon's questions.

'What are people doing in France?'

'Waiting for you.'

'What are they saying?'

'That you will return.'

'With which army?'

'You don't need one.'

'Why not?'

'Doesn't Your Majesty know what's happening in France?'

'I know they're doing lots of stupid things.'

'All parties agree: things can't go on in their current

state for another six months. People are discussing it freely in the cafés and the esplanades.'

'I abdicated.'

'No one is concerned in the slightest about your abdication.'

'Come now!'

'Show your face and you'll have an army.'

'By what miracle?'

'I have travelled through France, everyone is complaining, and they're waiting for you everywhere.'

'Even in the South?'

'Even there. They thought quails were going to tumble ready-roasted into their mouths, they're disenchanted now. That's the South for you.'

'What are they saying about the King?'

'That he's a good man, but his ministers are asses and rogues. They're complaining that only traitors and noblemen are given a decent welcome at the court: there isn't a village where they're not ready, at the first signal, to overturn the apple-cart.'

'How long did it take you to get to Nice?'

'Twenty days, sire. I was ordered to stick my nose in everywhere, and I assure you there are very few inns, taverns, wine-shops or billiard-halls that I have not been into. I only ever took the diligence with me from one town to the next.'

'I'm getting old,' said the Emperor. 'I need to rest.'

'Old, sire? You're the same age as me. Come and deliver us from this evil crew of aristocrats, who have started making so much noise, and who are talking of re-establishing feudal laws. The priests have even started calling for tithes.'

'Pamphlets?'

'They're pouring in from all over the place.'

'Have you brought me any?'

'I have a few in my wallet, but they're a bit ragged, and they don't all sing your praises . . .'

'I'm happy to read the pros and cons.'

'You've left it a bit late. You should have listened to everyone when you were in a position of strength.'

'Have you read Chateaubriand?' asked the Emperor, to avoid explaining his behaviour over the past few years.

'Chateaubriand?' echoed Marceau. 'Far from loyal, and he's got it in for you.'

'He's a genius: the purists don't like him, but he carries you along.'

'I should like, sire, to be able to carry you along as his style does.'

'Fine. Go and rest. We'll give you ten thousand francs.'

'Sire, one doesn't come to the island of Elba for money, unless one has been sent to betray you.'

Octave was summoned and attended to the messenger, lending him the room in the Mulini Palace that he himself shared with Monsieur Marchand, the first valet (when Octave did not sleep in town with Gianna, 'on a mission', as he put it). Alone at his window as dawn broke, Napoleon considered the information he'd gleaned over the previous two months — brought to him by travellers or sailors whose tongues were loosened after a few glasses at the Buono Gusto (on whom Octave gave him daily reports), as well as the comments from well-known visitors and articles, however biased, from the foreign newspapers that were translated for him. Piecing everything together, Napoleon was able to form a fairly accurate opinion of

France, and pondered it as he looked through the window, admiring the flowers in his little garden.

In Vienna, at the beginning of autumn, the allies had formed a congress to divide up Europe among their nations; they seemed to be spending their time on trivialities, they gave dances, galas, hunts, but the real work was being done behind the scenes: treaties, promises, deals, threats, lies, verbal agreements, alliances forged and broken. Everyone was taking advantage of the negotiations to increase their influence over their territories. Napoleon knew the kings were dismantling his Empire, but he also knew that this would lead to future wars and quarrels among his adversaries. Did Tsar Alexander want the Duchy of Warsaw; would he try to consolidate a vassal Poland? Austria dreaded this new state when, in Saxony, Prussia was already threatening its borders. England, for its part, was interested in strengthening Prussia as a bulwark against Russia. The powers were lining up in rival clans. Talleyrand, who had been invited as a spectator because he reluctantly found himself in the losers' camp, played the disinterested witness while at the same time stirring up discord. His sly talent was practised with pleasure, even if France had nothing to say; it had no army now.

'France has no army now,' Napoleon repeated to himself – but the soldiers who'd returned to civilian life, the prisoners of war who'd been repatriated, all dreamed of his return. The Emperor learned that in the Ain region, working-class gangs were roaming the villages shouting his name and braying Bonapartist chants. That in Rennes a play called *The Return of the Lily* had been booed and whistled. That St Napoleon's Day had been celebrated in the Vosges. That in Auxerre, some enthusiasts had walked through the streets with a mannequin of the King in women's skirts. An architect from Calais, commissioned to build a column commemorating the landing of Louis XVIII, had received an anonymous letter: 'Put some trundle-wheels on your column, and it can follow your fat king into exile!' The garrison soldiers waited dejectedly, keeping tricolour cockades hidden in the bottom of their haversacks. If the marquises who had been appointed as officers forced them to shout 'Long live the King!', they added in an undertone the words: 'of Rome'. When playing cards, they called not the king but the 'pig' of spades or clubs. Often, in the barracks, trumpets played 'He will return'. And in the evening, the old soldiers of the Grande Armée raised their glasses to the Absent One.

*

'Sunday 1 January 1815. I'm opening a new notebook for the New Year, which was, for reasons of economy, celebrated modestly in the Mulini Palace. What we have at present in our coffers will only last us a year. The Emperor is whittling away at the military funds, has sold his plough horses, cut wages by half, and got rid of the post boat to save 4,200 francs. Despite the priests' sermons, taxes aren't coming in as well as they might be, and he has even had to send the gendarmes to some recalcitrant villages. The grenadiers who have chosen to go back to France have a fine certificate to hang on their walls but not a penny in their pockets, and they are being replaced by mercenaries, Hungarians, Tyroleans who've come to offer their services, and large numbers of French officers fleeing the royal army: soon we will have more officers than soldiers. The men of the Corsican battalion are

deserting, and the Elbans only ever don their uniforms for the Sunday parade, and spend the week in the fields.'

Then Octave finally jotted down some personal observations, as though he were no longer concerned about malicious glances that might fall upon his notebooks. Thus, on Thursday 5 January, after writing: *'Yesterday we paid a visit to the forts because vigilance never relaxes now, even though the three French ships disappeared a long time ago'*, he added: *'The more worried the Emperor is in private, the more impulsive he is in public. He is concealing his anxiety behind exaggerated bonhomie, or practical jokes unworthy of his proper rank. As Colonel Campbell brought him the* Morning Chronicle, *an English periodical unfavourable to the Bourbons, His Majesty adopted a cynical pose, scorning the paper and saying, "From now on I want to live as a justice of the peace, Sir Neil. Nothing interests me now as much as my little house, my cattle and my mules." As soon as he has an audience,his personality changes. As he puts it, this island is a drum, and you need only strike it to make the sound you wish to hear. On his last outing to the farm of San Martino, because a group of tourists was watching him from a nearby hill, he started running around the vines after some chickens that had escaped from their pen; he knew that the visitors, startled by this unexpected and far from Imperial spectacle, would later tell stories about the Ogre being toothless, and in no fit state to govern an Empire. In the middle of a stroll, out he gets from his barouche, pounces on a ditch full of water, sits down, splashes about, gets back on his feet and asks to travel along the coast in a boat. He does not complain his boots are damp until the evening. Some people think he is going mad, but as soon as he is back in the small circle of his confidants, at the Mulini, he is serious and often irritable.'*

Clearly and bluntly, Octave gave an account of the fits of fury he had witnessed. When, for example, the Emperor learned that the King of France had just issued naturalisation papers to Masséna, because he was born in Nice on Italian territory, the Emperor was livid: 'These people have lost their minds! After all the Battle of Zurich and the defence of Genoa didn't naturalize the Prince of Essling!'

Or else it was Princess Pauline who infuriated her brother. She thought she was doing the right thing in asking His Majesty's bookseller in Livorno to change his bindings to make his library prettier. She thought, but she thought wrong, and Napoleon was so displeased that he called his guards and had them use their bayonets to rip to shreds some thirty geographical and medical textbooks before his very eyes.

'The Emperor's life is shrinking', Octave recorded, 'and as the assassination threats accumulate he barely leaves the Mulini Palace, where he lives a cloistered life. His mood sours over the merest trifles.'

This dismal climate did not prevent balls and receptions, however, which were to present the outside world with an image of serene and joyful royalty. It was up to Bertrand to organize such parties, and more particularly to assess their cost, which the Emperor was to approve. He brought his big accounts book and some invoices to the study for a signature of approval. Napoleon studied them in detail, crossed out some expenses and corrected others.

'Sunday evening, sire . . .'

'Mustn't cost more than a thousand francs.'

'Just the refreshments we agreed before . . .'

'Get rid of the ice cream.'

'The buffet . . .'

'Not before midnight, in the town hall. The guests aren't going to spend a whole evening nibbling away at our supplies!'

'If Your Majesty would care to look at the guest list . . .'

'Vicentini? No,' said the Emperor, glancing through the list. 'He takes advantage, that one does, he stuffs himself and costs us a fortune for nothing.'

'He'll sulk . . .'

'Find a mission for him, Bertand, get him away from the Mulini on the day of this damned party.'

'I'll come up with something . . .'

'Baroness Skupinsky?'

'Not her, sire, she's the wife of a Polish commander. She'll dance a fandango at the end of the party, as she always does. It's very amusing and it doesn't cost us a penny.'

'And that? What's that?'

'The invitation card, Sire.'

'Remove that idiotic phrase!'

'Which one, sire?'

'*Sovereign of the island of Elba.*'

'To put what in its place?'

'*The Emperor* invites you, etc., etc. That's sober and less ridiculous. And what about this invoice?'

'Ah, the invoice is something else, sire. Her Highness the Princess Pauline has had eight blinds put up in her drawing-room.'

'Sixty francs?'

'She supplied the fabric, but making and installing them cost sixty-two francs.'

'That expense isn't within the budget, the Princess can pay it herself. Ha? Look who's here.'

Monsieur Pons was crossing the garden, and in a moment would present himself before the Emperor, who said to Bertrand, 'You can give him his invitation, it will be one less to carry.'

Monsieur Pons de l'Hérault's face looked different. A man of strong convictions, he thought only in terms of black and white. After remaining hostile to the tyrant for a long time, the Emperor's familiarity and trust had turned him into a fervent Bonapartist, and now he was worried.

'Do you know, sire, what they are chattering about in town?'

'A lot of old nonsense!'

The Emperor gestured to Bertrand, who slipped out with his files to leave Napoleon in a tête-à-tête with his devoted administrator, who had difficulty finding his words.

'Well, sire, they're saying that at the Congress, in Vienna, our enemies are trying to remove you from the coasts of Europe, to take you away from Elba and put you on some incredible island . . .'

'I know.'

From letters sent by his brothers sewn into the lining of a messenger's clothes, Napoleon had learned that Talleyrand was demanding that the Emperor be deported to the Azores or the Antilles, or worse, to St Helena, as some English travellers had specified. The Emperor had immediately done some research. St Helena was a wind-battered, fog-bound, volcanic rock between Africa and Brazil, far from the normal maritime routes. A tomb. Pons asked in a faint voice: 'So it's true?'

'Yes, but they won't do it.'

'St Helena, sire, I've looked it up in my books, and it's an island shat out by the devil!'

'I can hold out here for two years, and anything can happen in two years.'

The Emperor mentioned the treaty that the King of France was refusing to respect, the subsidies he was refusing to pay in order to starve his enemy; this attitude was a declaration of war: by betraying his word, he said, the King was putting the Emperor back on the throne, and suddenly, mid-sentence, he asked:

'Were you a sailor, Pons?'

'In the Republic, you know that.'

'I have a mission for you.'

'Sire, I thank you for your trust . . .'

'Don't say a word about it.'

'I will be silent as the grave.'

'Without saying a word to anyone, you will organize an expeditionary flotilla.'

'An expeditionary flotilla? With my barges?'

'You put ore on them, why not men? And you'll find other boats to fit out.'

Monsieur Pons withdrew, puffed up with his mission. He imagined landing in Italy, where Napoleon was considered as a potential saviour in the major regions, where patriots were working to turn public opinion in his favour. Throughout the whole of the peninsula, Austria had revived the smaller states the better to control him, but some of those states were resisting the occupying forces. Murat did not bow, but he knew he was threatened. His Kingdom of Naples was to revert to the Bourbons, whose police were printing pamphlets presenting him variously

as a commis chef, a cut-throat, a butcher, and the man
who shot the Duke of Enghien. Even if his sniggering
wife Caroline, the Emperor's sister, was backing Austria
because Prince Metternich had been her lover, Murat still
felt isolated. Talleyrand's support? He would have had to
pay him, but how much, and with what? So Murat
became Napoleon's subject once more. Was Napoleon
going to land in Naples? Pons wondered.

*

Octave was doing his rounds as the Emperor came back
to his bedroom in the Mulini Palace. Each evening Octave
cursed because of a door that hadn't been properly closed,
or guards who were missing from one side of the fortifications. Now he leaned over the parapet and studied the
piles of rocks at the bottom of the cliff: no sentry there,
despite his recommendations, and a rope ladder and a
grappling iron would be enough for killers to climb up
from the sea unseen, tiptoe across the garden, and disperse
around the drawing-rooms to attack first the guards and
then the Emperor in his bed. Octave immediately put his
mattress outside, on the ground in the promenade gallery,
beneath the windows of the Imperial bedroom.

One January morning, he was pulled from sleep by a
raging gale. He got up. Because of a thick mist he couldn't
see six feet in front of him, but he heard the gusts, the
foliage being blown about, a clattering shutter, orange-
trees being toppled by the gale. Huge waves crashed
against the walls and rained back down on the terrace.
Octave listened hard, and discerned a loud report amid all
the hubbub, but it wasn't the rumble of thunder; it was
crisper than that, and repeated at almost regular intervals.

It sounded like a cannon. Doubled over by the squall, he walked to the edge of the fortifications. The noise was coming from the sea: a ship in distress was signalling for help. The mist faded away, the sky brightened. Lashed by gusts of wind, Octave clung to the stones of the parapet. He could just make out the shape of a brig washed up on a beach in the bay of Bagnajo. Lying on its side, battered by malevolent waves, one of the ship's masts was dislodged or broken, its sails in shreds. Napoleon had heard the cannon too, and he now, in his dressing-gown, a knotted madras scarf on his head, and a pair of opera-glasses in his hand, joined Octave.

'A ship in distress, sire! But take care! The wind is very strong!'

'What's that you say?'

With his hair in his eyes and his coat flapping around like a cape, Octave relinquished his grip on the parapet. He tried get the unsteady Emperor to crouch close to the ground lest he be blown over, but His Majesty refused, protesting that he wanted to go straight there, and back he went along the walls, bent so low that he was almost on all fours. Inside the palace he dressed and, before the gale subsided, jumped on his horse and galloped towards the wreck with a platoon of his grenadiers.

Below, dozens of Elbans were at work, fishermen, soldiers, miners. They couldn't put in their boats, because high and powerful waves tipped them over or threw them back on to the shore.

At that moment, the Emperor recognized the ship with its sides thrashed by the crashing sea: it was the *Inconstant*. Issuing orders with hands and voice, yelling himself hoarse, Napoleon ordered that ropes be thrown – but how? On the overturned ship half-naked sailors, constantly tossed about by the wind and the sea, were trying to save their passengers and help them to the shore, but those boats that had not been smashed already were wedged immovably against the upturned hull. As the squall finally began to ease, the rescuers prepared to tackle the wreck, although her planks were groaning, and she was still being lashed by a heavy sea. One man fell shivering on his knees on the beach and thanked them. On some flat rocks, the Emperor spotted Monsieur Pons, whose miners were scaling the wrecked ship. He approached him.

'Does this sad picture pierce your heart?'

'I would say that I'm choking back my anger, sire. If you hadn't appointed that fool Taillade as captain, your brig would be safe in the roads of Portoferraio.'

'You're getting as cross about Taillade as Monsieur Sénécal does.'

'He's incompetent and corrupt! I've just learned some amazing things about him from some of the passengers whose lives we've saved. Taillade has gone on holiday to Corsica, and had dinner there with one of Bruslart's aides-de-camp . . .'

'Pfft! He's more of an idiot than a danger.'

'Idiots are always dangerous, sire!'

The sea grew calmer, although the waves were still grumbling offshore. Harbour pilots arrived to tow away the wreckage.

'Give me your opinion, Pons. How long will it take us to raise it?'

'If the hull isn't broken, about three weeks.'

'Make sure that the hull is intact, oversee the work,

stay within your time limit. And you will have the *Inconstant* repainted in black and white.'

'Like an English merchant ship?'

*

Princess Pauline acted as a screen. Napoleon needed her lightness to hide his angers, his worries, his fears for the future. Everyone felt sorry for Paoletta, who was in poor health; previously a regular visitor to spa resorts, she nevertheless persisted in a state of morbid languor even though she had nothing in particular to worry about: she was wealthy, and no one wanted her dead. She wished only to amuse herself and, for the duration of a quadrille, she radiated wit and vivacity. The Emperor had put her in charge of entertainments, so she rehearsed little comedies in the old Mulini barn, organized concerts of flutes and fifes which were attended by the fashionable people of the island. Young lieutenants argued over her, billing and cooing (but none of them got into her bed, since the rooms of the palace were so noisy and all intercommunicated. Even where love affairs were concerned, a minimum of discretion was required so that gossips did not circulate bawdy rumours). The old soldiers of the Guard called her Paoletta and adored her: the tourists admired her when she took a gondola around the gulf or passed through the town lying in a palanquin, the Elbans loved her from the moment she opened a ball by inviting poor, clumsy Cambronne to dance, and had been amused to watch the General trying not to crush her pink silk ballet shoes.

Octave knew that the Princess's stay in Naples had helped to reconcile Murat and the Emperor, and he gave her credit for that but, if he had been dazzled by her beauty on the road into exile, just before Fréjus, he now saw the goddess from close to – and every day. Even if he did have hot flushes at the sight of those maddening dresses of hers, he was tired of her whims, her pretend sulks, her exaggerations, her perpetual moans.

The Emperor often tried to persuade his sister to take the air, to move around a little, to discover her island. Up until now Octave had escaped the chore of outings, but today Napoleon had deliberately singled him out. The more threats built up, the more severe they grew, and the more the police turned away undesirables – some of whom were found to be carrying sharpened knives – the more specific Napoleon's plans became (although he didn't discuss them with anybody), and the more he wished to be surrounded by a carefree atmosphere: Octave among the ladies in waiting, holding Pauline's arm, signified to the outside world that no major operation was under way, and that the death threats were not being taken seriously.

Octave climbed the steep pink marble staircase leading to Pauline's apartment on the first floor of the Mulini Palace. His name announced, he entered the large and luminous drawing-room to find some young women dressing the Princess, knotting a draped tunic around her shoulders.

'I am at Your Highness's command,' he said, slightly embarrassed.

'Where does Nabulione want you to take me?'

'His Majesty thought the heights of San Martino would bring Your Highness back to health . . .'

'It's terribly far away!'

'An hour by road, at the very most.'

'But I've nothing to wear for the journey!'

'It's not really a journey, it's an outing to the country-side, and the weather is mild . . .'

'You don't understand a thing, my poor friend!'

Pouting and acting like a girl, Pauline opened a case and rummaged through some scarves, complaining: 'Everything in France is going to the dogs, Monsieur, no one knows how to bleach malines or scallop a ribbon. Mme Ducluzel sends me lace that isn't properly white, my dresses don't fit, I've lost lots of weight, and all the hats that come from Leroy are terrible, they're two inches too big!'

Octave stood patiently while the Princess chose an outfit appropriate to the season and the weather, her hair-dresser arranged her curls and a light but skilful application of make-up brightened her complexion. Then, with the help of a valet, he carried the Princess down-stairs on her portable cushion – because she was afraid of wearing out the soles of her laced boots – outside to her café-au-lait landau, where two titivated companions waited for her.

On horseback, with an escort consisting of a few gendarmes, Octave guided the coach along the new road that ran close to the salt-works. Strolling visitors greeted them as they passed, and peasants raised their hats. They soon arrived at the villa of San Martino, built on a hill; it was a very plain house with whitewashed walls. The landau stopped among the recently planted pines and acacias, and Pauline said wearily, 'Help me to the house, Monsieur Sénécal.'

Dismounting, Octave opened the door of the landau. He picked up the Princess and carried her to the entrance, which was so narrow they had to squeeze through it sideways. With an indolent gesture, Pauline asked her retinue to wait outside, and they joined the gendarmes and the caretaker of the villa, who were setting up trestles for the picnic table, so mild was the winter. Beside the square of turned earth that was the kitchen garden, the Emperor's six milch cows distractedly assessed the intruders as they chewed the hay from their byre.

Octave deposited the Princess on the floor, at the foot of a staircase as steep as a ladder, which she then climbed, asking him to follow her. Octave had never been inside San Martino, a place to which Napoleon came very seldom, and where he hardly ever lingered for any length of time. On the first floor, which opened out on to a garden at the back (the red-tiled house was built on the slopes of a hill), he found himself in some small rooms furnished in the Florentine style, with sofas and chests of drawers stolen from Prince Borghese, Pauline's husband, who was now cavorting in Rome with his young Italian mistress.

'It's as though I'm in my palace,' said Pauline, throwing down her wide-brimmed hat and loosening her laces. 'Look, this divan could tell you an awful lot about me.'

'What about this statue?'

'Isn't it a good resemblance?'

Octave studied Canova's statue for a long time. The Trevisan sculptor had shown the Princess in a complicated pose, crouching with one knee on the ground, one arm behind the back of her neck and the other holding her breasts. Octave was about to ask, 'Is it you?' but by the time he turned around, Pauline had adopted the same pose, as naked as her effigy.

'*Non essere sciocco!* It's me, you fool! But look, the real Paoletta isn't made of white marble . . .'

*

Dr Foureau de Bauregard had no trouble identifying Octave's illness. He gave him a sly and disapproving look, sighed and offered him a scrap of morality.

'Obviously it was bound to happen to you sooner or later, sleeping with the whores in the harbour.'

'The whores in the harbour, yes,' Octave repeated, buckling his belt.

'The sailors who visit them don't just bring those girls souvenirs from their travels. All right. I'll prescribe you the same medication as I have done for His Majesty. Our pharmacist will prepare the mixture, he's familiar with it. Two injections a day.'

'With a syringe?'

'Well obviously, not with a flute!'

'I've never given injections . . .'

'You'll get used to it, my friend. You know, imitating the Emperor isn't always glorious.'

Thus Octave had to set about treating the disease, as embarrassing as it was venereal, given him by Napoleon's sister, and he would think often of that little mishap as he studied the comings and goings of the gallant officers that Pauline took for walks far from the Mulini Palace, to engage in her indiscretions far from wagging tongues. As one might imagine, not a trace of this bawdy episode featured in Octave's diary; instead, he recorded other events that were all happening at once, and which seemed to contradict one another.

'*Monday 13 February. The Emperor is going ahead with*

his major building project. He has set aside four thousand francs for bridges and roads, to be paid in monthly instalments until July. He wants to build a bridge near Capoliveri, and finish a road. He has already closed Cape Stella with a dry-stone wall and a long trench, and ordered that the whole island be beaten to enclose the rabbits and hares inside the reserve. That seems to herald festivities. This morning, I brought Count Bertrand a letter in which His Majesty asks him to prepare his summer residence at the hermitage in Marciana. Houses will have to be rented for his retinue, the hermitage will need to be repaired, the room that will serve as his study will have to be enlarged, and the kitchens moved from the far side of the chapel. Count Bertrand will have to produce an estimate. At the same time, and this seems to contradict the long-term changes, the Emperor has just asked General Drouot, in my presence, to arm the Inconstant, now repaired, with twenty-six guns, and to lay in three months' supplies for one hundred and twenty men . . .'

That same Monday, coming back from the town hall to the Mulini Palace, Octave bumped into Signor Forli, who was delivering his olive oil.

'Monsieur Sénécal, you who know everything . . .'

'As much as you, my dear fellow.'

'Don't be so modest. Tell me the identity of the false sailor that the Emperor is receiving as we speak.'

'I have no idea.'

'I saw you on the steps of the town hall, so you've had a meeting with Count Bertrand.'

'That's true. I gave him a letter from the Emperor about his holiday plans for next summer.'

'This morning Bertrand authorized an audience with someone disguised as a sailor.'

'Why disguised?'

'His hands were too fine to pull on ropes.'

The oil merchant had noticed the man in question beneath the Sea Gate, showing his passport at the customs office. From Genoa, he'd travelled to the town, where garlands were already being hung for the carnival on 15 February, then booked himself a bed in a hostel for passing sailors. An audience? An ordinary seaman? The sentry outside the Mulini Palace refused him entry. He was to seek authorization from the town hall, like everyone else. When the man came back two hours later with his authorization signed, the soldier looked surprised, but granted the man in his sailor's uniform access to the Palace.

'I'm surprised Bertrand didn't mention it to you.'

'I don't know everything, Forli, but I'm going to find out.'

At the Palace, the Emperor was locked away in his study with the visitor, and the conversation seemed to be going on for ever. Octave sat down on a garden wall until he saw the sailor leave; but the oil merchant was right, he didn't have the air of a sailor, and his disguise was thoroughly unconvincing. It was easier to imagine him in a tie and a black frock-coat. Octave wrote of him: *He's the former Sub-prefect of Reims, who resigned so as not to serve the King, come on behalf of the Duke of Bassano, and His Majesty reassured himself by asking precise questions to which the Sub-prefect replied in a convincing fashion. The Duke of Bassano tells us through him, among other things, that Fouché is plotting with the former Jacobins and a coterie of officers to get rid of the highly unpopular Louis XVIII, to establish a regency but send Napoleon to St Helena, as*

*Talleyrand has proposed. This confirms what we have known
for some weeks.'*

*

The following Wednesday, which was Ash Wednesday,
the god of carnival was ceremoniously buried. Masked
balls were planned at the Mulini Palace, at the Forte
Stella, and at some private homes which were to be opened
specially for the occasion. The population had massed in
the streets, where happy tourists rubbed shoulders with
Elbans. They danced, laughed, drank, and ate traditional
rolled tripe sprinkled with salt from the stalls — and then
drank some more. In the square in front of the church,
which had been turned into a fairground, street vendors
in baroque costumes sold toys and hats, while little boys
set off firecrackers. Octave strolled from group to group
always alert and suspicious of joyful multitudes since any
murderer could slip in wearing a mask, but he had advised
the Emperor not to show his face in Portoferraio —
chewing on one of the skewers of baby octopus grilled
over coals that vendors were offering at the crossroads.
He was amused by an astrologer in a pointed hat, false
cardboard nose, and a long robe patterned with silver
moons and stars, who was bragging about his elixir of
life. An onlooker bought a flask, which he wanted to try
straight away; he drank from it and spat it out with a
grimace: the celestial mixture was nothing but olive oil.
Octave recognized the barker by his voice, even if he was
distorting it: it was Signor Forli. While the laughing
crowd waiting for the next dupe to come along so they
could mock him in chorus, the astrologer turned towards
Octave, and adopted an incredible accent to shout: 'My

elixir, noble my lord?' (and in a whisper), 'I need to talk to you.'

Their playlet was interrupted by a fat and jovial fellow who was being dragged towards the platform by his neighbours. He wore a comical hat and was enjoying himself hugely. He demanded a flask, but cries and music distracted everyone's attention: 'The procession! The procession!' Inquisitive bystanders pushed their way to the other end of the parade ground, where the street fell steeply from the ramparts. 'There they are!' They hurried towards the route of the procession, applauding and climbing up trees and ladders.

The colonel of the Guard, normally so austere, appeared first, dressed as a pasha, with a disproportionately large turban rolled on his head, his moustache twisted into points, puffed breeches and a curved sabre lent him by a Mameluke. Just behind him, to great cheers, a spindly Polish officer was dressed as Don Quixote, wedged into some botched armour, with a paunchy catering officer following him on a donkey to embody the role of Sancho Panza. Then came the regimental band – grenadiers in Pierrot costumes strummed guitars and waved tambourines without much conviction. Behind them came some twenty carts arranged on gun carriages, on which other soldiers, wrapped in muslin and cashmere or fringed curtains, played at being odalisques, trying out lascivious poses, writhing their hairy arms and performing failed arabesques as they threw flowers at the laughing crowd. Next came a cart of bohemians waving mimosa branches, and everyone tried to guess which one was Paoletta. Finally, heads lowered, to round off this risible procession, Bertrand, Drouot and Cambronne marched in full uniform.

While the inhabitants of Portoferraio were concentrated around the festival, the oil merchant had rolled up his astrologer's robe and doffed his pointed hat. He led Octave down to the port, saying, 'You'll have to explain to me!'

They entered one of the warehouses, which was not guarded that day, and in front of a stack of numbered cases, Signor Forli asked, 'Do you know what they are?'

'These packages? No.'

'Some workmen told me. They're the two gilded berlins that came to Fontainebleau with the Guard: they've been dismantled.'

'You know more than I do.'

'Read this inscription on the cases.'

'*For Rome*,' Octave read.

'For Rome, that's exactly it! And why is the Emperor sending his coaches to Rome? To have himself crowned King of Italy?'

'How would I know?'

'Stop play-acting, Sénécal!'

'I'm not play-acting.'

'Come, come! You're always around Napoleon!'

'He's miserly with his confidences, and anyway I'm not really part of his inner circle.'

'Find out more, damn it! For some time now you've barely been informing me at all.'

'You know more than I do, Forli,' Octave replied with a laugh.

'What are you laughing at?'

'Your cardboard nose. You've forgotten to take it off.'

Furiously, the oil merchant took off his false nose and hurled it to the ground. But he had noticed suspicious movements. He knew that the horses of the Polish cavalry had been moved from Pianosa island where they had been stabled. The previous night he had witnessed the loading of sixty cases of ammunition on to the *Inconstant*. At the tavern, he listened to the sailors who claimed to be well informed. They all claimed that the Emperor was about to leave. Some said, 'He's going to escape to America.' Others contradicted them: 'No, he's going to reconquer Italy with Murat. Murat is already in Tuscany.'

Octave and Forli walked side by side along the quays. Some launches were coming and going from the port to an English ship called the *Partridge*.

'You want me to keep you informed, Signor Forli? That I can do. Colonel Campbell is setting off for Livorno tomorrow.'

'Will he report to the Austrian chargé d'affaires?'

'That's what he claims every time. In actual fact he's joining Signora Bartoli in Florence. Poor man, he's bored on this island. And if he's leaving, it's because he has no suspicion. That should reassure you about the Emperor's intentions. Campbell knows everything, much more than you and I.'

The oil merchant did not seem convinced.

*

The next day and during the days that followed, Signor Forli's doubts were reinforced. He became less and less convinced of Octave's ignorance, and Octave avoided him by no longer going to the port, always claiming that he was detained by some mission or other. 'Dust in the eyes!' Forli thought as he travelled with the tourists to visit the fallow land that the Guard units were transforming into a vegetable garden. He had even surprised a brief conversation between the Emperor and one of his guardsmen.

'Are you bored?' Napoleon had asked a digging grenadier.

'Why yes, my Emperor, I'm not enjoying myself too much.'

'Here you are, take this gold coin while you wait.'

'Wait for what?'

'Spring!'

The oil merchant had immediately communicated this exchange to Livorno: was Napoleon preparing to land in Italy in the spring? The garrison soldiers were no longer found idling in the taverns, but not for reasons to do with vegetable-growing, it was because they were now consigned to barracks in the evenings. Passing sailors were now the only ones Forli could question, but all he ever collected was endless boasting; he heard that King Louis XVIII had almost been kidnapped from his apartments in the Tuileries, or that Masséna, Governor of Toulon, had flown the tricolour. Forli also skimmed the pamphlets that had been brought from the Continent on the trading vessels, which portrayed Napoleon as a grotesque pot-bellied figure: a caricature showed him as an obese Robinson Crusoe lying his back on a beach with a parasol in his hand and his plumed eagle on his shoulder like a parrot; in another drawing he was shown ordering a round-up of thirty men, and in front of him marched a procession of people with goitres, hunchbacks and amputees holding sticks. This did not make Forli laugh, and he turned pale when a fisherman of his acquaintance pushed open the door of the Buono Gusto and yelled inside: 'The island of Elba is cut off from the world!'

'What does that mean?'

'Explain yourself, Tonino!'

The drinkers put their cups down, and urged the man to go into further detail about his bizarre claim.

That Sunday, 26 February, the Emperor had decreed an embargo on all shipping in the roads of Portoferraio and Porto Longone. The police would not be issuing any more passports and the cannon were ready to open fire on any ship that left the harbour. The tavern emptied immediately as its occupants headed outside and Forli hurried with the others towards the Sea Gate, which was now closed off by a line of grenadiers. He saw Gianna standing against a wall, sniffing and drying her eyes with a lace handkerchief. He took her by an arm and asked her distractedly in Italian, 'Have you seen Sénécal?'

'Not for a week. He's staying up there.'

She pointed her chin towards the hill and the Mulini Palace, and added, 'He's going to leave, they're all going to leave.'

'But where to? Do you know? Did he talk to you about it? Did Sénécal give you any clues to his destination?'

'He said nothing, but everyone's repeating it, and it's obvious, isn't it? They're going to go.'

Obvious it was.

Soldiers in battalions were emerging from the rear entrances to the forts and following the stepped streets to the harbour. Grenadiers were wearing their blue travelling hoods, muskets over their shoulders, their bearskin caps lined up under white canvas covers; the Polish lancers were carrying their saddles on their heads while four-pound loaves, sausage and bottles of wine protruded from their pouches.

To lend additional gravity to the moment, the call to arms began to ring out in the four corners of the town. The whole population silently escorted these determined-looking men, and there was a great deal of sadness in the faces of the Elbans – particularly the women. In their hundreds, the town's residents climbed up on to the ramparts and roofs. Taken unawares by this abrupt departure, Signor Forli ran back and forth: how would he join Consul Mariotti in Livorno? A fishing boat? The Sea Gate had now reopened, and he scrambled on to the quays with the tide of people. Beside the *Inconstant*, repainted as an English ship, other boats also lay at anchor, smaller but equally seaworthy, and launches were transporting the soldiers to those vessels in a constant frenzy of coming and going. Signor Forli noticed a boat that was being boarded by some fishermen.

'Hey!'

'Me?' asked the owner of the boat.

'Can you take me out of the roads?'

'That's forbidden, Monsieur Forli, as you very well know.'

'For fifty francs?'

'Even for fifty francs, and it's not as though I don't need them, but we're not doing it.'

'Sixty francs?'

'You can risk it, but that's not to say that we're going to get very far with all these soldiers about the place . . .'

The oil merchant jumped nervously into the boat,

and the oarsmen took their places. The boat moved slowly through the middle of the chaos. The *Inconstant* was very close, and they would have to skirt her, but as they drew level with her bows, some sentinels leaned from the ship's rail and shouted, 'Turn around!'

'Are they talking to us?' replied Forli, looking innocent.

'No ships are supposed to be leaving Portoferraio!'

'It's not a real ship, just a fishing boat . . .'

'Turn around!'

'I was going for a trip around the roads.'

'No trips! Turn back!'

'Don't you recognize me? I'm Forli, the oil merchant.'

'Get back to the quay or we'll shoot!'

'Careful,' the owner of the boat said in a quavering voice, 'they have itchy trigger fingers.'

'No, come on, we'll get through.'

'Seventy francs?'

'Fine.'

Splashed by some roundshot fired into the water, the boat was forced to return to the docks, and Signor Forli hurried away from the fishermen, who were shouting after him: 'Our money!'

'You haven't earned it!' he called back.

Forli saw some Poles boarding a vessel from Marseille that was moored near the mole. The cavalrymen strode back and forth from the hold, throwing part of the cargo into the water to the whoops of the sailors, and then Monsieur Peyrusse and Octave climbed on deck, negotiating for a long time with the captain, finally convincing him with some piles of gold coins. Thus it was that the oil merchant, who had stayed on the quay until the end of this scene, found himself face to face with Octave once more.

'You knew!'

'That we were going to leave? No. No one knew apart from the Emperor.'

'Are you going to sail for Italy?'

'Perhaps.'

'It's urgent that I alert Livorno.'

'That strikes me as difficult, Forli. Unless . . .'

'You have an idea?'

'Come with us.'

'You've got a nerve!'

'You've often protested your devotion to Bonapartism, I'll mention it to your friend Cambronne, he would be delighted to have you on board the *Inconstant*.'

'Come on, that's out of the question!'

It being February, the sun set early and thousands of paper lanterns lit the ramparts. Red and green Venetian lamps hung in the windows, and a roar announced that the Emperor was coming. Wearing his hat and his grey frock-coat, he passed through the Sea Gate in Pauline's landau, pulled by two ponies. Behind him, on foot, came Bertrand, Drouot, Pons and the valet Marchand, who was carrying a black leather case holding the jewels that Pauline had given to her brother. A slight breeze rose up, and a fisherman said to Forli, enraged by his impotence, 'There's a southerly wind blowing up off the coast.'

Six

THE RETURN

A SOUTHERLY WIND, light but favourable, had risen up in the middle of the night, and it drove the flotilla forwards (while at the same time keeping Campbell's ship in the port of Livorno). Five hundred grenadiers were huddled on deck and amid the cannon in the hold of the *Inconstant*, while the chasseurs, lancers and volunteers were aboard small, slow boats that followed in her wake. No one knew their destination, but everyone had had a guess.

'The army of the King of Naples awaits us.'

'We're going to Viareggio.'

'No, to Vado.'

'At any rate,' said a grenadier, 'we're ultimately going to Paris, the route's irrelevant.'

The moon was bright, no one slept. The Emperor went up on deck around dawn, where he watched the rising sun cast a yellow light on the top of the mountains of the island of Elba, twenty miles away. The previous day, in the launch on the way to his brig, an impromptu rendition of the 'Marseillaise' had rung out on all the ships, to be taken up in chorus by the Elbans on the quays and ramparts, and the song had run from hill to hill – that old hymn of the Revolution which had been forbidden under the Empire and which Napoleon would appropriate as a symbol of his return: was he not going to fight against kings as he had before? Of course, he was aware of the possibility that his enemies might have a trap set for him: by not paying him the income they had promised him, by sending him emissaries, not all of whom were honest, to paint him a terrible picture of the nation's condition in his absence, by provoking his return, weren't they trying to turn him into an outlaw so that they might more easily destroy him? It wasn't unthinkable. He watched the last stars fading in a sunlit sky. He was not the kind of man to be daunted. He would force the hand of chance one more time.

Napoleon had been thinking of returning like this since September, when a wealthy glove-maker from Grenoble, Monsieur Dumoulin, had visited the Emperor to tell him that the towns in the Alps were his already. And so Napoleon had planned his route to Paris, avoiding the suspicious South, preferring instead to travel along the byways in the snow, skirting the big cities, as far as Grenoble, where he hoped some men would be waiting for him: the soldiers serving the King of France against their will were his, first of all, and none of them would raise his musket against him. He discussed this now, on deck with Drouot – who was unsure but obedient – and with Cambronne, Bertrand, Octave and Pons, who still had his republican reflexes of honour and sobriety.

'Your Majesty has thought only of enriching his marshals, they wanted to retain their fortunes, even if it meant betraying you.'

'You're right, but I've never been able to bring myself to punish men who betrayed me after they had served me. It's a great weakness of mine.'

'What about Marshal Ney!'

'He doesn't like anybody.'

'Masséna's the Governor of Toulon, how's he going to react?'

'He has the soundest judgement and the quickest eye when the shooting starts.'

'Your former generals will resist you!'

'Maybe they will, but their regiments won't. They won't follow them.'

'And what about Augereau and his wretched proclamation?'

'It's not wretched, it's stupid. He'll write another saying the opposite, you'll see.'

They were going to land in France, and they no longer needed to ask to be sure of it. The conversation continued in the same vein when Napoleon sat down at the table on deck. About fifty officers were lunching with him, standing up, plates in their hands and loaves under their arms. About to raise a toast to the Emperor, they each poured wine into a glass on the deck. The lookout suddenly shouted, and they raised their heads instead. The man was pointing at a frigate off the coast of Livorno: 'They're coming towards us!'

'Full sail!' ordered the Emperor, untying his napkin.

Captain Chautard was in command of the *Inconstant*. A retired seaman from Toulon, who had come to Elba to ask for a job, he was just as poor a sailor as Taillade, whom he had replaced, but more reliable. Trembling, he suggested, 'Why don't we go back to Elba?'

'Prepare for battle!' cried the Emperor without hearing him.

'They're moving faster than we are . . .'

'Lighten as much as you can, come on, get moving, Chautard! Scuttle the heaviest boat.'

False alarm: the frigate was heading eastwards. Later in the day they saw the *Fleur de Lys*, one of the French ships that had circled Elba for a while, but she was at anchor. Until the evening they encountered no further obstacles, when they saw a brig heading straight for them. The two ships would soon be side by side. One of the sailors climbed down from the topmast and said, 'I know this ship, it's the *Zéphyr*. There's no danger, Captain Andrieux won't harm us.'

'Why don't we hoist the tricolour, sire?' suggested Chautard.

'No. Pick up your loudhailer.'

The captain obeyed, and Napoleon ordered the grenadiers who were massed on the deck: 'Take off your hats and hide.'

He did the same, his back to the rail, and when the *Zéphyr* drew level with them, he said, 'Chautard, repeat what I whisper to you.'

'Aye, aye . . .'

Captain Andrieux, as the two boats passed, put his loudhailer to his mouth.

'Who are you?'

'Captain Chautard . . .'

'I mistook you for an English brig.'

'It actually is an English ship,' whispered the Emperor to Chautard, who echoed what he said word for word.

'Flying the Elban flag?'

'It's a present from the King of England,' replied Chautard, still speaking Napoleon's words.

'And you're bound for Italy?'

'We're going to get some trees from Genoa.'

'And how's Papa?'

'Supremely well.'

'When you get back to Portoferraio, tell him we miss him!'

After these brief pleasantries, the two ships set off again on their opposite courses; Chautard bent down to the Emperor crouching behind a crate.

'Did you hear that, sire, he called you *Papa* . . .'

*

The lightened *Inconstant* outdistanced the boats of the convoy during the night. The light was on in the Emperor's cabin. Through the open hatch, the soldiers could see him walking up and down, one hand behind his back and the other under his waistcoat, dictating to Octave, who was leaning over a shelf. They also saw Count Bertrand, deathly pale, squeezed into an armchair, exhausted by the rolling of the ship. Octave emerged carrying a piece of paper, and headed for Monsieur Pons, who was issuing candles and lanterns. 'Time to go,' said Octave simply, and on the forecastle, overlooking the passengers on the deck below, he spoke.

'His Majesty has just written some proclamations. As soon as we land, we will put them up in the towns and villages we come across.'

'We need copyists to reproduce them in large numbers,' Pons said.

'Me! Me! Me!'

Dozens of soldiers and officers rose to their feet, to be handed white paper, pens and inkpots. They set themselves up where they could, kneeling against a drum, or lying flat on their stomachs, and, beneath the various lights placed near them (or held by those unfortunates who did not know how to write, and were furious about the fact), they began, forming their letters to the best of their abilities, writing out the texts read out to them by Octave and Pons.

> Frenchmen, from my exile I have heard your laments and your wishes. I have crossed the seas, I am arriving among you to reassume my rights, which are also yours . . .

And at the same time, Drouot and Cambronne had converted the hold into an impromptu study.

> Soldiers, the eagle with the national colours will fly from belfry to belfry to the towers of Notre-Dame . . .

When each man had finished his one poster, he made as many more copies as possible. Monsieur Pons and Octave also joined in, leaning on the steps of a ladder, beneath a dim lamp that swayed with the rhythm of the ship. Pons raised his pen and asked his companion: 'Do you still think we don't exist next to the Emperor?'

'I never said anything of the kind . . .'

'Oh yes, you did, my dear fellow, the first time I took you to the Buono Gusto. It's true, though, that you were a little the worse for wear.'

'Really? I still believe it, even stone-cold sober, but at least we've been through some things. In one year, I've lived a hundred.'

'I'm not sure we'll ever see such a great age . . .'

'What do you mean? A civil war when His Majesty lands in France?'

'Drouot predicts a universal war.'

'And that everything will start up again, yes, but for how long?'

The travellers on the *Inconstant* thus spent a second night without closing their eyes, too excited about the unknown. *'On Tuesday 28 February,'* Octave wrote, *'the wind is blowing again after abandoning us for a whole day. We've seen the coast of Noli and the mountains over the Cap de la Garoupe – The crew and the grenadiers got to their feet to yell a terrible 'Vive la France!' They have laughed, drunk and eaten, and in some cases danced like devils. On Wednesday 1 March, when the weather is calm, here we are in sight of the coast of Provence, and an extraordinary agitation is taking hold of us . . .'*

The Emperor rewarded the first lookout to sight land by giving him all the gold coins he had in his pockets, and then he called Captain Chautard.

'Fetch up the material we have in our suitcases, and distribute it so that everyone can make himself a tricolour cockade.'

'Is it worth it, sire?' asked Cambronne, pointing to the grenadiers, who searched their haversacks and took out their old and slightly battered cockades. One of them even offered his to Napoleon, and cheers rang out when the Emperor pinned it to his hat, in fact the clapping of hands and stamping of feet could have capsized the brig.

The homecoming called for a celebration, and His Majesty's chief steward, on His Majesty's orders, shared His Majesty's personal supplies. Bottles of champagne, claret and tokay were passed around, and Monsieur Pons improvised:

The Eagle of our nation dear
On mighty wings ahead doth race
Aloft it soars, our beacon bright,
Soon to reclaim its rightful place.

He had to be interrupted in the end, however, because he was starting to add endless couplets.

It was two o'clock in the afternoon when the vessel dropped anchor in the gulf of Juan les Pins. From the deck, everyone looked at the beach, the Tour de la Gabelle, which seemed empty of troops, and the warehouses that lay between the shore and the main road that led from Antibes to Cannes.

'Cambronne,' said the Emperor, 'choose forty men and take up position on this road, but be careful, I know you're impulsive, so just don't use your weapons. I want to get back on the throne without a drop of blood being spilt. Tell your soldiers.'

A boat set off towards the shore carrying Cambronne and his grenadiers while the others were preparing to follow, bringing luggage and ammunition. Napoleon smiled to Monsieur Pons.

'You seem very agitated.'

'Yes, sire, I am extremely moved. After a long absence, I am returning to France behind an army.'

'Where do you see an army? We'll get to Paris without firing a shot.'

*

Octave was resting, arms crossed, against the twisted trunk of an olive tree. The flotilla had assembled, and the brig had displayed a tricolour flag on her gaff then the boat had set sail again and they set off after unloading the equipment and the 1,132 men who made up the expedition. The Emperor was in the vineyard, standing on a wooden walkway between the rows of vines, dispatchng emissaries around the region. Cambronne had headed for Cannes with a detachment to buy mules and horses; some plain-clothes officers had headed for Antibes, with proclamations under their arms; the surgeon Emery had requisitioned a passing coach to take him to Grenoble, his home town, where he was to alert the Prefect of the Isère to the situation.

The first curious villagers who had arrived to investigate didn't seem particularly enthusiastic, in fact they seemed rather worried at the sight of the grenadier guards, even though they had thought at first, spying the ships through their telescopes, that they were Algerine corsairs who'd captured the boats of some Genoese fishermen, and were putting in at Juan les Pins to renew their supplies of water.

The men cleaned their weapons, ate soup and set up camp at the bottom of a creek. Peyrusse had given them two weeks' wages, and they could hardly see two feet in front of them. At a loose end, Octave walked a few hundred yards along the road, to an inn that would not have been noticed from the shore, behind a clump of pines with grey foliage. On the sign, he read the strange name of the establishment: *On the dot*. He planned to improve his rations by allowing himself a chicken and some wine, and in he went. The main room was deserted, but a delicious smell of chicken soup drifted from a cauldron in the hearth. Octave called out. No one answered. He ventured further, pushing doors open, and found himself in a gloomy chamber where the innkeepers sat at the bedside of a little girl whose face was dotted with red spots, like flea-bites. A serving-wench he hadn't noticed dragged him from the room. Carrying an empty cup that she was going to fill from the cauldron, she said crossly: 'What d'you want? The inn's shut.'

'What about this soup?'

'It's for the girl.'

'Is she ill?'

'Very ill, Monsieur. She has measles.'

'The Emperor has landed today . . .'

'What Emperor?'

'What do you mean? We've only got one!'

'So?'

'I thought I could buy some food and wine from you . . .'

'It's shut, I told you.'

'Aren't you moved?'

'Of course I am, measles is dangerous.'

'I mean by Napoleon's return.'

'Whether he comes, whether he goes, whether he comes back, it doesn't change anything for us, and I told you before, the girl has measles.'

'Yes, I heard . . .'

'Heard but didn't understand.'

'What am I supposed to understand?'

'As far as we're concerned, there's nothing more important in the world than that horrible measles.'

Disarmed by the situation, Octave thoughtfully set off again. He crossed the road amidst carts and horses: Cambronne's detachment was returning from Cannes as night fell. The moon was bright, but the air was icy.

Octave turned up his collar and walked towards the bivouac, where piles of vine shoots were burning. The Emperor had pulled on a woollen jumper and was sleeping on his folding armchair, his boots on a chair, his grey frock-coat wrapped around him like a blanket. His face was peaceful. Napoleon was dreaming of Bonaparte.

On 20 March the Emperor returned to the Tuileries, supported by a popular movement, and one hundred days later came Waterloo.

Notes for the Curious

1. The Ancestor Cult: Conversation with Myself

'Another historical novel?'

   'No.'

   'What do you mean, "no"?'

   'I don't write historical novels.'

   'Are you joking?'

   'Not at all.'

   'Come on! I have the novel in front of me. You take us on a tour of 1814, or am I mistaken?'

   'Your definition's at fault.'

   'What definition?'

   'The definition of the historical novel.'

   'Let's have it!'

   'The term, certainly reductive, even contemptuous, refers to adventure stories telling timeless tales of love and revenge in exotic settings. The hooligan suddenly assumes nobility in his disguise as a medieval cut-purse, he lends colour to an ordinary yarn. This donning of gilded folderols is very contrived. Personally, it doesn't interest me in the slightest: the chosen era serves as a backdrop, you can easily replace the fortified castle with a Florentine palace or an English building: it doesn't change anything.'

   'An example, please.'

   'Take *Romeo and Juliet*. Shakespeare sets his historic drama in Verona during the Renaissance, because he wants to stay close to the Italian story from which he drew his inspiration, written by Matteo Bandello in the sixteenth century. Bandello himself has taken it from a story by Luigi Da Porto. And in any case, love thwarted by parents was hardly a very new theme. You find it in Ovid, with the misfortunes of Pyramus and Thisbe. In this case, the age in which the action takes place is unimportant. Throw Romeo and Juliet into fifties New York and you get *West Side Story*.'

'I can see that, but nonetheless your novels are historical!'

'Because history isn't the setting but the theme. In actual fact, I'm trying to stage little fragments from our past.'

'Why?'

'It's a matter of personal taste, first of all, then curiosity, and finally the desire to communicate what I think I've understood, as best I can. It's the European version of the ancestor cult. I feel quite close to those Indonesian villagers, on certain islands, who take it in turns, day and night, to protect the wooden effigies of their dead against antiquarian tomb-raiders. The ancestors are part of our lives, as in Asia, as in the Rome of the Caesars.'

'Let's run through that again. You said "personal taste" . . .'

'In the fifties, children were immersed in history. Comics taught us about it every week. Thanks to things like *Tintin* and *Spirou*, by the age of seven we were familiar with Soucouf, Vauban, the Boxer Uprising, Marco Polo. We knew Samarkand, Babylon and Shanghai. *L'Oncle Paul* and *Alix* extended our Latin classes. That was when I learned the names of the seven hills of Rome, which I've never managed to forget . . . And then there were books like *Salammbô*, the works of Dumas . . .'

'Dumas, exactly! The cycle of the *Three Musketeers*, that's the historical novel in its pure state!'

'No, I don't think so. His characters can't be transposed in

time. You can't imagine them in our own time, or in ancient
Greece, during the crusades or among the pirates of the
Caribbean. They tell us of the transition, in France, from the
Baroque to the Classical age.'

'I don't see . . .'

'At the beginning we're in the reign of Louis XIII, an age
damaged by feudalism, and Richelieu knows it, he fights the
feudal lords. You have a sense of bravado, of sworn oaths,
emotional outbursts and decent food. You have panache.
Twenty years later, it's all changed. Under Mazarin, our musketeers are out of step: honour has been replaced by cunning,
negotiation and politics. With the accession of the young Louis
XIV, in the novel *Le Vicomte de Bragelonne*, the state wins the
day, the aristocracy makes way for the bourgeoisie, and Colbert
installs centralized power. You have to adapt or go under. Our
musketeers pass through that precise age, when society is being
transformed around them. They are nostalgic, they have plenty
of regret but no remorse. By the end they have lost their
illusions. It's the finest novel of passing time.'

'Like Proust? Are you joking?'

'I'm not joking at all. And anyway, Proust was thinking
about Dumas when he wrote the *Recherche*.'

'Really?'

'One day he revealed his project to his friends. To help
them understand, he said, "You see, it's like *Vingt Ans Après*."
Léon Daudet was there, and he corrected him: "No, it's more
like *Bragelonne*."'

'Whatever. Go on. You say you write to learn, as well.'

'Of course! It seems quite clear that when you set about
reconstructing the past, with a bit of imagination thrown in,
you make discoveries, you move from one surprise to the next.
The reality, seen from close up, by eye-witnesses, is more
complex, more unexpected, funnier or harsher. Each book, for
me, is based on questions. What's a battle? What was Moscow

like before the fire? Was Berezina really a defeat? How can a man who governed Europe end up on a little island with the power of a sub-prefect?'

'And those are the curiosities that you hope to pass on?'

'I want to imagine where we come from. Roots aren't innocent. And yet ignorance is manifest these days. One Saturday evening, on an Antenne 2 radio broadcast, a former Culture Minister revealed his ignorance of the fact that 4 September celebrates the birth of the 3rd Republic. On a television quiz, the contestant was asked: "What tribe did Vercingetorix command?" He replied without hesitation: "The Romans." We "old Europeans" are ending up like the American students quoted in the *Süddeutsche Zeitung* in 2001. When they were being welcomed on to a campus, some young Germans were startled by the things the students wanted to know: "Is Hitler still your president?" or: "Are there problems on the border between Germany and China?"'

'It's a long way from there to sacrificing at the altar of the ancestor cult.'

'Not at all: it's a good perspective. And the further we go in life, the more we are surrounded by the dead. There even comes a time when we know more dead people than living. Everywhere we go, we are surrounded by this procession of familiar phantoms, and books can awaken them. When I leave my Paris street, near Les Halles, I know that Victor Hugo, in 1832, when he was at work on *The Hunchback of Notre Dame*, saw with his own eyes the barricade in the rue des Petits-Carreaux that he would use in *Les Misérables*. I also know that on the quay, there, opposite the Tour de l'Horloge, during the Terror there were people who sold the hair of the beheaded to be made into wigs. The walls of our cities, the hills, the villages, are impregnated with very strong memories.'

'All the same, the contemporary world has little in common with those revolutionary centuries ...'

'Wrong again. The fundamentals haven't changed, and we've barely evolved since Homer. If formidable technical advances change the brains of future generations in due course, it's always worth mentioning that Cicero predicted the harmful employment of screens.'

'Could we be serious for five minutes? Cicero lived in the first century of the common era, and I can't imagine him sitting in front of the TV!'

'He could, though. In *The Pursuit of Unhappiness*, by the excellent Paul Watzlawick of Palo Alto University, I read this short and rather disturbing text from Cicero: "If we are forced, at every hour, to watch or listen to horrible events, this constant stream of ghastly impressions will deprive even the most delicate of us of all respect for humanity.'"

'Are you sure your professor hasn't been tinkering with his translation?'

'That wouldn't be like him.'

'Fine. But what about now?'

'Journalism deals with the question. I like Dos Passos's reportage better than his novels.'

'What if I'm not convinced?'

'I'm not trying to convince you.'

'Really?'

'I couldn't care less, I couldn't give a fig, I couldn't give a tinker's curse. Time travel is a gourmet delight.'

2. WHAT BECAME OF THEM?

Count Jean-René Pierre de SÉMALLÉ left the court with some haste, and his plot remained a secret. Extracts from his memoirs were published in 1826, and used in notes in a volume on Talleyrand published in 1853 by the printer Michaud. He died in Versailles, in Madame de Pompadour's old home, at the age of ninety-one: he had caught a cold at mass. His grandson finally published his *Souvenirs* in 1898.

In 1815 DESFIEUX-BEAUJEU, Marquis de la GRANGE, was given the task of whipping up a number of départements in favour of the King, but never received his travel expenses. Neither did he receive his pension as a royal commissioner.

MORIN became head of the 1st division in the Ministry of Police. He died in poverty.

Marie Armand de GUÉRY DE MAUBREUIL settled in England after his release from prison. He denounced the Tsar of Russia, the King of Prussia and the Bourbons to exculpate himself of the planned assassination attempt on Napoleon.

The Chevalier GUÉRIN DE BRUSLART was appointed camp marshal in 1816 by Louis XVIII, but given nothing to do. His past as a conspirator was too compromising. He died in Paris on 10 December 1829, in his home at 74 rue Saint-Dominique. He was not considered worthy of a funeral oration.

Hugues-Bernard MARET, Duke of BASSANO, was given back his job as Secretary of State during the Hundred Days. After Waterloo he was exiled to Austria, where he stayed until 1820. Louis-Philippe made him a peer of France in 1831. He died in Paris eight years later.

ANDRÉ PONS DE L'HÉRAULT was appointed Prefect of the Rhône during the Hundred Days. He asked to go with the Emperor into his exile on St Helena, but his request was refused. He himself lived in exile until 1830, when Louis-Philippe granted him the Jura Prefecture. He was soon fired from the post because of his poor character, and he died in 1853 after refusing to recognize Napoleon III.

Marie WALEWSKA married the Count of Ornano. She died in childbirth in 1817.

Contrary to legend, CAMBRONNE never said '*Merde!*' at Waterloo. The story was made up in 1830 by the bohemian Genty, in
the Café des Variétés, as a trap for Charles Nodier, who duly
passed it on.

Antoine DROUOT, the day after Waterloo, where he was in
charge of the Guard, refused to be reintegrated into the royal
army. He retired to Lorraine, where he died in 1847 after
rejecting all kinds of honours.

Henri Gatien BERTRAND followed Napoleon to St Helena. In
1830 he was appointed rector of the École Polytechnique. He
died in 1844. Four years before that, he organized the return of
the Emperor's ashes.

Michel NEY had promised Louis XVIII that he would bring
Napoleon back in an iron cage. He fell into the Emperor's arms
upon his return from Elba, pushed, it is true, by his troops.
At Waterloo, he behaved in a hot-headed fashion and contributed to the defeat. He was shot upon the King's return, at
the emplacement where his statue stands today, in front of the
Closerie des Lilas, near the Paris Observatory.

Louis Alexandre BERTHIER accompanied Louis XVIII when
Napoleon returned. He fell from a window in Bamberg Castle
in Bavaria, in 1815. He is thought to have been pushed.

Étienne Jacques MACDONALD led Louis XVIII to the border,
and became an ordinary grenadier in the National Guard. On
his return, the King appointed him Minister of State. He died
in 1840, near the Loire.

Armand Augustin Louis, Marquis de CAULAINCOURT, became
Minister of Foreign Affairs once again during the Hundred
Days, before retiring to die in Paris in 1827 – after writing
memoirs that would only be published long afterwards.

Auguste Daniel BELLIARD died of apoplexy in Brussels, where Louis-Philippe had made him ambassador. That was in 1832.

Charles Pierre François AUGEREAU did not live long enough to enjoy his vast fortune: he died in 1816.

Auguste Frédéric Louis Viesse de MARMONT because a peer of France under Louis XVIII, then Minister of State and Governor of Paris. As Duke of Ragusa, he was stuck with his reputation of having betrayed the Emperor, and the word *raguser* was invented, to mean *betray*. In 1830 he followed King Charles X into exile and died in Venice in 1852.

And PAULINE? Dear Pauline brought a legal case against the Prince Borghese, her husband, who was living with a certain Duchess Lanta della Rovere, moved to Rome for a while, made up with the Prince and perished of languor in the Villa Strozzi in Florence, in June 1825, four years after her brother, whose name she uttered with her final breath.

3. USEFUL BIBLIOGRAPHY

Most of the characters in this novel bear their real names, except for the main character, whom I use to articulate the story. I called him Octave Sénécal for two reasons. Octave was the part played by Jean Renoir himself in his film *La règle du jeu*. Sénécal I took from *Sentimental Education*, where Flaubert turns him into a troubled extra in the 1848 Revolution, half cop and half member of the secret societies. Otherwise, as usual, I have sought out the witnesses of the adventure. There are many of them. They allowed me to put in Napoleon's mouth remarks that he is really supposed to have made, or at least those that have been passed down to us. I should also like to thank the Clavreuil Historical Bookshop in the rue Saint-André-des-Arts in Paris, for the treasures that it offers manic devotees of French history. Come on! It's better to lose your fortune in a bookshop than in a casino. So I have reconstructed this episode, this dead period in Napoleon's life, with the help of the following books.

General Works

Henry Houssaye, *1814*, Librairie Académique Perrin, 1925.

Henry Houssaye, *1815*, same publisher, 1900. These two volumes seem to be the most complete and the most vivid books on the period.

Fain, *Mémoires*, republished by Arléa in 2000.

Fain, *Manuscrit de 1814*, Paris, Bossange frères, 1825.

Méneval, *Napoléon et Marie-Louise*, Vol. II, Librairie d'Amyot, 1844, and 1845 for Vol. III.

Caulaincourt, *Mémoires*, Vol. III, Plon, 1933.

Marcel Dupont, *Napoléon et la trahison des maréchaux*, Hachette, 1939.

Louis Chardigny, *Les Maréchaux de Napoléon*, Flammarion, 1946.

Lamartine, *Histoire de la Restauration*, Vols. 17 and 18 of his complete works, published in Paris by the author, 43 rue de la Ville-l'Evêque, in 1861. It is not sublime, like *L'Histoire des Girondins*, but intelligent and lively despite a number of minor mistakes. Thus the inn of La Calade becomes the inn of l'Accolade, but Lamartine was short of money at the time, and writing at great speed.

Philippe de Ségur, *Du Rhin à Fontainebleau*, Édition Nelson (undated).

Jean Thiry, *La Chute de Napoléon*, Vol. II, Berger-Levrault, 1939.

Henri d'Alméras, *La Vie parisienne sous le Consulat et l'Empire*, another volume about the Restoration, Albin-Michel, undated.

The *Napoléon* presented by Jacques Godechot (Albin-Michel 1969) includes a text about Paris in March 1814 written by an eye-witness, Julian Antonio Rodriguez.

Amédée Pichot, *Chronique des événements de 1814 et 1815*, Dentu, 1873.

Macdonald, *Souvenirs*, Plon, 1892.

Frédéric Masson, *Napoléon chez lui*, Fayard, 1951.

In the July–August 1922 issue of the *Revue d'études napoléoniennes* (librairie Félix Alcan) one may read a *Napoléon à Fontainebleau en 1814* by G. Lacour-Gayet and *San Martino et le muse napoléonien de l'île d'Elbe* by Ch. Saunier.

I don't wish to forget the volume devoted to *La Campagne de France* in the indispensable collection of Tranié and Carmignani, republished by Pygmalion. Jean Tranié died when I was writing this novel. I would have appreciated his enlightened opinion once again. In his Montmartre house he had a profusion of objects and books devoted to the Empire, but he viewed his collection with both interest and distance, for he had a good sense of humour.

About the Royalists

Counte de Sémallé, *Souvenirs*, Alphonse Picard et fils, Paris, 1898.

Indiscrétions 1798–1830, souvenirs tirés du portefeuille d'un fonctionnaire de l'Empire, Dufay, Paris, 1835. These two anonymous volumes are thought to be the memoirs of Count Réal, former Chief of Police, collected by his son-in-law Musnier-Desclozeau.

Mme de Chastenay, *Mémoires*, Perrin, 1987.

Mémoires of the Countess de Boigne, Vol. I, Mercure de France, 1971.

Mémoires of the Duchess d'Abrantès, Vol. 10, Garnier frères (undated).

Chateaubriand, *De Buonaparte et des Bourbons*, collection Libertés, Pauvert, 1966.

Souvenirs du chancelier Pasquier, Hachette, 1964.

Léonce Peillard, *Vie quotidienne à Londres au temps de Nelson et de Wellington*, Hachette, 1968.

Maubreuil, *Extrait de l'examen de l'Adresse au Congrès et à toutes les puissances de l'Europe, envoyée à Aix-la-Chapelle à tous les souverains, à leurs ambassadeurs, à leurs ministres et aux différents cabinets, relative à l'assassinat de Napoléon et de son fils, attentat ordonné par la Russie, la Prusse et les Bourbons...* Düsseldorf, 1820.

G. Lenotre, *Vieilles maisons, vieux papiers*, third series, Perrin, 1911. Long portrait of the *chouan* Bruslart.

G. Lenotre, *La Révolution par ceux qui l'ont vue*, Grasset, 1934, republished in Cahiers rouges. This fifth volume of the 'Petite Histoire' includes a portrait of Champcenetz based on the *Notes d'un émigré* by Pradel de Lamase.

About the Island of Elba

Pons de l'Hérault, *Souvenirs et anecdotes de l'île d'Elbe*, édition de Léon G. Pélissier, Plon, 1897.

Mémoire de Pons de l'Hérault aux puissances alliées, Paris, Alphonse Picard et fils, 1899.

Paul Gruyer, *Napoléon roi de l'île d'Elbe*, Perrin, 1947.

Marchand, *Mémoires*, Vol. I, Plon, 1952.

Baron de Vincent, *Mémorial de l'île d'Elbe*, published in around 1850 in an unidentified journal.

De l'exil au retour de l'île d'Elbe, contemporary accounts, Teissedre, 2001.

Waldburg-Truchsess, *Nouvelle relation de Napoléon de Fontainebleau à l'île d'Elbe*, Paris, Panckoucke, 1815 (lengthy extract in *Le Consulat et l'Empire* by Alfred Fierro, collection Bouquins, chez Laffont, 1998).

La Déportation de Napoléon à l'île d'Elbe, issue 11 of 'Toute l'histoire de Napoléon', April 1952. Account by Captain Ussher and diary of Vicomte Charrier-Moissard.

La Vérité sur les Cent Jours, par un citoyen de la Corse, Bruxelles, H. Tarlier, 1825. I took the dialogue in Chapter 5 with the messenger who has come from Portoferraio to meet the Emperor. He himself would have authenticated the text, if I am to believe this note on page 176 in the same book: 'The messenger recorded this dialogue, at the very moment when he left Napoleon, and showed it, upon his return, to those who had entrusted their dispatches to him. One of them copied it, and when the Emperor was in Paris, he gave it to him. Napoleon read it, was greatly amused, and often said while reading it: *That's it, that's exactly it.*'

A. D. B. Monnier, *Une année dans la vie de l'Empereur Napoléon (1814–1815)*, Paris, Alexis Eymeery, 1815.

Sophie et Anthelme Troussier, *La Chevauchée héroïque du retour de l'île d'Elbe*, Imprimerie Allier, Grenoble, 1965.

Pierre de Gumbert, *Napoléon de l'île d'Elbe à la citadelle de Sisteron*, éditions du Socle, Aix-en-Provence, 1968.

About some of the characters

Comte d'Ornano, *Marie Walewska*, Hachette, 1938.

A. Augustin-Thierry, *Notre Dame des colifichets*, Albin-Michel, 1937.

Fleuriot de Langle, *La Paolina, sœur de Napoléon*, éditions Colbert, Paris, 1946 (terribly like the previous book . . .)

A. Augustin-Thierry, *Madame Mère*, Albin-Michel, 1931.

On the subject of the injections that the Emperor administered to himself, Dr Patrick Laburthe provided me with their content, and I am indebted to the Countess de Ségur for the chicken soup that is supposed to cure measles. The final idea of measles, incidentally, belongs to Anatole France: he wanted to use it to conclude a novel on the island of Elba of which he never wrote a single word.